Elvi Rhodes was th
in the West Ridi
between the wars.
Grammar School a
her family. A wide
Her other novel
Appleby, *Madelein*
The Rainbow Through the Rain,
Mountain, *Portrait of Chloe* and *Spring Music*. A
collection of stories, *Summer Promise and Other Stories*,
is also published by Corgi Books.

THE GOLDEN GIRLS

Elvi Rhodes

CORGI BOOKS

THE GOLDEN GIRLS
A CORGI BOOK : 0 552 13185 7

First publication in Great Britain

PRINTING HISTORY
Corgi edition published 1988

11

Copyright © Elvi Rhodes 1988

The right of Elvi Rhodes to be identified as the author of
this work has been asserted in accordance with sections 77
and 78 of the Copyright Designs and Patents Act 1988.

Set in 10/11pt Plantin.

Corgi Books are published by Transworld Publishers,
61–63 Uxbridge Road, London W5 5SA,
a division of The Random House Group Ltd,
in Australia by Random House Australia (Pty) Ltd,
20 Alfred Street, Milsons Point, Sydney, NSW 2061, Australia,
in New Zealand by Random House New Zealand Ltd,
18 Poland Road, Glenfield, Auckland 10, New Zealand
and in South Africa by Random House (Pty) Ltd,
Endulini, 5a Jubilee Road, Parktown 2193, South Africa.

Printed in Great Britain by Clays Ltd, St Ives plc

FOR ANTHONY, WITH MY LOVE

THE GOLDEN GIRLS

PART ONE

CHAPTER ONE

Throwing potatoes into the big scale, Dick Fletcher silently cursed the sharp March wind which whipped around the corner of his market stall. His pitch in the Akersfield market was not an ideal one. Apart from the fact that when the wind was in the east it tore at him all day long, the position was too far to the outside, away from the heart of things, so that sometimes he had to sell his produce a ha'penny a pound cheaper, thus cutting his profits. He had complained to the council and would do so again, claiming that when they dealt with the tenders it was his turn to have a spot in the centre. Apart from the better trade, he thought as a fresh gust of wind sneaked between his cap and his scarf, it would be a sight warmer, hemmed in by other stalls and with more shoppers around.

'There you are, missus,' he said, tipping the potatoes into the large straw bag which the woman held open for him. 'That'll be twopence. And you won't find better quality in the whole of the West Riding.'

He could say that with confidence. He was fussy about quality, using only the best seed in his market garden and, when he had to buy in, taking only the best from the wholesalers. Apart from his own pride, he hoped that if the quality was good his customers would return. If it were not, if the produce was bad in the middle, then they'd come back to throw it at him! Akersfield housewives were sharp, fussy. They wouldn't put up with being cheated.

'How about a few cut flowers?' he said persuasively. He picked up a small bunch of daffodil buds, posing them in his outstretched hand for the best effect. 'Brighten up the house for the weekend!'

'I've no brass for flowers,' the woman said. 'Times is hard. A nice joint of beef would brighten *my* house best!'

'I'm sorry, missus,' Dick said. 'Perhaps things will look up.' But she had already moved on. He was truly sorry. He saw too many women with pinched, harassed faces. He'd have liked to have given them all a bunch of flowers apiece.

He might as well begin to pack up. It was nearing the end of the afternoon and there'd not be much more trade now. Not that he'd done all that badly. He could tell by the feel of his jacket pockets, weighted with coins. Coppers mostly, but amongst the pennies and ha'pennies, some sixpences and shillings, even a few half-crowns. People didn't shop for vegetables with sovereigns. He usually did all right in the Akersfield market on a Friday. And what he didn't sell there he'd get rid of in Skipton on the Saturday morning.

He sold in three markets most weeks; Akersfield, Otley and Skipton, travelling from his home in Felldale early in the morning. Three markets was as much as the horse could manage, for, though she was willing, she was getting old, and a bit slow. Besides, he had to have time to grow the stuff, didn't he? Growing was what he liked best; planting the seeds in the dark earth, seeing the first, pale green shoots appear, nursing the plant right through to harvest. But if you wanted to get on you couldn't just grow. You had to sell.

Bending down to the boxes at the back of the trestle tables he didn't see the next customer approach. When he straightened up again she was there, at the far end of the stall, standing with her back to him as she sifted through the produce. He recognised her at once, though he had scarcely seen her since she left Felldale five years ago. Indeed on the few occasions when she came back there he had avoided her. He knew she lived in Akersfield now, though she had never visited his stall. Once, when he was serving a customer, he had seen her hurrying past and, on an impulse, had called out to her. She didn't answer, and by the time he'd finished serving she was out of sight.

She was still easily recognisable, standing there, even

12

though her face was hidden. For a start she was tall for a woman. Five feet seven or eight. And then, though she was dressed in black from head to foot − shabby black at that, he thought − she had style. She wore her fringed woollen shawl as if it were a sable cape. Oh, she had style all right!

You could tell that by the angle at which her wide-brimmed hat was perched on the top of her head. It was far too fashionable a hat for one of her station, though he guessed she had made it herself. And from beneath her hat, if further proof were needed, her hair − a rich dark gold − escaped in tendrils down the back of her neck and over the top of her shawl. No-one else had hair so vibrant, so singing with colour. A swift arrow of longing went through him like a sharp pain. He knew, as really he had known all along, that he should never have let her go.

Should he let her go again? Should he busy himself with the boxes, pretend not to see her, hope that she'd pass by? She wasn't for him. She was a married woman. But in the second that it took the thoughts to go through his head she turned and faced him.

'Why, it's Dick! Dick Fletcher!'

There was pleased amazement in her voice, but her face was more honest than her words and he knew at once that she had been certain she would see him there. Her eyes − those amazing green eyes, thickly fringed with lashes of a darker gold than her hair − told the truth. Her eyes spoke apprehension, unhappiness, fear; as if the brightness in them might be that of tears ready to fall.

'Eleanor! This *is* a surprise! What brings you here?' He was at a loss for the right thing to say.

'Absolutely nothing!' she said lightly. 'Sheer coincidence! I was walking past the market when I remembered I needed vegetables. This was the first stall I came to.'

She was all innocence, but he didn't believe her. He saw the chalky whiteness of her face, the fine lines of worry developing on her broad forehead. Her hands were clenched so tightly around the handle of the basket that the knuckles showed white. He knew trouble when he saw it. But he knew pride too; heard it in her chirpy voice, saw it in the smile which widened her mouth but did not reach her eyes. And, seen closer to, she was so painfully thin.

'It's nice to see you. It's been a long time.' It wasn't what he wanted to say. He was shocked by her appearance. She was twenty-three and looked ten years older, though she was still as beautiful as ever. And would be if she lived to be a hundred, he thought. It was in her bones, those high, rounded cheekbones, the long, clean lines of her jaw, the delicately moulded chin. Now, though, what had been the slightest of hollows beneath her cheekbones were too deep and the skin was stretched too tight over her jaws. Gaunt was how he would describe her now. It was not the look she had had when she'd left Felldale at the age of eighteen.

'Have you been keeping well, then?' he asked.

'Very well, thank you,' Eleanor said brightly. 'And you?'

'The same.'

'Good!'

They stood looking at each other, Eleanor with a fixed smile on her face, neither of them knowing what to say next.

'Well now . . . Let me see. I don't need much. Carrots, an onion; perhaps a small turnip.'

He weighed them out, dropped them in the empty basket she handed to him.

'A nice stick of celery?' he suggested. 'Crisp. Picked with the frost on it.'

She hesitated. 'I don't think so, thank you. But . . . perhaps two apples . . . no, three. Small ones. Red ones.'

'Jonathans,' Dick said. 'Can't beat 'em. You choose.'

As she picked out three red apples Dick watched her tongue lick over her lips, saw the eager look on her face. She was hungry! He was looking at sheer, naked, deep-down hunger and the sight shocked and disturbed him. But it would never do for him to show his feelings.

'Try one,' he said. 'Go on, try one. See if they're to your taste.'

There was only the slightest pause before she bit into the apple. She took a large bite, chewed rapidly, swallowed,

14

bit again. Her eyelids drooped as if she was in ecstasy. She
ignored the tiny trickle of juice which ran from the corner
of her mouth. She bit and chewed with amazing speed, until
in no time at all the apple, core and all, was gone, swallowed.
Then she licked her fingers, opened her eyes, looked Dick
straight in the face.

'Very good! Really very good. I can recommend them.
Now how much is all that – including the apple I've eaten?'

'No charge for tastings,' Dick said. 'That'll be eleven-
pence altogether.'

She put her hand into her pocket and an expression of
horror spread over the face.

'My purse! I've lost my purse!' She looked quickly around
where she was standing, then felt again in her pocket. 'It's
gone! Do you think it's been stolen? There are pickpockets
in the market. Everyone says so!'

She was so transparent, Dick thought. Of course there
was no purse, and never had been. Watching her eat the
apple he had guessed the truth. She was on her uppers.

'Perhaps you left it at home,' he said gently. 'Perhaps
you never brought it with you?'

She clutched eagerly at his explanation.

'You're right! I know now! I left it on the sideboard! Oh,
what a silly fool I am!'

'Easily done, easily remedied,' Dick consoled her.

'But I can't pay you. I couldn't get home and back before
you left – and I really need the things!'

I'll bet you do, Dick thought. He would willingly have
given her the contents of his entire stall, but there was the
matter of her pride.'

'That's all right,' he said. 'You can come back next
Friday, pay me then. Any Friday. I'm always here.'

Eleanor gave a great sigh of relief. He believed her. For
one moment she'd thought he'd seen through her – and
small wonder after the way she'd gone at the apple. Oh,
but it had been good. She hadn't been able to resist it. And
tonight, after the vegetable stew she'd make the minute she
got home, they'd all feel better. And of course she would pay

15

him back, though right now she didn't know how. It was true that she had left her purse at home, but it was also true that it was empty.

'As a matter of fact we might have missed each other,' Dick said. 'I was just packing up to go home. A cup of tea and a bite to eat in the cafe around the corner, and then I'll be away.'

'Lucky for me you hadn't gone,' Eleanor told him. 'Who else would have trusted me?' But there was no chance that he would have left. She'd been watching, waiting until the coast was clear. She knew he had his stall here. She'd been tempted more than once to stop, especially that time when he'd called after her and she'd pretended not to hear. But she'd had her pride, still had. She hadn't wanted him to know everything, carry the news back to her family. Her mother was the only one who wouldn't have said 'I told you so,' but her mother was under Clara's thumb.

'I'm sure anyone would have trusted you,' Dick said. 'You'd only have to . . . ' Open those big green eyes was what he nearly said.

' . . . Yes?'

'Explain. You'd only have to explain.'

'Well I'm glad it was you, Dick.'

'Perhaps you'll come with me for a cup of tea and a bite to eat? It'll not take me a minute to pack the boxes and I can leave them behind the stall. Nobody'll touch 'em.'

Eleanor hesitated.

'For old times' sake,' Dick said.

She smiled – her swift, bright smile, though this time open and honest.

'Why not?' she agreed. 'Like you said, for old times' sake.'

'Then if you'll just wait on a minute or two,' Dick said.

He busied himself packing the boxes, wondering how he could fill up her basket without offending her.

'I'll not get everything in,' he lied. 'I hate throwing stuff away unless there's no help for it.' It was a feeble excuse. Common sense would tell her that as he'd brought everything on the cart from Felldale, there was bags of room for

16

the return journey. But if she wanted to accept a few things he'd made the opening for her.

'Ma always told us it was wicked to waste food,' Eleanor said seriously. 'A sin against the Holy Ghost or some such. I wouldn't like to think of you doing that.'

'Well, if I could put a bit in your basket,' Dick suggested. 'Maybe I wouldn't waste too much.'

She watched with eagerly parted lips while he filled her large basket. Carrots, onions, leeks, oranges, apples. It looked for all the world like a harvest thanksgiving. When it was full to the brim he said, 'I'll just lay this bunch of daffodil buds over the top. They'll come out nicely in a vase of water.'

When the stall was emptied and packed, and he had called out to a neighbouring stallholder to keep an eye on his boxes, Dick picked up Eleanor's basket and led the way out of the market. That was another thing about Dick Fletcher, Eleanor thought. Men in the West Riding never carried shopping baskets, that was women's work, but Dick didn't seem to mind. With his long strides he forged ahead through the Friday shopping crowds, past the meat and fish stalls which always caused Eleanor to hold her breath. She realised they were heading for the covered market in Church Street. Though her own strides were long, she was tired and found it difficult to keep up with him. There was certainly no breath left for speaking and nothing was said between them until they had climbed the steps into the market – everything was hilly in Akersfield, even the market entrance – and made their way to the far aisle which was lined with small open-fronted cafés for almost its whole length. Delicious smells floated out from every café and there were tantalising glimpses of steaming steak-and-kidney pies, and legs of pork encased in golden crackling. It was almost unbearable. Eleanor's stomach contracted and she could hardly stem the flow of digestive juices in her mouth.

'Butterfields. That's the one I always go to,' Dick said. 'They do the best hot pies in Akersfield, and that's what I'm going to have after a day's work. I hope you'll keep me company, Eleanor.'

17

'Well, a cup of tea would do me nicely,' Eleanor said.

'Oh no, we can't have that! How am I going to sit here eating hot pie if you're doing no more than sip at a cup of tea? I'd not be comfortable.'

And how could I possibly watch you doing it, Eleanor thought. 'Very well then,' she conceded. 'If you'd rather I did.'

'I couldn't eat otherwise,' Dick assured her. 'So is it to be a hot meat pie?'

'Yes please.'

'Mushy peas and gravy?'

'Oh yes please!'

She could no longer keep the enthusiasm out of her voice and when the food came – juicy pork encased in crisp brown pastry, flanked by green marrowfat peas, with a generous amount of rich thick gravy poured over – she fell to without even waiting for Dick to start. Afterwards they had apple pudding with custard and a cup of strong, milky tea. No meal she had ever eaten in her life had tasted so good. King Edward in his palace could not have wished for more.

Almost nothing was said between the two of them while they ate. Without seeming to, Dick watched Eleanor, marvelling at her appetite, though he was concerned at the degree of hunger which caused her to fall on the food almost with the speed of an animal. What was her husband doing that she went so hungry? And what about the children?

'Another cup of tea?' he said presently.

Eleanor shook her head. 'I couldn't take another thing. It was . . . delicious! Thank you very much.' Her thanks were genuine. She had shed her pretence of not having been hungry.'

'You're welcome. And now how about catching up on each other. How's everything with you, Eleanor?'

The mask came over her face again, the withdrawn look into her eyes. But he had no intention of letting her get away with it.

'How's your husband?' he asked.

At Dick's question the colour which had come into her

18

face as a result of the warmth of the little cafe, and the food she had eaten, drained away again. Her eyes swam with tears.

'Ben's dead!'

'Oh no! I'm sorry. I didn't know!' It was unbelievable, Dick thought. No-one in Felldale, where news spread like a forest fire, had said a word. It must have happened in the last few days. He had not been into the village since Monday. And yet, curiously, though Eleanor was clearly upset, she did not have the manner of someone very recently bereaved – and so closely. She was distressed, but he doubted that she was suffering from shock.

'When? How? Was it an accident?' The tears were spilling down her face now. She looked in vain for a handkerchief, and he passed her his.

'Thank you,' Eleanor said. 'No, it wasn't an accident. He had a chest cold and it turned to pneumonia. He only lived ten days after. It was in January. He was buried the same day as Queen Victoria.'

But there, Eleanor thought, all similarity between the Queen and her subject had ended. The elaborate preparations for the Queen's all-white funeral, with its pomp and circumstance – the bands, the muffled drums, the daily accounts in the newspapers, the crowned heads of Europe flocking to the scene – had culminated in the long procession through streets lined with sorrowing, weeping people. Ben had been buried with only Eleanor and two neighbours to follow him. But not in a pauper's grave. They had paid their burial club dues every week, so there was enough. In Akersfield, and in the West Riding generally, the snow had been heavy in January, so that even if she had let her family know, she doubted if they'd have been able to get down from Felldale. She had never felt so alone in all her life as in the hours after the neighbours had gone home and she had put the children to bed.

'But . . . I never heard anything. I haven't seen your ma lately, but I've seen Albert. I've been in the shop. He never said a word.'

'He doesn't know. I never told them.' she was calmer

19

now. She handed Dick's handkerchief back, determined she wasn't going to cry again. Crying would get her nowhere. Her situation was too bad to be remedied by tears.

'You never told them? Why ever not? I don't understand.'

She looked across the table at Dick. He was so kind. Yet he was kind without being weak, which was why there was a note of censure in his voice. He believed in families sticking together – well, it was what most Yorkshire people believed in. He didn't approve of what she'd done – or rather, what she'd failed to do. Not to let your family know of a birth or a death, even if you were estranged from them, as she was to a certain extent since she'd left Akersfield, was not right.

The waitress came to give Dick the bill.

'Bring us two more cups of tea, Polly,' he said.

'Right you are, Mr Fletcher.' He was one of her favourite customers; so handsome and well set-up; so polite. And not without a bob or two, she wouldn't wonder. It was the first time she'd seen him bring a lady in here, though she couldn't believe he didn't have one somewhere. And this lady was in trouble. One woman to another, she could tell that at a glance.

'I don't understand,' Dick said to Eleanor when the waitress had gone. 'They're your kith and kind. They'd have wanted to help you, stick by you.'

How could he understand, Eleanor thought. Sometimes she didn't understand herself, didn't know why for five years she'd let pride cut her off. And now here she was, sitting in this little café booth, just the two of them and his eyes, sympathetic and caring, inviting her to tell. But it was when his hand reached across the table and covered hers that she melted inside. Everything that she had endured welled up in her. She bowed her head, leaned her face against his hand, and, in spite of her resolve not to do so, wept. She was still weeping when the waitress brought the tea.

'Here, love,' Polly said. 'Drink it while it's hot. There's nowt like a cup of tea!' She was a pretty little thing, Polly thought; too much sorrow on her for her years.

20

When the waitress had left Eleanor raised her head. 'The truth is . . .' she began hesitantly.

'Have a drink of tea,' Dick said. 'Here, put plenty of sugar in it. Now come on, out with it, love. You'll feel better after.'

'The truth is,' Eleanor said, 'it never worked out with Ben. Well, I say never – I mean not after the first few months. The streets of Akersfield weren't paved with gold, the sky wasn't the limit. In fact, he couldn't get a job. The most he had was part-time work with Mr Northrop, the undertaker. You'd never think you could come to being pleased if more people than usual died, would you? But I did, because it meant money in my purse, food on the table.'

'And did you never say – when you wrote home, when you visited Felldale?'

'No. We'd boasted so much when we'd left Felldale: what we were going to do, how much better off we were going to be. I couldn't lower my pride. I pretended everything was fine. I gradually stopped writing, stopped visiting, made the excuse that it was difficult with the children. Then when things got much worse, when I wanted to ask for help, Ben forbade me.'

'Forbade you?'

'He said it had been my choice to cut myself off from my family and now I had to stick to it. He said they'd always been against him and my first loyalty was to him. I was to have no truck with them, he said.'

'And you obeyed him?' Dick asked. It was difficult to believe. All their lives he'd known her as a spirited person, someone with opinions of her own which she'd never failed to express. It had been one of her great attractions. And an hour ago, in the market there, the same spirit had shone out of her.

'He was my husband,' Eleanor said.

How could she explain that in the first year of their marriage she would have done anything for Ben? He was the sun, moon and stars for her. She would have swum an ocean for him. Still less could she say to anyone that in the

21

marriage bed he had had her enthralled. She had entered a new world. They could never have enough of each other. And that even when their love had died and most of her respect for him had gone, the sexual attraction was still there, as strong as ever.

'I feel the most guilt about my mother,' Eleanor said. 'Even when I stopped going to see her, she would have come to Akersfield to visit me. But I put her off. I always put her off. In the end she knew she wasn't wanted. And yet she was. I longed to see her, but I didn't want her to know how things were. It's too late now.'

'Too late?' Dick queried. 'But your mother's still in Felldale. And Albert and his wife. Of course it's not too late.'

Eleanor shook her head.

'When Ben died in January he left no money. But I was lucky. I got one or two jobs, cleaning, so we just managed. But I was pregnant, and just six weeks ago I had the baby. Our third daughter. After that I couldn't work. I sold Ben's tools – he had good tools and he looked after them – and one or two pieces of furniture he'd made. The money's all gone now and I owe two months' rent. It was true I left my purse at home today. I left it because it was empty. I don't have to tell you what will happen to us now.'

She didn't. He knew well enough. Except for the kindness of friends or family, or the occasional handout from a charity, there was no help for those who were destitute.

'It's the workhouse, that's all.' Her lips were stiff. She tried to keep all emotion out of her voice, not to show any. But the thought was too much for her. She cried out in agony. 'Oh, I could bear it for myself! They'd give me a roof over my head and let me work for my keep – but they'd separate me from the children! I'd never see my children. I'd die without my children!' She was wild, frenzied, and then as she saw the customers in the opposite booth raise their heads, she was quiet again.

'I'm sorry! I'm showing you up!'

Dick shook his head. 'You don't have to apologise to me.'

He wanted to put his arms around her, comfort her. He

22

wanted to take her and her children home with him, care for them, give her a new life. And it was totally impossible. There was Jane Lawrence. He and Jane had a firm understanding. Under no circumstances could he, or would he, ever let her down. He was fond of Jane and he had looked forward to their marriage as much as he knew she did.

'There's only one thing for it,' he said. 'Eleanor you've got to go back to Felldale!'

'Do you think I haven't thought about it?' Eleanor replied 'Of course I have. But how could they keep us? How could Albert keep me and mine?'

'But he's your brother,' Dick said. 'He wouldn't see you want.'

'He's got a wife, and children of his own. And my mother living with him. How could he do it? The shop doesn't make much – a village store, that's all.'

'Nevertheless, you should give him the chance,' Dick persisted. 'How would he feel if he learned that his sister had been taken into the workhouse?'

'He wouldn't hear it from me,' Eleanor said. 'I'd never tell. Oh, if it weren't for the children . . . !'

Dick took her hand. 'Listen, Eleanor. For the sake of the children you *must* go to Felldale. There's no other way.'

She fell silent, the thoughts whirling in her head until she felt she must burst.

'Very well,' she said sharply. 'I'll do it. But how? Do I just turn up on the doorstep? Is that what you suggest?'

'Well, if you did, they could hardly turn you away. But no, that's not what I suggest. I reckon that I should go around and see Albert and Clara, and your mother. Tell them the circumstances. Then when they agree to have you . . .'

'You mean *if*.'

'I do not. It strikes me I know your family better than you do, Eleanor. When they agree, I'll make arrangements to take you and the children up there. It will have to be next Friday because that's the only day I can come to Akersfield. And we'll have to travel on the cart, children and all. And whatever bits and pieces you want to bring

23

with you, although I shouldn't make it too many if I were you. Can you manage that?'

She leaned back, closed her eyes, drew a long breath. For the first time in many months she was no longer terrified of the future. She knew that in the next week, while she waited to hear from Dick, the fear would return, but for now, for this moment, it had left her. Someone else had taken a decision. All she need do was follow.

'Oh yes,' she said. 'I can manage. I don't have much to take, anyway. But will you put me a line in the penny post, tell me what happens? I'll be anxious.'

'Of course I will,' Dick smiled. 'Did you think I'd keep you in suspense?' He felt in his pocket, brought out some money. 'Here's thirty shillings. Buy some food, and whatever else you need for the children until next Friday. Where are the children, by the way?'

'With a neighbour,' Eleanor said. 'And I must go now and fetch them. Dick, I don't know how to thank you. What would I have done if I hadn't seen you today?' But she knew that in her desperation she had planned to see him, and one day when she had the courage, perhaps next Friday, she would tell him the truth about that.

Dick fished in his pocket again. 'Here, he said, 'you'll need a penny for your tramfare!'

CHAPTER TWO

It was already dusk by the time Eleanor reached home. She had stopped at Hardy's, the butchers at the corner of Albert Street, for six pennyworth of scrag end of mutton, and Bert Hardy's eyes had nearly dropped out when she offered him a half-sovereign in payment. He knew her circumstances and would often let her have pie bits for fourpence if she went late enough on a Saturday night.

'Been backing the horses have we, Mrs Heaton?' he joked.

She smiled, and said nothing. He'd be even more surprised when she came back tomorrow. She might well buy a couple of nice chump chops, or some sausages, instead of the 'penny ducks' they usually had on a Saturday. Penny ducks were a sort of mish-mash of odds and ends of meat all minced up together and highly seasoned. Goodness knew what went into them – you could never tell what you were eating. Still, they were tasty, and many a time two of them had made a meal for herself and the two girls. But chops tomorrow, as a special treat, and after that she'd have to go easy on the money Dick had lent her, make it last.

Home was number fifty-two, Elliot Street, one of a long row of stone, smoke-blackened terrace houses a mile from the centre of Akersfield. It was an uphill mile, which would have seemed twice as long with the weight of her basket had not her new lightness of spirit given wings to her heels. Nothing was solved, she told herself firmly. There was trouble ahead of one sort or another, that was for sure; but for the first time in weeks she had hope in her heart.

She turned the key in the lock and entered, lighting the gas at once, so that the small square room, once the mantle was hissing and glowing, was bathed in a soft, pale light. It was icy cold though, and since the evening was by way of a special one she would borrow a bucket of coal from Mrs Baxter and they would have a fire. A good mutton stew inside them, a fire in the grate and the blind drawn against the March chill, and they'd be as snug as bugs in a rug. Just for this evening she'd let the future take care of itself. She'd done all she could.

First off she must fetch the children. It was way past the baby's feed time, and if the alarm clock on the shelf hadn't said so she'd have known anyway by the fullness of her breasts. Right now she needed the baby as much as it needed her.

Mrs Baxter lived three doors down the street. She was a kind friend as well as a neighbour, always ready to do Eleanor a good turn as long as it didn't cost money. With a houseful of children and a husband on short time at the mill, she had none of that to spare.

'Of course you can borrow a bucket of coal,' she said to Eleanor. 'And welcome!'

'He comes in the morning. I'll get a bag and pay you back.'

'Why don't you leave the children here until you've got the roomed warmed?' Mrs Baxter suggested.

Eleanor hesitated. 'Well, it would be nice if Becky and Selina could stay a bit longer, though I'll have to take Jenny. She needs feeding. I can wrap her up warm in her shawl.'

The baby was already whimpering. It was a mewing, hungry sort of cry. When Eleanor picked her out of the cradle she nuzzled into her mother's breast, seeking the source of the food she so urgently desired.

'I'll not be long,' Eleanor promised. 'I'll feed Jenny and get the fire going and then I'll be back.' She turned to her two older daughters who were playing on the floor with some of the Baxter children. 'Be good until I get back,' she cautioned them.

She always enjoyed feeding the baby, trying, even when she was not alone as now, to create a little oasis of peace around the two of them as she did so. Jenny was a swift

26

and hungry feeder. Sometimes Eleanor worried that because she herself went so short of food, her milk might dry up. But there was no sign of that yet. She hoped she'd be able to go on feeding her for months to come. And then, with the thought, came the awful dread which she had managed to put away for the last hour. It rushed back to fill her mind. Supposing the children were taken from her! Supposing Albert and Clara wouldn't have her after all! Would the authorities take away a child at the breast? Would they be so inhuman? But even if they didn't, they'd take Becky and Selina, put them in an orphanage. That was for sure.

The baby, sensing Eleanor's distress, feeling the stiffening of her body, arched her back and drew away with a cry. Eleanor looked down at her.

'I'm sorry,' she said out loud. 'No more thoughts like that this evening – especially when I'm feeding you. It's going to be a good evening – and be damned to tomorrow!'

When the fire was burning and the pan of stew on the single gas ring was filling the room with delicious smells, and Jenny was sleeping the sleep of the deeply satisfied, Eleanor fetched the girls.

'I'm going to get you washed, and into your nightshifts,' she said. 'And by the time you're ready there'll be a lovely supper ready. So come on, jump to it!'

She half filled the enamel bowl at the tap in the cellarhead, then set it on the table and warmed it up from the kettle, already singing over the fire.

'Now who's first?'

'Becky first,' Selina said. Selina didn't like water, made a fuss every time her face was washed. Becky, on the other hand, loved it. She would have liked the big zinc bath out on the hearthrug every night of the week instead of only on Saturdays.

Her children were unlike each other, Eleanor thought, except that they were all fair-haired. Even then it was with different degrees of fairness. Becky's hair was a gold which leaned towards copper; Selina's was a much paler shade, like

27

the outer petals of a daffodil. Jenny's hair, what she had of it, was so fair as to be almost white. Ben, in one of his good moods, looking at Eleanor with Becky and Selina, had said, 'You're my golden girls. That's what you are. My golden girls!'

'How long will the supper be?' Becky asked. 'I'm hungry!'

'I know you are, love,' Eleanor said. 'But it'll be a while yet. It's meat – and you can't cook scrag end quickly, else you wouldn't be able to chew it. I'll tell you what – we'll sing!'

It was a while since they'd had a sing-song. She'd been too down-hearted even for that, though it was one of the things she liked doing best of all and she knew that when she did make the effort it never failed to lift her spirits. It took her away from her troubles and into a sunnier world. It didn't matter whether the songs were happy or sad, comic or tragic, it was the act of singing which made her feel better. It was simply making the effort to begin the first song which was difficult, but tonight she was stronger.

She sang 'Daisy Bell' and 'Ta-ra-ra-boom-de-ay', which the girls liked because it made them laugh and they could both – even Selina at only two and a half – join in the 'boom' with a great shout. She sang 'Dolly Gray' which the soldiers were singing in the Boer War, still being fought. Halfway through 'Dolly Gray' her voice wavered and she had to stop for a minute, remembering her brother David, who had been killed crossing the Tugela river on the way to relieve Ladysmith less than eighteen months ago.

Becky tugged at her skirt.

'Keep singing!' she ordered.

'What a bossy child you are!' Eleanor said. But Becky was right. To keep singing was a good idea. How else would you get through life?

They sang 'Jesus bids us shine', which Becky knew from Sunday school, and then Eleanor struck up with her own favourite – 'My love is like a red, red rose'.

Her voice rang out, clear, rich, powerful. 'And I will love thee still, my love, though all the seas gang dry!' She sang the words as though she meant them, yet there was no-one she loved like that. Once they could have been for Ben, but that was a long time ago. Even if he had lived, she could not truly have sung those words for him now. 'And I will love thee still, my dear, while the sands o' life shall run.' She wished there was someone, some man who meant the whole world to her, and she to him. She brought the song to an end and said, 'That's all for tonight. Supper's ready.'

It was Tuesday when the letter came. She had hoped it might be from Albert, welcoming her. It was short and to the point.

'I will fetch you and the children Thursday, not Friday, so that we can travel in daylight. Will arrive about noon. Hope this suits.

Your mother is looking forward to seeing you.'

She read it twice through, looking for a sign that everything was all right, that they were going to be welcome. 'You're mother is looking forward to seeing you.' Well, she was glad about that – but what about Albert, what about Clara? Her sister-in-law wasn't the easiest person in the world. If only Dick had been more explicit! But it was no use trying to read things into the letter that weren't there. What really mattered was that they were leaving in two days, lock, stock and barrel.

The first thing was to get Mr Earnshaw, from the second-hand furniture shop, to come and put a price on her bits and pieces. There was no hope of taking furniture with her. Albert's house had been crowded with things even before their mother had moved in. Now she doubted there was room for one extra eggcup. All that was left, all her material possessions of five years' marriage would have to go, and she'd get very little for it. But as long as she could pay the back rent and have a little, just a little, in hand to pay Clara for a week or two's keep.

'Right, Becky, Selina, finish your breakfasts. We have to go out.'

'To the park?' Becky asked.

29

'Not today. We shan't have time.' Austen Park was fifteen minutes walk away and it wasn't much of a park at that. Still, it was the only green oasis in this part of Akersfield, even if the green was dark laurels and rhododendrons and a few areas of grass on which one was not allowed to set foot. Eleanor was country born and bred. When she had first come to Akersfield she had desperately missed the fields and trees of Felldale, the wide skyscapes and empty spaces. But she had grown used to it. You could get used to anything in time. And the people of Akersfield were warm and friendly. They'd never treated her as a stranger, even at the beginning.

She finished changing Jenny and put her back in the baby carriage which stood at one end of the living-room, taking up a lot of space, and was the baby's daytime bed.

'Selina, you'd better go in the pram this morning as we're in a hurry,' Eleanor said.

'*I* want to go in the pram!' Becky demanded.

'You're going to walk, like me,' Eleanor said. 'You can help me push.' Her eldest daughter was in an awkward mood, which wasn't unusual if she couldn't have her own way.

'Why can't Selina walk?'

'Because she's too little. Besides, even if she did, you're too big for a baby carriage. There'd be no room for Jenny.'

She was lucky to have the carriage, Eleanor thought. Not every mother in these parts had one. Ben had made it for her when Becky was born, so that she could wheel the baby in the park. At that time he had sometimes even accompanied them – but never after Selina was born. He had fashioned the carriage from wood, and had made it well, as was his way. He had a talent for working in wood and dreamt always of making beautiful things: chairs, delicate tables, carved screens, intricate boxes. His dreams never materialised. It seemed the only way he could earn enough money was by making work benches, putting up kitchen shelves, helping the undertaker when the sharp northern winter took the frail and elderly and Mr Northrop was rushed off his feet. Perhaps, Eleanor thought, that was why Ben had turned so bitter, so morose. He was a man thwarted.

They set off; the two youngest in the carriage, Becky walking, tugging all the while at her mother's skirts because she was fed up. When they reached the second-hand shop Mr Earnshaw emerged from behind cupboards, chests, chairs with the stuffing bursting out of them. He gave the impression that he didn't actually want to sell anything, and when Eleanor told him the purpose of her visit he sounded equally reluctant to buy.

'I'll come and have a look' he said gloomily. 'Don't build up yer hopes, missus. There's not much call for owt second-hand.'

'You'll come today? It's urgent.' And that, Eleanor thought, would knock the price down still further – but there was no help for it.

'Aye. This afternoon. But don't expect much.'

Back home, she viewed the contents of the living-room. An armchair covered in horsehair, which had been Ben's. In the centre of the room a deal table, covered with a dark red plush tablecloth; three chairs around it, plus the high chair, first made for Becky. There were pots and pans, the copper kettle over the fire, the tabbed rug in front of the hearth. Standing in the window, in pride of place, was her beautiful plant stand. It was in polished mahogany, with turned legs. A crocheted mat protected the top, on which stood a flourishing aspidistra, fed with the occasional cup of tea, its leaves polished regularly with a drop of milk. Well, Mrs Baxter would give the aspidistra a good home. She had often cast envious eyes over it. But how can I part with the plant stand, Eleanor asked herself? Nevertheless she'd have to. It was probably worth more than all the rest put together, including the two beds upstairs, and she needed the money.

Mr Earnshaw looked in the bedroom first. It took him ten seconds flat before he clattered downstairs again. He took a gloomy look around the living-room. Eleanor felt everything in it diminished by his gaze.

'I'll give you eight pounds for the lot!' he said.

'Eight pounds!' She couldn't believe her ears. 'But the

31

plant stand alone is worth five pounds! You mean not including the plant stand.'

'I mean including the plant stand,' he said dourly.

'But it's mahogany! It was one of my husband's best pieces . . .'

'It's nicely made, and well kept,' he said. 'I'll grant you that. But there's not much call for them. I'd get next to nothing for it. So eight pounds, missus, take it or leave it.'

But she had seen his beady eye light on the stand when he'd first looked around and she knew he was cheating her.

'Then I'll leave it,' she said firmly. 'I'll go elsewhere. Thank you for calling and I'm sorry we can't do business.' She moved towards the door and held it open.

'Well now,' he said. 'Not so fast! I know you're in a bit of a spot and I'm a sympathetic man. I'll give you ten pounds, including the plant stand, and I'll not charge you a penny for taking them away, which by rights I should. What's more, I'll not collect until Thursday morning, after breakfast. How's that?'

She could have murdered him. She wanted to order him out of the house and have nothing more to do with him. But how did she know she'd fare any better with another dealer? And time was so short.

'Very well then,' she agreed reluctantly. 'Ten pounds.' That would be two pounds for the back rent and eight pounds left to keep them, for who knew how long?

He counted out ten gold sovereigns on to the table.

'I'm a fool to meself,' he said gloomily. 'But there you are. It's the way I'm made!'

By eleven o'clock on Thursday morning the house had been cleared. Mrs Baxter, delighted with the aspidistra, had offered to take Becky and Selina until Dick should arrive, and the baby was asleep in the pram.

'Come round and have a cup of tea while you're waiting,' Mrs Baxter invited. 'You don't want to be here on your own.'

'I'll be round presently,' Eleanor said. She *did* want to be on her own, just for a little while. She was sad at leaving

32

Elliot Street. She had grown used to it, though not all the times had been happy ones. And now the fear of the future, which, except when she lay in bed at night, she had kept at bay over the last few days by being busy, was back on her with a vengeance. She sat on the window sill in the empty room in a state of terror. Every conceivable ill that could happen to her seemed certain to do so. What if Albert said it was impossible, if Clara said she couldn't do with them? However much her mother welcomed her, she had no say in the matter. She herself was a guest in her son's home. He had looked after her in the ten years of her widowhood, before his marriage and since. It wasn't fair to ask him to take on more. But only a fool thought life was fair. Life was cruel, unjust.

At a point where Eleanor felt she could face no more, a cry from Jenny, in the pram, pulled her back. She had almost forgotten the baby, and it would make sense to feed her now, before Dick arrived. She went to the pram and lifted her, sat down on the window sill again and put the baby to her breast. Miraculously, the feel of the soft warm bundle in her arms brought, if not tranquillity, then resolve; banished, for the time being, the worst of her fears.

'It won't do,' she said out loud to the child. 'Self-pity never got anybody anywhere. We won't have it, will we? We'll make out somehow – you and me, Becky and Selina. See if we don't!' All she needed was a little bit of time to sort things out, a breathing space. Surely they'd give her that in Felldale? 'So buck up, my girl,' she admonished herself. 'Stop moaning!'

She winded Jenny, put her back in the pram, took her round to Mrs Baxter's and stayed long enough to drink a cup of tea.

'I'd best get back now,' she said. 'Else Dick won't know where to find me. And I can't thank you enough, Mrs Baxter, for all your kindnesses to me.'

'Get along with you!' Mrs Baxter smiled. 'I'm only sorry you're going. But I daresay you'll turn up now and then, like a bad penny!

Eleanor had been back in number fifty-two no more than a minute when, from the window, she saw the cart, Dick sitting up front driving a dappled grey horse, turn the corner of the street. She watched him as he drew nearer, saw him looking for the number. Her knight in shining armour, she thought fancifully, come to rescue her. She smiled at the thought of a knight sitting on a cart, pulled by an old horse. Still, Dick himself was attractive enough for the part, with his dark curly hair, not totally hidden by his cap, his skin evenly tanned from his open-air life. He held himself well, his head lifted almost proudly. And when he stopped the cart in front of the door and jumped down it was, in spite of his height, with the lightness and skill of an athlete. Yes, she thought, in different circumstances he could have been a knight, come to rescue his lady. Not that she was his lady.

She ran to open the door.

'You're in good time,' she said. Then – 'Is it all right? Is everything going to be all right?' It was the only moment of anxiety she was going to allow herself. She had vowed she would not let herself slip back into that earlier dark mood.

Even so, she couldn't keep the nervousness out of her voice, nor the fear from showing in her eyes. Dick saw it at once as he looked at her, and determined immediately that he would not tell her the whole truth. Leave it at the fact that she was going to Felldale, never mind saying that her welcome wouldn't be a warm one, at least not from Clara, who was the one who counted. Don't tell her that they'd agreed to her coming only to save the disgrace of Albert's sister in the workhouse, and they certainly didn't want her for long – though where else she could go, nobody was prepared to say. So he'd keep quiet, let her at least have the journey in peace. She'd find out soon enough.

'Everything's all right,' he assured her, and was rewarded by seeing her face light up. With her fear banished she was again her strong, radiant self. Shabby as she was, he thought, she was a wonderful-looking woman. There was an air about her. 'Your Ma is looking forward to seeing you and the children. It was all I could do to stop her coming with me,' he said. At least that was true. 'I told her I didn't think there'd be room. I didn't know how much stuff you'd have.'

'Only these few bundles,' Eleanor said. 'Clothes – mine and the children's – a bit of bed linen I thought might be useful. And then there's the pram. I couldn't manage without the pram. But I sold everything else – which reminds me that I can pay you back your thirty shillings.'

'There's no need,' Dick told her. 'Leave it be for now.'

'No,' she said. 'I want to pay you – and to thank you again. You'll never know what it meant to me. That and the meal. That hot meat pie, those mushy peas! They put new life into me.'

Though he still demurred, she counted out the money into his hand. Of the rest of the sum she had ten shillings in her purse, to give immediately to Clara so that they shouldn't be too beholden, and the remaining six pounds sewn into a bag which she fixed on a cord around her neck, underneath her dress. Every time her hand strayed towards it, which it did often, she was comforted by its weight against her skin.

'I'll fetch the children,' she said. 'They're with a neighbour.'

While she was gone Dick loaded the bundles on to the cart and spread a tarpaulin over them. As the total of a woman's possessions, he thought, they were meagre. When he turned, Eleanor was walking towards him, a child on each hand. He caught his breath at the sight of the older girl. She was the spitting image of her mother and the double of Eleanor as he remembered her when they'd both been children.

'No need to go back into the house,' Eleanor was saying. She didn't want them to see that bare room. But though Selina stayed obediently outside, Becky was too quick for her. She broke free from her mother's hand and ran into number fifty-two. Then she stopped in amazement, her eyes widening as she stared around the empty room.

'The table's gone!' she cried. 'Mother, where's the table? Why is there no furniture?' As long as she lived she was

35

to remember the shock of that bare room, which only that morning had been her home. Where was her home?

Eleanor bent down and put her arms around her daughter.

'It's all right, Becky. Don't you remember, I told you all about it. We're going to live with Grandma Foster, and with Auntie Clara and Uncle Albert. You'll like it there. You'll be able to play with your cousins.'

'I want my table,' Becky said. Her eyes, meeting Eleanor's accusingly, brimmed with tears. Eleanor swallowed hard, and managed a smile.

'One day you shall have a table which is really your very own. I promise you. And now we must go. We mustn't keep Mr Fletcher waiting – or the horse. Come and see the horse!'

Becky, turning her head for a last look at the room which had been so familiar and was now so strange, followed her mother outside. The man swung her through the air and up on to the cart, then Selina beside her.

'You can call me Uncle Dick,' he said. 'Now Eleanor, if you'll take the baby out I'll lash the carriage on to the cart.'

He lifted the baby carriage as if it weighed no more than a couple of pounds, then he jumped after it and secured it with a rope. 'Now give me the baby while you climb up,' he instructed, 'and then I'll hand her to you.'

'You make it seem so easy,' Eleanor said when they were all settled.

'That's because it is.' He clicked his tongue and the horse began to move away.

Even at the horse's slow pace they quickly left Akersfield behind.

'It's a bigger town now than it was even five years ago, when I first set foot here,' Eleanor said. 'New houses spreading over the hills all around the town. They keep extending the tram routes, and you can get buses now to some places.'

'Trams and buses today, motor cars before you know where you are,' Dick observed.

'But not for you and me,' Eleanor said. 'Nasty, smelly

things, motor cars. Though I wouldn't mind having a go. They go ever so fast. Do you know, there's talk of raising the speed limit to twenty miles an hour! Can you imagine? It's true – I read it in the *Akersfield Record*!'

'Ah, Well in that case it must be true,' Dick said, grinning. 'I'll tell you what, when I get *my* motor car I'll take you for a ride and we'll go at twenty-*five* miles an hour!'

Eleanor laughed. 'That'll be the day! And I'll get myself all togged up in a long dust coat and a motoring veil!'

'You think I don't mean it?'

Eleanor turned and looked at him, hearing the serious note in his voice.

'I mean it all right. One day, I don't know when, I'il have a motor car. And one day, instead of a horse and cart I'll have a motor lorry. I mean to get on, Eleanor!'

'Oh Dick, I didn't mean . . . I didn't know . . . I'm sure you will get on if that's what you want.'

He sounded so determined.

'So things are going well with you?' she asked.

'Reasonably well. I rent five acres now, further down by the river. I can grow more things than my dad ever could.'

And I work a damned sight harder, he thought. While he had worked for his father, which he had done straight from school, no-one had realised the ambition in him. But it had always been there under the surface, waiting for a chance to break out. He had a long way to go yet – a long way, he knew that – but he'd go it, he'd get there.

'I'd like more land,' he said. 'And I've got the money my father left me, when I can find the right place. I'd like to do more growing, employ a man to take the stuff to markets. In fact, *seed* is what interests me. I'd like to concentrate on seed. Have you ever thought, it's all there, the whole plant, inside one small seed, maybe no bigger than the head of a pin? And have you ever thought that the seed's all there for the taking – hundreds, maybe thousands, of seeds from one plant?'

'No, I hadn't thought,' Eleanor said. 'So what would you do with all that seed?'

'Sell it!' he said. 'Pack a teaspoonful in a fancy packet and sell it! And experiment. Try to get different seed, better plants.'

'I'm hungry!' Becky announced loudly. The grown-ups were talking all the time. No-one was taking any notice of her. She didn't like no-one noticing her.

'Well now,' Eleanor said. 'I can do something about that. I've got a nice thick slice of bread-and-dripping each in my basket! Are you hungry too, Selina?'

'Yes.' Selina's pronunciation was clear and precise, though she was not one for wasting words. So far she had found she could get most of what she wanted without much speech. 'Uncle Dick' she added.

'Yes, I have one for Uncle Dick,' Eleanor assured her.

'There are some apples in a box there,' Dick said when they'd eaten the bread. 'Help yourselves.'

The baby continued to sleep. Perpetual motion was what Jenny liked, and Eleanor was glad of it. If she wakened she'd be hungry and she'd have to be fed. Somehow Eleanor didn't want to do this in front of Dick. With the old Dick it wouldn't have mattered, she thought. She'd not have taken much notice. But with this man who seemed almost new to her it was different. He was . . . an attractive stranger, almost. She realised she knew nothing of what had happened to him in the last five years. Why, he might even have a wife and children!

'Are you married?' she ventured.

'No.'

She could tell by the tone of his voice that there was more to it than that, but the firm monosyllable precluded further questioning so she said nothing more. For a while they rode in silence, but then suddenly he spoke, and she realised that he had not stopped thinking about their earlier conversation.

'A man's got to have confidence,' he said. 'He's got to have confidence in himself, and in the future. And he's got to work to make it come true.'

What about a woman, Eleanor thought? A woman needs a future too. I need a future. But without a man, what could

38

she do? Nevertheless she had to make a future, not only for herself but for her golden girls. She owed it to them. She couldn't let them down.

The jogging of the cart, the rhythmic clip-clop of the horse's hooves had now lulled Selina to sleep also. But Becky was still awake. She seemed to need little sleep at any time. Her eyes were always open, taking everything in. Judging, it often seemed to Eleanor. Sometimes finding wanting.

She raised her eyes to Eleanor's now. When Becky's eyes met hers, Eleanor thought, it was like looking in a mirror, except that the child's were a hazel green instead of the pure green of her own, and her long curling lashes and fine wings of eyebrows were darker than those of her mother. Sometimes Becky's face seemed dominated by her eyes, though her other features were striking: the finely-sculpted nose with its flaring nostrils, and the pale mouth, prettily curved, but a little too determined for one so young. 'Becky is all you,' Ben had once said. So was Selina, but a gentler, paler edition. It was too soon to know about Jenny.

They were nearly there. The main road ran through the bottom of the valley, almost parallel to the railway, and a bridge took the canal over them both. Away to the west a long line of hills separated Yorkshire from Lancashire and to the east, starting in the valley and then climbing and clinging precariously to the hill, was Felldale. Eleanor's stomach lurched at the sight of it. She felt sick − but sick with longing and sick with fear at one and the same time.

They had turned off the main road now, crossed the river bridge. The horse, knowing every foot of the way, slowed down in preparation for the steep hill. As they climbed, the different parts of the village came into view. The huge church, the Methodist chapel, the public house, the school, the forge; the cottages and a few larger houses, and Albert's shop. They were all clustered together, all built of the same dark stone, the millstone grit of the West Riding, darkened still further by the smoke which the wind brought from the towns. But behind the village, beyond where Royd Manor kept an eye on everything, the fields were of a spring green so brilliant as to dazzle the eyes.

'Whoa, Polly!' Dick drew up in front of the shop. He jumped down, then lifted the two older girls and stood them on the pavement.

'The pram next, and then the little 'un,' he said.

While he was unlashing it, Eleanor waiting on the cart, holding the baby tightly to her as if she was a talisman against what was to come, Albert emerged from the shop, followed closely by his wife and mother.

CHAPTER THREE

'Why, our Eleanor!' Albert said, his voice full of surprise, for all the world as if he hadn't expected her.

'Well don't just stand there,' his wife admonished him. 'Give Dick a hand wi' the baby carriage!' Her sharp voice and thin features matched her skinny appearance.

'Let me take the babby,' Mrs Foster said.'

Eleanor handed Jenny over to her mother. 'There you are then,' she said. 'Go to Grandma.' The baby, wide awake now, seriously studied the new face looking into hers, and approved it.

'Well, there's no call for everybody to stand on the street,' Clara said briskly. 'Dick, you'll stop and have a cup of tea?'

'I'd best get on,' Dick replied. 'There's always something to do.' The next half-hour wasn't going to be easy for the Foster family, he thought. Aside from Eleanor, they'd prefer his room to his company. And it would be best for her to get it over quickly. He jumped back on the cart and took up the reins. As he began to move away, Eleanor ran after him.

'I can't thank you enough, Dick, for all you've done for me and the children. I'll never forget it!' She didn't want him to go. She felt a security in his presence, as if just by being there he could protect her from the difficulties she knew were waiting for her the minute she stepped inside the house.

Seeing her standing on the pavement, her anxious face lifted towards him, he felt he wanted to shield her from the whole world. It was a strange feeling to have about Eleanor Foster (he could never think of her as Eleanor Heaton)

41

because if ever a woman was strong, she was. Always had been, even as a child. But she was feminine too, and now it was her femininity which reached out to him, called to him so that he wanted to bend down and snatch her up; drive away with her, he didn't know where. He felt knocked sideways by the suddenness of his feelings, and his bewilderment at himself made it difficult for him to reply to her. In any case, he thought, bringing himself back to earth, there was nothing he could do. He was out of it now. He had commitments of his own.

'Promise me one thing,' he said. 'Promise you'll keep your pecker up. Don't let your spirits go!' He raised his hand to her, pulled on the reins and moved away. Eleanor watched him out of sight. By the time she turned away the others were going inside. She followed them through the shop – redolent of bacon and candles and cheese and a score of other things which were the smells of her childhood – and into the back parlour.

Mrs Foster, already seated and still holding the baby close as if she would never let it go, looked up and smiled as her daughter entered.

'Well, it's grand to see you, Eleanor love,' she said.

They were words of defiance. She knew well enough that Eleanor was not welcome in that house. They had been through it all a dozen times – she, Clara, Albert – from the first minute Dick Fletcher had brought the news. She had been deeply saddened to hear of Eleanor's plight . . . and yet, and yet. Until Dick had brought the message she had sometimes thought that she was never to see Eleanor again. She had been angry when her daughter had left Felldale with Ben Heaton. He was the wrong man for Eleanor. As time passed she reckoned that it was Ben who forbade Eleanor to visit Felldale and when, though too late, she learned from Dick of Ben's lack of success before his death, she was sure of it. Ben Heaton was a proud man – false pride, Susannah Foster called it. But it was a wife's duty to obey her husband – didn't she promise that in church? – and she didn't blame Eleanor for doing so.

But now, she thought, though she wished it could have been by different circumstances, she was reunited with her daughter.

'Everyone knows that Eleanor was always your favourite,' Clara had said in the course of all the arguments they'd had. 'But who was it *really* cared for you, looked after you when you needed looking after?'

'Albert,' Mrs Foster said promptly. 'And I love him and honour him for it.' She couldn't bring herself to deny that Eleanor was her favourite. Eleanor and then her younger son David, but David was gone now. She could not tell a lie, though she had tried always not to make any difference between her children. And Albert, had his mother but known it, had realised while he was still a child that he and his sister Madge came second to Eleanor. He accepted it. Who would not love bright, beautiful Eleanor best? And she herself, if indeed she realised it, had never taken advantage of the situation.

'It's grand to see you,' Mrs Foster repeated. She made no move to kiss her daughter, or to embrace her. Kissing was for children and courting couples. But her round face beamed with pleasure in the happiness of the moment. Never mind what was to come.

'It's lovely to see you – all of you,' Eleanor said. 'I can't tell you what it means to me, the fact that you've let us come.'

'Yes, well,' Clara said quickly. There was no point in anybody taking anything for granted. She hoped she wasn't a hard woman, but you could say Eleanor had made her bed when she'd left Felldale behind; so full of herself, so sure of everything. Pride went before a fall, though as Albert had said it wasn't Eleanor's fault that she'd been widowed. And to be widowed, if you were poor, was a terrible thing.

'I daresay you're all hungry,' Clara said. 'Well, tea'll not be long. I've got the kettle on.'

She poked at the fire until it glowed more red, wedged the kettle more firmly into the coals. Then she checked the heavy black iron fireguard, making sure that the hook was securely fastened to the ribs of the fire grate. She was always careful with her own two children, though they were older, seven and five. With Eleanor's she reckoned she would have to be extra watchful. Becky, she had already decided, was going to be a handful. You could see it in her face.

'I'm hungry, Ganna,' Becky announced.

'I'm afraid she's always hungry,' Eleanor apologised.

'She a growing girl,' Mrs Foster said indulgently. 'She shall have a nice piece of oven-bottom cake until the proper tea is ready. It's not long out of the oven.'

When she split the flat circle of bread through the middle with a long sharp knife, deliciously scented steam arose from it in a little cloud. In fact, the whole room smelled of newly-baked bread; of spiced currant teacakes, and of the tin of gingerbread which was cooking right now in the cooling oven. Eleanor had overlooked that it was Thursday, the traditional baking day. All over the West Riding the same wonderful smells would fill every house.

She was suddenly ravenous. When she saw the fresh butter, which her mother spread generously, melt into the softness of the bread, watched while it was topped with home-made rhubarb jam, she could stand it no longer. 'Could I have a piece too?' she asked.

'Proper tea won't be long,' Clara said. If Flo saw everybody eating, then she'd want some – which meant she would have no appetite for her tea. Clara didn't hold with eating between meals. There was a time and a place for everything. Routine was important – she hoped Eleanor realised that. On the other hand, those poor fatherless mites certainly looked hungry. Well, it wouldn't hurt just this once, she supposed!

'Here you are, love,' Mrs Foster said, handing Eleanor a generous chunk of oven-bottom cake. 'A biting-on.'

Eleanor sank her teeth into the heavenly mixture. It was bliss! No-one, but no-one, made oven-bottom cake like her mother: the base crisp as could be, the inside soft, the whole cake exactly the right thickness – an inch and a half, so that when it was split, and you bit into it, you could taste

44

can sleep with Ma, with Selina between you. We can make up a bed for the baby in a drawer in your room.'

'I'm very grateful,' Eleanor said. 'We don't mind where we sleep, and I'll see to it that the children behave themselves. Also, I've got a bit of money towards our keep.' She held out a half-sovereign to her sister-in-law but stopped herself – just in time – saying 'There's more where that came from' as her hand strayed towards her neck and she felt the purse of coins beneath her dress.

Clara put out a hand to take the money, and then drew back. She didn't want anything settled as quickly as that. If Eleanor felt she was paying her way . . . but there was more to this situation than money. Nothing could compensate for sharing her home. It was bad enough having her mother-in-law, but you expected to be burdened with parents when they were older and couldn't earn. And no-one could say she didn't do her duty. But a sister-in-law and three children was another matter. She didn't intend it to last and she wasn't going to compromise herself from the start.

'It's not necessary,' she said. 'We can manage the food. It's not as if it was for long.' She gave Eleanor a straight look and saw that it was immediately understood.

'Happen you'll want to go and stay with your Madge for a while,' she suggested.

And happen I won't, Eleanor thought. Madge was eight years older than she, separated from her by Albert and David. They had never been close, even as children, and Madge had married while Eleanor was still at school. John Brookfield was a successful sheep farmer in Wharfedale. It was Eleanor's opinion that as well as running her husband, Madge ran the entire village in which they lived. Anyway, Madge wouldn't have her.

'We'll see,' she said quietly. 'I'll not outstay my welcome anywhere. You can be sure of that. And now if there's nothing I can do for you I'd best be getting the baby to bed.'

When she went upstairs to the back bedroom which was her mother's, Mrs Foster had already emptied a drawer from the large chest and had balanced it across two chairs so as to keep it clear of draughts from the floor.

'She'll be as snug as can be,' she said. 'Bless her little heart! Here, give her to me for a minute and I'll change her while you get ready to feed her. And Eleanor . . .' she was suddenly hesitant.

'What?'

'Try not to mind Clara too much. Try to fit in with things.'

'But of course I shall!' Eleanor said sharply. 'What else do you think? I'll not argue, I'll keep quiet, I'll keep myself and the children out of the way! Is that what you want?'

'It's not what I want,' Mrs Foster said. 'Don't blame me. I know how you feel.'

'No Mother, you do *not* know how I feel! No-one knows how I feel, though at times I'd like to shout it out to the whole world. I know you sympathise, but you do *not* know how I feel!'

'Perhaps you forget I was widowed too,' Mrs Foster said quietly. 'I was only forty when your father died. I know what it's like to be without my man. You were still at school and David only just apprenticed at the forge. If it hadn't been for Albert earning a wage with Mr Braithwaite, we could have been in the workhouse. Do you think I liked taking from Albert, and him saving up to get married? Do you think when he got wed I liked moving in here with him and Clara? You were away in service by then. Did you know how I felt? But I tell you, I know how *you* feel, and my heart aches for you. Aches all the more because I can't do anything.'

'Oh Ma, I'm sorry! I really am. But the difference is, you didn't have little children. We were nearly all off your hands.'

'And the other difference is, I was forty. No hope of me getting another husband. I knew when Ted died I'd have to be dependent for the rest of my life. You're young and good-looking. Given just a bit of time, you'll get married again.'

'You're wrong, Ma,' Eleanor said. 'I shan't get married again. Not from choice anyway. Not unless I have to for the sake of the children. I soon found marriage isn't all it's cracked up to be.'

50

'Well I'm sorry about that, lass,' Mrs Foster replied 'Marriage has its ups and downs, but me and your dad were happy together. Perhaps you will be second time round.'

'I've told you, there's not going to be a second time,' Eleanor snapped.

She crossed to the window and looked out over the garden. It was a long, fairly narrow garden, with a paved path leading to the privy at the far end. There were currant bushes – red and black – three or four gooseberry bushes, and rows of various vegetables. In the middle of a grassed area was an old, contorted apple tree, around which Becky, Flo, and her elder brother Jimmy played some game of their own devising while Selina tried in vain to keep up with them.

Beyond the garden, down the hill, a line of trees – alders, oaks still black, a few willows – marked the line of the river. And beyond the river, beyond the flat land where Dick Fletcher had his market garden, the land rose again to more hills. It was a scene of total peace, the evening sun catching everything with gold, and in spite of herself some of it invaded Eleanor's spirit. She should not have spoken so to her mother. It was unnecessary, unkind.

'I'm sorry, Ma! Truly! Now give me Jenny and I'll feed her. She's a patient little soul.'

'Then make yourself comfortable on the bed,' Mrs Foster said. 'And I'll hand her to you.'

Eleanor held the baby close, soothed by the feel of it in her arms, heartened by the way its blue eyes looked so calmly into her own. She marvelled again that this child, the whole of whose short life had been spent in an atmosphere heavy with trouble and grief, should be so serene, so accepting.

When she had fed Jenny she put her into the makeshift bed where she fell asleep at once. Mrs Foster crossed to the window and called out to the other children. 'Time to come in! It's dropping cold.'

'You see to Selina, I'll look after Becky,' she said to Eleanor. 'She's a little treat, that Becky!'

Downstairs she unhooked the tin bath from its nail, carried it into the living-room and placed it on the rug in front of the fire. After filling it, she undressed Becky and Flo and sat them one at each end. They giggled with delight at the mere fact of being together.

'There you are,' their grandmother said when they finally emerged from the water, smelling of carbolic soap. 'Now finish drying yourselves while I make you some pobbies. Bread-and-milk pobbies is the best thing in the world to go to bed on! It poultices the stomach and helps you to sleep.'

'I hope that last bit's true,' Clara said. 'They look a long way from sleep to me. And mind you, I want no fun and games when you get upstairs. Straight to sleep!' She hoped Becky wouldn't keep Flo awake. If Flo went short of sleep she was impossible to deal with next day.

She hoped, too, that Eleanor wouldn't want to stay up until all hours. They were early-to-bed and early-to-rise, she and Albert. And although her mother-in-law, in the early days, had liked to stay up late, she had quite soon fallen into the pattern.

She needn't have worried. Not long after nine o'clock, when Albert had pulled down the shop blinds and locked the door, Clara yawned and said she didn't know when she'd felt so tired and it really wasn't worthwhile mending the fire at this time of night. Mrs Foster asked who wanted cocoa and said she thought she'd take hers up to bed with her. Eleanor bade everyone goodnight and went upstairs. It was not quite ten.

In the bedroom Mrs Foster prepared herself for the night slowly, with deliberate routine. Interrupted by sips of cocoa, the steelboned stays were abandoned, the hair, once as golden as Eleanor's, was brushed. That done, Mrs Foster climbed into bed, sighing with contentment as the feather mattress adapted itself to her ample contours. They were old friends, she and the feather mattress. She had slept on it since she was a bride and every night she was grateful that Albert and Clara had let her bring it with her.

'Blow out the candle when you're ready,' she said to Eleanor, 'Goodnight, God bless!'

She was drifting on the edge of sleep when she heard

Eleanor's stifled sobbing. She dragged herself back to wakefulness again, then reached out for the matches and the candle.

'No, don't light the candle!' Eleanor cried. 'Please don't!'

Mrs Foster put the matches down again, sat upright in the dark, aware that Eleanor was tossing her head from side to side against the pillow.

'What is it, doy? What is it?'

'Oh Ma! You've got to stand by me! You've got to help me!' Eleanor sobbed.

'Of course I'll stand by you. You're my bairn, aren't you. No matter how old you are, you're my bairn. And I'll always help you.' But even as she spoke a feeling of deep helplessness, as impenetrable as the darkness of the room, filled Susannah Foster. What could she do? What in God's name could she do?

Eleanor wept as she had not done since Ben's death; deep, despairing sobs which shook her body. Mrs Foster took her in her arms, stroked her hair, felt the tears soaking the front of her own nightshift. It was, for a moment, as if her daughter was the little girl she had once been and she herself was the young, confident mother she had been then, knowing that she could put right whatever ailed her child. But the feeling went quickly. It was not so, not any longer.

'Hush love,' she whispered. 'We don't want to waken anyone, do we?'

Though Mrs Foster had thought she could do nothing for her daughter, it was surprising what strength and hope came to Eleanor from the feel of her mother's arms around her, the softness of her voice, her comfortable lavender smell. Her sobs lessened, and subsided. Somehow . . . somehow . . .

'Perhaps I could get a job? Earn enough to keep us, rent a little cottage in Felldale? If you would help with the children.'

'Well of course I would, love. But a job in Felldale?' All the same, it was not the moment to show the pessimism she felt.

'Perhaps I'd get something at the Manor. Or better still, perhaps Dick Fletcher would give me a job? He was telling me he'd got more land – and it's a busy time of the year.'

'Market gardening? It's hardly the job for a woman,' Mrs Foster said dubiously.

'Anything's a job for a woman if it means keeping herself and her children. I'd go down a coalmine, break stones on the road!'

'Well, we'll see, love.' Mrs Foster summoned all the confidence she could muster into her voice. 'I think for now we should get a bit of sleep. Things might not turn out as bad as we think. It's always darkest before the dawn and tomorrow is another day!'

Eleanor found the clichés surprisingly comforting. Totally spent with emotion – she felt as though she had travelled a thousand miles since leaving Akersfield that morning – she fell suddenly into a sleep of exhaustion. Not so Mrs Foster. She lay awake waiting for the new terrifying day, pondering deeply on her own impotence.

CHAPTER FOUR

In the first moments of Eleanor's wakening she was confused as to time and place. She thought she was back in Elliot Street, and that if she put out a hand she would touch Ben beside her in the bed. She had been dreaming of him again, something she had done several times since his death, though less frequently in the last few weeks. He had been making love to her but she had wakened, as she always did, just before the climax came. She was glad, if she had to dream about him, that it was of the thing which had been best between them, the only thing which in their last three years together had made the marriage bearable. That and the children which resulted.

How could she possibly have been as mistaken in the character of a man as she had been in Ben Heaton's? It was true what her mother said; she had been infatuated, blind. What she had taken for strength had been bigotry and obstinacy; what she had seen as devotion was jealousy; jealousy which made him query every step she took without him, every person she spoke to; a stifling, smothering jealousy, and without cause, though he himself had been unfaithful. His infidelity was never mentioned between them, but she had known it just the same. But in bed together, in the darkness, they were the two people they had been in the first days of their marriage, never failing to give pleasure and satisfaction to each other.

She had been wakened, she now realised, by the small noises which the baby was making to greet the new day. Each day now Jenny found a new sound with which to express herself. Looking across the room, Eleanor saw two arms and two legs waving and kicking in the air, the movements of the tiny limbs punctuating the child's peroration.

Mrs Foster stirred in her sleep. 'What's that?' she mumbled. 'Did you say something?'

Eleanor raised herself on one elbow and gazed down at her mother. How tired she looked! Her face was full of worry lines which Eleanor didn't remember having seen before. Lacking teeth, her mouth was sunken, nothing more than a thin line, the lips sucked in. She looked old. Was fifty old? Eleanor couldn't imagine herself ever being old. There was so much living to do before then. And, strangely in view of the circumstances, she felt in herself this morning a new optimism, almost a zest for living, which she had not experienced since before the baby was born. Things *would* come right. She had only to make it so.

'It was only the baby, Ma,' she said. 'Go back to sleep.'

The sounds from Jenny were changing. She was getting querulous. The last thing Eleanor wanted was for the household to be wakened before time, and right now everything was silent. She hopped out of bed, changed the baby where she lay, and then carried her back into the bed, managing not to disturb Selina who still slept peacefully against the wall.

When Mrs Foster opened her eyes and saw her youngest granddaughter her face cleared; the worry lines momentarily vanished and her brown eyes were soft. She held out a hand to the baby and Jenny took her finger and grasped it firmly.

'My word, she's got a strong grip,' Mrs Foster said. 'She'll hang on to life all right!'

She got out of bed, drew the blind up a little and looked out at the day. It was going to be fine, but there was no sun on this side of the house in the morning. She badly wanted to go to the lavatory but with Eleanor there she couldn't bring herself to use the chamber pot. In spite of having lived all her life surrounded by family, she was a private person. She believed Eleanor was too. It was one of the traits she had inherited from her mother. They never discussed intimacies. It had not been easy for her last night to undress in her daughter's presence, more especially since she was conscious that, unclothed, she was no longer pleasant to look upon. She was fat and shapeless, where once she had been slim, with a tiny waist, slender hips, a firm, high bosom – the kind of figure Eleanor had now.

'I'm just going down the garden,' she said. 'You stay where you are. If I can stir the fire without waking anybody I'll make a cup of tea – bring you one up.'

When she brought the tea, Eleanor said, 'Ma, I've decided what I'm going to do. I'm going to see Dick Fletcher, ask him if he'll give me a job. I can't see him today, he'll be at Akersfield market, and tomorrow morning at Skipton. But tomorrow afternoon I'll walk down to his place.

Mrs Foster shook her head. 'Well I don't know, love . . . Would you not think it might be better to go up to the Manor? They might have a job for you.'

'I don't think so. Even if they didn't want me to live in, they'd want me there from morning until night and I'd have to leave all three children. If Dick would give me work I daresay I could take Jenny in the pram. She'd be no trouble either to him or to me. She'd be out of Clara's way and it would only leave you with the two older ones.'

'Well, if you think that's best,' Mrs Foster said doubtfully.

'Will you walk down with me to Dick's tomorrow, Ma? You could wait nearby with the children while I went in. And I don't want to say anything to Clara or Albert until after we've been. Pretend we're just going for a walk.'

Mrs Foster sighed. 'All right then. There's one thing I almost forgot, though, what with so much happening. Our Madge is coming over tomorrow afternoon with John and the children. You'll want to see her.'

'To be truthful, not really,' Eleanor said. 'Though I daresay I'll have to. But I shall be glad to be out when she arrives. That way they can discuss me to their heart's content!'

'I had thought Madge might be able to help. Maybe let you stay on the farm for a while. Perhaps find you a job in Faverwell?'

'That's wishful thinking, Ma, and we both know it. She'd like it even less than Clara does. She'd not rest until she'd got the children into an orphanage – and I'm not letting them go! I'll never let them go, do you hear! Never!'

If only there was something she could do for Eleanor, Mrs Foster thought. That was one of the worst things about having children. When they were little you somehow managed to do most things for them – feed them, clothe them, love them. They could bring their childish troubles to you and you could cope with them. When they were grown it was another matter. You loved them as much as ever, but sometimes that was all you *could* do.

When they went downstairs Clara was already up and doing. There was a pan of porridge on the hob and the appetising smell of home-cured bacon filled the air, teasing at Eleanor's nostrils. She didn't know how, in the face of everything, she could be hungry, but she was.

'Where's Albert?' she asked.

'He's already in the shop. He likes to get it all shipshape before the first customer arrives, and they start coming early. It's amazing how people run out of things last thing at night or at the break of day. A shopkeeper's life would be a sight easier if only people had a little forethought!'.

I'll bet you'd never run out of anything, Eleanor thought. Clara was as organised as Madge. She couldn't imagine either of them ever being left a penniless widow. It would be inefficient.

'You could go and get Becky and Flo up, if you've a mind,' Clara said. 'Then we can get breakfast over with. Flo goes to school now and I like her to eat properly before she sets off. Jimmy is already in the shop. He does an hour or so before school to earn a bit of pocket money. He's like me, our Jimmy; likes to make best use of his time.'

'I shall be glad when Becky is old enough to go to school,' Eleanor said. 'She gets fast with herself what to do. But only a month or two now.'

'Perhaps . . .' Clara stopped herself. She didn't want to encourage anything which might sound like a long-term

58

arrangement. That had to be made quite plain. On the other hand, it would be one less person underfoot.

'Perhaps if you asked Miss Lawrence she might take Becky on temporarily. As a sort of visitor . . . short-term, if you see what I mean.'

'Oh I do!' Eleanor said. 'Well, I can ask her, and I will. I'll go up to the school this morning.'

At ten o'clock, having given Clara what little help she would accept in the house, Eleanor set off with Becky, the latter wildly excited at the thought of going to school.

'Will I sit with Flo?' she asked. 'Shall we be able to play with the dolls' house?' She had heard all about the dolls' house. It had been there when her mother had gone to the same school.

'First of all we'll have to see if Miss Lawrence can do with you,' Eleanor said. 'She might not have a place.'

'Do you mean she might not have a chair for me to sit on?' Becky asked. 'I don't mind. I can sit on the floor.'

'That's not what I meant. Anyway, the children sit on benches, not chairs. But your best plan is to be a good girl and keep quiet while I talk to Miss Lawrence.'

When Eleanor pushed open the heavy, green-painted door which led directly into the school hall, it was for a moment as if she'd never been away. Nothing, as far as she could see, had changed in the slightest. The same pictures on the walls, the tonic sol-fa modulator hanging there, even the same sentences written on the blackboard. And the same smell, exactly, of chalk and dust and children.

A singing lesson was in progress and the boys and girls, from the youngest to the oldest, sat cross-legged in a circle on the floor. They were singing the same song that she, Dick, her brother David and all the others had sung.

'Cherry ripe, cherry ripe, ripe I cry
Full and fair ones, come and buy!'

And the piano sounded the same; as tinny as ever, and slightly off-key, even though she felt sure the same blind piano tuner came once a year to see to it. But, off-key or not, she wanted to join in, and might well have done so had not the pianist, who presumably was Miss Jane Lawrence, broken off her playing at the sight of a stranger, and held up a hand to silence the children.

'Can I do something for you?' she called out.

'Please don't let me interrupt,' Eleanor said. 'I can wait. I wanted a word with you when it's convenient.'

'We were just about to finish.' The woman turned to the children and clapped her hands. 'Little ones, get your slates and draw me a picture. Something you saw at Easter. Older children, you can read for a few minutes.'

They set about doing exactly as they had been told at once. Miss Lawrence had them completely under control, though with her slight figure, her clear, unlined complexion, and not being one iota over five feet in her rather dainty shoes, she looked little more than a schoolgirl herself. Her abundant dark hair was piled more fashionably high than might have been expected for a schoolteacher, perhaps to give her extra height. Fine, dark eyes mutely questioned Eleanor.

'I'm Mrs Eleanor Heaton. I'm staying with my brother, Albert Foster. I daresay you know him?'

The teacher held out a hand. 'Jane Lawrence, and I'm pleased to meet you, Mrs Heaton. Of course I know your brother and sister-in-law, everyone in Felldale does. And I had heard you were coming.'

Just what had she heard, Eleanor wondered? Had her own family spread the news, or could it be that Dick Fletcher had told this self-possessed, undeniably pretty, young woman about her? Whoever it was, she hoped they had not gone into details. There was no need for the world and his wife to know her whole situation.

'I heard you had been recently widowed,' Jane Lawrence said. 'I am so sorry. I hope a short stay with your family will help you to recuperate.'

'Thank you, Eleanor said. 'I'm sure it will.'

'But . . .'

'You are wondering why I'm here? In fact I came to ask a favour of you. This is my eldest daughter, Becky. I wondered if you might have her here? She's four and a half and she's more than ready for school. She's – I suppose I shouldn't say it, but she's quite bright and can read well. I'm sure she wouldn't be any trouble to you, Miss Lawrence!'

Jane Lawrence smiled. 'I'm sure she wouldn't. But then I wouldn't let her be. As well as reading and numbers, I try to instil discipline and good manners into my pupils, no matter how young they are. But I'm sure Becky has all of that!' She smiled encouragingly at the child and Becky gave back her most winning look.

I wouldn't be too sure about that, Eleanor thought. She knew that look. It was the one her daughter used when she wanted something badly.

'Of course, as you know, the starting age is five . . .' Miss Lawrence began.

Tears welled up in Becky's eyes. She looked up imploringly at Miss Lawrence and then lowered her gaze and stared dejectedly at the floor.

' . . . But some rules are made to be broken. And as you're only here for a short time I think this is one we might break. I'm sure if the Inspector should choose to visit us, he would understand. So you may stay, Becky. I see you are already wearing your pinafore, so that's all right. And for today you may sit next to your cousin Flo, who will show you where to find a slate and slate pencil.'

Becky let go of her mother's hand, and without a backward glance, trotted across the room to join Flo.

'I'm really most grateful,' Eleanor said. 'You must let me know at once if Becky is any trouble.'

'Oh, she won't be,' Miss Lawrence replied with confidence.

'Then I mustn't take up any more of your precious time.'

Jane Lawrence watched the other woman recross the room and go out of the door. So that was Eleanor Heaton. When word had got around the village a day or two ago that she was returning, widowed, more than one person had taken the trouble to tell her that Eleanor Foster, as was, was the girl they'd all expected Dick Fletcher to marry. He'd been real cut up when she left, which was no doubt, they said, why he hadn't looked at anyone else in the last five years.

Well, now that she had seen Eleanor Heaton in the flesh, Jane had to admit that she was every bit as beautiful and attractive as she'd been described. But it's all right, she thought; Dick and I will be married soon. Really, the sooner the better. There was no reason to wait.

She called the children to order again.

'Little ones, bring your slates and let me see what you've done. Those of you who are reading, continue to do so quietly, and I shall test you later.' It was no easy task to teach children of differing ages, but she loved it. It was a pity that when she married she would have to give it up. Married women were not allowed to stay on. In any case, Dick would not wish her to. Her job would be to look after her husband and home and, later, their children. She felt, as always, a stab of fear at the thought of children. Not of children once they were there, but at the prospect of actually giving birth. She had no idea where the roots of her fear lay and she knew that she would have to get over it. She pushed the thought away and concentrated on the children's drawings. They were all remarkably similar, and mostly of Easter eggs, which had clearly meant far more to them than the religious festival.

Saturday was fine and bright.

'There's even a bit of warmth in the sun,' Mrs Foster said, coming in from the garden. 'Not bad for April.'

Eleanor was glad, now, of every bit of fine weather which meant she could get herself and the children out of the house. As there was no school today, and Becky had been in a fractious mood from the moment of waking, it was more important than ever. Clara still insisted that there was really nothing her sister-in-law could do to help in the house – weren't there already two women? – and that Albert could manage very well in the shop with her own and Jimmy's assistance. She spoke pleasantly enough, and expressed thanks for the offer, but Eleanor understood the message behind the words. You don't belong here. How long would it be before they were said out loud? She must do everything she could to prevent that. Once the words were spoken, once the veneer of politeness was cracked, things would be much worse.

'Can I do nothing more to prepare for Madge coming?' she asked. Last evening she had actually been permitted to stir jellies for today's tea.

'Everything's done, thank you,' Clara replied.

'Very well then,' Eleanor said evenly. 'I'll take the children out for a bit of fresh air.'

'I don't want to go,' Becky objected.

'Fresh air will do you good,' her aunt said firmly. Though she would not admit it, even to Albert, every minute they were out of the house was a bonus. Also she could see that Becky was going to be a bad influence on Flo. If she was with her long enough she'd turn her into a cheeky little monkey like herself. Flo had been a nice quiet child up to now.

They left the house fifteen minutes later, Clara watching them as they went down the street. Selina and the baby were in the pram, Becky, still protesting, trailed by its side. Eleanor walked very upright as she pushed the pram, her head held high. She wore her hat and gloves, just as if she was in the town instead of in the village street. She always did act as though she *was* somebody, Clara thought. And look where her airs and graces have got her in the end! She turned away and went into the shop. With any luck they'd not be back before dinnertime.

Becky dragged her feet, pulled at Eleanor's skirt.

'Don't want to go on a silly walk! Won't go!'

'Oh yes you will,' Eleanor said sharply. 'And stop acting like a baby. You're worse than Jenny and Selina put together!' She could do without Becky's tantrums at the moment.

They walked for a while in silence. The only thing wrong with the carriage was that, being so strong, it was heavy to push; also, bigger wheels would have made it easier to manage along this rough country lane they were now traversing. But Ben had envisaged it being wheeled along

63

the flagstoned pavements of Akersfield, and he had made it strong to last, expecting that every two years or so it would have a new occupant. Neither he nor Eleanor had thought, when they'd left Felldale, that they would ever return to the country.

'We'll rest for a bit,' Eleanor said presently. 'Sithee, if you like you can take your stockings off and dip your feet in the stream.' She knew that would please Becky. 'But I warn you, the water will be cold.'

It was hardly a stream, no more really than a trickle of water which in the spring came down from the fell, filling the ditch which ran between the grass verge and the thick hawthorn hedge which bordered the neighbouring field.

'Want to paddle! Want to paddle!' Becky cried. 'Unbutton my boots!'

When Eleanor had helped with the boots, Becky tore off her garters and her thick ribbed black stockings and handed them to her mother.

'Go carefully,' Eleanor warned. 'It's sure to be stony.'

Selina raised her arms to be lifted out of the carriage. She didn't speak. Sometimes Eleanor worried that Selina spoke so little, but perhaps that was because she got what she wanted by other means. Maybe I should take no notice until she learns to ask, Eleanor thought. Nevertheless, she lifted the child, and gave her a quick hug before setting her down, whereupon she immediately began to draw with her finger in the dust of the lane.

'You'd better come out now, Becky,' Eleanor said after a few minutes. 'We don't want you catching cold, do we?' Usually, though she loved them dearly, she didn't fuss about the children, wasn't over-protective; but it was different now. She mustn't, couldn't, let them get ill.

'I want a towel!' Becky demanded.

'I haven't got one. How did I know you were going to paddle? You must run on the grass for a bit until your feet dry, then I'll finish them off with my petticoat.'

She did so, then helped Becky with her stockings and boots and put Selina back in the pram.

64

'Now we'll walk a bit quicker, and we'll sing,' she said. 'What shall we sing?'

' "Onward Christian Soldiers", ' Becky demanded.

'A good choice!' Eleanor approved.

Side by side they marched, singing, until Eleanor guessed by the height of the sun in the sky, not to mention the hunger in her stomach, that it was time to go back for dinner. She wondered what time Dick would be back in Felldale. Perhaps by about three o'clock? If he wasn't, then they'd wait around until he came. Might he have Jane Lawrence with him? Though she didn't know why, she hoped not.

After dinner she helped to clear away and then fed Jenny. If Dick gave her a job, even if he let her take the baby, she supposed she'd have no alternative but to wean her. She put Jenny back into the carriage and turned to Becky.

'Now fetch your bonnet and coat and we'll go for another nice little walk, and when we get back your Auntie Madge will be here!'

Madge and her family would have taken the train from Grassington to Silton, where the railway ran along the valley the best part of a mile from Felldale. Eleanor hoped she wouldn't meet them as they walked up the hill from the station.

'I don't want to go!' Becky protested.

'That's what you said this morning,' Eleanor reminded her. 'You enjoyed it when you got out.'

'I didn't! And my head aches.'

Mrs Foster looked up anxiously. 'She didn't eat much dinner,' she pointed out. 'Happen she's a bit tired. It'd be best if you left Becky and Selina wi' me and just took t'babby.'

Eleanor was doubtful. She wanted them to be out of the way as much as possible. But if Becky really wasn't up to it . . .

'Very well, Ma. If it won't be too much trouble then.'

She saw the wary expression on Clara's face and prayed that Becky wasn't sickening for something; but as likely as not it was nothing more than a cold, combined with Becky's worse-than-usual awkwardness.

She was too late to avoid the arrival of Madge and her family. As she opened the door to leave, there they were, walking towards her up the street. She hurried out, resolutely pushing the pram, though she would have to pass them so there was no pretending she hadn't seen them.

'Why, our Eleanor!' Madge cried. 'What in the world are *you* doing here?'

'Hello then, our Madge! Same as you – visiting!' So no-one had rushed to write to Madge to tell her the news. Eleanor was thankful for that. They could chew it over while she was out of the way. 'I'll not stop,' she said. 'The baby's a mite fractious. I want to get her to sleep. I'll see you all a bit later.'

When she reached Dick's place, to her relief he was already back from market, busy stabling the horse. He looked surprised to see her.'

'Is everything all right?' he asked.

'Yes. Well, more or less. I wanted to ask you about something.'

'Then you'd best come into the house.' He had no idea what it could be, but when he'd looked up from fixing the horse's feed and seen Eleanor walking into the yard a sharp feeling of pleasure, and of something more than pleasure, which he didn't care to define, had run through him.

She left the baby carriage in the porch and followed Dick into the cottage. It was dark inside and the smell of tobacco hung in the heavy curtains at the window.

'Sit down,' Dick said. 'I'd offer you a cup of tea, only I don't light the fire afore I go to market.'

'That's all right,' Eleanor replied. She sat herself in the high-backed Windsor chair and looked around her. The room was tidy enough for a man living on his own, no dirty crockery lying around and everything dusted, but the furnishings were shabby and old-fashioned and she guessed that he had changed nothing since his parents had died.

'Did you have a good morning in Skipton?' she asked.

'Aye. Sold up! That's the trouble. I could sell more if I had a bit more land and could produce more, but then it'd be too much for me to manage on my own.'

'Then you might be glad I've come,' Eleanor said. She was surprised at the confidence she could hear in her voice. She felt nothing like that inside.

'And what does that mean?'

'You need help. I need a job!'

It was not the way she had intended, blurting it out in that brusque manner. She had meant to approach it more politely, grateful for all he had done for her so far, but anxiety had got the better of her.

'Whoa there!' He held up a hand. 'Who said I needed help?'

'You did. Well . . . that is . . .'

'I said if I had a bit more land I couldn't manage on my own.'

But it was true, he thought, that even with his present parcel of land he could produce more if he didn't have to do everything himself. He was aware that sometimes seed didn't get sown as early as it might, seedlings weren't transplanted or produce harvested exactly at the right time because he was too busy. It all made a difference to what he had to take to market. Vegetables were sometimes a little later than those of his rivals, sometimes a proportion of the soft fruit was lost because he didn't have time to pick it at the precise time of ripening, and he would never jeopardise his reputation for quality by selling things overripe.

'I'd work hard, and I wouldn't want much,' Eleanor said. 'You'd make my wages out of the extra profit, if you had more help.'

He might at that. It had already occurred to him. But when he'd thought of help, he hadn't envisaged a woman. His thoughts had run to a strong lad.

'I'm as strong as an ox,' Eleanor went on, reading his mind. 'I doubt there's anything you'd need doing that I couldn't manage!'

Even if he did employ a woman, he thought, which he

had no mind to, he wouldn't want that woman to be Eleanor Foster. She was too – he sought for the word to describe his feelings – she would be too . . . distracting. That was it. With Eleanor around he knew he wouldn't be able to concentrate on his work. Her presence, even now, just sitting there, played tricks with his thoughts. And it was not fitting. There was Jane. Though as yet they'd not named the day, they were promised. No doubt Eleanor didn't know that – for if she did she'd never have made the suggestion.

'I don't think . . .'

'Dick! Please!' She reached out and touched his hand. Her eyes were filled with tears, brimming over so that two large teardrops ran down her cheeks.

'Dick, I'm desperate! Truthfully I'm desperate. I know that Clara's not going to let us stay long. I can see it in her face and hear it in everything she says. The minute I put a foot wrong . . . well, that will be it!'

'How will working for me help?'

'If I have a job maybe I can get a place to live, even if it's only a room in someone's house. Just somewhere where I can be independent. It means everything to me – and there's no-one else I can turn to. Dick, I'll work my fingers to the bone . . .'

How could he refuse her, he thought. Sooner rather than later he'd have had to set on a lad to help him, and it was true that there were plenty of tasks which were within Eleanor's physical capabilities. And much of the time, he told himself, he wouldn't be working with her. He'd be off to market. Maybe with more help he could do a fourth market.

'There'd be no need for you to work your fingers to the bone,' he said. 'But there'd be plenty to do and I couldn't afford to pay you much. Six shillings a week.'

She jumped up from the chair and hugged him. 'Oh Dick, I can't thank you enough! I really can't!'

Her arms were around his neck but he kept his own arms straight by his sides, his fists clenched. Aware of the soft curves of her body against his, he turned away and put a match to the fire laid in the grate. The flames leapt up, as

68

they had in him a minute ago. He had done the wrong thing. He knew it now, but it was too late.

'When can I start?' Eleanor asked. 'Can I start on Monday?'

She hardly noticed the reluctance in his voice when he agreed. Everything was going to be all right again. She just knew everything would be all right.

When she arrived back at the house they were about to sit down to tea. 'We have to have it early,' Madge's husband John explained, 'because we have to get the train back.' She saw sympathy in his eyes as he spoke to her, and knew at once that she had been discussed. But there was none on her sister's face.

'Well, so you've got yourself into a pretty pickle!' Madge said as they sat down. She believed in calling a spade a spade.

Eleanor bit back a sharp retort. It would not do to start a quarrel at Clara's table, a quarrel for which she would undoubtedly be blamed.

'I always said no good would come of marriage to Ben Heaton,' Madge went on. 'Wasn't that what I said, John? You remember at the time?' She looked to her husband for confirmation.

'I daresay you did,' he said quietly. 'Sometimes you say too much.'

His wife appeared not to have heard him.

'Well, I'm sorry we can't help,' she said firmly. 'We haven't a spare inch of space at the farm. What with the children growing up, we're more than pushed for room. I'm sorry, but there it is!'

You are not in the least bit sorry, Eleanor thought. You want to rub my nose in it. But nor was she sorry, herself. If it came to it, she'd be hard pushed to choose between living with Madge and going to the workhouse. But now, thank God, there was no need for either.

'Don't apologise, Madge.' Eleanor said sweetly. 'I know if you had the room you'd be only to delighted to have me.' She paused for a moment, watching with pleasure the colour rising in her sister's face. 'As it happens, I couldn't come. I couldn't come however much you wanted me.'

'Couldn't come?' Clara said sharply.

'That's right I couldn't come. I've got a job. I'm going to work for Dick Fletcher. I start on Monday.' She realised as she was speaking that she had forgotten to ask Dick if she might take the baby. But she would just do so. She knew it would be all right.

'In a week or two I'll find a room, and be off everyone's hands,' she said. How she was going to do that on six shillings a week she wasn't sure, but she knew it would be all right in the end. All she had needed was a start, and now she had it.

'Working for Dick Fletcher?' Clara said. How would Miss Jane Lawrence take that?

CHAPTER FIVE

'There isn't any doubt about it,' Clara said. 'The child's got measles! Or something worse!' Her face was flushed almost as red as Becky's, but Clara's was the flush of anger at the sight of this . . . this *awful* child lying there in the bed right next to her daughter. Whatever it was – could it be scarlet fever? – Flo would catch it, and Flo took things badly. Oh, what a fool she had been ever to take on her sister-in-law and her brats! She should have put her foot down from the beginning, and would have if it hadn't been for Albert. He was too soft-hearted by far. But why should he be responsible for his sister? She'd gone her own way when it suited her and never mind the rest of them.

'Measles is what it is,' Mrs Foster said, surveying the small red spots which covered Becky's forehead and were spreading over her body. Gently, she touched the child's face, felt the burning fever. 'But it's nowt to worry about. A childish ailment, no more.'

'How do we know?' Clara snapped. She looked balefully at Eleanor. 'Whatever it is it's been brought here from Akersfield; nasty dirty place!' If she dared she'd say nasty dirty people, Eleanor thought.

'It's not the plague, Clara.' Eleanor spoke as calmly as she could, though inside herself she was far from tranquil. There was little hope that the illness wouldn't spread to Flo and the other children.

'That is not funny,' Clara said sharply. 'We have the shop to think about, you know! Who wants to come and buy food from a place full of infection?'

'Nay, Clara lass,' Mrs Foster remonstrated. 'I daresay

there's not one of your customers hasn't had measles in the family already.'

'Well, I'm going to call in Dr Hardy,' Clara said. 'We'll see what he says.'

Mrs Foster shrugged. 'He'll not thank you for calling him out on a Sunday; not for measles.'

'It might *not* be measles,' Clara persisted.

Almost as if she wanted it to be worse, Eleanor thought, so that she can blame me even more.

But Dr Hardy quickly agreed with Mrs Foster.

'Keep her quiet. Plenty of fluids. Draw the blinds and keep the room dark,' he said.

'What about the other children?' Clara asked.

'As likely as not they'll go down.' He turned to Eleanor. 'Are you breast-feeding your baby?'

'Yes, doctor.'

'Then she won't catch it.'

'Well then,' Clara said when the doctor had left, 'that'll put paid to your job with Dick Fletcher. You'll have to stay and look after Becky. I shan't have time, that's for sure.'

Oh no! She just *had* to go to work tomorrow. She had to earn the money. The job was her only way of getting out of this household where she was so unwelcome. Yet Clara was right. Becky was her responsibility. Oh my dear Becky, she thought ruefully, trust you to throw a spanner in the works!

'There's no need for anybody to fret themselves,' Mrs Foster broke in. 'I'm more than capable of looking after Becky, and the rest if they happen to go down with it — though there's no saying they will.'

'Oh Ma! Are you sure it won't be too much for you?' Eleanor felt frantic with relief.

'Of course I am! I haven't got to my age without being able to nurse a straightforward case of measles.'

'And who's to say it'll be straightforward?' Clara demanded. 'You heard what the doctor said. Keep out the daylight. It can affect the eyes. And I've heard you can get bronchitis, pneumonia even, after measles.'

'My word, you're in a mood for looking on the black

72

side,' Mrs Foster said. 'Well, don't worry. I know exactly what to do and I'll not need any help.' She bent over Becky. 'Grandma'll have you better in no time, won't she, little love?'

Eleanor, pushing Jenny in the pram, was at Dick's place early next morning. She had left Becky sleeping peacefully, though during Sunday the rash had spread over her body until she was covered in it.

'All to the good,' Mrs Foster said. 'Better out than in!'

Dick was coming out of his cottage as Eleanor arrived. She noted the surprise on his face as he saw the pram.

'I'm sorry, I forgot to ask you if I could bring the baby. She'll be no trouble. As it happens I couldn't have come without her. Becky's got measles and Ma has her hands full.'

'I'm sorry to hear about that,' Dick said. 'Do you want to leave the baby in the house?'

'No. I'll just put the pram near to where I'm working so's I can keep an eye on her. Don't worry, you'll hardly know she's there.'

She felt irritated that she had to apologise for her baby. Not that Dick was being awkward — but it was always like this. And there was the other matter.

'There's just one other thing,' she said hesitantly. 'I'm still feeding her. I mean to wean her but it takes time. So if I could just go into the house at the time . . .'

'Of course.'

'Good. Then I'm ready to start work.'

'There's plenty to do,' Dick said. 'It's where to begin is the thing. Now let's see! There's another lot of gladiolus corms to plant. The flowers sell well in the market come the summer and autumn. I try to plant them every two weeks so I'm never without on the stall.'

'So show me where and how.'

He led her to the bottom of the garden and indicated a strip of land.

'Against the wall,' he said. 'They'll be sheltered from the wind there.' He went away and was back again in a minute with a large box of corms.

73

'Plant them deep,' he instructed her. 'They're tall flowers so they need to be firm in the ground. Like this, see.'

She watched him while he quickly planted half a dozen corms, taking pleasure in observing the movements of his well-shaped hands; so deft; so sure. Could she ever work fast enough to please him?

It was his turn to watch while Eleanor, kneeling on the ground, planted the first few corms.

'Is this right?'

'A bit deeper, and a bit farther apart. Plants all need their fair share of ground, otherwise they won't give of their best. You do right by them and they'll do right by you.'

As he handled the brown, dry-looking corms he saw in them the tall, sword-like green leaves, the exotic flowers which they would bear when the summer came. He watched Eleanor as she made a further attempt, noted that her wide black hat threatened to fall off as she bent low, saw the gold of her hair against the white skin at the nape of her neck, took in the length of her back and the narrowness of her waist. Feelings – they were too instinctive, too incoherent to be thoughts – came unbidden to his mind, raced and tingled in his body. He jumped to his feet.

'I'll leave you to it.'

She looked up, hearing the roughness in his voice.

'Am I not doing it right? I'll get quicker with practice.'

'You're all right. But I must get on with my own jobs. When you get tired come and tell me and I'll set you on to something different.'

It was a back-breaking job all right. In no time at all from her neck to the bottom of her spine was one big ache. She wondered if she'd ever be able to straighten up again. But she had no intention of giving in. She'd keep on until she'd planted the very last corm. And at the rate she was going that would be some time yet.

Momentarily she sat back on her heels, raised her hands and unpinned her hat. She should have had more sense than to wear it. A kerchief would have been better to keep her hair in place. She was conscious that it was coming down, falling around her face. She pushed a few hairpins more firmly in and went back to work.

In the end, at long last, the box was empty and the corms all planted. She leaned back and gave a deep sigh of exhaustion. Oh, but she hadn't known there were so many muscles in her body, and every one of them aching!

She was struggling to her feet when she felt Dick's strong arm under her elbow, helping her up. She stumbled against him and gave a little yelp of surprise.

'Oh Dick, you made me jump!'

'I'm sorry, Ellie. I came to tell you it was dinnertime.' He saw the empty box and nodded his approval. 'You've done well there.'

He was the only person who called her Ellie. Mrs Foster chose her children's names with care and let it be known that she disliked having them shortened or changed in any way. Eleanor was Eleanor, and it was surprising that she had always let Dick Fletcher get away with the diminutive.

'Have I really?' She smiled with pleasure at his praise, while stretching her back, massaging the nape of her neck to ease the pain. 'What do I do next?'

'You have your dinner. I usually have a bit of bread and cheese and a cup of tea. If you . . .'

'Oh, I've brought something,' Eleanor interrupted. 'I can eat it out here.' Packing herself some food to take to work had not been easy. It was bad enough to sit at Clara's table every day, but that could be counted as hospitality. To take food out of the house seemed different. She had seen Clara's eye on her and had almost felt guilty of stealing. For that reason she had taken nothing more than two slices of bread and butter, though she knew quite well that Albert wouldn't have begrudged her a slice of ham to put between them. Right now she would have given her back teeth for a good, thick ham sandwich with plenty of Colman's mustard. She was clemmed.

'Might as well have it inside,' Dick said.

So, pushing the pram, she followed him up the long path and into the house.

75

She sat down at the table and began to eat. Though she was ravenously hungry she ate as slowly as possible, trying to make the food last.

'Have a bit of cheese,' Dick offered.

'I couldn't. I'm full to the brim!' she lied. Something in her said she couldn't be beholden to him for her food. He was kind enough already. Also, she was sick of being beholden to people.

They ate in silence for a while, then he said, 'You're not going to find it easy, bringing up three children on your own.'

'I know,' Eleanor agreed. 'But others have done it and so will I. You'll see.'

'Happen you'll marry again?'

He didn't know what had driven him to say it. There were good reasons why he shouldn't do so. There was the renewed attraction Eleanor had for him, the strength of which had shaken him as he had watched her this morning. Perhaps that attraction had never died, only lain dormant over the years? More to the point was the irrevocable fact that he and Jane Lawrence had visited the vicar last night. Everything was in train and the banns were due to be called for the first time of asking next Sunday. There was no turning back.

'Not me!' Eleanor said firmly. 'I've neither the wish nor the intention to marry again!'

He wanted to ask why, but there was something in her face which told him not to.

The baby started to cry; desperate, hungry cries, impossible to ignore. Eleanor looked at Dick in embarrassment.

'Would you mind? I have to feed her.'

'Go ahead. I'll be making a pot of tea.'

Eleanor lifted the baby out of the carriage. When her fingers went to undo the buttons of her bodice, Dick turned away, took the kettle to the sink. But the sounds – the baby's cries, mews, then its gasp of satisfaction as it found the breast, and the regular rhythm of its suckling – filled his ears. As he waited for the kettle to boil, and mashed the tea, all the while not looking in Eleanor's direction, the sounds continued. Then they stopped. He thought it was over, and the excitement was so high in him that he could not forbear to turn around.

It was not over. The child had finished at one breast and was about to be put to the other so that for a moment Eleanor sat with both breasts bared: the nipples, deep rosy pink, engorged, set in a circle of paler pink, like the styles of exotic flowers; the breasts themselves, round, milk-white globes, with the faintest delicate tracery of fine blue veins.

He stood rooted, gazing at her magnificence, the desire to touch, to cup, to hold and caress, even to hurt, filling every corner of him. His body was hard with almost uncontrollable need. Only with difficulty did he raise his eyes from her breasts, and look into her face. She had ceased all pretence of feeding the child. She was staring at him, and in her eyes he saw the hunger that he knew must show in his own. She made no attempt to cover herself.

With superhuman effort, he spoke.

'I'll be in the greenhouse. When you've had your tea there are some jobs to be done there.' Then for the second time that day he turned and fled.

Eleanor watched him go. The baby had fallen asleep on her lap, no longer searching for food. She touched her breasts, touched the nipples. How long since anyone had done that to her? But the feeling and the longing didn't die. If Dick had stayed . . . if he hadn't run away . . . for she knew he'd been running.

She laid the sleeping baby in the pram. It was clearly satisfied. She was the one now gasping with hunger – but for a man's body. She had not thought, until today, that she would ever feel this hunger again.

She did up her bodice, though something made her leave undone the top two buttons, so that the shadowy cleft between her breasts was visible. She was not sure why she did this; perhaps to assert that she was a woman, and desirable.

But she must get back to work. Leaving the baby tucked in its carriage in the cottage she went to join Dick in the greenhouse.

77

He was bending over a plant as she entered, but when he heard her step he straightened up and turned to face her. There was no mistaking the message in his eyes: she recognised his yearning because it was matched by her own. Excitement tingled through her body from head to toe, and then Dick moved towards her, his hand outstretched to touch her.

'Ellie!'

With the one word, the speaking of her name, though it was little more than a whisper, he gave voice to the longing which showed in his face. Eleanor tried to speak – and could not, not even to say his name. She could scarcely breathe.

Then on the very point of touching her he drew back, lowered his hand and held his arms rigidly by his sides. She saw the whitened knuckles of his clenched fists.

His nerves were taut with his desire for her, and yet in spite of the passion he saw in her – because of it – he knew he must not give way. There was no end to that.

He turned away from her and began to speak – quickly, stumbling a little over the everyday words but trying hard to sound casual, as if nothing whatever had been felt between them.

'I'd like you to nip out the side shoots from the tomato seedlings. They grow just here, see, in the axils of the leaves. I daresay you'll do this job better than me. You've got smaller fingers.'

And breasts like round, ripe fruits, eyes the sea-green of the ocean, he wanted to say. A body I want to touch and hold. But now his thoughts were hidden behind an impassive face, though he felt his hands tremble as he fingered the plants.

How could he have such control, Eleanor asked herself? How could he? Only a moment ago . . . Then with a tremendous effort she managed to speak normally, even lightly.

'It's nice in here. Nice and warm and out of the wind.'

'Just you wait until the summer comes,' Dick replied.

78

'It's a sight too hot in the greenhouse then.'

Shall I be here when the summer comes, Eleanor wondered? When these seedlings are fully grown, bearing fruit, where shall I be? She couldn't envisage being in Clara's home then.

'Well, you seem to have got the idea,' Dick told her, watching the deft way she handled the young plants. 'I'll leave you to it.'

'Everything smells so nice,' Eleanor said.

He nodded. 'You don't need to wait for flowers and fruit to get perfume. The foliage of every plant has its own special scent. And tomatoes as much as any.' Their sharp, aromatic scent was one of his favourites.

He would have liked nothing better than to have worked side by side with her in the warmth of the glasshouse, breathing in the fresh smell of young plants. But he could no longer trust himself to stay so close, though not for the life of him could he leave her altogether. The sensible thing would be to go the farthest end of the garden, dig the hard, unyielding soil, make a trench for sowing the peas. Instead he moved no farther away than the other end of the greenhouse.

Once she had calmed down, Eleanor found the work pleasant, and less exhausting than being on her knees, planting – though now her back ached from standing. It had never occurred to her that gardening was such a physical thing, that every bit of it would affect her body while leaving her mind to roam free.

Why had she been so adamant in telling Dick that she had no desire to marry again? She knew now that it wasn't true. To be married to a good man was surely a blessing? And with marriage would come what she knew she wanted – the excitement and fulfilment of the marriage bed. Oh how she wanted it! But with three small children and not a penny to her name, who would want to marry her?

Then sun had moved round now and the greenhouse was hot. She pushed back her hair, rolled up her sleeves to leave her arms bare. She had worked methodically along the row of plants until she'd reached the far end where Dick was.

79

'There! I think that's it!'

He turned around, and at the same moment she turned to him. In the narrow gangway of the greenhouse they were unavoidably close, and this time there was no denial of that which instantly flared between them. She was in his arms. She tilted back her head and her lips opened to him as his mouth sought hers, bruising it with the strength of his kisses. She pressed herself against him. She wanted to melt into him, wanted her body to be fused with his. She felt his hardness against her own yielding and knew that his desire equalled hers.

His hand went to the neck of her bodice and as he fumbled with the tiny buttons she moved to help him, and all the while he was covering her with hungry kisses. When his hand cupped her breast she thought she would faint. She wanted to lie down on the hard flagstones of the greenhouse floor and let him take her there and then. And then suddenly he let go of her.

'What . . .? Why . . .?'

'Not here! Not here, we must go to the house!'

He took her hand and began to lead her, she half stumbling against him, towards the cottage; through the living-room where Jenny still slept in her carriage, into the bedroom. She would have lain on the bed at once, but he stopped her.

'No! I want to undress you, Ellie.'

She stood in front of him while he took off her garments one by one; not hastily but slowly; exulting in the beauty of her body as, little by little, it was revealed to him. In the end she stood before him mother-naked while he looked at her. Then he went on his knees and buried his face in the softness of her thighs.

'Oh Ellie! You are exquisite! You're everything that's perfect!'

She was trembling, shuddering at his touch. She wanted him so badly.

'Let me take off your clothes,' she said. 'Quickly, quickly!'

80

Then they were on the bed together. He began to make love to her, she responded eagerly. The climax came quickly for both of them, It was a climax towards which they had both been moving since she had observed him watching her as she gave the breast to the baby.

Then everything began again and this time, though in the end passion flared between them as hotly as before, there was sweetness, tenderness, exploration. Their coming together this second time had in it the seeds of love.

But they were seeds which, Dick thought as they lay together when it was over, could not be allowed to grow. The thought came to him like a blow.

'Dearest Ellie,' he said. 'What have I done to you?'

'You've given me yourself,' she murmured. 'What else would I want?'

He sat up abruptly.

'It's no good, Ellie. I'm to marry Jane Lawrence. Everything's settled. There's nothing I can do. I'm not prepared to jilt her.'

So it was true, Eleanor thought.

Slowly, she rose from the bed and began to dress. She was cold now, shivering a little, as if the blustery April wind had stolen into the house.

'I'm not seeking for you to marry me just because we made love,' she said. 'But I don't regret what we've done. I never could. Not ever.'

In her own ears her voice sounded so flat, so matter-of-fact. She was trying to tell herself that what had happened was simply a physical thing. They had been for all the world like two animals mating, she like a bitch on heat. It was nothing more. That was what she told herself, but it wasn't how she felt. It was a lie. It had been the most wonderful lovemaking of her life.

'Nor could I,' Dick said. 'Ever! But supposing . . .?' He looked at her, leaving the question in the air.

'You mean supposing I have a child? Well, don't let that thought worry you. I'm safe. They say a woman can't conceive while she's breast-feeding.' Yet she knew with every bit of feeling in her body that she wanted his child. She wanted also to be back in the bed with him, the two of them loving each other again. It was Jenny's wailing cry from the next room which stopped her.

She dressed quickly now, leaned over and kissed Dick where he lay, before going to Jenny. When she had seen to her she pushed the pram down to the bottom of the garden and went back to work with a will. She felt curiously light, every faculty sharpened.

So busy was she that she didn't hear Jane Lawrence arrive, didn't know she was there until she saw her walking down the garden towards her.

'Hello,' Jane said pleasantly. 'I didn't know you were working for Dick. He forgot to tell me.' She looked with surprise at the baby carriage.

Eleanor stood up. 'He was kind enough to give me a job. I had to bring the baby because, as you know by now, Becky has measles and my mother is fully occupied.'

'I see.'

Dick came down the path and stood behind Jane.

'It's time you were off,' he said to Eleanor. 'I reckon you've done enough for your first day. I'll expect you at half-past eight in the morning.'

Thank heaven for that, Eleanor thought. She had wondered, after what had passed between them, whether Dick would think it right for her to continue working for him. It wouldn't be easy, there was too much feeling, but he knew and she knew that she had a desperate need of the job.

'I'll be here,' she said.

The banns had been called for Dick and Jane and the wedding fixed for the first Saturday in June, to take place in Felldale. Jane had no relatives other than an aunt in Skipton, but almost everyone in the village would attend. After the ceremony there would be a sit-down tea in the village hall and even now a large ham was hanging from the rafters in Albert's shop, waiting for Clara to cook it. Mrs Foster had been roped in to bake and ice the cake and

Eleanor, in a weak moment, had agreed to the vicar's request that she should sing in the choir.

'One likes to have boy trebles, of course,' he said. 'But most unfortunately both Tom Whitfield and Sam Carter have chosen this moment for their voices to break and we are left with only four youngsters. So if you would help us on the soprano side . . .'

It seemed to Eleanor that everything in Felldale revolved around plans for the wedding. No-one seemed to think of anything else. But worse was to come. When she arrived home from work one day – hot, tired, dirty; pushing the heavy perambulator – Becky rushed out of the house to greet her.

'I'm to be a bridesmaid!' she cried. 'Miss Lawrence has chosen me and Flo and two others to be bridesmaids! I shall wear a new blue dress and flowers in my hair!'

'Don't shout,' Eleanor said wearily. 'You'll waken the baby.'

Jenny had been unusually fractious all day. Thank heaven she had at last fallen asleep. A crying baby would only add to the tense atmosphere in Clara's home, an atmosphere which seemed to get worse all the time. And though Eleanor had tried desperately hard to find another place for them to live in Felldale – even one room would have sufficed – there had been nothing. No-one would take them in for the small amount she was able to pay. So she was still dependent on Albert and Clara.

The atmosphere had not been helped, either, by the fact that, though Jimmy had escaped, both Selina and Flo had taken the measles and, true to Clara's predictions, Flo had indeed taken it badly, ending up with a nasty bout of bronchitis. Becky and Selina had sailed through the illness with very little trouble to themselves, though they had upset the routine of the household. They were now as fit as fleas, while poor Flo was still pale and chesty. Every time she had a spasm of coughing Clara shot an accusing look at Eleanor; and she clearly resented Becky, so bright and happy while her own daughter languished.

It sometimes seemed to Eleanor that Clara hated Becky,

and Becky did nothing to improve matters by her own noisy exuberance. She didn't mean to be naughty – well, not always – but when there was trouble it was usually Becky who was at the bottom of it. And lately Becky and Flo, from being bosom pals, had started to quarrel; and every time they did so it ended with Flo in a paroxysm of coughing. I'm a nasty suspicious person, Eleanor thought, but sometimes it seemed that Flo could cough to order. But how ridiculous that a small child's cough could be the cause of so much friction!

'Is it true,' Eleanor asked as she entered the house, 'that Becky and Flo have been asked to be bridesmaids?'

'Yes,' Clara said.

'I told you so! I told you so!' Becky cried. Her face was pink with excitement, her eyes shone. 'I have to have a new blue dress and a wreath of flowers in my hair!'

'A new dress?'

'Naturally. You'd hardly expect them to wear their school pinafores, would you?' Clara said scornfully.

'I'm not sure that I can afford . . .'

'Well, then, that's it. If she can't have the dress there's only one answer, isn't there. And don't forget there's a dozen other little girls waiting for a chance.' Clara was implacable. She couldn't for the life of her think why Becky had been picked. She didn't belong here, and never would.

'I *have* to have the dress!' Becky cried. 'I *have* to have it! If Flo can have a new dress, why can't I?'

Because your father was thoughtless enough to die, Eleanor said to herself. But meeting the angry disappointment in her daughter's tear-filled eyes, she knew that somehow she must get the dress. Her fingers went towards the neck of her blouse, felt the cache of money which lay hidden beneath it, to which she had managed to add just a little each week from her wages. Clara, tight-lipped, still refused to take money for their food, though she knew that Eleanor wanted her to do so. She would gladly have handed over every penny Dick paid her in order to lighten her obligation. But the precious hoard was not for fripperies like bridesmaids' dresses. It was for an important emergency. Though when, she asked herself, would there be an emergency more important than this in her small daughter's life? So she would break into the money and buy the dress.

'You shall have it,' she said. 'Don't take on so.'

'And flowers for my hair and new slippers?' Becky asked quickly.

'Whatever the other bridesmaids are having,' Eleanor agreed. 'I will tell Miss Lawrence tomorrow that you may accept.'

She offered no explanation in answer to Clara's puzzled look.

Almost every day now Jane came down to Dick's house as soon as afternoon school was over, and was still there when Eleanor left. Mostly Jane occupied herself indoors. She was trying to get it ship-shape and more to her liking before she moved in permanently. New curtains were hung at the windows; mats, which she had skilfully crocheted and stored in her bottom drawer long before she'd met Dick, went under every plantpot and ornament; new antimacassars protected the chairbacks and a bobble-fringed valance was hung around the mantelpiece. It was all looking much smarter.

Eleanor no longer went into the house. She had taken to using a small hut at the bottom of the garden to attend to Jenny, who in any case was now almost weaned. To drink with her dinnertime sandwiches she took a bottle of cold tea. Nor did Dick invite her in. In any case, it seemed no longer Dick's place, but Jane's. Nothing more had passed between Eleanor and Dick, not a word was said. They seemed further apart than they had been before the afternoon of their lovemaking, though sometimes Eleanor caught a look in Dick's eye which made her heart beat faster. So she kept out of the way and got on with her work. Heaven knew there was plenty to be done – weeding, planting, hoeing, staking. She worked as long as the daylight lasted. She was getting better at it too.

'You can also tell the weeds from the precious seedlings,'

Dick teased her. 'I might let you thin out the lettuces!'

On the day after Becky had announced that she had been invited to be a bridesmaid Eleanor saw Jane coming down the garden towards her. She noted the elegance of her new sprigged cotton dress and was struck, not for the first time, by the radiance which these days seemed to surround Jane like an aura. Here was a happy woman.

'Ah, Mrs Heaton!' Jane greeted her. 'I expect you can guess what I want to see you about? I'm sure Becky must have told you. She was beside herself with excitement yesterday.'

'She certainly was,' Eleanor agreed. It would have been better, she thought, if you'd consulted me first, found out if I could manage it.

'Well, I hope you're going to say yes,' Jane smiled.

'There'd be no living with Becky otherwise,' Eleanor answered.

'There is one thing, Mrs Heaton. I want you to know that it won't cost you anything. I will be entirely responsible for Becky's outfit.'

There was no denying the relief which swept over Eleanor, yet at the same time she felt wary.

'Are you doing the same for the other bridesmaids?' she asked quietly.

'There's no need to. They have fathers in work. I know how hard it must be for you, Mrs Heaton. I hope you won't refuse me. Naturally the arrangement will be a secret between the two of us. Not even Becky will know.'

'It's extremely kind of you, Miss Lawrence. I accept with gratitude.' It would be churlish to refuse. Also, beggars couldn't be choosers.

'Then that's that,' Jane said. 'I shall be going into Skipton to choose the material for the dresses when Dick goes to market on Saturday morning.'

The wedding day dawned bright and clear, the sky deep blue and cloudless. Eleanor was woken early by Becky.

'Wake up, Mama! I have to get dressed!'

86

Eleanor squinted at the clock on the chest of drawers. 'Nonsense, Becky! It wants ten minutes yet to seven o'clock. The wedding isn't until noon. Go back to bed for at least another hour or you'll be tired all day.'

She was about to rise herself, get ready for work, when she remembered that there was to be no work today. Dick had declared a holiday for her as well as for himself. Today he would not even go to market.

'I'm not tired!' Becky protested. 'I want to wear the dress!'

'Not yet,' Eleanor said firmly. 'You'll have it all mussed up by midday.'

'I will not,' Becky declared. 'I'll sit still and not move until it's time to go.'

'Get back to bed,' Eleanor commanded.

There was no need to think about her own dress. It was the same black one she had made for Ben's funeral and had alternated with her older skirt and blouse ever since. In a way, she was glad that with Ben dead only six months she must still wear mourning, since she could not have afforded anything else. She had carefully sponged and pressed the dress, and added a bunch of artificial violets at the neck, and a new swathe of violet tulle around her hat. Violet was permissible for half-mourning and for a wedding. In any case it wouldn't matter what she wore in the church since her choir robes would cover her shabbiness, and at the reception who would look at *her*?

By ten-thirty Becky would be put off no longer. With a sigh, Eleanor gave in and helped her daughter into the bridesmaid's dress. Then she proceeded to release the child's hair from the rag curlers in which she had slept all night.

'Will my hair be *really* curly?' Becky asked.

'Really and truly,' Eleanor promised. 'And when you put your headdress on . . . well . . .!'

She brushed Becky's fine, golden hair around her fingers, making ringlets which fell over her forehead and hung softly into her neck, before fixing the wreath of tiny pink rosebuds in place. She caught her breath at the picture her daughter presented. Oh, but she had been right to agree to all this, and credit had to go to Jane Lawrence, not only for her kindness, but for her good taste in choosing such an outfit. Becky had never looked lovelier.

'Do I look beautiful?' Becky asked solemnly. 'Really beautiful, Mama?'

'You do, my pet!' Eleanor assured her. 'If you ask Auntie Clara nicely, she might let you look at yourself in the long mirror in her room.'

'Handsome is as handsome does,' Clara said. 'And now you've set Flo off wanting to be ready hours before time. But you can go and take a peek at yourself,' she added grudgingly. She had to admit that the child looked nice. No more so than Flo would, of course. They were just different – the one so dark and the other so fair.

'After which,' Eleanor said, 'you come downstairs again and sit and look at a book until it's time to leave. Don't you dare get into mischief!'

It was really not her fault, Becky thought afterwards, when the trouble was at its height. It was that silly Flo's cough. All right, she'd teased her a bit, and then they'd started to shout at each other, but she hadn't moved from her chair, not once.

'It's not *my* fault if shouting makes Flo cough,' she complained.

'And coughing makes her sick, and she's sick all over her bridesmaid'a dress and on to her bronze slippers!' Clara stormed.

Becky had never seen Auntie Clara so angry, or Mama so upset, with bright red cheeks and her voice all shaky – and Selina and the baby both crying as well.

'You are a menace!' Clara yelled. 'That child is a menace! She'll come to a bad end, that's for sure!' She swung around to Eleanor. 'Why can't you control her?'

'I'm sorry,' Eleanor said. 'I'm very sorry indeed!'

'Sorry won't do this time!' Clara shouted. 'I can't put up with it any longer. You should never have come here in the first place. Heaven knows I didn't want you!'

'I realise that only too well!' Eleanor was shouting now and

88

Selina, terrified, ran and clung to her mother's skirt. 'You've made that much plain from the minute we arrived. And we'll leave the minute we can. You can take that for certain.'

'Well, it can't happen too soon for me!' Clara retorted.

She was ugly with rage. She's twenty-five, Eleanor thought, and anger makes her look forty. But she had no sympathy to spare, except for poor little Flo.

'Nor me!' she snapped.

'And now if you've anything about you you'll forbid that monstrous child to go to the wedding!'

Becky started to cry. They were not, like Selina's, tears of woe, but of fury.

'I didn't mean it! I didn't! I didn't! I want to go to the wedding more than anything in the world!'

'Don't worry,' Eleanor said grimly. ''You shall go to the wedding if it's the last thing you do in this village!'

Mrs Foster had listened in silent dismay to the quarrel – but not with any surprise. I was a wonder it hadn't happened sooner; they were always bickering, sniping at each other. She was filled with a sick foreboding about the future – Eleanor's future – but now wasn't the time to give way to it.

'Strip off quickly and give me the dress,' she said to Flo. 'I'll sponge it down and dry it in front of the fire.'

'It's ruined! That's what it is, ruined!' Clara cried dramatically.

'Nonsense! It's no such thing!' Mrs Foster said. 'I'll have it right, see if I don't!'

When she had dealt with the dress she held it up for Flo's inspection.

'There! It's not too bad now, is it? Just a slight mark on the front – and if you hold your bouquet there no-one's going to notice a thing!'

'You are the best grandma in the world!' Flo said.

'She's my grandma too!' Becky said.

'Don't start again! Do *not* start again!' Mrs Foster begged.

Eleanor saw and heard little of the wedding ceremony. She

was too troubled in her mind. This was the end of the road with Clara, but where would the road take them now? Something had to happen.

She was dimly aware of Jane Lawrence, radiantly pretty in her wedding gown; of how big and handsome Dick Fletcher looked standing beside his petite bride. Eleanor knelt, stood, sat at the right times; her beautiful voice poured out the hymns and psalms as if she hadn't a care in the world. 'God be merciful to us, and bless us . . . be merciful unto us!'

'Be merciful to *me*!' she wanted to cry. But however loud she cried it seemed that God never heard her. If he did she would not be destitute, cast out with her children. When had she been so wicked that she must be punished like this?

The vicar was pronouncing the blessing when she glanced up and, without meaning to, looked straight across at Dick Fletcher, standing there at the chancel steps with his new bride.

His eyes were on Eleanor, and for a moment – it could only have been a moment, though when she remembered it afterwards it seemed to have lasted hours – his gaze held hers, and it was as if they were the only two people in the world. For the time that they looked at each other Eleanor had only one thought, and she knew, instinctively but surely, without any shadow of doubt, what was in Dick's mind. A physical thrill ran through her as if he had indeed touched her, the way he had on that April afternoon. Then Jane took his arm, he looked down at his new bride, and they began to move towards the vestry.

It was that, the moment she had just experienced, which above all – far more than Clara's screams and tantrums earlier in the day – convinced Eleanor that she must leave Felldale. There were forces far stronger than Clara at work which now made it impossible for her to stay. How could she not have known until now?

She excused herself from the festivities after the wedding on the grounds that she had to take the younger children home. The truth was, she couldn't bear to be present.

Waiting for the others to return, she thought desperately about what she might do – and by the time they arrived she had made up her mind. The scene which followed their homecoming, though no worse than a dozen others recently, only confirmed her in her decision.

'You look tired,' she said to Becky as they came in.

'And well she might,' Clara grumbled. 'Running around the hall like it was the school playground, making a nuisance of herself.'

Eleanor looked at her mother.

'Was Becky naughty, then?'

'Not a bit,' Mrs Foster replied. 'Childish high spirits, nothing more. Nobody minded.'

'Well, I did for one!' Clara said. 'She's too forward by half. Why, even in church she pushed herself forward, taking the bride's bouquet like that when everyone knows it should have been Flo!'

'I didn't!' Becky said. 'Miss Lawrence handed it to me!'

'Don't you answer me back, young lady!' Clara fumed. 'And while we're at it, I don't want you to share Flo's room any more. You're a disturbing influence. Flo's not getting her proper sleep!'

'Where *will* she sleep then?' Eleanor asked. There were already four of them in the small attic.

'It's not up to me or mine to find a place for you or your children to sleep!' Clara retorted. 'Sort it out for yourself!'

Becky started to cry. In spite of their arguments, she loved her cousin Flo and they enjoyed sharing a room. What had she done to be kept out?

'I will' Eleanor said furiously. 'And sooner than you think!'

'I've heard that tale before,' Clara scoffed. 'I wish I could believe it!'

'You're taking it out on Becky because you don't like me,' Eleanor said. 'I consider that despicable!' Oh what joy it gave her to say what she thought to her mean-spirited sister-in-law!

'I wasn't despicable when I took you in, saved you all from the workhouse, was I?'

'I'll grant you that, Clara. And I was grateful and always will be. But you've made me pay for it, and now you're making Becky pay. I'll not put up with that.'

'Won't put up with it indeed! Listen who's talking! Madam High-and-Mighty. You always were above yourself, Eleanor Heaton.'

'And you always were a vinegar-faced sourpuss, if you want to know. I don't know how our Albert stands you!'

Becky's cries grew louder, and Flo joined in. Eleanor put her arms around her daughter.

'Don't cry, pet. You can sleep with me and Grandma and Selina. We'll be ever so cosy.'

Later that night, when the girls were asleep and she and her mother were preparing for bed, Eleanor said:

'Ma, will you look after the three children on Monday? I want to go to Akersfield.'

Mrs Foster looked at her in astonishment.

'Akersfield? Whatever for? And how will you get there?'

'On the train. I've a bit of money saved, money I'd gladly have given to Clara but she wouldn't let me have that satisfaction. As to what for – I'm going to find a job.'

'A job? What sort of a . . .?'

'Any sort. I'll do anything.' She spoke bravely, but she was filled with a cold fear. What about the children? 'But however awful it is, Ma, it can't be worse than staying here. You do see that?'

'Aye lass, I do.' Mrs Foster shook her head sadly.

'Oh Ma, it's you I'll miss! I'll miss you so badly! And there's no telling when I'll see you again.' It was suddenly all too much for her. She put her arms around her mother and cried against her shoulder, as she had not done since she was a small child.

Mrs Foster held Eleanor and let her have her cry. It would do her good. And as she felt the tears soaking her shoulder, she made up her own mind.

'You'll not miss me, lass, for I'm coming with you. As soon as you've found a place, I'll be there. I've got my bed, and a few bits and pieces. I don't eat much. And if you're going out to work you'll need me to look after the bairns.'

'Oh Ma, you wouldn't? It'll be hard.'

'Of course I would. To tell the honest truth, I'll be glad to get out from under Clara's feet!'

Eleanor had never thought she'd be glad to see Akersfield again, but she was. Even the sooty buildings and the cobbled streets looked better in the June sunshine, and the tall mill chimneys were quite striking, silhouetted against the clear blue sky. She had forgotten, too, that even from the centre of the town, if you looked up you could see the tops of the green hills which surrounded it. Her spirits lifted. If necessary she would visit every factory, every shop, knock on every door, until she had found a job and a room.

But by the middle of the afternoon she was less confident. She had been to five factories where the story was always the same, even when the notice on the gate said 'Hands wanted'.

'We're taking on skilled weavers, burlers-and-menders, spinners. Nowt else, love.'

At a laundry she missed a job by minutes.

'Nay, I've nobbut just set a lass on! Now if you'd come a bit earlier . . .'

There were no vacancies in the shops or on the market stalls, though a man on the pot stall nearly took her on, and then thought better of it.

'Come back in six weeks,' he said. 'We're a bit slack now.'

Six weeks was an eternity she couldn't live through. But it was four o'clock now; she had had no dinner and her feet were killing her. The grit from the pavements had worked through the newspaper with which, before leaving Felldale, she'd stuffed her shoes because of the holes. Even though it took precious money she'd have to stop for a cup of tea and a bite to eat.

She entered the first cafe she camed to. Kramer's it was called. It looked a bit fine for her, but she really couldn't go a step further, not if it was to cost her double here.

A young man came to take her order, which she thought seemed unusual. In Akersfield it was always waitresses, and anyway, he looked a cut above that. He was well-dressed, and when he asked what she'd like he was polite and well-spoken.

'I'd like a cup of tea and a slice of toast, please.'

'A cup of tea, or a pot?'

'I'll have a pot,' she said recklessly. Two or three cups of tea would help to fill her up.

She had to wait a long time. The man was over-busy, dashing between the tables and the baker's shop part at the front.

'I'm sorry to have kept you waiting,' he apologised when at last he brought her order. 'My waitress has left and I'm without help in the cafe.'

'That's quite all right,' Eleanor said.

It was more than all right. It was an opportunity sent straight from heaven. All she had to do was pluck up the courage to ask him. But supposing he enquired if she was experienced? She caught his eye and asked if she might have some more hot water. When he brought it she said:

'Excuse me, but are you looking for a new waitress?'

'I am,' he said. 'I should get one within a day or two.'

'Only I was wondering . . . I'm not engaged at the moment, and if I could help . . .'

She saw him looking at her wedding ring.

'I'm widowed.'

'I see.' Poor little thing, to be widowed so young!

'You are experienced in this kind of work?' he asked.

'Oh yes,' she lied. Only it wasn't quite a lie. Hadn't she served hundreds of meals to her husband and children? There was nothing to it.

'Where did you work last?'

'In the country,' she said truthfully. 'In Felldale. You might not know of it.'

She hoped this was so, or he'd know it didn't boast a cafe.

'The vicar there will give me a reference,' she said.

'Come to the counter when you've drunk your tea, and we'll discuss it,' he told her.

He liked the look of this young woman. She seemed

94

bright, confident, but not cocky. She was also very pretty, with her golden hair and green eyes. His customers would appreciate that as much as he did. And she had assured him she was experienced. But by the time she came to the counter he seemed less certain.

'I'm not convinced that the job would suit you,' he said doubtfully. 'You see, it isn't just being a waitress. I want more of a general help, from quite an early hour really. It would be more convenient to have someone who could live on the premises. There are two rooms over the cafe which come with the job, and I'd pay a fair wage. But perhaps that arrangement wouldn't suit you?'

Surreptitiously, Eleanor pinched her arm to make sure she wasn't dreaming. Oh please God, let it happen!

'It is *exactly* the arrangement which would suit me best, because I want to move back to Akersfield,' she said. 'When would you like me to start?'

'Tomorrow, ideally.'

'Then tomorrow it is. But I can only come as early as the first train. I'll move in in a day or two, if that will suit?'

She wasn't sure whether he'd offered her the job or whether she'd pushed him into it, but he seemed quite pleased.

'That will be splendid,' he said.

She took a deep breath.

'You'll find the children no trouble. They're as good as gold and as quiet as mice!'

'Children? I didn't realise . . .'

'Don't worry, Mr Kramer. You'll hardly know they're there. The eldest goes to school and my mother will be here to look after the other two.'

'Your mother?'

'Yes. So's I can give my full attention to the job here. Now how much do I owe you for my tea and toast?'

'Oh! Oh, nothing at all. Since you are going to work here.'

'Thank you very much then. It seems to be my lucky day!'

Probably it would be all right, he thought as he watched her leave. Though he had not envisaged a waitress with a mother and three children, it might well work out.

CHAPTER SIX

'Good night then, Mrs Heaton! I'm just leaving!'

Eleanor, on her knees washing the linoleum-covered floor to the accompaniment of her own spirited rendering of 'Bobby Shafto', sung in the exact time of her use of the scrubbing brush, didn't hear Mr Kramer's words; not until she paused at the end of the verse to draw breath and to wring out the floorcloth, at which point he repeated them.

'I'm just leaving!'

'Oh! I'm sorry, Mr Kramer!' She knew he didn't mind her singing as she worked, not once the shop was closed, or if she chanced to be in the bakehouse, where the customers wouldn't hear her and be disturbed. 'I didn't hear you.'

He smiled and nodded. 'It's a cheerful little song, that one.'

'But did he come back and marry her?' Eleanor wondered out loud. 'The best songs are often the sad ones.'

'You know a great many songs,' Mr Kramer said. 'I wonder if you know the composers of my parents' country – Schubert, Handel?'

Eleanor sat back on her heels. 'I don't know anything about composers,' she said. 'I just sing the songs. I never really know where I pick them up!'

'Well, you sing them very beautifully,' Mr Kramer told her.

She had worked for him for more than a year now and it seemed to him that everything she did was touched with beauty, which was the more moving because she was unconscious of it. Sometimes, in the dinner-hour rush in the cafe, he stopped what he was doing and watched her moving around among the customers, taking orders, serving plates of food, making out the bills which she always did with a frown of concentration on her face. She was so tall, so graceful in her movements. She had a smile for everyone. She was quick and competent, too. Even now, in the small act of rising to her feet because she had finished washing the floor, her movements were fluid and balanced, like those of a born dancer.

'I've left you a few things, on a tray on the counter,' he said.

'Oh thank you, Mr Kramer. You must let me pay you.' Eleanor replied. She knew he'd refuse, though sometimes she insisted on paying him twopence, which he accepted reluctantly, for a bag of stale buns and teacakes. It couldn't be said that the goods were really stale. Usually they'd been baked that morning, but Kramer's cafe and bakery had a reputation for freshness and Mrs Kramer would seldom stock anything which was more than a day old. The only problem about the leftovers was that they were often an unbalanced assortment, and this led to fierce quarrels between Becky and Selina when there was only one cream horn.

To Eleanor's secret relief, Mr Kramer waved away her offer of payment.

'I'll say goodnight again, Mrs Heaton. My mother will have prepared a meal and she doesn't like food to be kept waiting.'

'Doesn't Mrs Kramer get tired of cooking?' Eleanor asked. 'All the dinners in the cafe, and then another meal at night!'

It was Mrs Kramer's practice, now that she was getting older, to leave the cafe towards the end of the afternoon. She had done her share, starting early in the morning to bake for the shop, and then cooking the dinners. They did very few teas and her son, or Eleanor, was quite capable of dealing with those.

'Ah, but for supper she cooks the dishes she used to make for my father when they were in Germany. Pork with sauerkraut, fried herrings with onion sauce, sauerbraten. To tell you the truth, I am not so keen on them myself. I have seen enough food by the time I get home at night, but my mother would be disappointed if I did not eat.'

What a good son he was, Eleanor thought. He was a good man altogether. She admired and respected him, and wondered why he wasn't married. Though he was not strikingly handsome, and did not have quite the height and breadth she herself liked in a man, he was pleasant to look upon, with his light brown hair, blue eyes and clear skin. And his speaking voice was so attractive. He had no trace of the German accent of his mother, nor did he have a pronounced West Riding accent, though Eleanor knew he had been born and brought up in Akersfield. Perhaps, she thought, there *was* a young lady in that other life he lived away from the cafe.

When he had left the premises and Eleanor had locked the door behind him, she went quickly to see what was on the tray. Unlike her employer, however much food she served during the day it didn't take the edge off her appetite. She was always hungry.

There were three teacakes – two currant, one plain – a curd tart, two coconut buns and, to her delight, two small pork pies. It was seldom that any of Mrs Kramer's pork pies were left over. If she put them in the bakehouse oven now, for it seldom lost all its heat, and made some gravy from an Oxo cube, the four of them would have a good supper. And they could have the coconut buns to follow. The curd tart would keep for another day.

She walked through the cafe, the kitchen, the washing-up pantry, to the bakehouse at the far end of the building, making as much noise as she could as she went, for there were mice in the bakehouse and she liked to warn them of her coming so that they could get out of the way. In Felldale, in the country, she never bothered about mice, but town mice were different and she hated them. One of the things she disliked most was going to the privy late at night. The privy was across the yard, and you had to go through the bakehouse and out of the back door to reach it. On these occasions she sang at the top of her voice from the moment she left her own rooms to the second she was safely back again. 'All the world will know when you're going down the yard!' her mother said disapprovingly.

While the pies were heating she went upstairs and made the Oxo gravy, laid the table.

'He's very good to you, Mr Kramer,' Mrs Foster said. 'You lit on your feet when you came here!'

'I know. There's no denying it, though I don't think Mrs Kramer likes me.' Mr Kramer's mother wasn't a bad old stick, but Eleanor thought she would have preferred a middle-aged, spinster waitress.

The work was hard. She had to be downstairs early in the morning to light the baking oven before Mrs Kramer arrived on the first tram of the day. The Kramers had been one of the first businesses in Akersfield to install a gas-fired oven. Although it was physically easier than stoking the coke-fired ovens still found in the town, Eleanor was mortally afraid of the great iron beast. She jumped sky-high every time she put the taper to the long burners, and they popped, and shot out threatening tongues of blue flame.

From that moment she was on the go constantly. She greased the tins and laid out the ingredients for Mrs Kramer, while that lady, the minute she arrived, donned a white apron, white cotton sleeves and a white cap over her hair, and set to. The fixing of the cap was Eleanor's signal to make herself scarce. Mrs Kramer liked the bakehouse to herself. Her recipes, she said, were secret – especially that for the puff pastry. No-one since Mr Kramer had passed on had been allowed to watch her make the pastry.

Sometimes Eleanor stopped to do a job in the pantry next to the bakehouse, and tried to work out from the thumps and bangs heard through the wall, just what her employer was doing. Mostly she hurried back upstairs where she would make a cup of tea for herself and her mother before getting Selina and Becky up and dressed. Albert had sent his mother's bits and pieces by carrier, including her bed which she shared with Eleanor and Selina, while Becky slept on a narrow straw mattress on the floor, and Jenny in an iron cot. With the money which she had saved in the purse around her neck, Eleanor had been able to buy the bare necessities of furniture for the two rooms. They had chairs to sit on, beds to sleep in, a table at which to eat and enough pots and pans to manage with.

'School's on holiday,' Mrs Foster said when Eleanor brought her cup of tea on the morning after Mr Kramer had given them the meat pies. 'Let the children lie. I'll see to them later.'

Eleanor frowned slightly, 'I don't like to give you the trouble,' she said.

'Nonsense!' Mrs Foster sipped her tea. It was the nicest of the day, this first one in the morning. 'What else am I here for?'

'A lot better reasons than that,' Eleanor replied.

She didn't know how she would have managed without her mother. When she looked back on those last few days in Felldale, she knew she could never have endured them without Mrs Foster's support. Her mother had been so cheerful about it all, looking forward to the future as if it was all a big adventure, encouraging Becky and Selina to do likewise.

It had been a relief to Eleanor to make her farewells to Clara, and in the end they had parted civilly; but no-one, not even her mother, knew what it had cost to say goodbye to Dick. She hadn't wanted to go to his house so she had watched for him returning from market, and had run out and stopped him in the street. He jumped down from the cart and they stood close enough to touch, but not touching, conscious of the eyes of the village.

'I'm sorry, Ellie,' he said when she told him she was going.

'So am I, Dick. Ever so sorry. But it's for the best, Dick. We both know that. There's no more to be said except that I don't have any regrets, nor ever will.'

'Nor me!'

When she told him about the job he said, 'I know

Kramer's. I pass it on the way into Akersfield.'

Her face lit up, then clouded again when he said, 'I shan't call in, Ellie. Best not.' But perhaps, she thought, he might on some occasion have to bring a message from Felldale.

'Do you want me to take you on the cart?' he asked.

'No thank you. We're going on the train. Albert's very kindly paying the fare.'

There were no words left to say. Everything was there in the too-brief look which passed between them before Eleanor turned away and went back inside.

The first year in Akersfield hadn't been easy. The un-accustomed work, the summer heat of the overcrowded bedroom which was situated above the bakehouse; the bitter winter which followed; the mice which began to stir as soon as the candle was blown out at night; the daily struggle to make ends meet. It was her mother's calm, cheerful presence which helped Eleanor to face it. It was not so much what her mother did for her, though that was plenty; it was what she was, and the fact that she was there.

'Have a bit of a lie-in,' Eleanor suggested. 'Why not?'

'I thought happen I'd take the children in the park,' Mrs Foster said. 'I reckon it's going to be another hot day.'

'As you like,' Eleanor answered. 'Only don't go tiring yourself out, Ma. Any road, I'm going downstairs now. Mrs Kramer'll have the first batch ready for the window and Mr Kramer'll be here any minute.'

There was, also, the cafe to set out. Chairs to lift down from the tables where they were always stacked while she did the floor. Tables to wipe over; salt cellars, pepper and mustard pots, sugar basins to fill. And then a start to be made on the vegetables; mounds of potatoes and carrots. Fresh peas were too expensive for their trade but she'd had the dried marrowfats in soak overnight with a pinch of bicarb. And a score of other jobs which didn't meet the eye, though Mr Kramer would write out the menu boards, one for outside, the other for inside, in his meticulous script, and he'd be the one to see the butcher and sort out the meat order.

101

Eleanor put on the blue overall with which she'd been supplied, took a critical look at herself in the mirror, pulling her hair back from her face, then ran downstairs just as Mr Kramer let himself in. He greeted her cheerfully, thinking how fresh and pretty she looked.

'Good morning, Mrs Heaton! Another fine day. Let's hope it keeps it up for the coronation! Only a few days now!'

'Good morning, Mr Kramer!'

It was funny how he was getting so excited about the Coronation. Most people were, of course; perhaps because hardly anyone could remember a coronation in their lifetime, perhaps because the King might well have died from that awful new illness before ever he'd been crowned. But he hadn't, and everyone was thankful and now it was all 'Good old Teddy!' But you wouldn't have expected Mr Kramer to be so interested because, really, he wasn't English. Well, not quite. Of course, he'd been born here – he'd told her that right at the beginning. But his mother and father were German. But then the King had foreign blood in him. They said he spoke German better than he did English. Perhaps that was why Mr Kramer was so loyal.

'Yes, I hope the weather holds,' Eleanor said. 'Fireworks in the rain won't be much good.'

'Shall you go the the firework display?' Mr Kramer asked.

'Oh I expect so! It is a special occasion, isn't it? I wouldn't like Becky and Selina to miss it, even if it does mean keeping them up late.'

She would dearly have loved to buy each of the children some special souvenir, something expensive and beautiful which they could treasure all their lives, but it wouldn't be possible. What she had seen, however, was a special set of coloured postcards of the King, Queen Alexandra, and the Prince and Princess of Wales. When she drew her wages on Friday she intended to buy a set for each of the children, the baby included.

'I've finished the cafe,' Eleanor said. 'I'll go and see if Mrs Kramer needs a hand. There should be something ready to come out.'

102

She met Mrs Kramer who was coming from the bakehouse carrying a large wooden tray filled with scones, plain and fruit, and richly-smelling Eccles cakes. Eleanor's mouth watered every morning at the fruity, buttery smell of the Eccles cakes. She always hoped there would be one left over at the end of the day but there seldom was. Anything made with Mrs Kramer's special pastry went like the wind.

'Fruit pies next,' Mrs Kramer said. 'The teacakes not for an hour and a half. I am behind myself, as you so strangely say. When Mr Franz can spare you, you should put the steamer on for the puddings. Suet pudding must not be rushed.'

She always referred to her son as Mr Franz, though he had told Eleanor that his name was Frank. 'Because I am as English as the next person!' he said.

'Unless you're standing beside your mother!'

They had both laughed immoderately at that. It was one of the things she liked about Mr Kramer. He didn't mind a joke now and then.

The morning went by in a multitude of jobs. When the mill buzzer went at noon Eleanor put on a clean white apron and prepared to be a waitress, which was the part of her job she liked the best. They wouldn't get many people from the mill in the cafe, just some of the overlookers and one or two of the lower ranks of managers. Overlookers and managers didn't mix. They sat at two separate tables. The mill workers, those of them who hadn't brought their 'jock' to work, often came into the shop to buy one of Kramer's threepenny ham sandwiches in a fresh teacake, with mustard. The other customers in the cafe were usually commercial travellers, or perhaps office workers, and mostly they were regulars. There were very few women, just the occasional one brought in by one of the commercials, Eleanor suspected illicitly.

She took another quick look at the menu, chalked on the blackboard. The main course was either roast beef and Yorkshire pudding or fried haddock, followed by steamed jam pudding or plum pie and custard. Not bad for tenpence, including a cup of tea. She wondered what would be left over when the customers had gone, for from that she was allowed to select her own dinner. The Kramers ate in the back of the cafe, with one eye on the shop, but usually Eleanor was permitted to take her dinner upstairs, and this meant she could share it with her mother and the children. Mrs Kramer was sometimes surprisingly generous when she doled out Eleanor's meal, especially if it was food which wouldn't keep or couldn't be made up into something else next day, and Eleanor thought she guessed about the sharing.

'It will be haddock today,' Mrs Kramer said when two o'clock came and the last dinnertime customer had gone. 'It hasn't gone as well as the beef. Could you eat two pieces?'

'Yes please, Mrs Kramer!'

There were boiled potatoes, also some jam pudding, and one piece of pie which Eleanor thought she would let her mother have. Her mother missed being able to bake such things herself, but there was no oven in the upstairs rooms.

Mrs Kramer glanced over the dinner tray and then looked directly at Eleanor. 'I don't know where you put it!' she said dryly. 'You are as thin as a rail!' Her own rounded shape was a tribute to her good cooking.

When Eleanor got upstairs with the tray Mrs Foster had plates warming on the trivet, and they shared the food out equally and fell to.

'Did you go to the park?' Eleanor asked.

'No. We didn't get there. It was that hot! But we called in the mission.'

'And there's going to be a party on Saturday!' Becky broke in. 'And me and Selina can go. And everyone will get a present from the King! And can I have a new dress? I want a pink one.'

'You cannot have a new dress,' Eleanor said. 'If anyone's having a new dress it's Selina. It's her turn. But you may wear your bridesmaid's dress in honour of the King. I think you can just get into it, though it might be a bit short.'

Becky smiled happily. 'I expect the King will like me in my bridesmaid's dress!'

'I'm sure he would if he could see you,' Eleanor agreed. She had almost given up trying to impress upon Becky that the King would not be appearing in Akersfield in his robes and crown. She turned to her mother. 'Is is true about the party?'

'Yes. And they can go. It's for the poor children of Akersfield – and orphans.' It shamed her that her own grandchildren were numbered among the poor, but not so much that she had let her pride prevent her from gritting her teeth and walking into the mission hall to apply for tickets, the minute she'd seen the notice.

'Shall you mind going?' Eleanor asked. 'I shall be working.'

'I'll take them,' Mrs Foster promised.

'Then could you go down to the market today or tomorrow and get me a cheap fent of material, pink if you can? I could make Selina a little frock before Saturday. She hasn't anything good enough for a party.'

When Eleanor had gone back to work Mrs Foster carried Jenny down the stairs and put her in the carriage. 'Now you hold your whist while I get the other two ready,' she said lovingly.

They set off a few minutes later, Becky and Selina clinging to either side of the pram. Mrs Foster kept well away from the pavement edge. She didn't trust the trams which careered down the hill every few minutes. Nasty, noisy things, with their bells clanging. People said they were as safe as houses, but who could be sure that one of them wouldn't, one day, leap off the rails and go right out of control? And then there were the horses and carts, and sometimes even a nasty, smelly motor car. So she played safe and kept close in to the buildings.

As a matter of fact, though she would never tell Eleanor, who had enough on her plate already, she didn't like Akersfield. She couldn't take to it at all. Every time she went out she saw hundreds of faces, not one of which she knew. She hated the traffic and was scared of crossing the street. Most of all she disliked the noise. Even at night it was noisy, with

105

trams running late and people always on the street. She thought of Felldale, of the deep quiet of the countryside at night, with the only sound that of nocturnal animals.

She missed the green of the dales country, on which she had feasted her eyes every time she looked out of the window or stepped out of the door. Here, the only bit of green was to be found in the park, and it was a sooty green at that. If she set the children down to play there – always supposing she could find a patch which didn't say 'Keep off the grass' – then they'd be dirty in no time at all.

But though she missed Felldale desperately, she didn't regret coming to Akersfield, not for one minute. Eleanor needed her. Her grandchildren needed her. She had a part to play in all their lives. When she was a young woman she'd been happy with her husband and children, it was the best time of her life. But those days were gone and nothing could bring them back.. A few months ago, when the war in South Africa had ended, she had faced the fact that she must now put her son David to the back of her mind – not forget him, she could never do that – but she must concentrate on the living. She would live a day at a time, and look forward to whatever future was left to her.

'Can we buy some humbugs in the market, Grandma?' Becky asked. 'Striped ones?'

'Nay lass, you know I've no money for humbugs,' Mrs Foster said.

She never had money, except for the coppers Eleanor spared whenever she could. If you were too old to earn, there was no money. It was as simple as that. There were folk who said that the government, up in London, should give you some when you couldn't earn, but that was a far-fetched idea. She couldn't see that ever happening.

On the fent stall in the market she found exactly the right material for Selina's dress, fine pink cotton printed with blue rosebuds. The fent cost tenpence, which left her twopence from the shilling Eleanor had given her. She made a bold decision.

'Right, children! We're going to buy some humbugs! A

pennyworth for you to share and a pennyworth for your mother and me to eat this evening!'

If it had been a Friday she might have walked around to speak to Dick on his stall, gathered news of what was happening in Felldale. If only Eleanor and Dick . . .

That evening, after the children were in bed, Eleanor made a start on Selina's dress. She had a talent for making clothes – not so much for the stitching, she had won no prizes for childhood samplers – but for design and originality, so that whatever she fashioned, even if the material was cheap, seemed a cut above the rest.

They were sitting, now, in front of the open window in their room over the shop, trying to get a little air from the hot summer's night.

'I think I shall scallop the edge of the yoke,' Eleanor said, 'and do some shaped smocking.'

'I don't know where you get your ideas,' Mrs Foster said. 'Certainly not from me. All I'm good at is darning and hemming sheets.'

Eleanor smiled. 'Well, we'll strike a bargain, Ma. You do the darning, and as soon as I can scrape enough together for the material, I'll make you a new blouse!'

She longed for a new dress herself, but she didn't have the money. She supposed it would have to be black, though she was no longer in mourning and she was sick to the teeth of wearing black. Actually, except for the sake of her children, she didn't mourn Ben. So much had happened since his death that her life with him seemed in the distant past. Now she had this fanciful notion that as the King was starting out on *his* new life, so she would start hers. She had no idea what it was to be; common sense told her that nothing was likely to change from the present state of affairs, but deep inside her she had this unquenchable hope. Even so, a new dress, preferably in some beautiful, glowing, if impractical colour, would have to wait.

It was almost midnight before she put away her sewing.

When she went to close the window she stood for a moment looking out on the street. This was the road which eventually led to Felldale. Dick still travelled this road, every week. Sometimes on a Friday, in those first few months, when she judged the time was right, she hovered near to the shop window in the hope of seeing him pass. She never did see him. He never called, not once in all this time.

She fastened the window catch and turned back into the room. 'We must get to bed, Ma,' she said. 'I'm that tired I could sleep on a clothes line!'

But she knew that however tired she was, for the last few minutes, in the darkness before she fell asleep, she would think about Dick.

When Mrs Kramer arrived next morning she said, 'Mr Franz will be late today. We are to open the shop at the usual time. He has this idea that he wishes to trim up the shop and cafe for the Coronation and he has gone to buy things for it. Though every drop of his blood is German, my son is more English than the English!'

'He's certainly a very loyal subject,' Eleanor replied. She admired him for it. She wondered if Mrs Kramer had ever been really happy since she had left Germany, if she had been dragged here, unwillingly, by her husband.

When Mr Kramer arrived he was laden with streamers, paper chains and flags. He set to at once, trimming every part of the premises. The centrepiece of his efforts was the shop window, where he displayed a portrait of the King and his beautiful queen, with red white and blue streamers and chains radiating from it to every point of the compass, and underneath the portrait the words 'God Save the King!'

'I notice that some have put "God Bless Good Old Teddy",' he said. 'But I think that is perhaps a little disrespectful.'

'I daresay you would have liked me to ice all the cakes in red white and blue icing,' Mrs Kramer said dryly.

Her son's eyes sparkled at the thought.

'What a pity we did not think of that earlier, Mother!

But perhaps you could still ice a large cake for the centre of the window?'

'Not if anyone is to have any dinner today,' Mrs Kramer said. 'And even if I had the time, who can see what is in the window through all that lot hung across it?'

On Saturday, the day of the Coronation, after the early morning rush there was very little trade in the shop, and even less in the cafe. Dinnertime brought no more than a dozen customers and Mrs Kramer left the moment it was served. 'No doubt the trams will stop when the procession starts,' she said. 'And I have no wish to walk home through the crowds.'

The moment the last customer had swallowed his pudding Mr Kramer said, 'We, too, will have a little holiday, Mrs Heaton! I shall close at once so that we may join in the celebrations. Leave all the cleaning until Monday and take yourself off to whatever you have in mind!'

'I'm very grateful to you,' Eleanor said. 'If I go now I can join my mother and the children at the mission party before it's all over. Then this evening I plan to take Becky and Selina to the fireworks in the park.' It had also occurred to her that since there had been so few takers for Mrs Kramer's excellent dinner, there would be enough food left over to feed them for the whole weekend.

'I hope to go to the firework display myself,' Mr Kramer said. 'Perhaps I shall see you there.'

Then he opened the till drawer and took out three silver sixpences. 'One for each of the children,' he smiled. 'There are sure to be stalls, with things they would like to buy. They can choose something for the baby to keep.'

'You really are most kind,' Eleanor said. 'My children have never had so much money to spend at once in the whole of their lives!'

'Then promise you won't insist on them spending it wisely,' Mr Kramer said cheerfully. 'This is a day to do special things!'

When Eleanor reached the mission hall she spotted her mother at once, sitting on a bench down the side of the room, the baby on her lap, the carriage parked in a corner.

'There are the girls,' Mrs Foster pointed out. They were sitting in the front row, their heads tilted back, their eyes wide open and shining as they watched every movement of the clowns and jugglers on the stage. They laughed and clapped and shouted with an abandonment Eleanor had never before seen in them, Selina every bit as much as Becky. When the final turn was over they found their way back to their mother and grandmother.

'We had jelly and sweets and sandwiches, and there was a great big thing where you turned a tap on and tea came out!' Becky cried.

'Jelly,' Selina said.

'And we're going to get a coronation mug with a picture of the King and Queen!'

'Carnation mug,' Selina echoed dutifully.

When they were home, Eleanor said to Becky, 'I hope you'll never forget this day. I hope you'll remember it when you're an old, old lady.'

'You'll be dead then.'

What a matter-of-fact child her eldest daughter was, Eleanor thought.

'I suppose so.'

'Can I have your gold ring when you're dead?'

'Yes.'

'When do you think that might be?' Becky asked hopefully.

Eleanor laughed. 'Not for a long time yet! I daresay you'll have a gold ring of your own long before then.'

'I shall have a gold ring and a pearl necklace and a big hat with feathers,' Becky said confidently.

'Right! But for now, if you want to stay up for the fireworks you and Selina must both lie down and have a little sleep.'

While they slept, Eleanor got herself ready. Not that there was much she could do to her appearance, she thought, staring into the mirror. She looked so dull, so drab. She failed to see the clear skin, the pink cheeks and shining eyes

110

or the rich golden hair which showed under her hat. Nor could she see, the mirror was too small, her graceful figure, slender, yet sensuously curved.

She stuck out her tongue at herself, in disgust – and then she had the bright idea! She ran downstairs, and from the lavish decorations in the shop she took three large paper flowers in red, white, and blue. And on a second thought she took a further supply. Back upstairs she pinned the three largest flowers in her black hat, two on the front of the crown, the third trailing over the brim. 'Splendid!' she said out loud. The remaining flowers she would pin on the girls' sailor hats.

There were other happenings in the park before the fireworks were due to begin. A choir sang patriotic songs; children wearing appropriately-coloured paper hats formed the flag; Akersfield's heaviest men struggled against each other in a tug of war. The Akersfield Town Silver Prize Band struck up, first with yet another selection of patriotic songs, and then, as the last, lingering notes of 'Rule Britannia' faded reluctantly away, the tempo changed and the music began for dancing.

How she would love to dance, Eleanor thought. Though she frequently dusted the furniture in waltz time or made the beds to a stately minuet, all to her own sung accompaniment, she had hardly ever danced in public.

She stood with the children on rising ground, with a good view of the dance area. Next to them were a young man and woman with their two children, a little older than Becky and Selina. The man and the woman looked at each other, then glanced towards Eleanor. Presently the man raised his hat and spoke.

'We were wondering, my wife and I, if you would be so very kind as to keep an eye on our children while we had just one dance?'

'We would be so very grateful,' his wife chipped in.

'Of course I will,' Eleanor said. 'With pleasure. Your children will be quite safe with me.'

The man led his wife away. Eleanor watched them as they

joined the dance, her own foot tapping with the rhythm of the music. Oh, but the Akersfield band was a good one! No doubt about it!'

So immersed was she in the dancing that she failed to see Frank Kramer approaching, and when he spoke to her she almost jumped out of her skin.

'Good evening, Mrs Heaton,' he said formally. 'I hope you are enjoying yourself?'

'Oh! Oh yes I am. Very much, thank you.'

The man and his wife returned, out of breath and smiling happily.

'We can't thank you enough,' the man said. 'It was most kind of you.'

'I kept an eye on the children while this lady and gentleman danced,' Eleanor explained to her employer.

'Ah! Then I wonder . . .' Mr Kramer turned to the couple. 'I wonder if you might be so kind as to keep an eye on this lady's two little girls while we too dance. That is,' he said to Eleanor, 'if you will do me the honour?'

'Why of course,' Eleanor replied. It was most polite of him to offer, but who could imagine Mr Kramer dancing? She took his arm and was escorted to the dance platform. The band had started to play a waltz. He placed one hand correctly at the back of her waist, and began to dance.

She could not believe it, she had never in her wildest dreams imagined anything like it! He whirled and twirled and spun and swung, taking her with him so that at times she wondered if her feet touched the ground. She felt like thistledown in his arms, as if she was dancing on a cloud. His timing was perfection and, in spite of the movement, his balance so controlled that the flowers on her hat remained as secure as the moment she had pinned them on. When the music came to a halt he spun her skilfully around, and then bowed to her.

'Thank you, Mrs Heaton. I hope you found that as enjoyable as I did?'

'It was . . . yes, indeed I did. I had no idea you were such a good dancer, Mr Kramer!'

112

'I get it from my parents,' he said modestly. 'Remember that the waltz came from Germany. My mother and father were champion dancers in their time.'

Mrs Kramer a dancing champion? Whatever next? What a strange day it had been!

'You yourself are a good dancer,' he told her. 'I can see you enjoy it.'

'I could dance all night!' Eleanor said.

So could I, he thought. I could dance forever with this young woman who these days is seldom out of my thoughts. Out loud he said nothing, but took her back to rejoin her children.

CHAPTER SEVEN

Eleanor, balancing a tray piled high with dishes on her left hand, in the skilful manner she had now acquired, moved towards the shop door to close it yet again.

'Drat this door!' she said. 'There's something wrong with the sneck.'

The trouble was that if a departing customer didn't quickly give the door a good hard pull behind him, the curtain of fog, which hid everything outside beyond the pavement's edge, immediately began to creep in. You could see it, see the curls and twirls and folds of it as it insinuated itself into new territory. It was like a living thing, an evil spirit on the prowl. And even if you hadn't been able to see it, the proof was right here in the cafe – everybody coughing. Except for two or three days when a wind had arisen to disperse it, the fog had been with them for the whole of November. Sometimes it thinned a little, so that you could see the gaslit windows of the shops across the road; sometimes, as today, it came down again in a thick, impenetrable blanket. All you knew of the trams today was the warning clang of their bells as they inched their way down the hill.

'I'll see to the door as soon as the rush is over,' Mr Kramer said.

Oddly enough, in view of the weather, they were busier than ever in the cafe. All this week every seat had been taken at midday, as if Mrs Kramer's solid food was the best defence the customers could find against the elements. And it seemed as if she quite enjoyed pitting her culinary skills against such nastiness. The November menus had been full of nourishing things like rich beef stew with dumplings, meat-and-potato pie with thick suet crust, steamed currant puddings.

Eleanor took the tray of dirty crockery into the washing-up pantry, then went into the kitchen to give more orders to Mrs Kramer.

'One apple pie, four syrup rolls. Extra custard for Mr Carter. I swear that man has custard running in his veins!'

'All the English are soaked in custard sauce,' Mrs Kramer said. 'But Mr Carter is a good customer, five days a week as regular as clockwork and never a complaint. we should not begrudge him a little extra custard.'

'Oh I don't!' Eleanor replied.

She begrudged Mr Carter nothing, partly because she liked him, partly, she had to admit, because every Friday, without fail, he left her sixpence under his plate. Very few people left tips, it wasn't that sort of trade, though had it been she might have done quite well since she was popular with the regulars. But the odd pennies and twopences which did come her way were welcome and, together with Mr Carter's weekly sixpence, she saved them in a jug upstairs.

Mrs Kramer sounded snappy. She was often a little short of temper in the heat of the cramped kitchen, but the last few days she had been more so. Eleanor thought she didn't look well. The flush on her face was angrier than that normally caused by the cooking and she had a tight, persistent little cough. In the few spare moments she had from her own work Eleanor had offered to give a hand in the kitchen, but Mrs Kramer had not accepted.

'I prefer to be on my own when I cook,' she said. 'Two women in one kitchen can never succeed.'

Frank Kramer had been in the kitchen when Eleanor had made the offer. 'My mother is too independent,' he said.

Mrs Kramer heard the note of apology in her son's voice and it niggled at her. There was something in his attitude towards this young woman which disturbed her. She had seen the way he looked at her, the way his eyes followed her as she went about her work. She wondered if the girl herself was aware of it. If so, she gave no sign. Mrs Kramer wished that Eleanor Heaton had never come to them. She was a good enough worker, she couldn't be faulted on that score, but she was a disturbing influence.

Mrs Kramer knew that her whole life depended on Franz. Though she had been in England now for more than twenty-five years, she still felt herself a stranger. She had never made friends, had never wished to. When her husband was alive that had not mattered. They had been all in all to each other. Now there was only Franz, and she was afraid, in her heart she was desperately afraid, that she might lose him. Perhaps she should tackle him about it, ask him outright? What could be worse than not knowing, than living with this ache of apprehension? But if she spoke to him too directly, might she not drive him into the very action she dreaded? Was it better not to know . . . to persuade herself that it was all in her imagination? But she knew it was not.

Frank came into the kitchen.

'Mother, I think you should leave now. Everyone has been served. It will be dark early this afternoon, and when darkness falls the fog will be thicker than ever. The trams will probably not run.'

'If I wait until closing time it won't matter about the trams. I can walk home with you,' Mrs Kramer said.

Frank shook his head. 'Mother, you are not fit to walk in this weather. Though you won't admit it, you know you're not well. It's my opinion that you shouldn't be here at all. You should be in bed. I wish I could take you home myself, but it's too early for me to leave.'

'You could go, Mr Kramer' Eleanor interrupted. 'I can look after things here. There won't be much more trade on a day like this.'

How dare she, Mrs Kramer thought furiously. How dare she give her employer permission to leave his own business? Before they knew where they were the girl would have made herself indispensable. Was that what she was trying to do?

'Thank you, that will not be necessary,' she said. 'I can manage very well on my own. Or if my son prefers it I can

116

wait until closing time. It is up to him to decide.' She wished she did not feel so unutterably tired, didn't have this nagging pain in her side. At this moment she wanted, more than anything in the world, to be in her own warm bed.

'I'm glad you say that, Mother,' Frank answered. 'And I *have* decided. I shall accept Eleanor's kind offer and I shall take you home in a few minutes. What is more, we shall not go on the tram. If I can get one to make the journey in the fog, I shall call a cab.'

Mrs Kramer shrugged. 'If you think Mrs Heaton can manage . . .' She was ashamed that she should sound so ungracious – but why had he taken to using the girl's Christian name? It was not fitting. 'Then you had better cash up first,' she added.

Eleanor flushed. What did Mrs Kramer mean by *that* remark? That she was dishonest?

'Whatever Mr Kramer wishes,' she said frostily.

Frank smiled at her. 'I think you are as capable of cashing up as I am and I'd be grateful if you'd do it, and take the money upstairs with you. Thank you very much, Eleanor. Oh yes, it is possible that the traveller from Hopkins Baker's sundries will call, in spite of the fog. I have left his account, with the money to cover it, in the back of the till. I don't think we need any further supplies this week, but if you think of something, feel free to order it.'

He didn't want to leave. It was only that he was worried about his mother. He would have preferred to stay as long as ever Eleanor was there. Since the night of the Coronation dance, since he had held her in his arms in the waltz, he had never wanted her out of his sight. It was no good, of course. He could offer her nothing. He was young, he had a thriving business, he had a heart full of devotion towards her, but he could give her none of it. He had been brought up to put duty before everything, and his duty was towards his mother.

It would have been different if his father had lived. On several occasions since his father's death Frank had thought – hoped, almost – that his mother might decide to return

117

to Germany, leaving him in England. Had her sister there, her only relative, not died, she might have done so. But it would never happen now. He loved his mother, but sometimes in recent weeks there had been a bitterness in his thoughts which was new, and disturbing, to him.

It was perhaps as well, he thought, though it would have given him infinite pleasure, that Eleanor showed no signs of returning his feelings, or even of recognizing them. At least she would not be a partner in his sadness. And if he could not make her happy, as he wanted to, then the next best thing was to spare her pain, and make her life easier in whatever small way he could. This was the only means he had of expressing his love.

There was little doing in either the shop or cafe after Frank Kramer and his mother left, and soon after darkness fell on the November afternoon the trickle of customers ceased altogether. Eleanor looked out of the window. The fog was not quite as thick as it had been. There was the odd patch where it moved a little, was not quite so solid. But it was still impossible to see across the street. The trams had stopped running and there was neither traffic nor people around. It was all uncannily quiet. She might as well close. It was highly unlikely that Hopkins' traveller would call now. She was glad that she lived on the premises and would not have to turn out in the fog to get home.

She cleared the remaining goods from the shop window – there wasn't much because Mrs Kramer had baked short today. That done, she stacked the cafe chairs on the tables and began to sweep the floor. She would be glad to finish. Becky and Selina were not well, she had had to keep Becky home from school with a cold, and it would have been a hard day for her mother.

She was in the back part of the cafe when she heard the shop door open. She put down the sweeping brush and went towards the shop as the man walked in. He had a large cotton handkerchief tied around his face, but it was not that which frightened her. That was a common precaution against the fog. It was the eyes which showed above the

118

handkerchief: hard, dark eyes. He wore a cloth cap, pulled well down over his forehead, so that he seemed to be nothing but eyes: eyes which stared and threatened.

'I'm sorry,' she said. 'We're closed.' She was amazed how steady her voice sounded. It gave away nothing of the fear inside her. But why should she be afraid? He was just a man, just a customer.

'I'm not after a cup of tea!' the man said. He had a low, quiet voice, which was somehow more disturbing than if he had shouted. 'All I want is whatever's in the till. So you just stand right here, lady, and don't move and you won't get hurt!'

Fear left her, was instantly replaced by a burning indignation that he should dare to do this thing. She ran to the till and stood in front of it, barring his access with her body.

'Move out of the way,' the man ordered her. 'Don't play games with me. I can be rough!'

'Get out! Get out of here!' She spat the words at him, refusing to move.

'All right,' the man said. 'Don't say I didn't warn you!' He struck out and pushed her savagely aside, so that she fell to the floor, hitting her forehead against the corner of the counter as she went down. She felt blinded by pain, felt the blood trickle down her face; nevertheless she tried to rise, aware that already his hands were in the till. She must stop him! At all costs she must stop him!

By the time she was on her feet he was heading for the door, and before she could take a step – she was so dizzy – he had gone. She moved to the door, went outside, but there was no sign of him. There was no sign of anyone, and the only sound, coming through the fog, was that of running footsteps in the distance. And then they too died away. It was no use calling for help. There was no-one to answer. In any case, it was too late.

She went back into the shop, locked and bolted the door, drew the blinds, and all the time her body trembled from top to toe and the blood ran down her forehead. She should have washed the blood off in the kitchen before going upstairs to her mother, but somehow she wasn't thinking straight. All that mattered to her now, the only thing in the world that mattered, was that she must get to Mr Kramer, tell him what had happened.

When she dragged herself upstairs and into the living-room, her mother screamed at the sight of her and Selina started to cry. Becky, Eleanor remembered afterwards, did not do so. She seemed to have more curiosity than fear. She listened avidly while Eleanor related what had happened.

'I'm all right,' Eleanor assured her mother. 'It's nothing more than a cut. But I have to go to Mr Kramer. I have to let him know at once what's happened!'

'You can't do any such thing,' Mrs Foster protested. 'You can't go out in that state, and on a night like this!'

'I must!' Eleanor said. 'I can't let it wait. I shall manage well enough. It's no more than a mile to Ashfield Road. I shall be there as quickly as I could get to the police station. Then Mr Kramer can inform the police.'

'You're not going out without having that cut attended to, and swallowing a cup of tea!' Mrs Foster declared.

'I haven't time to wait for tea,' Eleanor said.

'Then I'll dab a bit of witch hazel on the cut,' Mrs Foster insisted.

Eleanor stood impatiently, trying not to wince as the witch hazel stung her face. Then she put on her jacket, wrapped a scarf around her throat, pinned on her hat.

'Take care!' Mrs Foster said anxiously. 'I don't like you going out like this. I don't like it at all!' Who knew what other villains were about? But she didn't voice that fear. There was no stopping her daughter and therefore no point in making things worse for her.

'I'll be careful,' Eleanor promised. 'And I'll be back as quickly as ever I can.'

In the street, hurrying towards Ashfield Road, the horror of what had happened struck her afresh: not the horror of what had befallen her, that didn't matter, and was easily remedied – but the theft of the cash, and not just the day's takings, but the money for Hopkins' bill. She should have locked the door and pulled down the blind the minute the last customer had left. She had been a fool, a negligent fool! She had been left in a position of trust and she had failed that trust. What would Mr Kramer say; what would happen to her?

Panic at the thought of telling him swept over her and she began to run through the fog. Away from the town it was a little thinner. There were patches where it was just possible to see the street names. She knew where Ashfield Road was, she had sometimes passed the end of it when taking the children to the park on a Sunday. There was a large chapel at the bottom of the road and that would be her guide. She kept on running, though she had a stitch in her side now, and the cut on her forehead was bleeding again. When the chapel building loomed up out of the fog she felt a spasm of relief, which changed quickly to fear as she turned into Ashfield Road; fear of the confrontation which must happen any minute now.

The numbers on the doors were not visible, but the houses had iron railings and gates, enclosing small front gardens. She touched and counted each gate until she knew she was at number seventeen. She rang the bell, then beat on the door, then rang the bell again. There was scarcely any breath left in her body now; if he didn't come soon she must collapse! Oh why didn't he come?

At the moment the hammering on the door, the insistent pealing of the bell, impinged on Frank Kramer's ears, he was listening to the songs of Schubert on his phonograph. The sounds at the door were so insistent, so urgent, that he turned off the singer in mid-song and hurried into the front hall. His mother was almost certainly asleep. He hoped the noise wouldn't waken her.

The sight which met his eyes when he opened the door was like something in a nightmare; yet it wasn't a nightmare, it was really happening.

Eleanor Heaton stood there, her golden hair, streaked with black from the soot-laden fog, wisping damply about

121

her face, tumbling down on to her shoulders. Her hat was awry. But it was her face, her lovely face! On her forehead was a swollen, black and blue bruise, with a gash in the centre from which blood had trickled down her chalk-white face. There was another bruise on her cheek. Her lips were bloodless and her eyes, deep, dark green now instead of their usual shining emerald, were full of terror. Her breathing was shallow, laboured, as if she had no strength for it.

There was no question of waiting to be invited in. She was over the dootstep and without a word, other than his crying out of her name, he had taken her in his arms. He felt her whole body trembling, shaking as she burst into tears. He held her close, waiting anxiously for her weeping to subside, yet at the same time with part of him exulting that whatever terrible thing had happened, she had turned to him, that it was his arms which sheltered her.

Mrs Kramer had been not quite asleep when the hammering on the door aroused her. She was slower to move than Franz but even so, when she had put on her dressing-gown and slippers and reached the top of the stairs, it was in time to see, down below in the hall, Eleanor Heaton in her son's arms. She stood without moving, not understanding any of it. The girl's face was invisible, buried in Franz's shoulder. It was not until they moved apart and the light from the gas mantle fell on Eleanor's face that she saw the damage, and cried out aloud.

'Gott in Himmel! Was ist denn los?'

The two in the hall heard her and looked up, and then, at the sight of the fear in Eleanor's face, Mrs Kramer descended the stairs.

'What is it? What is happening?'

'Eleanor is about to tell me,' Frank said. 'Let her do so in her own time.' He turned back to Eleanor. 'You are with friends now,' he soothed her. 'Whatever it is, you are with friends.'

'Now,' Eleanor said. 'But not when you have heard what I have to say.'

She told him.

She told him, looking him straight in the face. She could hardly believe it when she saw that his expression of concern and compassion did not, for one second change. It was not so with Mrs Kramer.

'You stupid girl!' she cried. 'I knew we were wrong to leave you in charge! How do you suppose we can afford a loss such as this? Why did you not lock the door? Why did you not draw the blinds?'

'Do you think I haven't asked myself those questions?' Eleanor said quietly.

'And what is your answer?' Mrs Kramer persisted.

'That will do, Mother!' Both Eleanor and Mrs Kramer looked in surprise at the sternness of Frank's voice. 'What happened to Eleanor could have happened to anyone. At whatever time one chose to lock the door, it could happen five minutes sooner. It could happen to you. It could happen to me, if the man was stronger and took me by surprise. I am sorry it had to happen to Eleanor while she was being kind enough to take over *my* responsibility.'

'But the money!' Mrs Kramer persisted. 'And Hopkins' account? how shall we make it up?'

'I would make it up to you if I could,' Eleanor said. 'As it is . . .'

The only money she had in the world was the tips she had saved, and those were for a very special purpose. Albert and Clara − it seemed impossible to believe but it was true enough − had invited them to visit Felldale at Christmas. The money was for the train fares. Without it they couldn't go, and her mother, who longed to see her son and her other grandchildren, would be bitterly disappointed. Even so . . .

'Even if you could, I wouldn't hear of such a thing,' Frank said. 'Money is only money. We shall recover from the loss. And now, Mother, I intend to give Eleanor a little brandy, and to take her home. I suggest that you go back to bed as quickly as possible. It isn't suitable for you to be standing around in this draughty hall.'

While Mr Kramer was seeing to his mother, Eleanor sat in the dining-room and sipped the brandy he had poured for her. She had never tasted the stuff before and it took her by surprise, catching her in the throat so that she gasped, and almost choked; but within minutes she felt its glow spread right through her body. Now she felt not only warmer, but more confident. Rising, she went to look at herself in the mirror over the fireplace – and was horrified by the sight. It was not only the bruises, which seemed to be ripening by the minute, it was the state of her hair and the angle of her hat. What must Mr Kramer have thought of her? Quickly she took off her hat, drew back her hair and pinned it up as well as she could, then replaced the hat at a straighter angle. There was nothing to be done about her face, but at least she looked a little more respectable.

'And now I shall take you home,' Mr Kramer said, coming back into the room.

'Thank you, but there is absolutely no need. I shall be perfectly all right. And you have already been far kinder than I deserve.'

'Nonsense!' he said. 'And I wouldn't dream of letting you walk through the streets alone in your state. Why, your mother would never forgive me! Are you sure you feel well enough to leave, or would you like to rest a little longer?'

'I'm perfectly all right, better than I look. And I must go. It's true that my mother will be worried.'

When they left the house he offered her his arm. The fog had thickened again. They could see for no more than a few yards. But for the occasional sound of footsteps they might have been alone in the world. Once, they heard footsteps running, and Eleanor was momentarily filled with panic, so that she clutched at Mr Kramer's arm. He put his hand over hers and spoke comfortingly.

'There's no need to worry. You are quite safe with me.'

'I know. I'm sorry. But that was what *he* sounded like!'

'Try to forget,' he said. 'Let's talk of other things. For instance, next week I am going to a performance of the "Messiah" at the Akersfield Central Hall. Have you ever been to hear the "Messiah"?'

He was talking for her sake. He felt no need of words

between them. It was enough for him just to be with her, to feel her arm in his, to have her turn to him in her moment of fright.

'No,' Eleanor said. 'But I know some of the music, and love it.'

'Ah! Then as it is the season of the year, perhaps we may expect a few excerpts as you wash the cafe floor!'

For the first time since the robbery, Eleanor smiled – and then found that it was painful to do so since one side of her face was stiff and aching.

For the rest of the way Frank Kramer kept Eleanor occupied with chat, and gradually he felt her arm relaxing in his. All too soon they were at the shop. For his own sake he would have liked the journey to be twice, three times as long. But an idea was shaping itself in his mind.

They entered by the back door. When they went through to the shop he did not even glance in the direction of the till, though he saw Eleanor do so.

'Never mind that now,' he said. 'If you will allow me, I am going to take you upstairs and deliver you safely to your mother.'

Mrs Foster, white-faced and anxious, came to the top of the stairs to meet them.

'I've been that worried!' she confessed. 'It's very good of you to bring our Eleanor back, Sir! Can I give you a cup of cocoa before you set off again? I'm afraid we've nothing stronger.'

'Thank you, but no. I daresay my own mother is awake, and anxious. We all know what mothers are like!' He spoke pleasantly and Mrs Foster warmed towards him.

'Now there is a good man, a gentleman!' she said to Eleanor when he had departed.

'The very best,' Eleanor agreed.

As he walked back to Ashfield Road Frank Kramer asked himself many questions, and found no satisfactory answers. He knew more than ever now that he loved Eleanor, that he wanted her and always would. Was it possible, was it just possible, that she would consent to live in the same house as his mother? It was a big house, they needn't be on top of each other. But his mother's attitude earlier this evening appeared to rule that out. It was strange how his mother had changed towards Eleanor. At first she had seemed quite to like her, had often been kind to her.

Why should his mother not live on her own? She would hate it, but other women managed it. He would still support her, though in a more modest style. But if he settled the question of *his* mother, what about Mrs Foster? He knew she was totally dependent upon her daughter. For one moment he, who had all his life been a dutiful and loving son, hated all parents. The moment passed, but not his resolve to find a solution. It might be a slow process, and he wasn't clear how he would bring it about, but he determined that, if she would have him, one day Eleanor would be his.

As he turned the corner by the chapel and began the walk up Ashfield Road, the fog began to clear. He took it as an omen that his own life, too, might do likewise.

Both Eleanor and her mother had been surprised by Albert's letter, inviting them all to visit Felldale at Christmas. And not only to visit, but to stay two nights. 'If you could get away in time for a train on Christmas Eve,' he'd written, 'then you could stay over Christmas Day and go back Boxing Day. Clara and me would be pleased to see you all.'

It was the only letter they had had from him since they'd come to Akersfield.

'What's come over him after all this time?' Eleanor said. 'Suddenly to invite us?'

'What's come over *her* more like! Guilty conscience, I should think. Anyway, she's safe enough. We can't afford to go.' But Mrs Foster desperately wanted to do so. It would be the second Christmas of her life spent away from Felldale.

'We might just afford it, Ma!'

Eleanor told her about the tips in the jug. 'And coming up to Christmas, Christmas week, folks might be a bit more generous. I reckon I'll just be able to afford the train fare, but with nothing to spare.'

'It would be grand if we could go,' Mrs Foster said. 'Apart from anything else, I don't like families falling out and this could patch things up again.'

'I'd have to ask Mr Kramer if I could leave a bit early on Christmas Eve, so's we could catch the train,' Eleanor said. 'I'm not sure what he'll say. It'll be a busy day, what with the special dinner in the cafe and Christmas orders in the shop.'

'It's my belief he'll agree,' Mrs Foster declared. 'You've already said you'll be in the bakehouse at five-thirty that morning to help Mrs Kramer with the mince pies. He'll take account of that.'

'He might, but Mrs Kramer won't,' Eleanor said. 'She seems to have taken against me – I'm sure I don't know why.'

Except that she still had a cough, Mrs Kramer seemed back in normal health again. There was, however, a distance between the two of them that had not been there in the beginning. Though it was never mentioned – Frank had forbidden his mother to speak of it – Eleanor thought that Mrs Kramer still blamed her for the till robbery. There must have been some reason for her attitude, and Eleanor could think of no other.

'Mrs Kramer doesn't get it all her own way,' Mrs Foster said. 'I'm sure he'll let you go.'

She was proved right, though Eleanor herself was correct in thinking that Mrs Kramer would protest.

'It is the busiest day of the year,' she grumbled. 'Busier even than Easter with its hot cross buns! How can we manage if you are to take the half day off?'

'It won't be a half day, Mrs Kramer,' Eleanor pointed out. 'The train doesn't leave until four-thirty and it takes only a quarter of an hour to get to the station.'

'There is no problem,' Mr Kramer said. 'I shall see to it that you finish work at three-thirty prompt.'

He was also the means of solving another problem. On the Saturday before Christmas week, when he paid her wages, he included an extra half-sovereign in the envelope in which he always put her money. When she had counted out the money she took it back to him at once.

'You've made a mistake, Mr Kramer. You've given me too much!'

'It is not a mistake, Eleanor,' he said. 'The extra money is a small Christmas present – a thank-you for all your hard work.' He was happy at the pleasure in her face, but he stopped short her thanks and turned away, busying himself with something else. He really was the kindest man in the world! Sometimes Eleanor thought she would do anything for him.

It is nothing to what I would like to give you, he thought. He would have given her everything he had. He wanted to give her a real Christmas present – a beautiful dress, a brooch – not a half-sovereign in her wage packet. But the time was not yet ripe for such gifts, though one day it would be.

'With that and what's in the jug,' Eleanor told her mother, 'we've got enough for the fares and a bit left over for presents. I'd rather not go empty-handed.'

She was lucky in other ways too. The customers turned up trumps and gave her more in tips than she have ever hoped for; and on Christmas Eve Mrs Kramer provided the greatest surprise of all by giving her a beautifully iced Christmas cake. Eleanor could hardly believe her eyes.

'It's wonderfully kind of you, Mrs Kramer,' she said. 'I hardly know what to say!'

'It's Christmas!' Mrs Kramer replied briefly.

The English could not understand what Christmas meant to the Germans. They were cold, they did not have the soul. She could not come to Christmas without this truce.

Christmas Eve was a bright, clear day. As they had expected. every seat in the small cafe was taken for the special dinner, goose and all the trimmings, which Mrs Kramer so skilfully cooked and Eleanor served. The trouble was, everyone seemed to take twice as long over eating it and Eleanor began to fear that she wouldn't finish her work in time to catch the train. The shop was busy too, never cooled from early morning until mid-afternoon, but fortunately (so she thought) by that time everything had been sold, every last mince pie and sausage roll from the famous pastry.

At three o'clock Mr Kramer said, 'You must finish now, Eleanor. I'm sure you have things of your own to see to before leaving. I wish you and all your family a very happy Christmas.'

'You too,' Eleanor said. 'And thank you for letting me go.'

'Not at all,' he replied. 'You have already done a good day's work.'

It was true. She had been in the bakehouse not long after five o'clock, had skipped breakfast and taken her dinner on the hop.

'Then I'll just say goodbye to Mrs Kramer,' she said. She popped her head around the kitchen door.

'Mr Kramer has said I can leave. I wish you a merry Christmas, Mrs Kramer. Thank you for letting me go.'

She was off like a shot before Mrs Kramer could think of anything else to be done.

It was dark when they set off for the station, the sky high and starry.

'If we hurry,' Eleanor promised, 'we can go up to the front of the train and you'll see the engine; see where the man lights the fire and shovels the coal to make the train go.' To Becky and Selina there was no delight in the world to be compared to that of going on the train. Becky was entranced by the engine and was loth to be dragged away.

'If we don't get the perambulator into the guard's van, and find ourselves a compartment, the train will leave without us,' Eleanor threatened.

They found a 'Ladies only' compartment and settled in, Becky and Selina on either side of their grandmother, Eleanor sitting opposite to them with Jenny on her lap. 'There's no point in squabbling over the window seat,' she told the children. 'It'll be much too dark to see anything.'

The lights of Akersfield quickly gave way to the thick blackness of the countryside, a blackness only broken, every so often, by the shower of red sparks from the engine, which

129

Becky hailed with a squeal of delight.

'It's like the fireworks on Coronation Day!' she cried.

'Fireworks!' Selina echoed.

That had been a happy day, Eleanor thought. And a day not without surprises, especially Mr Kramer and his dancing. Who would have thought it? But she had discovered that, though sometimes he might seem staid, he was a man full of surprises. Such a nice man, and so kind. She was really fond of him.

In spite of their excitement, or perhaps because of the rhythm of the wheels on the track, Selina, Becky and Mrs Foster quickly fell asleep once they had left Akersfield behind. Mrs Foster snored a little, in a quiet manner, but it didn't matter, there was no-one else in the compartment. Jenny was awake, gazing up at her mother from wide, blue eyes. It was so seldom, Eleanor thought, she had time to hold Jenny like this. She contemplated her family and thought how much she loved them. They were the world to her. In her present mood she felt kindly even towards Clara, and vowed that she would do everything in her power to make the short holiday go smoothly.

Thinking of other things, she failed to notice the stations through which they passed, and was taken by surprise when the train pulled into Silton. Hurriedly, she wakened the others and ushered them out of the train, then saw to getting the carriage from the guard's van.

'We'll squeeze Selina and Jenny into the carriage, and I'll push,' she said to her mother. 'You can take Becky's hand.'

They had known there would be no-one to meet them at the station. Albert and Clara would still be all hands aloft in the shop. But it didn't matter. The night was fine and Eleanor and her mother knew every inch of the way. 'Off we go, then!' she said as they started the climb up to Felldale.

They were warmly welcomed. The cousins greeted each other with enthusiasm. It seemed impossible that they could ever quarrel about anything, but Eleanor knew better. She could only hope for the best. Albert came in for a few seconds from the shop, kissed his mother and smiled happily at everyone else. Even Clara seemed pleased to see them.

'Kettle's on,' she said. 'I'll have a cup of tea ready in no time. But perhaps you'd like a glass of ginger wine, Ma, to warm you up? After all, it *is* Christmas!'

'That would be very welcome,' Mrs Foster said. 'And a cup of tea to follow.'

She glanced appreciatively around the room, noting the familiar plush tablecloth, the horsehair sofa with the antimacassar she herself had crocheted. And now the room was enhanced with paper chains everywhere and a sprig of red-berried holly tucked into the top of each picture frame. She liked plenty of pictures, especially those which told a story. They helped to furnish a room.

The evening passed quickly, there was so much to do. First off there was a lavish supper spread, which Eleanor ate with gusto. She was famished. Then the children had to be put to bed, though with a visit from Father Christmas in mind they were less reluctant than usual.

'But mind you, straight to sleep when you do get to bed,' Clara warned them. 'Father Christmas does not stop at beds where the child isn't fast asleep. And it's no use pretending, neither!'

When the children had settled down, the shop was finally closed, and the last carol singer had departed, the four adults sat around the fire, exchanging news.

'I must say, you seem to be doing middling well in Akersfield,' Albert said. 'And your Mr Kramer sounds a nice chap!'

'He is,' Eleanor agreed. 'He's a real gentleman.' She had not told them about the robbery, she didn't want to think about it. Nor had she mentioned the half-sovereign, though the spending of that would show up in their presents the next day.

'So what's the news in Felldale?' Mrs Foster asked.

Clara laughed.

'You know Felldale, Ma! Nothing ever happens in Felldale!'

Later, in bed, Mrs Foster thought to herself that almost everything which had happened to her had happened in Felldale. Births, marriages, deaths, friendships – happiness and sorrow. Was it all nothing? She lay there, savouring the deep quietness of the countryside after the noise of Akersfield. No trams, no late traffic; no singing drunks going up the street under her window. Not that the men in Felldale didn't take a drop, but somehow they seemed quieter about it. Or maybe it was that she knew them, so their occasional noise didn't matter. She turned over on to her side. The last sound she heard before she fell asleep was a fox barking, but that was all right. That was a proper sound to hear at night.

Eleanor lay awake. Alone now, she could let the thought which had been in her mind all day – to tell the truth, in her mind ever since they had received Albert's invitation – come to the surface. She would see Dick Fletcher tomorrow. He would be in church, and so would she. She knew it was no good, nothing could come of it. But miracles *did* happen. Christmas was a time for miracles.

CHAPTER EIGHT

No-one knew when the snow started to fall. Even if it had not been soundless, unaccompanied by the least breath of wind, everyone in the house was deeply asleep.

'But it must have been early on,' Clara said. 'There's a good three inches, and it's lying. Well, thank goodness it's stopped now! The best place for snow is on Christmas cards! Nasty wet stuff!'

Eleanor disagreed, though silently, since she was determined to keep the peace. On rising – it had been only just daylight – she had looked out of the window from the room she was sharing with her mother at the back of the house, down the steep hill and west across the wide valley towards the distant hills which separated Yorkshire from Lancashire. Except for the line of the canal, and beyond that a few bare trees where the river ran, everything was a startling dazzling, untrodden white. She had caught her breath, felt the tears in her eyes at the beauty of it.

Becky, Selina and Flo had been awake since before daylight. She had heard their excited cries as, in the dark, they had felt the contents of their Christmas stockings, and their squeals of pleasure as Clara went into them with a candle and everything was revealed. Jenny, sharing her mother and grandmother's room, slept on, unaware of the excitements of Christmas.

It was what she would like to do, Eleanor thought. She was bone tired after yesterday's early start and busy day.

'Have another half-hour,' Mrs Foster suggested. 'You've earned a bit of a lie-in.' She herself was already wide awake and getting out of bed. She seemed to need less and

133

less sleep.

When her mother had gone downstairs Eleanor lay between waking and sleeping, waiting for the daylight to come, thinking about what the day might bring. In less than three hours now she would see Dick, perhaps speak with him. But even a few minutes – and she knew it was all she could expect, all she was entitled to – would sustain her for who knew how long to come? She got out of bed quickly, ashamed of the direction in which her thoughts were taking her.

'The vicar called yesterday,' Clara said later. 'He said he'd be glad if you'd take your usual place in the choir this morning.' She turned to her mother-in-law. 'You'd sit with the children, wouldn't you?' She had no time to go to church, what with the Christmas dinner and everything, but it would be good to have them out of the house for an hour.

'Wouldn't you like me to stay and give you a hand?' Mrs Foster made the offer but she knew what the answer would be.

'I'll manage,' Clara said.

And complain afterwards, Mrs Foster thought. It was difficult to please her daughter-in-law.

Eleanor made no such offer. She was set on her course. When she couldn't entirely put Him out of her mind, she hoped that God would forgive her for her ulterior motive in going to church. But since she was not really and truly sorry that was probably too much to hope for.

Processing down the aisle, part of the choir which the vicar had augmented as much as he possibly could for the occasion and which was now giving a full-throated rendering of 'Christians Awake', Eleanor saw Dick, Jane by his side, in the third pew. Only the back of his head, bent over his hymn book, was visible to her. His hair was longer than she remembered it, curling into the nape of his neck where it met his jacket collar. She longed to touch it, and was aghast at the temerity of her thoughts at such a time. It was not until she was in the choir stall, that she noticed Jane, to whom she had not given a thought. But when she did notice her, the sight caused Eleanor to falter in her singing,

134

and then to stop, the breath seeming to leave her body. Jane was clearly, boldly, and by the look on her face, blissfully pregnant. Very pregnant.

Much later, Eleanor asked herself why the fact should have so surprised her, shocked her. Nothing could be more natural than that a young married woman should be pregnant. But in the first moment that Eleanor saw Jane standing there, her cloak failing to meet over the ripeness of her figure, her neatly-gloved hands holding the hymn book resting where the baby would be, she felt that she had been dealt a sharp blow between the eyes.

She realised then that in her mind she had never allowed the possibility of Dick making love to another woman, not even to his own wife. It had never been a conscious thought – it was absurd, and she was not so stupid – but clearly it had been there. She felt, irrationally, betrayed, sick at heart – and when Dick's eyes met hers in a long, steady look she told herself that she saw shame and betrayal in them. What, she wondered, did he read in hers? She hoped that she had not shown her true feelings and vowed that from now on she never would. She looked purposefully away from him and began to sing again.

By the time the service was over and everyone was meeting in the porch she had herself in hand. She had joined up with her mother when Dick and Jane came to greet them, Jane clinging to her husband's arm.

'A merry Christmas!' Jane said. 'I didn't know you were in Felldale.'

A merry Christmas to both of you,' Eleanor replied. 'You're both looking very well.'

Only Dick heard the over-brightness of Eleanor's voice and noticed the unusual pallor of her face.

'Oh we *are*!' Jane agreed. And I expect you've noticed marriage suits us, doesn't it, my dear?' She looked up adoringly at Dick. 'And Dick takes such care of me, because of the baby. I expect you've noticed about the baby?'

'Yes indeed! Congratulations,' Eleanor said brightly. 'When is it to be?'

'Early March.'

Mrs Foster was shocked at the openness of Jane Fletcher's conversation. Everyone knew women had babies, but it wasn't something to talk about in mixed company. Nor was it seemly to be seen in public when she was six months gone and showing so much. But Mrs Fletcher was a mite over-pleased with herself, as if no-one else had ever been in such a condition before.

'Let's hope pride doesn't go before a fall,' Mrs Foster said as they walked home through the snow.

Against Clara's wishes Albert had made both Jimmy and Flo sledges for Christmas and all the children could think about was trying them out. All through the delicious dinner which Clara had prepared they nagged and nattered. And it did seem as though the snow was providential.

'Carr Side is the best place,' Jimmy said. 'I can go on my own, but I'm not taking a bunch of girls!'

'I'll go!' Eleanor offered. 'Wrap up well and we'll set off the minute you've finished eating. It'll get dark early this afternoon.'

She would be glad to get out of the house, to let the winter air cool her thoughts as well as her body.

Carr Side was a long sloping field on the edge of the village. It was common ground. In the spring and summer one could pick flowers there; in the winter, slide or sledge.

'I used to sledge here when I was a little girl,' she told the children. They looked at her in disbelief. 'Come on then,' she said. 'Let's sort you out. You'll have to take turns.'

In the Fletchers' cottage Jane dried and put away the last of the dinner pots.

'You didn't eat much,' she said to Dick. 'Didn't you enjoy your Christmas dinner?'

'Of course I did. It was grand. For some reason or other I just wasn't hungry.' He knew the reason, but it would remain buried deep inside him. The sight of Eleanor,

136

watching her in church, seeing her eyes meet his and then turn away; standing with her in the porch, she more beautiful than ever, and finding nothing to say to her – it had all been unbearable. And now he couldn't get her out of his mind, though he must, for Jane deserved better of him than this.

Jane crossed to where he stood in front of the fire, twined her arms around his neck, pressed her swollen body against his.

'You mustn't let worry about me put you off your food. I'm going to be all right.'

'Of course you are! And I'm not worrying.'

But a great deal of the time he was, and so was she. They didn't share their anxieties about the coming baby, but sometimes in the middle of the night he was aware, by the stiffness of her body beside him, that she was wide awake, and he could guess at her thoughts. In the daytime she was different; cheerful, confident. Only once had she confessed to him that she was afraid of childbirth.

'But I'm not now,' she said. 'Not with your baby. You'll have strength for both of us.'

She was a good wife. He couldn't fault her. She wasn't to blame that the spark wasn't there, and hadn't been since Eleanor had returned to Felldale in the spring of 1901. He had been wrong to marry Jane, but at all costs *she* must not suffer for it.

'I think I'll go out for a walk,' he said. 'Sharpen my appetite for the teatime spread!'

'But it's cold!' Jane objected. 'And snow on the ground. Do you want me to go with you, dearest?'

'Better not. It's slippery underfoot. You should stay indoors and keep warm. I shan't be long.'

He supposed it was the sound of children's voices which drew him towards Carr Side. Though Eleanor was in his mind he had not expected to find her there. When he saw her standing alone at the top of the hill, and she turned and recognized him, shock ran through both of them. And yet to both of them the meeting seemed inevitable. He walked

137

towards her and they stood looking at each other, not speaking. He wanted to take her hands in his, and knew he must not; and as if she read his thoughts she tucked both her hands out of sight, inside the muff which hung around her neck.

In the end, the silence which seemed to go on and on was broken by Eleanor.

'The children have found friends,' she said. 'So there's enough room on the sledges for everyone. Jimmy has Selina with him. He's very good with her.'

It was not what she wanted to say. The words sounded banal. But even if she could find the words she wanted, how could she say them to Dick?'

'So how are you? How is life in Akersfield?' He asked.

'It's all right. I . . . we . . . thought you might have looked in the café.'

'It was better not,' Dick said abruptly. It was the nearest either of them came to an admission. If more was to be said, it was prevented by the arrival of the children.

'How is your business?' Eleanor asked politely.

'Doing well. But I'm ready to expand. I don't want to stay in Felldale forever.'

'*You* leave Felldale? But you've been here all your life!' She couldn't bear that he would be in some other place where she wouldn't know him, couldn't picture him.

'You did so. You sent to Akersfield.'

She felt that he was accusing her, that if she had not followed Ben, everything would have been all right. Well, perhaps it would, perhaps not. It was all too late now.

'What does Jane think?' She forced herself to include Jane.

'At the moment she doesn't think beyond the baby,' Dick replied.

'Is she . . . are you both . . . looking forward to the baby?' She didn't know why she had this need to torture herself.

'Yes.'

'Then I hope all goes well. And now I really must collect the children and leave. It's getting dark.'

138

'And you are shivering,' Dick said.

So she was, but it was not with the cold. She gathered the children together, and left Dick standing there. He stood for a long time, until it was quite dark and freezing cold, before turning to go home to Jane.

Sitting in the train, speeding back to Akersfield on Boxing Day afternoon, Eleanor wondered if she had done the right thing in going to Felldale for Christmas. On the face of it everything had gone exceptionally well. Clara had been agreeable, all the children had behaved perfectly, and not a cross word between them. Jenny had hardly cried at all. Her mother had taken pleasure in seeing a few old friends and neighbours, as well as her son and his family. So for all those good reasons, yes, she had been right to go. But what about me, she thought? In the weeks beforehand she had lived on the thought of seeing Dick Fletcher again. Now she had seen him, and it was no good. Whatever she felt, whatever he felt and whatever lay unspoken between them, it was no good. She had to put him out of her mind. He belonged clearly and firmly to Jane.

With an effort of will she turned her thoughts elsewhere, looked out of the window at the passing scene. They were close to Akersfield now and the snow which had been pristine white and beautiful in the country had already turned grey and sludgy here. The mills were at work again and the sky, which in Felldale had been clear and blue, was crisscrossed with clouds of black smoke from the tall chimneys.

The train drew into the station and they gathered their belongings together and alighted. When Eleanor came back from the guard's van with the baby carriage Mrs Foster said, 'Surely that's Mr Kramer waiting at the barrier? I wonder who he's meeting?'

'I can't imagine,' Eleanor said. She had told him, in conversation, which train they would catch back, but he would certainly not be meeting *them*. He must be expecting a visitor, though he had never hinted at such a possibility.

But as Eleanor went through the barrier, pushing the baby

139

carriage, it was to her he quickly moved. Face to face with him she realized at once that he was deeply troubled. She saw the anguish in his eyes, and was immediately and terribly afraid. Something had happened to the cafe! A gas had been left on and the whole place had been blown up! Or burnt to the ground! Her home and her livelihood gone in one terrible disaster! When she remembered the moment afterwards she was ashamed that she had thought only of her own loss, not of his.

'I must speak with you on your own,' Mr Kramer began.

Eleanor put her mother in charge of the perambulator. 'Wait just here,' she said. What would this do to her mother?

'I did not wish the children to hear,' Mr Kramer explained when they had moved aside.

'What is it? Please tell me quickly!' Eleanor implored him. 'I know something terrible has happened!'

'You are right,' he said. 'I have to tell you that my mother has died!'

For one, awful, shaming moment Eleanor felt a relief which was almost joy, that what she had feared had not happened. But the moment was soon over, and she was truly shocked by the news.

'But how . . . when . . .?'

'She died early on Christmas Day, in her sleep. I found her so when I went to take her a cup of tea. It was her heart, the doctor said. It had been weakened by the chest infection, which was clearly more serious than we had ever thought.'

'Poor Mrs Kramer!' Eleanor cried. 'Poor lady! I can hardly believe it. And I can't tell you how sorry I am, Mr Kramer! Is there anything at all I can do?'

'For today, no,' he said. 'In the next few days I dare say a great deal. But we will go into that later. The funeral is the day after tomorrow, and I shall close the shop and the cafe until after then. Perhaps you would put a suitable notice in the window?'

'Of course I will,' Eleanor promised. 'I'll do anything I can. I wonder . . .?'

'Yes?'

140

'Would it be all right if I came to the funeral? Mrs Kramer was often kind to me. She gave me such a lovely cake on Christmas Eve.'

'I would be pleased if you would,' Mr Kramer said. 'Will you come to Ashfield Road at one-thirty?'

The day of the funeral was bleak. A thin, sleety drizzle had been falling all morning and showed no signs of letting up. The funeral itself was even bleaker, attended by Frank Kramer, Eleanor, a few dutiful neighbours, the doctor, and one or two men mustered by the undertaker. Mrs Kramer had not gone through life making friends and there were few to mourn her. It being the depths of winter, the wreaths were of dark evergreens, brightened only, here and there, by the red berries of the holly.

'If my mother had had her choice,' Frank Kramer said after the funeral, 'I think she would have wanted to be buried in Germany. Perhaps I should have thought of that sooner.'

But he had not expected her to die like this. She had seemed to him to be indestructible, to be someone who would live forever. Now he felt guilty for the times when this belief had seemed a burden to him.

He had asked everyone back to the house for a glass of sherry, which was accompanied by the delicious biscuits and mince pies which Mrs Kramer had baked herself, only a few days earlier. Eleanor, though she was cold and hungry, choked on the delicate pastry and discarded it on an inconspicuous side table.

'My wife and I hope you won't think of leaving here,' a neighbour told Frank. 'Now that you're on your own, I mean. Though of course it's a fair-sized house for one person.'

'You'll need a housekeeper,' said the neighbour's wife. 'Let me know if I can help you to choose one.'

Frank Kramer shook his head. 'I have no plans at all. There has been no time.'

'That's right,' the doctor intervened. 'My advice is not

to do anything in a hurry. Take time to make up your mind. And now I really must be on my way. Patients to visit!'

I don't need your advice, Frank thought, seeing him out. I don't need time to make up my mind. All that he wanted to do was already in his mind. It was a question of waiting for the right moment. He moved back to where Eleanor stood on her own.

'Could you possibly stay for a few moments after the others have gone?' he asked. 'There is the question of what happens in the shop and cafe tomorrow, not to mention in the future.'

'Certainly,' Eleanor agreed. Ever since the fact of Mrs Kramer's death had sunk in she had not ceased to worry about the future. How could Mr Kramer keep the business going without his mother there – and if he didn't, couldn't, then what would become of herself, the children, her mother? The fears which swept over her when she had first seen Mr Kramer waiting in the station were now with her all the time. She wanted nothing more than to hear what he had to say, whether it was for good or ill.

In the end the mourners departed, though on the part of the neighbour's wife not without some reluctance. She had seldom entered the house in Mrs Kramer's lifetime and she would have liked to have taken a closer look. It seemed very well appointed.

'Please sit down, Eleanor,' Frank Kramer said. 'Let me give you another glass of sherry. Or perhaps you would prefer a cup of tea? I could make one quite easily.'

'Nothing, thank you,' Eleanor replied. All she wanted was to hear what he had to say. She sat on the very edge of an upright chair, her hands clasped tightly together.

'Then please sit somewhere more comfortable,' Mr Kramer suggested. He indicated a deep, well-upholstered armchair.

'No thank you,' Eleanor said. Oh, why didn't he get on with it?'

'Well then, decisions have to be made and I will tell you

142

what I have in mind. Then you can give me your thoughts on the matter.' He couldn't, of course, tell her all that he had in mind, though he longed to do so. But it was too soon. It would be improper. He knew, too, that she wouldn't be ready for it. He didn't want to frighten her off. He would therefore, confine himself strictly to business.

Hope sprang in Eleanor. If she was to be allowed to express an opinion, then he couldn't have decided to close down, to dismiss her.

'So you're keeping on?' she said quickly. 'The business, I mean?'

He looked at her in surprise.

'But of course! It's my living. And a very good living.'

'I just thought . . . without Mrs Kramer . . .'

'My mother contributed a great deal. Together with my father she built up the business, and she never ceased to work hard in it. Perhaps if she had taken more care of herself and less of the business she would be alive today. No, I am not thinking that my mother can easily be replaced, or that she will not be missed – but life must go on.'

'But who will do all that she did?' Eleanor asked. 'The baking for the shop; the dinners?'

'Probably no-one,' he admitted. 'But this is what I propose. I thought that I would engage a good plain cook who would take care of the dinners, and the few teas we do. Also, a young girl who would assist with waiting at the tables . . .'

'But I don't need assistance there!' Eleanor interrupted. 'I can manage that, *and* serving in the shop quite easily!'

'I know you can. But I thought you might like to help in a different way – though you must tell me at once if my idea doesn't appeal to you. I thought that perhaps you might like to take over the shop baking, though there would be no need for you to carry on exactly as my mother did, you could do things your own way. This would leave you free to help in the cafe at dinnertime, which I know you enjoy and which you are so good at. In addition, I would like you to have oversight of the female staff. So what do you say, Eleanor?'

He gave her no time to reply before he spoke again.

143

'Naturally, as this would be more responsibility for you, you would be paid more. I would not be ungenerous. And I do realize that it would mean an earlier start, but I daresay we could make some arrangement so that you could finish earlier, have some time with the children when Becky came home from school.'

'So what do you say?' he repeated. This time he paused, waiting for her reply. Eleanor wondered why he should look so anxious.

'Of course I'll do it!' she said. Did he have any idea what the extra money would mean to her? New clothes for the children, better food for all of them, and in time perhaps she would be able to furnish their living quarters a little more comfortably. An upholstered armchair for her mother! Why would she ever refuse such an offer?

'You are sure?' Mr Kramer asked. 'You won't mind the early start?'

'As long as I live I won't *enjoy* getting up early,' Eleanor admitted. 'But I'm already accustomed to it. Don't forget that I used to come down to light the oven before Mrs Kramer arrived.'

'I didn't know that,' he said.

'The only thing is . . .' Eleanor hesitated.

'What is it? You have only to say.'

'Mrs Kramer was such a good pastrycook. How shall I ever reach her standard? And what will it do to your shop trade if I don't?'

'I don't have any fears about that,' Frank assured her. 'You will have all her recipes . . .' he smiled. 'Yes, even the one for the famous puff pastry, the one which she had from a Swiss chef! I've heard my mother say that anyone who could read well enough to follow a recipe, could cook.'

'Well, I think there's a bit more to it than that!' Eleanor said. 'But I promise I'll do my level best. Perhaps I could introduce a few new lines where I can't come up to Mrs Kramer's standardds?' Her mother, though she could not write, had a head full of recipes, Yorkshire fare which might go well. She'd enjoy passing them on.

'That would be a splendid idea,' Mr Kramer agreed. 'And now we must talk about money.'

She was amazed at the generous wage he proposed, and deeply grateful. 'Why, that's almost as much as a man would be paid!' she exclaimed.

'And why not?' he asked. 'You will be doing as much work, and every bit as skilled.'

He was such a good, kind man. So thoughtful, so generous. Though she knew she could never have what she wanted from life − it was out of her reach − at least in this area she was lucky.

'Excuse me asking,' she said. 'I daresay I shouldn't . . .'

'Ask anything you wish!'

'Can you afford to pay me this? What with new staff and everything? I would be prepared to take a little less to start with.'

He smiled. He was feeling happier than at any time since his mother's death, also guilty at the lightness of his heart.

'That's most considerate of you, Eleanor, but not neces-sary. I can afford it. And let me tell you something else. I shall not always be the owner of one small cake shop and cafe in Akersfield. I have ambition. One day I shall own perhaps a chain of such shops, or a beautiful large restaurant or hotel where well-to-do people will come!'

Eleanor raised her eyebrows. What a flight of fancy, to be sure! Yet she already knew he was a man of surprises. It might just turn out as he said − and she liked a man with ambition.

'In the meantime,' she reminded him, 'we have to sort out how we'll get through the next few days, until you find a cook. I'll do as much as I possibly can, and I'm sure my mother will give a hand.'

'Then between us,' Frank Kramer said, 'we shall manage.'

After the first few hectic days, and apart from a few mishaps, the new arrangements went smoothly enough. Mr Kramer found a cook in a Mrs Eliot, a widow who, in spite of an occasional show of fiery temper, was both capable and willing. Maisie, the new part-time waitress, was less efficient. She regularly mixed up the orders. But since she was both pretty and pleasant, customers uncomplainingly accepted Irish stew when they had asked for cottage pie, and sometimes, if she smiled sweetly, tipped her into the bargain. Eleanor was always in the cafe at lunchtime to see that nothing went badly wrong, and to smooth over any rough patches. She really enjoyed being with the customers. It was far and away the best part of her job.

When, one day, she remarked upon this to Frank Kramer, he said, 'Yes, you have a talent for it. But it is not your only talent, Eleanor!'

'Oh!' she said. 'So what other talent have I, then?'

You have a talent to charm, to look beautiful even in your bakehouse overall and your lovely hair hidden under a cap; you have a talent to enchant a man – this man – every minute of the day. That was what he wanted to say to her. Instead he said, 'Think of the talent you have shown as a pastrycook. You are every bit as good as my mother was. And the new lines you have introduced – and the new routines in the kitchen. In only two months you have made so many changes, and all for the better.'

'Because you've been good enough to let me,' Eleanor pointed out.

She supposed what he said was true. She had surprised herself with some of the things she had found she could do. Why, there were now lines in the shop, like the new fruit malt loaf and the Yorkshire parkin, for which customers went out of their way to visit Kramer's. And she had made the place look better, too. She had persuaded Mr Kramer to have the walls painted a sunny yellow, and to buy new tablecloths for the cafe. Taken separately, they were small things, but added together they had made the last two months interesting and satisfying, in spite of all the hard work. And hard work it was, no doubt about that.

Only when she was working could she drive forbidden thoughts from her mind; thoughts which intruded and persisted at other times, no matter how much she tried to

146

banish them. When Mrs Foster came back from the market one Friday afternoon and said that she had seen Dick Fletcher, Eleanor found herself so filled with longing that she could hardly keep her feelings under control, hardly resist blurting out to her mother.

'I'd say Dick Fletcher's a worried man,' Mrs Foster declared. 'It seems things aren't going too well with Jane now that her time's near. Let's hope nothing goes amiss.'

'Yes indeed. Excuse me, Ma, there's something I have to see to!'

Mrs Foster's face was puzzled as she watched her daughter dash out of the room. She had been in two minds whether or not to tell Eleanor that she had seen Dick. There was something there she wasn't sure about.

Eleanor flew downstairs to the bakehouse. Though it was evening and there was no need for it, she started a furious batch of intricate baking, trying to calm the turmoil in her head.

Frank Kramer had no idea of his beloved Eleanor's innermost feelings. He would have said, had he been asked, that she was an open book to him, a book whose every fresh page was a new delight, one he could hardly wait to read. On a day early in March he realised that he could be patient no longer. He must ask her the question.

But how – and in what circumstances? They were scarcely ever alone together. There was no intimacy between them, though he liked to think they were friends. She remained on formal terms with him. Though he always called her 'Eleanor', to her he was 'Mr Kramer', her employer, to whom she deferred. He knew that in asking her so soon to marry him, he was running the risk of refusal – but he could not wait.

His mind made up, he delayed only until that evening. The last customer had gone, followed, the moment she had washed the floors, by Maisie. It was no longer Eleanor's task to do this but she always came downstairs before Mr Kramer left in the evening, to see that everything was shipshape. When she entered the shop through the staircase

147

door she seemed to him like a vision. Her golden hair was piled abundantly on top of her head, with a light fringe falling over her broad forehead. It was a style, even he knew, copied by thousands of women from the new queen, but not one of them could look more royal than Eleanor. She had no fine clothes – that was something he would give her – but freed from her daytime apron, her plain black dress was the perfect foil for her slender yet curvaceous figure. He stood immobile, watching her, worshipping.

'Are you ready for off, then, Mr Kramer?' she asked. 'Shall I lock the door behind you?'

'Yes. No. That is to say, not quite! If you can spare me a moment there is something I want to say . . . Shall we sit in the cafe?'

She thought nothing of his request. They often had little conversations at the end of the day, almost always about what might be done on the premises, what improvements made, what new ideas introduced. She enjoyed these times, partly because he was always so ready to listen as well as to talk. But he didn't usually look so serious about it, she thought as she took a seat opposite to him.

He came straight out with the question.

'Eleanor, will you marry me? Will you do me the honour of becoming my wife? I love you, Eleanor, and have since the first time I saw you!'

She couldn't believe what she was hearing. She opened her mouth to protest, but the words wouldn't come. It didn't matter, because he was still speaking.

'I have thought about everything – all your circumstances. I would take your children and love them as if they were my own. Your mother would be more than welcome to make her home with us. You have seen my house. It is big enough for all of us. As for you, my dear Eleanor, there would no longer be any need for you to slave in the business. As my wife you could live like a lady. I would work my fingers to the bone for you, Eleanor!'

He paused. In the silence between them she said the only thing she could think of.

148

'But I *like* working in the business! I wouldn't want to live like a lady, doing nothing all day.'

'Then you can stay in the business! Nothing would please me more than that we should be together all the time! Can you give me your answer. Eleanor? Can you say you will marry me and transform my life?'

She looked at him. She looked at him, but she did not see him. Instead of the pale face, the light brown hair, the steady, kind blue eyes of Frank Kramer, she saw dark, curling hair, eyes almost as dark set in a strong-featured, tanned face. She saw Dick Fletcher.

'I'm sorry, Mr Kramer. I can't. You see, I don't love you.' She spoke as gently as she knew how. She wished she *did* love this kind young man, whom she already liked so much.

'Then don't give me your final answer yet,' he said quickly. 'Think about it. Take all the time you need. I know you don't love me, Eleanor. How could I expect it? But I believe you do like me a little?'

'I like you better than almost anyone I know,' she replied truthfully.

'Well then! Many good marriages are founded on less. Love can grow from liking – and I have enough love for both of us.'

She shook her head and started to speak, but he silenced her.

'Don't decide now, Eleanor! Think about it. Discuss it with your mother, if you wish. She is a wise woman. And I will ask you again in a few weeks' time. For now, there is just one more thing, Eleanor.'

'Yes, Mr Kramer?'

'That is it. Could you bring yourself to call me Frank?'

'It doesn't seem respectful,' she demurred. 'But yes, if that is what you would like . . . Frank.'

She thought about the matter all night. It would be a better life for her children. It was something she could do for her mother, who had done so much for her. She even had it in her to be a good wife to Frank Kramer, she knew

149

that. But between the thoughts of Frank and herself, spinning around in her mind through the long night, came always the form, the features, the feel of Dick Fletcher.

Towards morning, when she could bear it no longer, she wakened her mother and told her of Frank Kramer's proposal, though she didn't mention the true reason which held her back.

'I don't love him, Ma. That's the long and short of it.'

'Are you sure?' Mrs Foster said. 'Though you've never told me – I think I can guess. I know what's in you. But it's no good, love. It never will be.'

'Then you think I ought to marry Frank Kramer?'

'I didn't say that. He's a good man, one of the best. And I saw long ago that he worships the ground you walk on. But there's only you can decide and you mustn't do it because you think it's better for me or the children. But kill the idea that you can ever have Dick Fletcher. You can't!'

But I can't kill the hope, Eleanor thought. I can't! I can't!

Next morning's post brought a rare letter from Clara which killed Eleanor's hope stone dead.

'Jane Fletcher has had her baby. A little girl. Weighed ten pounds. A difficult birth and the doctor says no more children. Both doing well though and Dick is the proudest man in Felldale. He walks ten feet tall. Hoping this finds you all in the pink as it leaves us at present.'

Eleanor's first impulse was to rush downstairs to Frank Kramer and tell him that she would marry him. She would marry him as soon as he liked, and the sooner the better.

'You mustn't do that,' her mother said sharply. 'He deserves better! You have to be sure you have something to give him, as well as taking.'

Her mother was right. He was too good to be taken advantage of. Eleanor vowed to herself that she would only consent to marry him if she was prepared to be a good wife. She couldn't love him, she thought she never could, not in the way he loved her. But if she was honest with him about that, and if he still wanted her, then perhaps something could come of it. She would say nothing until he asked her again, and she half hoped it would be a long time before he did so.

It was a month later that he proposed to her for the second time. When she voiced her doubts he swept them away with the strength of his own feelings.

'It will work! I know it will! We shall have the happiest marriage in England. It will be the beginning of a new life for both of us!'

'Then I will marry you, Frank,' she said. 'And I will do everything in the world to make you happy.'

He pulled her to her feet and took her in his arms. At first his kiss was gentle, and then it grew stronger, firmer as he felt the softness of her mouth under his and held her closer. With Frank's kiss on her lips, Eleanor said goodbye to Dick Fletcher.

On a Friday afternoon, the day after Eleanor and Frank had become engaged, Dick Fletcher packed up his stall in Akersfield market and prepared to go back to Felldale.

He would not do the markets much longer; a year or two at the most. He was determined to get into the seed business. But for that he had to find more land, and more fertile land, which would not be in Felldale. Logically, he should give up Akersfield soon. It was the least profitable of his markets and the furthest away from Felldale. But he knew well enough what held him to Akersfield. It was the thought of Eleanor, though he never saw her there, had never called on her since she'd come back to Akersfield. It was the knowledge that she was in the town, that he could find her if he wished to, which drew him back.

The pull was stronger than ever today. He felt that just to set eyes on her would be a balm to his spirit, a spirit which was unhappy, troubled. He had known at the time that he should have broken his promise to Jane, should not have married her once he had seen Eleanor again. The keeping of his word had been a stupid gesture. The only good to come out of it was that it had made Jane happy.

151

Had made her happy, for since the baby's birth she seemed to be so no longer. He had set all his hopes on the thought that with the birth of the child he and Jane would be drawn closer together. He had done his best to make it so. But since the baby was born Jane herself had changed. She was withdrawn, depressed. She didn't want him near her and more often than not, was not even interested in the baby. He himself loved the little girl, knew that in her, in watching her change and grow, was going to be his salvation; but he did not understand Jane now. Nor did the doctor; nor the neighbours nor anyone else, it seemed.

It was in this mood that, packing the boxes with what was left of the produce, he knew he had to see Eleanor. Just this once, and once only. Just to look at her, speak to her. He would call in at Kramer's on the pretext of wanting a cup of tea.

Eleanor was standing beside Frank when Dick came into the cafe. She felt the blood drain from her face and her head begin to spin as she set eyes on him. She thought for a moment that she might faint, and she stretched out a hand to feel the support of the counter. She was glad that Frank, shoulder to shoulder with her, could not see her face. Then she steadied herself and answered Dick's greeting.

'Good afternoon, Dick. Frank, this is an old friend of mine from Felldale – Dick Fletcher.'

Frank held out his hand. 'I'm pleased to make your acquaintance. You have come at a good time.' He turned to Eleanor. 'Tell your friend our news, then he can take it back to your family!'

'News?' Dick queried.

'We are to be married!' Frank announced. 'Eleanor and I are to be married!' He put an arm around her shoulders. 'She has made me the happiest man in the world!'

Dick looked at Eleanor and she at him. It was if Frank Kramer did not exist.

'Is this true?'

She was stabbed by the steel in his voice. No, she wanted to cry. No, you are the only one! But she hadn't

152

hadn't been the only one for him. He'd chosen otherwise.

She sought Frank's hand and held it in hers.

'Quite true! We are to be married next week!'

They were married in Akersfield Registry Office on the following Saturday, closing the shop and cafe for the day. On the previous day Eleanor had helped her mother to move, with the children, to Ashfield Road. Mrs Foster had insisted on taking her bed.

'I've had it since I was married,' she said. 'It's an old friend!'

After the ceremony Frank and Eleanor went to Scarborough for the briefest of honeymoons, from which they would return on Sunday night. She had wondered what it would be like with Frank. Would he be as shy as she, standing there in the hotel bedroom, suddenly found herself to be?

'But you must not be shy with me,' Frank said. 'I am your husband now, and you my beloved wife. Everything is open between us.'

He drew her towards him and began to undress her, slowly and gently until she was naked. Then he took the pins from her hair one by one until at last it fell around her shoulders and breasts like a golden silk curtain. When he had looked at her lovingly, he lifted her on to the bed and came and lay beside her.

She was astonished by the ardent nature of his lovemaking, the strength of his passion. He came to the act of marriage as if all his life had been leading up to it. Her passion rose to meet his; and again, and again. Perhaps, she thought afterwards as they lay quietly side by side, perhaps there is more hope for this marriage than I'd ever dreamt possible.

'We are going to be very happy together, you and I,' Frank said.

CHAPTER NINE

Mrs Foster dusted the last of the ornaments, a china shepherdess, and put it back in its place on the mantelpiece, exactly three inches to the left of the marble clock, to balance the china shepherd on the right. They were pretty little statuettes, though nothing like the real shepherds she had known all her life. These were fancifully dressed in blues and mauves, with touches of gold, had tidy hair and exquisite complexions, and wouldn't have lasted ten minutes on the tops of the fells on a rough day. But then they were foreign, brought by Mrs Kramer from Germany. (She still couldn't think of Eleanor as Mrs Kramer.) Perhaps that was how shepherds and shepherdesses went about in foreign countries.

The drawing-room was full of ornaments, mostly in pairs. For that matter, so was the rest of the house. She rather liked that. Also it gave her something to do, dusting them, and every so often taking them down and washing them carefully in warm soapy water. In spite of the size of the house, she didn't have enough to do, because at Eleanor's insistence a woman came in three days a week to clean.

'If I choose to work in the cafe,' her daughter said whenever she objected, 'then I'm not going to have you slaving away at home every day. There's no need for it. It's enough that you look after the children when they come home from school.'

But in between seeing the children off in the morning and welcoming them back in the afternoon – they stayed at school for dinner – there were too many hours to fill. She had never been much good at sewing or knitting. Her talents lay in housework, in cooking and baking, in growing vegetables and flowers. There was no baking to be done, everything was brought home from the cafe. And there was no garden, unless you could count the few square feet at the front, where Akersfield's smoke mottled every leaf and flower with black. All she could do in that line was look after the indoor plants, and that she did with a vengeance. She nurtured the ferns, polished the leaves of the aspidistras with milk, took endless cuttings of the geraniums and fed everything with cold tea.

'You have green fingers, Ma!' Eleanor told her. 'If you stuck a pencil in a pot of soil I daresay it would take root!'

Mrs Foster moved the shepherdess a quarter of an inch to the left, then stood in the middle of the drawing-room and surveyed her surroundings with some pleasure. Thick blue carpet, heavy blue curtains, braided and fringed, at the window; sofa and armchairs upholstered in blue plush. Plenty of nice crocheted mats, and antimacassars on every chair. And all was as neat and clean and shining as a new pin. She took an especial pride in this room. It was the only one which was in her sole care, because everything in it was precious and Mrs Carter, though a good worker, was clumsy. The trouble was, Mrs Foster thought, that since they so seldom used the drawing-room it took very little keeping up. But now she wanted it at its very best because on Sunday Albert and Clara *and* Madge and John, not to mention all four of their children, were coming for the day. Now that Eleanor was comfortably settled and couldn't possibly be a drain on them, all breaches had been well and truly healed.

It was ten past four by the marble clock. Any minute now Selina and Jenny would appear at the bottom of Ashfield Road on their way home from school. She went and stood by the window, peering through the lace curtains for a sight of them. No-one knew that she kept this eager lookout every day and she would never let on. Sometimes she was so impatient for their presence that she went to meet them, though pretending that it was quite accidental, that she had

155

been out for a walk, or to shop. Now as she stood there she saw them at the bottom of the road.

Selina walked decorously, her hat at the correct angle, her satchel hanging straight from her shoulder. She kept to the inside of the pavement because today was Wednesday. On Thursdays she had to touch, as inconspicuously as possible, every tenth railing, for luck. On other days she had to be careful about treading in the nicks between the flagstones, or had to walk a certain number of steps backwards. Every journey had its hazards. For Jenny, at eight and a half, life was not the least bit hazardous. She went happily to school every morning, did all that was required of her in the school day, and returned home just as happily every afternoon. Now she skipped her way up Ashfield Road, swinging her satchel shoulder high. The two sisters didn't speak to each other. They had no need. Though different from each other in character, they had a communion which didn't require words.

Mrs Foster stood in the open doorway to greet them. They never asked how their grandmother happened always to be on that spot at that time. She just was.

'Hello, loves! Did you have a nice day at school then?'

Selina nodded. She had to finish counting to one hundred before she was able to speak.

'I came top in spelling,' Jenny said. 'And I got a star for reading.'

'Well done!' Mrs Foster said. 'You take after your mother. She was always good at reading.'

'Who do I take after?' Selina asked, freed from her spell.

'I'm not sure,' Mrs Foster admitted. 'No-one in our family, that I can remember, has been as good at drawing and painting as you. But you're like your mother to look at. All three of you are. Your dad used to call you his golden girls, and he would have Jenny if he'd known her.'

'I've got a dad,' Jenny said. 'We all have.'

'He's our stepfather, silly,' Selina corrected her.

But as good as any real father could ever be, Mrs Foster thought, and perhaps a sight better than Ben Heaton might have been, God rest his soul!

'You're very lucky little girls,' she said.

'Can we have our tea?' Jenny asked. 'Or do we have to wait until Becky comes home?'

Selina and Jenny went to a small private school in the next road but Becky, at nearly thirteen, attended Akersfield Grammar School, which was in the town. Frank Kramer ungrudgingly paid fees for the education of all three of his stepdaughters.

'Not on a Wednesday,' Selina said. 'You know she has a music lesson.' She turned to her grandmother. 'We had macaroni cheese for dinner. I hate macaroni cheese!'

'Your tea will be ready in two shakes of a lamb's tail,' Mrs Foster promised.

They followed her downstairs. Tea, like most of the family's meals, was nearly always taken in the big living kitchen, and this suited Mrs Foster. She never liked it quite as well when, at weekends, holiday times, or on the rare occasions when they had visitors, they used the proper dining-room with its large walnut table and matching chairs. As for Eleanor and Frank, once they got home together from the cafe they couldn't have cared less about food.

When she had mashed the tea she put more coal on the fire and soon had a good blaze. It was May, but none too warm for all that. She reckoned May could be a treacherous month for weather. But at least the evenings were light. They'd have a nice long day when they all came on Sunday, especially if they made an early start.

'Can I paint?' Selina asked when the tea things were cleared away.

'As if I could stop you!' Mrs Foster said dryly.

She watched Selina get out her box of colours, fill a jam jar with water and set to work. The child was a real artist. Imaginative, too. She painted pictures out of her head – stormy seas with sailing ships, landscapes with turreted castles, things she could never have seen.

Jenny was already playing with her dolls. She had a family of them which she constantly dressed and undressed. Mrs

157

Foster wondered if she wasn't getting a bit too old for dolls.

'You make us a nice tea and then you let us do what we want,' Jenny said suddenly. 'You're a very *nice* grandma!'

Mrs Foster felt warm with pleasure, but then, unaccountably, the feeling turned sour on her. That's what I am, she thought. A grandmother. Sometimes a mother, sometimes a mother-in-law. Never me, never myself. Never Susannah Foster. She was only ever addressed as 'Grandma', 'Ma', 'Mother'. There was no-one in the world who called her 'Susannah', and as far as she could see, there never would be. She had been a little bit down for a day or two, and now the thought came as a crushing blow.

She was jolted out of her thoughts by the banging of the front door. Becky always arrived or departed in a series of bangs. You could never miss her. Now she bounded down the stairs and into the kitchen.

'You haven't waited tea for me!' she exclaimed. 'And I'm starving!'

'So was everyone else,' her grandmother said. 'It'll only take a few minutes and I'll set it to one side of the table. How will that do, miss?'

Becky sighed. 'I can't think *why* we always have to eat in the kitchen! It's so *common*!'

'Common, is it?' Mrs Foster said mildly. Becky could be very provoking but she had learnt not to rise to it. 'Well, I know someone not a mile from here who's getting a bit above herself!'

'I shouldn't think *any* of the girls in my form have tea in the kitchen,' Becky persisted. 'If *I* had a dining-room I'd use it all the time.'

'I wouldn't,' Selina said. 'It's warmer in the kitchen.'

'I'd have a fire in the dining-room, silly!' Becky retorted. Sometimes her family were a great trial to her.

'Well, here's your tea,' Mrs Foster said. 'Let's hope eating it at the kitchen table won't take away your appetite!' She was safe on that one. Becky, growing rapidly – she was going to be as tall as her mother – had an appetite like a horse.

158

'When will Mother and Father be home?' Jenny asked.

'Not long now, seeing it's Wednesday, and half-day closing. But they have jobs to do after everyone's left the cafe, you know. When you have a business you can't just turn the key on it.'

'Well, will they be in time to take us for a walk?' Jenny wanted to know.

'Of course,' Mrs Foster said. 'Don't they always on a Wednesday – and every Sunday afternoon too? You're lucky little girls that way.'

In fact, Eleanor and Frank were just about to leave the cafe. It was a cafe only now. They had dispensed with the shop part not long after their marriage – though Eleanor would always do special orders for old customers. It was the cafe which gave the best profit, Eleanor pointed out, especially if they could attract more customers for teas. Teas were easier to cater for, and there was less waste. And not having the shop, they could fit in three extra tables, twelve places.

'I'll just nip upstairs, see that everything's in order for this evening,' Eleanor said.

The accommodation upstairs had been adapted, changed, furnished, decorated, so that now there was one fair-sized room which would take a meeting, a whist drive, a small wedding reception or a party (Frank had purchased a second-hand piano), a second, smaller room for meetings, and a kitchen from which refreshments could be served. It was not only the rent from the two rooms – and they now had several regular bookings for meetings as well as an increasing number of parties – it was the fact that practically nothing took place in them which didn't include refreshments supplied by Kramers, which made the upstairs of their premises almost as profitable as the cafe below.

'Must you come back this evening?' Frank asked. 'Can't Mrs Eliot and Daisy manage? It's only a whist drive.'

Mrs Eliot was still with them, a tower of strength. Daisy was the fourth successor to Maisie, the waitress they had first employed.

'Of course they can manage,' Eleanor replied. 'But customers like to set eyes on you or me. They feel they're being looked after, even if we only say "good evening".'

'Then I will come down,' Frank said.

'No. You said you were tired and I think you have a cold coming on. I'll do it. I'm not in the least tired.'

She never was. Frank marvelled at her. Though without the shop she didn't have to make such an early start in the bakehouse, she was on the go all day and still had plenty of energy left for whatever the children demanded of her in the evenings. And for his needs too. In bed she never turned away, pleaded fatigue, though she might well have done. After six years she was as lusty, as vigorously loving as she had been in those wonderful first days of their marriage. He knew he was the luckiest man in the world.

If he had an unfulfilled wish it was that they might, from all their lovemaking , have had a child. It was not that he wasn't contented with Eleanor. He desired a child because it would be an extension of his wife. But there had never been a sign. He accepted now that it was not to be. Eleanor herself seemed not to mind, except for his sake. And he shared her children. He could not have loved them more if they had been flesh of his flesh.

'Everything's laid out ready,' Eleanor announced, returning. 'Shall we take the tram home, or shall we walk?'

'The tram,' Frank said. 'We'll be with the children sooner.'

'Akersfield's improved out of all telling in the last few years,' Eleanor remarked as they walked to the tram stop. 'More shops, better shops, even a good department store.'

It was Akersfield's blossoming which had been responsible for the increase in their cafe trade. Now that women didn't have to go to Bradford or Leeds to find what they wanted in the shops, they came to Akersfield. And tea at Kramer's, which was handy, pleasant, and gave good value, was a nice rounding-off to the trip, especially in the company of a friend.

When they heard the front door, Selina and Jenny ran upstairs to the hall. Becky was already hard at work on her piano practice. While Eleanor went down to the kitchen with the younger children, Frank went straight in to Becky. She was doing so well at her music. She had a real gift. Sometimes he forgot that he was not her father and wondered if she had inherited her love of music from him. He crept quietly into the drawing-room and stood behind her, but although she knew he was there, she didn't falter. She never minded him watching and listening.

'Very good!' he said when she had finished. 'I think you like "*Fur Elise*". You play it well, Becky.'

'I do like it,' she agreed. 'Shall I play some Schubert next?'

'We are going for a walk,' he reminded her. 'Perhaps, if there is time, when we get back.'

In the kitchen Eleanor said, 'Here is a copy of the *Daily Mail*, Ma. A customer left it behind. There isn't time now, but I'll read it to you later.'

'Perhaps one of the children could read it to me?' Mrs Foster suggested. It shamed her that everyone in the house except herself could read. She could make out no more than half a dozen words at most. Every day the *Akersfield Record* was delivered, and often Eleanor brought home a *Daily Mail* or a *Titbits*; but aside from a few photographs, or a comic drawing or two in *Titbits*, I might as well be blind, Mrs Foster thought. It was the second time today she had given way to self-pity, which was something she didn't hold with.

'I'm not sure that the contents will be fit for the children,' Eleanor said. 'But don't worry, I'll have time later. Would you like to come for a walk with us now? We thought we'd go along to the park. It's pleasant out.'

'Not at the moment,' Mrs Foster said. 'I've got a few things to do.' It was her firm belief that they should have time together, as a family, without her hanging around their necks. Also she couldn't keep up with them. Akersfield was a damp place and in the last year or two it had made her a bit stiff and rheumaticky.

The park was no more than ten minutes' brisk walk away. They often went there, especially on a summer Sunday when there was a band, and crowds of people parading around in their best clothes. On those occasions Frank liked to pay for a deckchair in the enclosure by the bandstand, so that he could turn his back on the fashion parade and concentrate on the music; but the others, though they enjoyed the music, preferred to mingle with the crowds.

There would be no band today. But if we're lucky, if we're there in time, Selina thought, the motor boat will still be running. It went twice around the lake for one penny, which was pretty good. Sometimes at the weekend the queues of parents and children waiting to board were so long that their mother wouldn't wait; but that shouldn't happen today.

'Can we go on the boat?' she asked.

'I don't see why not,' Eleanor replied, smiling. 'Would you all like to do that?'

Becky was the only one who demurred. 'It's really rather childish for me,' she said. 'But if you're all going on . . . She just hoped that no-one from school would see her, that was all.

'I hope *I* never get too old to go on the motor boat,' Frank teased. 'It must be an awful feeling!'

Becky blushed. She cared about her father's opinion – she always thought of him as her father and addressed him so. He was so kind, and sometimes she felt he understood her better than did her mother. Naturally she loved her mother, but they didn't always see eye to eye.

The boat was waiting at the jetty. It was almost full, and once Frank had paid the fares and they stepped aboard, it began to chug away. That was the magic moment for Selina. The lake, though in reality not large, was always an uncharted sea, their voyage one of discovery. There were two small islands in the middle of the lake where water fowl nested in the vegetation, but *she* knew that they were really desert islands where no white man had set foot, and who could tell *what* lived in those dense bushes? She said nothing of all this to the others.

Becky sat sedately, trying hard not to be the least bit interested, though until this, her thirteenth summer, she had always enjoyed going on the boat. Jenny's attention was taken by the boys who stood or knelt on the shores of the lake with their fishing nets in the water, and glass jars beside them awaiting the tiddlers, or the occasional minnow, they hoped to catch. She longed with all her heart to join them.

'Mother, *when* can I have a fishing net and a jar?' she begged.

'When you're old enough not to fall in,' Eleanor replied.

Becky was horrified. 'Mother, you are surely *not* going to allow her to stand on the edge of the lake and fish – and with all those boys?'

'Why not?' Eleanor asked.

Becky sighed in despair. Why could her mother not *see* that some things were simply not done?

'Because it's so *common*!' she explained.

'What does common mean?' Jenny asked.

'You're too young to understand,' Becky said impatiently. Not for the first time, she wished she was the only child of rich and noble parents to whom all the niceties of life were second nature.

When the boat trip was over they set off to walk around the perimeter of the park before turning for home. Frank tucked Eleanor's arm in his own as they strolled behind the children.

'Do you remember Coronation night?' he said. 'Do you remember when we danced?' He would never forget it. It had not been the beginning of his love for Eleanor, but it was the first time he had held her in his arms.

'Of course I do,' Eleanor replied. 'It was such a surprise. I had no idea you danced so well.'

It was only after the Coronation dancing that she had begun to think of Frank as a person rather than just an employer. Even then, it was not as a man she thought of him, just a person. The only man in her mind at the time was Dick Fletcher. She had been blind to everyone else. Well, she had not seen Dick Fletcher since the day he had

163

visited the cafe and Frank had told him of their forthcoming marriage. She could still see the look on Dick's face.

She had purposely not been to Felldale since her marriage. With so many changes, so much to do in the cafe, it had not been difficult to find excuses. Clara and Albert had been only too pleased to come to view the house in Ashfield Road. They had made a few visits, and on two occasions they had taken her mother back with them for a short stay. It was after one such visit that Mrs Foster had given Eleanor news of Dick and his family.

'They have the loveliest little girl,' she said. 'Emily. As dark as dark, with curly hair and great big eyes.'

'Like her father?'

Mrs Foster had given Eleanor a sharp glance.

'Yes. And he's mighty proud of her, I can tell you! So is her mother. It's quite a picture to see them all out together!'

Eleanor knew that her mother did it deliberately, and she understood that it was because she was still apprehensive. She wanted to say, 'Don't worry, Ma. I'm married to Frank now,' but she couldn't bring herself to utter the words, she couldn't bridge the gap which was between them in this matter.

She was surprised that Dick had not left Felldale, as he had talked about doing. Clara said it was because Jane was never too well and didn't want to move away, and he just went along with his wife's wishes. But Eleanor knew that he no longer came to Akersfield. He had given up his stall in Akersfield market at the time of her marriage to Frank.

Frank, too, seemed to have given up all idea of starting a business somewhere other than in Akersfield. She had almost stopped mentioning it to him, but, as they walked, it came into her mind again.

'The business is doing so well now,' she said. 'But there's no room for expansion. We could sell it at a profit and set up somewhere else, somewhere pleasanter than Akersfield. Perhaps a small hotel in the country. Now that people are buying motor cars there'll be a demand for meals and accommodation. What do you think?'

'You know what I think, my love.' It was about the only subject on which they disagreed. 'We're settled here, all of us. Akersfield has been good to us and I feel a loyalty to it. It's not an unpleasant little town and it's improving all the time. The children are at good schools. Your mother seems contented. I had thought you were happy, my love? Are you not happy?' He sounded anxious.

'Of course I am,' she reassured him. 'It was just a thought.'

There were times when she could hardly believe her good fortune. The years of struggling and poverty were behind her now, but she would never forget them; never as long as she lived.

'You know that if there's anything about the house you don't like, you're free to change it. You are not obliged to keep one stick of my mother's furniture.'

'I know.'

It wasn't the first time he had said it and she herself didn't quite understand why in almost six years she had made only the most minor changes in the house. Mrs Kramer's furnishings were not to her taste; she found them heavy and ornate. It was not that Mrs Kramer's presence hovered over the house, inhibiting her. She felt nothing of that: and Frank seldom showed any attachment for an item of furniture, except for the piano, which was a good one and had been brought by his father from Germany. Nor was it, Eleanor thought, that she had no ideas of her own about furnishing, decorating. She was always changing and improving things in the cafe. But at the very back of her mind, so deeply hidden that she was scarcely aware of it herself, was the feeling that she didn't belong in Ashfield Road; that number seventeen was a temporary abode, she wouldn't always be there.

'Why don't you do that?' Frank urged. 'Why don't you make changes?' She heard the anxiety in his voice.

'I daresay one of these days I'll get around to doing so,'

she answered. 'Don't worry, Frank. Truly, it was just a thought – what I said about moving on.'

It was a thought which had existed in her a long time ago, when all she had wanted was to run away, run to a place of which Dick Fletcher was no part, where she would have no memories of him. She knew now that there was no such place on earth. She could never run far enough. The way to banish Dick was in her own person, in nurturing the steady love she had come to have for Frank; feeding it, helping it to grow. She wished with all her heart that they could have a child, but she would never tell him, fearing that he saw the lack as his fault, and that this grieved him deeply.

Mrs Foster picked up the newspaper which Eleanor had brought home and willed herself to be able to read it, but it was impossible. Her eyesight was good enough, but the shapes of the words meant nothing at all to her. She flung the paper to the floor in a rare fit of rage – then when she had stared at it for a minute or two she picked it up and smoothed it out again. Temper and self-pity would get her nowhere, but she was so frustrated she felt she could burst.

'Pull yourself together, Susannah!' she said out loud. 'Take action!' The very sound of her own name, spoken, seemed to give her identity, put grit into her, so that when the family returned she could hardly wait for Eleanor to take off her hat and gloves before blurting out her decision.

'I want to learn to read! I've made up my mind. I know I can do it, I just need someone to teach me. I know you haven't time, but I could go to a teacher. I wouldn't be ashamed . . .' She broke off. 'That is, if you can afford it?' She had quite overlooked that it would cost money, and she was totally dependent on Eleanor and Frank for that.

For a moment Eleanor looked at her mother in astonishment, noting the flush in her cheeks and the suspicious brightness of her eyes. She was near to crying, and in her mother that was unthinkable. She never cried. Eleanor put out her hand and touched her mother's.

'Of course we can afford it! If that's what you want to do, Ma.'

'It is!'

'Then we'll find a teacher. The Reverend Parker might know of one. Shall you ask him, or would you like me to do so?'

'You ask!' Mrs Foster felt suddenly shy at the whole prospect, but not enough to make her change her mind. She would go through with it no matter what. She knew the Reverend Parker because she went to the Ladies' Sewing Guild every third Wednesday afternoon and he usually popped in for a few minutes, but he had never spoken to her. Well, she thought, if she was going to spend her time learning to read she could drop the hated Sewing Guild. All she ever made, and she did it badly, was white calico shifts for little black boys in Africa because the missionaries didn't like to see them naked. She'd be glad enough to drop that useless occupation.

'Then I'll see to it tomorrow,' Eleanor promised. 'I think it's a very good idea!'

'Fancy not being able to read!' Becky said.

Eleanor turned on her sharply.

'No more could you before you were taught, young lady! You weren't born able to read!'

'I expect you'll be ever so good at it, Grandma,' Jenny said kindly. 'And then you can read me stories!'

'You can read them for yourself,' Becky told her.

'I know. But I *like* being read to,' Jenny said firmly.

For her own part, Mrs Foster thought, she looked forward to the day when no-one would ever have to read to her again.

'Don't tell the others when they come on Sunday,' she said. 'I'd rather wait.'

The great excitement about Sunday was not that the family were coming, but that John Brookfield, with a legacy from his mother, had splashed out and bought a motor car! He and Madge, and their children David and Mary, would set off at the crack of dawn, picking up Jimmy and Flo from

167

Felldale, and they would drive down to Akersfield in style. It would be a bit of a squash. David Brookfield, at eighteen, was as tall as his father and Jimmy Foster was now a lanky sixteen-year-old. Albert and Clara would have to come by train.

'And I daresay they'll have the better journey,' Mrs Foster remarked. 'Especially if it rains.'

'If it rains they can put the hood up,' Eleanor said, laughing. 'It's quite waterproof!' Privately she thought that Madge would really be above herself now, going everywhere in a motor car.

'Do you think Uncle John will take us for a ride?' Becky asked. That really *would* be something to tell the girls at school.

'I daresay,' Eleanor replied.

Albert and Clara arrived first, getting a tram from Akersfield station.

'I wouldn't want to go in a motor car if you asked me,' Clara said sniffily. 'Nasty, dangerous things! I can tell you, I wasn't too happy about letting Jimmy and Flo go, but nothing else would please them!'

The Sunday joint was already overcooked by the time the motor-car party arrived.

'Sorry about that!' John said. 'Just a small breakdown – running repairs!' He had a new jauntiness, Eleanor thought. As for Madge, swathed in scarves and veils, her hat tied firmly on her head, she stepped down from the motor as if she was the Queen!

'It's quite the best way to travel!' she announced.

Except for Mrs Foster, who was attending to the Yorkshire puddings, and Clara, who showed what she thought by absenting herself, they were all gathered on the pavement, examining the new acquisition.

'It's splendid,' Frank said. 'You were wise to buy a Wolseley. I really envy you!'

Eleanor looked at him in surprise.

'I mean it,' he told her. 'I'd like us to have a motor car one day. We could get out into the country at the weekends.

168

You'd like that.'

Becky squealed with delight.

'Oh Father! You will buy one, won't you, Father! Say you will!' She danced with pleasure.

That would be truly wonderful, something, at last, of which she could be proud. It would almost make up for having a mother who made pastry in a bakehouse, even if it was their own bakehouse and their own café. It was all right that her father should be in such a business. Most of the fathers of her schoolfriends were in the wool business or in trade, but she didn't know a single girl whose mother went out to work every day. But a motor car would redeem her. And if were to be port-wine colour, like the King's cars . . .!

'Well, anyone who wants to can come for a spin,' John said.

'But not before dinner,' Eleanor warned him. 'If you keep Ma's Yorkshire puddings waiting she'll kill you.'

With some reluctance at leaving the motor car, they moved into the house, but the smell of roast beef which pervaded the air encouraged them into the dining-room. Eleanor, watching her nephews and nieces take their places, managed not to remark how much they had all grown. David Brookfield was a young man now, and Jimmy Foster not far behind. Flo, just a little older than Becky, seemed shy and quiet, quite different from her voluble cousin.

Mrs Foster sat impatiently while Frank said grace. Surely even the good Lord himself would not expect Yorkshire puddings to be kept waiting! But once the meal started, she was a happy woman. She had her family around her *and* she had a secret! It was a secret which gave her more pleasure than anything she had known for a long time. She had had her very first reading lesson and had read her first sentence. It had been as clear as clear, no hesitation. 'The cat sat on the mat.' Her teacher said she was a real quick learner. In a few months from now she would be able, except for the longest words, to read the *Akersfield Record* unaided.

'And now for a bit of news,' Madge said. 'Our David is

going into the army! He's joined the West Yorkshire Regiment and he goes off to camp next Thursday!'

'Good heavens!' Eleanor exclaimed. 'I thought you were going to be a farmer, like your father.'

'I never wanted to be a farmer,' David said. 'The army is the life for me, even though there isn't a war on.'

'Not this minute, there isn't,' his father put in. 'But it could come, and maybe sooner than you think. I read the papers and I know. Those up at the top are not too happy about Germany, I can tell you. There's a lot of fear that they might invade us.'

'Germany invade England?' Clara said. 'What rubbish you talk! Why, the Kaiser is the King's cousin!'

'You can't trust a German,' John Brookfield persisted.

There was a sudden silence. Everyone except the two youngest children stopped eating. Eleanor looked at Frank and saw his unusual pallor.

'I'm sorry!' John stammered. 'I wasn't thinking . . . I didn't mean anything, nothing personal. You know that, Frank.'

Frank seemed to recover more quickly than any of them, but Eleanor was not deceived.

'Of course you didn't! And there is no need to apologise, John. Besides, I am not a German. I was born here, right here in Akersfield. No-one could feel more English than I do.'

'And no-one could be more loyal to his country,' Eleanor said.

She turned to Jimmy. 'So what are you going to do?'

'He's already working in the shop,' Clara told her. 'And a real help to me and Albert.'

'But I'm not staying,' Jimmy said stubbornly. 'I've told you that before. I'm going into the Merchant Navy.'

'The army, the navy – whatever next?' Mrs Foster wanted to know.

'Not the Royal Navy, Grandma,' Jimmy said. 'The Merchant Navy isn't a fighting force.'

'Well, thank goodness for that,' his grandmother said.

170

'All this talk of war, it's quite spoiling my dinner!'

'Yes,' Eleanor agreed. 'Let's change the subject.'

'Let's finish our dinner and go out in the motor car,' Becky said. 'That's what *I* want to do, Uncle John.'

'And so you shall!'

With the four girls packed into the back seat and Frank beside John in the front, they set off in style. The day was fine and the hood down, and Becky desperately hoped that they would see someone she knew, so that she could wave to them. David and Jimmy went off for a walk while the four women cleared away and saw to the dishes.

'All these children growing up,' Eleanor said. 'It makes me feel ancient. I can hardly believe I'm only thirty!'

She never quite knew how old she felt. Sometimes it seemed as though she had lived her life and was already an old woman, that every day from now on would be the same and there was nothing to look forward to. At other times, and she thanked God that these were in the majority, she felt no more than eighteen, full of life and energy, sure that something good would happen. She didn't know it, but Mrs Foster recognised these happier moods by the fact that her daughter would burst into song, sing all around the house as she had done when she was a child. She loved to hear Eleanor singing.

'So what news is there from Felldale?' Eleanor enquired. It was not how she wanted to phrase it, but she couldn't bring herself to ask the direct question.

'Nothing much,' Clara said. 'Oh yes, there is one bit of news that'll interest you. Jane Fletcher's expecting again! You couldn't rightly say they're delighted about it. The doctor said she mustn't have another. But these things happen. It can't have been easy for Dick all this time; denied his rights, so to speak . . . And I suppose in the end . . .'

She went on and on. Eleanor wanted to shout at her to stop. She didn't want to hear any more.

'Excuse me,' she said. 'I think there's someone at the door.'

She hurried out of the kitchen, ran upstairs to the

bedroom, flung herself face down on the bed, burying her face in the pillow. She burst into sobs. She couldn't bear it. She could not bear it, this searing, tearing jealousy and longing. And then while she was still crying she really did hear the sound of the front door.

She was sitting in front of the mirror, putting herself to rights, trying to compose herself, when Frank came into the bedroom. She could not conceal her unhappiness, and the telltale signs of her tears. He put his hands on her shoulders and his eyes met hers in the mirror.

'I know what is wrong, my darling,' he said gently. 'You are upset by what was said at the table about the Germans. But there is nothing to worry about. I am as English as you are. All my loyalty is to this country. Everyone who knows me realises that.' He bent over her, and she closed her eyes while he kissed the back of her neck.

'And now come outside and take another look at this motor car. I am quite serious about us having one, my dear.'

She took his hand and went with him. As she always must, she thought, for the rest of her life.

CHAPER TEN

Mrs Foster sat at the kitchen table, the *Akersfield Record* spread out in front of her. She read slowly but steadily, her forefinger following the line of print, her lips, though she was unaware of it, silently shaping each word. Less than three months since that first lesson, she thought, and she had never looked back. She had read all Selina's and Jenny's schoolbooks and story books, and had dipped into Becky's, though she didn't always understand those of her eldest granddaughter. Such things they taught children nowadays!

But the greatest freedom her new skill had brought her was that she could now read almost all of the newspaper, or at any rate enough to make sense of it. She knew what was going on, not only in her immediate surroundings of Akersfield and the West Riding, but in the wider world as it was brought to her by occasional copies of the *Daily Mail*. She was privy to the goings-on in London, and even in foreign places with names she couldn't always make out. She knew what the latest fashions were and had added to her stock of recipes. Best of all, she followed avidly the doings of the King and Queen and the royal family. He was a bit of a lad, the King – and Queen Alexandra was such a beautiful, sweet woman.

'According to the *Record*,' she said, 'Akersfield Fair is going to be better than ever this year. More roundabouts and stalls, the Fat Lady, and a troupe of midgets. And I suppose the usual boxing booth, horrid thing!'

'Oh how I *long* to go' Becky sighed. 'Why do we have to go to silly Felldale when we could stay here and go to the fair?'

'I want to go to the fair too,' Selina said.

'And me!' Jenny echoed.

'We're going to Felldale on Sunday because, being Akersfield Feast week, the cafe will be closed on the Monday and Tuesday. It's about the only holiday your ma and pa get. Anyay, surely you want to see your cousins?' What an idiot she'd been to read out the announcement — though even if she hadn't they'd have found out. There'd be posters everywhere.

'Surely you want to see Flo?' Mrs Foster persisted.

'Flo is boring,' Becky said. 'Jimmy is a bit better because he talks about going to sea.' But she hadn't always thought Cousin Flo boring; not when they were both smaller. She supposed it was the result of living in a place like Felldale — only a village and nothing to do, nowhere to go. She would hate to live in Felldale, or any other little village, come to that. Akersfield was bad enough. When she was grown up — she prayed nightly for the years to fly by — she would live in London.

'Why couldn't we have gone to Morecambe?' she grumbled. 'Now that we have the motor car we could have gone to Morecambe, or even Scarborough, and stayed in a boarding house.' They had never, ever been away from home and stayed in a boarding house, and in her opinion it was high time they did.

'It's all of sixty miles to Morecambe,' her grandmother reminded her. 'And in any case, it seems your dad wanted to go to Felldale. He's the head of the family and it's up to him to choose. Anyway, the fair goes on for a week, so I daresay he'll take you when we get back from Felldale. Just you be a bit more patient!'

Mrs Foster had been rather surprised herself that Frank had chosen to go to Felldale for Akersfield Feast weekend. Though he got on well with everyone, she didn't think he had that much in common with Albert and Clara. But there, she thought, being the kind man he is, he's probably doing it to please me and Eleanor. There was no denying she'd be glad to set foot in Felldale again, and she was even happy

174

about going in the motor car. They had had the vehicle almost two months now and they'd had two trips to Baildon Moor and one to Bolton Abbey. Though she'd been petrified at first, in the end she'd quite enjoyed it.

Eleanor had come into the room while Becky was speaking. She, too, was not sure about going to Felldale, but Frank had sprung it on her as what he expected to be a pleasant surprise.

'It will be a very nice drive,' he'd said. 'And I daresay we'll be able to have the hood down. And perhaps there'll be an opportunity to take Albert and Clara for a spin!'

With part of her, for reasons which she hardly dared admit to herself, she longed to go. If she could just set eyes on Dick, just see him, not even speak to him. Surely there could be no harm in that? But what she knew she could not bear the sight of was Jane Fletcher on his arm; Jane in the seventh month of her pregnancy, carrying Dick's child for all the world to see. Such thoughts were wrong. She knew it, and she tried all the time to put them away from her. She *did* love Frank, she really did. If only she was carrying *his* child. It would be compensation – but for what or whom she didn't care to dwell upon.

She turned to Becky, who was standing by the window, sulking.

'Have you done your homework? If not, get on with it. The fact that school breaks up on Friday is no reason for neglecting Wednesday's homework. And then go and tidy your room. It was like a pigsty when I looked in this morning.'

'I've finished my homework,' Becky retorted. 'I did it as soon as I came in. And why don't you say anything to Selina and Jenny about their room? Why do you always pick on me?' Her voice was hard, her face flushed with anger as she faced her mother.

Eleanor felt the colour rise in her own face at Becky's accusation. It was true enough. She *did* pick on Becky. She tried not to but there were times when she couldn't help it. They rubbed each other up the wrong way.

175

They're too much alike, those two, Mrs Foster thought. Both wilful, wanting their own way, wanting it at once — no waiting. Eleanor, as a child, had been much like Becky was now, though not as hard, she'd had more feeling for others than Becky showed. Perhaps because Eleanor was her own child she'd been closer to her, had understood her better. It was difficult these days, though she loved her dearly, to get close to Becky. and it was clear that Eleanor had the same problem. Would Eleanor have got on better with a son, her mother wondered? She herself, though she had had a greater closeness with her daughters, had found her sons easier. Well, it didn't seem as though there were going to be either sons or daughters for Eleanor and Frank!

'I'm sorry,' Eleanor said. 'I didn't mean to. Selina and Jenny, of course you must also tidy your room. I daresay it's just as bad as Becky's.'

'There are two of us to make it untidy,' Selina said.

'And two of you to tidy it,' Becky added quickly.

'That's enough?' Eleanor said. 'We'll have an end to this bickering. Off you go and do as you're told, all three of you.'

Sunday, as Frank had hoped and expected, dawned bright and sunny. The moment breakfast was over he strapped their two suitcases on to the luggage grid at the rear of the motor car and carefully lowered the hood. Then he walked around the car to inspect it, giving it an occasional surreptitious, loving pat. Oh, he was so pleased with it!

'Come along,' he said, going back into the house. 'We don't want to waste time on a lovely day like this!'

'We just have to tie our hats on, since you've put the hood down,' Eleanor explained. 'No matter how fine the day, there'll be a breeze when we start to move.'

'Blow the cobwebs away, do us all a power of good!' Frank said. 'Now pile in. A bit of a squash, but we'll manage.'

Though they stopped on the way to get out and stretch their legs, it still wanted more than an hour to dinnertime when they turned off the main road and started up the hill to Felldale.

'Look at that!' Frank enthused. 'She goes up the hill like a bird! What a real beauty she is!'

'I think you love this car more than you love me!' Eleanor teased. She was pleased to see him so happy.

'Never!' He took his eyes off the road long enough to turn and smile at her. 'I could never love anything or any one as I love you, and you know it.' He spoke quietly, so that the sound of the engine almost drowned his words.

They were words Eleanor didn't want to hear, not as they were driving into Felldale. Her mind was filled with all the wrong thoughts and she wished she had persuaded Frank not to come here, to go somewhere else. She knew she could have done so, but she had allowed herself to be tempted. She didn't deserve him. He was too good for her.

As the car, chugging and puffing from the steep climb, turned into the village, Albert came out of the shop to meet them.

'I heard you,' he said. 'You're in good time. My word, she's a little beauty, isn't she!'

'I take it you don't mean me or any of my daughters?' Eleanor laughed. 'Are we too early then?'

'Not a bit of it. It means there's time for me to take Frank for a pint in the Feathers.'

To Eleanor's surprise Frank, who didn't usually bother with public houses, accepted with alacrity. It was the car, of course. He wanted to talk about it, have it admired. No-one in Felldale had a car yet, not even the doctor.

'I'll be in time to give Clara a hand,' Mrs Foster said as Albert handed her down.

'There's no need, Ma,' Clara replied when the offer was made. 'You're supposed to be here for a holiday. But if you want to make the Yorkshire pudding batter . . .'

Mrs Foster sat near the open back door so that she could beat fresh air into the pudding mixture. Eleanor took a chair nearby, drawing in deep breaths of the pure air, so different from Akersfield. No wonder it made the puddings rise!

'So what news is there in Felldale?' Mrs Foster asked.

Clara paused in the act of laying the table.

'Not good I'm feared! Jane Lawrence had her bairn two months premature. She'd been warned she'd never carry it full term.' She broke off, saw the anxious faces turned towards her.

'Do you mean . . . the baby died? Poor lamb!' Mrs Foster said.

'A deal worse than that, Ma. The bairn lived. A little boy. It was Jane who died.'

Eleanor caught her breath, felt the colour drain from her face, gripped the sides of her chair as her head spun. She was aware, in the moment's silence which followed Clara's words, that her mother was looking at her, but she couldn't meet her eyes.

'They say Dick has taken it hard,' Clara went on. 'Well he would, wouldn't he, because he should never have put her in the family way. But these things happen. Any road, he won't talk to anybody, won't let anyone near him.'

'I must go to him!' Eleanor stopped herself in time from saying it out loud. But go to him she must. She must comfort him. He couldn't refuse to see *her*. The need was so strong in her that she had to force herself to stay seated, remind herself that no-one else would understand the urgency of this desire which gripped her. But turning her head she saw knowledge, if not understanding, in her mother's worried face.

'So where is the baby?' Mrs Foster asked Clara. She was thankful that Frank had gone with Albert and couldn't see his wife's state. He was a loving, sensitive man, and though Eleanor, she knew, was trying to keep control, he wouldn't fail to notice. Clara, thank goodness, had no such sensitivity. She wouldn't notice a thing.

'Dr Bell and the midwife took charge. They put the bairn to wet-nurse with Mollie Laycock. She's feeding one of her own. When isn't she? Those Laycocks breed like rabbits. But of course she can't keep him long. And who'd want a child left in that house – not that Dick cares. He won't so much as look at the little lad, hasn't since the moment

178

it was born!'

'Poor little thing!' Mrs Foster said. 'What's to become of it?'

Clara shook her head. 'Who knows, Ma? Who knows?'

'And the little girl — Emily, isn't it — what about her?'

'An aunt of Jane's, over Skipton way, has taken her. For the time being, that is,' Clara replied.

My poor Dick, Eleanor thought. My poor Dick! She was filled with sorrow for his sorrow. She must find an excuse to go and see him, alone. She would go for a walk the minute dinner was over.

In the event, it was not difficult. As soon as the dishes were cleared, all who could do so packed into the motor car. Selina and Jenny, left behind, chose to take turns on the garden swing while their grandmother looked on.

'I think I'll take a walk, Ma. Stretch my legs,' Eleanor said.

Mrs Foster looked her daughter straight in the face. 'Don't try to pull the wool over my eyes,' she admonished her. 'I know what you have in mind — and you're wrong. Leave it alone.'

'I must go and see him!' Eleanor said. 'You don't understand.'

'I understand only too well,' Mrs Foster replied. 'I haven't been your mother for thirty years without knowing how your mind works. You're playing with fire — and you'll get burnt. If you can't think of yourself, think of Frank.'

'I'll do nothing or say nothing to hurt Frank,' Eleanor said. 'I promise you that. I love my husband.'

'I know you do. So why not leave it at that and stay where you are? There's nothing you can do for Dick Fletcher. Nothing that you're free to do.'

'Maybe I can get through to him. You heard what Clara said, that no-one else can. Maybe I can convince him that people care. At any rate I'm going to try. You can't stop me, no matter what you say.'

'I never thought I could,' Mrs Foster acknowledged. 'I

179

had to try. If you manage to talk to him, give him my deepest sympathy.'

Eleanor bent over and kissed her mother on the cheek. 'I will,' she promised.

He was working in the garden, deep digging a patch of ground, plunging the spade in, lifting and turning the heavy soil. Throwing it down again as if he hated every grain, wanted only to wreak vengeance on it. Why was he deep digging at this time of year? Every other square inch of the garden was clearly in various stages of production, early produce ready for harvesting, seedlings pushing their way in long straight lines through the soil, and fruit, flowers and vegetables at every stage in between. It was more orderly, everything in greater abundance, than in those few weeks she had worked with him. It was seven years now, but watching him as she walked up the path, the time in between seemed to melt away.

Every ounce of energy concentrated on his digging, he neither saw nor heard her approach. She was standing now no more than a few feet away from him, still unseen. She could leave, change her mind and return home, and he would be none the wiser.

'Hello, Dick!' she said quietly.

He turned at the sound of her voice, and when she saw his face it was difficult not to cry out. It was not his physical appearance which shocked her, though he was much thinner, with deep hollows beneath his cheekbones and the flesh drawn tight beneath his jaw; it was the look on his face. He was a man ravaged by grief, haunted and possessed. But worst of all was the look in his eyes when he saw her. On first lifting his head he had stared blankly, but when he recognized her his eyes filled with anger.

It couldn't be anger, Eleanor told herself. It was grief, despair, hurt. She wanted to step towards him and throw her arms around him, hold him close. She wanted to hold him and comfort him as a mother would a child, stroke his head and soothe his spirit. But it *was* anger, and it was turned on her. It flashed in his eyes as he looked at her.

'Dick, I had to come! I couldn't bear not to!'

'Leave!' he said. 'Go back where you came from!'

'Why? I came to try to comfort you.'

'There's no comfort,' he said. His voice was flat, dull. She almost preferred the rage in his eyes to the deadness of his voice. 'If there was, it wouldn't come from you.'

'But why? Dick, what have I done? You've got to tell me. You've got to talk to me, for your own sake as well as mine. Dick, please leave the digging, please come into the house with me and talk. At least tell me what I've done, why you're angry with me.'

He looked at her without speaking. The seconds seemed to go on forever, but Eleanor held his eyes with hers and saw a little of the hostility go from them. They looked at each other in silence for a moment longer, and then Eleanor held out her hand to him.

'Let's go into the house,' she said.

He made no move, so she stepped towards him, pushed the spade he was holding to the ground and took his hand in hers. She expected resistance, but there was none. That in itself distressed her. It was so unlike him. Dick had always been the strong one, firm of purpose, in charge. Now only the trembling of his hand in hers showed that he felt anything at all. She drew her arm through his, felt his body shaking against hers, and began to walk towards the house.

Inside the cottage everything looked neglected; a loaf of bread going mouldy on the table, dirty dishes, a smell of sour milk, dust over everything. It would have broken Jane's heart, Eleanor thought – and realised that it was the first time she had allowed Jane to enter her mind. There had been room only for Dick.

They stood awkwardly, side by side in the litle room. With all her heart she wanted to help, to do the right thing, but she didn't know how to begin. She felt that whatever she said would be wrong, would only rouse the anger which was simmering in him. Not knowing what to do, she began to clear the table, picking up a dirty mug and plate and taking them to wash at the sink.

181

'Put that down!'

She turned quickly at the harshness of his command – and obeyed him.

'Don't touch anything, do you hear. Anything!'

'I'm sorry. I was trying to help. I want to help, and I don't know how to unless you tell me, talk to me.'

'Nobody can help,' he said. 'Least of all you!'

'I don't understand,' Eleanor protested. 'What have I done?'

'You know I killed her? You know I killed my wife? Everybody knows that!'

'I know nothing of the kind,' Eleanor said. 'Nor have I heard anyone else say that. Why do you say you killed her?'

Instinct told her that to keep him talking was the right thing to do. She wondered if he had spoken to anyone at all in the fortnight since Jane had died. The wildness of his talk, his seeming hatred of her, didn't matter if only she could keep him talking, help him to vent his bitterness.

'Why do you say you killed her?' she repeated.

'I knew she mustn't have another child. The doctor had made it quite plain. It was touch and go with the first one.'

'But these things happen . . .' Eleanor interrupted.

'No they don't happen!' he shouted. 'You're wrong! We make them happen. I made it happen. What's more, she didn't want it. She was afraid. I forced myself on her. That's how I killed her, as surely as if I'd put a knife in her heart. When she was carrying the child I let myself hope that it would be all right. She pretended to believe that, but I knew she was afraid. When I saw her lying dead I knew I was a murderer!'

He dropped to the sofa, buried his head in his hands, his whole body shuddering. Eleanor sat beside him, again and all the time wanting to hold him but knowing that she mustn't.

She felt helpless.

'Some would say it's God's will,' she said. 'We don't always understand these things.'

'It's not God's will! I tell you it was my will! God had nothing to do with it – the devil, more like!'

'All right then, the devil,' Eleanor said. 'You know when we were children we always believed in the devil. I used to believe he'd come out of the mirror and get me.'

'I never did. I believed in myself. I reckoned I was responsible for my own actions.'

'But we all fail,' Eleanor told him gently. 'We have to forgive ourselves.' Here in this room she remembered that April day when they had made love. She had learned to live with the memory, but it would never die. She stretched out her hand and stroked his arm. He flung her away and jumped to his feet.

'You'd better leave,' he said. 'Please go!'

While he'd talked about Jane, Eleanor had thought that a little of his animosity towards herself had gone, but now it was all back again. It was there in the harshness of his voice. She had to know why.

'Very well, I'll go,' she replied. 'But there are two things I have to ask you. Please tell me the truth, Dick. Why are you so angry with me?'

He paused a long time; she thought he was never going to reply.

'Why?' she persisted.

When he did speak he was quieter, calmer, as if bringing it out into the open was the relief he needed.

'Can't you guess why?'

Eleanor shook her head.

'Because when I made love to Jane, when I forced myself on her, planted the seed which killed her, it was you lying there. It was you I saw. I never thought of Jane. It was desire for you which drove me. I didn't even kill my wife in love!'

It was Eleanor who buried her face in her hands now. Her body trembled as a great wave of desire swept over her. She raised her head and looked at Dick, and saw that the same desire was in him, clear and strong. She held out her arms to him and he moved towards her. Then suddenly, instinctively, and against her desire she turned her outstretched hands, palms towards him, as if to push him away, though he had not yet touched her.

183

'No, Dick! No!' She felt, in her own body, his pain at her rejection of him. She wanted to weep at the sight of the hurt and confusion in his face.

'I'm sorry, Dick!'

How could she explain to him that though her longing for him was still there, there were even stronger feelings of guilt and remorse which rose between them like a high wall. And it was not a shared guilt for what Dick had done, his feelings about Jane and her part in them. It was guilt and remorse entirely personal, known only to her.

It was remorse for all those times when, lying in her own bed with Frank making love to her, she had substituted Dick's face for that of her husband, had imagined Dick's hands on her body. That she had seldom done so deliberately didn't absolve her now. Her guilt and Dick's seemed one and the same, and made worse because she still wanted him, wanted to give in to him. Physically to reject him now, when he had need of her comfort, was the hardest thing she had ever had to do. Yet she had no doubt that she must. She must turn away.

She knew also, with great clarity, that it was not for her sake or for Dick's that she did so. It was for Frank. Her atonement for what she had done to Frank, even though he would never know about it, was that from this moment on she must be entirely his, true to him in the spirit as well as in the flesh, for the whole of their future together. At the very moment when Dick needed her most she must turn away from him and commit herself wholly to Frank. She had made her choice.

'So you do condemn me?' Dick said quietly.

Eleanor shook her head. 'I don't at all. Who am I to do that? And I understand more than you might think. There are things for which I have to forgive myself, and I *shall* do so. You must learn to do likewise.'

He shrugged. The mask came over his face again and she knew she hadn't convinced him.

'There's something else I have to ask you,' she said. 'It's about the baby.'

She had had this idea in her mind since the moment Clara had talked about the baby. Now she was no longer sure that it would be right. It could only be right if her own motives were sincere, if she thought only of the baby, and of Frank and herself. It mattered more than anything now that it should be right for Frank.

'I don't want to talk about the baby!' Dick's voice was hard again, withdrawn.

'You have to sooner or later,' Eleanor said firmly. 'Whatever else you are *not* responsible for, you are responsible for him. He can't stay with Mrs Laycock forever, and I doubt if Jane's aunt in Skipton is young enough to have him. You've got to do something.'

'I suppose you have the solution? You seem to think you know the answer to most things.'

Eleanor flinched at the sarcasm in his voice.

'I might be able to solve this. I don't know. If my husband is happy about it, and only if he is, I thought perhaps you might let me take the baby. Frank and I don't have a child of our own. He'd be well looked after. And when you wanted to, you'd be able to see him.'

She was not sure about that. She was not sure that she would be strong enough to see Dick again.

'May I go and see the child? she asked. 'May I take my husband?'

'I can't stop you,' Dick said. 'I can't think about the baby. I don't want to see him.'

CHAPTER ELEVEN

Eleanor knocked for the second time on Mrs Laycock's door, then, realizing that she couldn't be heard above the bedlam going on inside, she lifted the latch and went in. The door opened straight into the living-room of the small cottage and as she stepped in she was assailed by a cacophony of sound and a strong smell of ammonia. The latter, she saw at once, came from the steaming baby nappies draped over the big iron fireguard. It was obvious by the yellow stains on them that most of the nappies had been put to dry without first being washed. The smell was choking. With an effort, she resisted the temptation to hold a handkerchief to her nose.

The noise, which did not diminish in the slightest with Eleanor's entry, came from children fighting, children playing, babies crying – and from Mrs Laycock trying, in a good-tempered though totally ineffective way, to make herself heard above it all. As well as being noisy and smelly, the room was incredibly untidy and downright dirty but, as far as Eleanor could see, Mrs Laycock was unperturbed by any of it. She herself was dirty and untidy to match. How could anyone bring up children in such conditions, Eleanor asked herself; but oddly enough they all looked healthy, and not at all unhappy, even those who were quarrelling.

Mrs Laycock looked up from the child she was nursing and saw Eleanor.

'Why, if it isn't Eleanor Foster that was! This is a right surprise. What brings you here, then? Are you visiting your Albert?'

'Yes. I heard the sad news about Mrs Fletcher, and that you'd kindly taken the baby. I wondered if I could see him?'

Mrs Laycock gave Eleanor a curious look.

'Of course you can. He's right there in the cradle.'

Eleanor picked her way across the room. Mrs Laycock put the child on her lap down on the floor and joined her as she stood looking down at Dick's baby.

'He's so tiny!' Eleanor said. 'So frail!' But when she held her finger against his small clenched fist, he opened his own fingers and took hers in an unexpectedly strong grasp.

'He's all that,' Mrs Laycock agreed. 'But he's hanging on to life, bless his little heart!'

'It was very kind of you to take him,' Eleanor said.

'Well I don't know what he'd have done else,' Mrs Laycock admitted. 'And I had enough milk for two, what with feeding little Violet. I always have plenty of milk. But of course I can't keep him. I have six of my own and not much coming in.'

'So what will happen to him?' Eleanor asked.

Mrs Laycock shook her head sorrowfully.

'Who knows? His dad won't look at him, hasn't since the day he was born. They say he's grieving something cruel over his wife, which is natural I daresay, but we have to look to the living, don't we? Sooner or later I'll have to wean this little fellow, then it'll be the orphanage for him if his father won't have him. I wouldn't want one of mine to be brought up in an orphanage, I can tell you!'

'But if someone adopted him?' Eleanor said.

Mrs Laycock laughed.

'You've been reading fairy tales! That doesn't happen in real life, not unless there's grandparents, which this little mite hasn't got. In real life they go into the orphanage and that's that! How his poor mother would have grieved!'

Pity for Jane Fletcher suddenly overwhelmed Eleanor. Her eyes filled with tears. She had given so little thought to Jane in all this, but now the knowledge that the dead woman would never see either of her children grow and develop seemed unbearably cruel.

'Has he been given a name?' she asked. He was still clinging to her finger as if he would never let her go.

187

'Oh aye,' Mrs Laycock said. 'T'vicar insisted on baptising him fairly quick, him being so weakly. His father wouldn't have anything to do with choosing a name, wouldn't even be here at the christening, so t'vicar picked between Peter and Paul, it being nearest to their saint's day, he said. He chose Peter.'

'Peter. It's a good name. Thank you for letting me see him, Mrs Laycock.'

'You're welcome I'm sure. Though I was a bit surprised. I must admit.' She gave Eleanor a direct and questioning look.

'I knew Mrs Fletcher,' Eleanor said. 'And I've known Dick Fletcher all my life.'

Mrs Laycock loked vaguely dissatisfied with the explanation, but it was clear it was all she was going to get.

By the time Eleanor got back to Albert's they had all returned from their spin. Mrs Foster looked up anxiously as her daughter walked in but Frank greeted her with a smile.

'You went for a walk?' he said. 'I'd have gone with you if you'd waited, my love.'

'I went to see Dick Fletcher,' Eleanor replied straight out. 'I thought there might be something I could do.'

'That was thoughtful of you,' Frank said. 'And were you able to help?'

'Not really,' she admitted. She would say nothing about the baby, not even that she had seen it, until she was alone with Frank.

'Then perhaps you and I will go tomorrow and see him together,' Frank suggested.

The rest of the day, until bedtime, seemed to drag on forever. There was the usual splendid tea, and afterwards the children to see to. 'The children' could no longer include Jimmy. The Merchant Navy had accepted him and he was due to join his ship in two weeks' time.

'I was lucky to get with the Cunard line,' he said happily. 'I never thought they'd take me on. *And* on the *Lusitania!* I shall be able to go to America!'

'Why anyone would want to go to America I can't think!' Clara said acidly. Eleanor was sure that her sister-in-law's sharpness was a cover for the unhappiness she was feeling at the thought of her son's departure, but Clara would never admit to that.

With the children finally settled, Albert suggested a game of whist. Mrs Foster opted out, so that Eleanor was obliged to play. She couldn't concentrate for the thoughts which whirled around in her head.

'You revoked again, our Eleanor!' Albert complained. 'You did have a spade after all!'

'I'm sorry,' Eleanor said. 'I really am tired. We were up so early this morning.'

'Then perhaps we should go to bed when this round is over,' Frank proposed.

She waited until they were in bed and Frank was about to blow out the candle.

'No, leave the candle,' she said. 'I want to talk to you.'

He looked at her with concern.

'Is something wrong? You haven't been yourself all evening.'

'Not really wrong,' Eleanor said carefully. 'But I have an idea I want to discuss with you. It's very important – to both of us.'

'Then by all means let's discuss it, my love.'

'I went to see the Fletcher baby,' she began.

'That was kind of you,' Frank said. 'How was it?'

'Very small, very frail. After all, it's two months premature. But hanging on to life, I think. You know that Mrs Laycock is looking after it?'

'I didn't,' Frank replied. 'I don't know Mrs Laycock, do I?'

'No. She means well, but she's not a suitable person. The house is filthy and I'm afraid the baby might catch something. If so, it would be too weak to fight.'

'But Dick will know this,' Frank said. 'He won't let the baby stay if it's in any danger.'

'Dick will have nothing to do with the baby. He won't

189

go near it. It was having the baby which caused his wife's death. He holds himself responsible for that, and the thought of the baby is all mixed up with it.'

'But what can we do, my dear? Do you want me to go and talk with him, persuade him to change his mind? I'll willingly try.'

'It would do no good,' Eleanor told him. 'I've seen him. He's in no mood to change his mind. He's adamant. It's Mrs Laycock's opinion that the baby will have to be put into an orphanage.'

'That's terrible!'

Eleanor turned towards him. His face was filled with compassion.

'But I don't see . . .'

Eleanor took a deep breath. There was no point in beating about the bush.

'I thought we might take the baby!'

'Take him?' He stared at her in disbelief. 'My dear Eleanor . . . ! How could you cope with a young baby, even for a short time?'

'I could cope quite well. And I didn't mean for a short time, Frank. I meant we could adopt him. Bring him up as our own. He would be the child you and I have always wanted and never had.'

He was at once deeply troubled.

'Oh my dear one, I didn't know that you wanted a child so badly! You never said so.'

'Not so badly that I was very unhappy, Frank. Please don't think that. But yes, I did want our child, and I think you did too. Though you seldom said anything, sometimes I saw the look in your eyes when other couples had children.'

'I thought of your children as mine also,' he said.

'I know. I'm everlastingly grateful to you for that, and they regard you as their father. But you never knew them as babies. They haven't always belonged to the two of us.'

There was a long silence between them. He took her hand and held it tightly in his, then raised it to his lips and kissed her fingers.

190

'It's not just for me,' Eleanor said. 'It's for both of us. And more than that, it's for the baby. Think what we could do for the baby. You could say it's for Dick, too.'

'Perhaps it's Dick I'm most worried about,' Frank confessed. 'I'm not sure that it would be right to take the child away from him when he's in such a condition. Later on he might change his mind. He might marry again – some woman who would look after both his children.'

It was an idea she couldn't yet face. She pushed it from her. 'But in the meantime,' she said, 'what is to become of the baby?'

'Perhaps we could offer to take the baby for a period of time, say for a year – but only if you are totally sure that you can manage such an undertaking. At the end of a year we could see how Dick felt.'

It was not what she had envisaged, Eleanor thought, but it made a kind of sense, though how she would face giving up the baby after caring for it as her own for a year, she didn't know. But if it was best for the baby, and best for Dick . . . and if Frank agreed . . .

'I'm not sure that your way is best,' she told him. 'But if that's what you think . . .'

'It is,' Frank said. 'But, more important, we must see what Dick thinks. We'll go together tomorrow to see him. And now, my love, you must get some sleep. I don't like to see you looking so weary.'

But the short summer night was over and it was morning before either of them slept. They lay still, with closed eyes, not talking, pretending sleep, until the daylight came and he took her in his arms and began to make love to her. Dear God, she prayed, let it be Frank. From now, and for always, let it be my husband.

They went together to see Dick, soon after breakfast the next morning. Eleanor could not eat a thing and was impatient to be off. 'We don't have much time,' she said.

a pause now in the men's conversation, so she pour the tea and take it to the table. When she ont of them Frank gave her a brief nod, which she could sit down with them. She was pleased ised to see Dick pick up his cup and drink, but nk offered him the biscuits he turned his head away.

have one if you don't mind,' Frank said. 'They icious, and I'm sure your dear wife made them.' or held her breath. How could Frank be so tactless? ick merely nodded.

k has been telling me that he is to leave Felldale,' k went on, turning to Eleanor.

ave Felldale?'

e intends to . . . But let him tell you himself,' Frank

When Dick began to speak, Eleanor knew that there had en a change in him, perhaps not so swift as to have ppened since their arrival, but he was different from esterday.

'It's not a new idea,' he said. 'I told you once before I wouldn't stay here forever, but then somehow I settled down again. But just before . . .' He paused. He couldn't bring himself to say her name, though how could he expect anyone to understand that? How could a man like Frank Kramer ever understand the kind of guilt that he felt? It was not in Frank to act as he had done. And sitting with Frank, he had a double guilt – that he loved this man's wife. Not had loved her, but still, right now as she sat there looking at him. He would never act on that love and nor, he believed now, would she. After her visit yesterday he had stayed awake all night, thinking. He knew, when morning came, that he had to accept this love which was in him. He knew that it would not go away, that he would never forget her, though he could never do anything about it. He could not even tell her. That good, kind man, Frank Kramer, stood between them, a guardian on both their hearts.

'We go home tomorrow.' She felt that if something was not decided before they went back to Akersfield, then it would be too late. She also doubted, having seen Dick's mood, that one visit from herself and Frank would be enough to persuade him.

Frank seemed to read her thoughts.

'You must be patient, Eleanor,' he said. 'In the first place I am not going to persuade Dick to do something which might be very much against his wishes. In the second place, even if he agrees that we may take the baby, we cannot do so at once. You said yourself that the baby must be weaned – and on our part there are preparations to be made.'

'I know all that,' Eleanor agreed. 'But if there is to be a plan, it's better for everyone's sake that it should be made before we leave Felldale.'

There was no sign of Dick on his land so they went at once to the cottage. Their repeated knocks on the door were not answered.

'What can have happened?' Eleanor whispered. She was filled with fear, remembering his desperation.

'I daresay nothing more than that he has gone out,' Frank said. 'But we'll step inside and leave a note for him, arrange to call later.'

When they went in Dick was sitting at the table, staring into space as if he had not even heard their knocking. His untouched breakfast was in front of him, as if, having taken the trouble to prepare it, he couldn't make the further effort to eat. He spoke without turning his head towards them.

'Go away!'

'We will go shortly, my friend,' Frank said quietly. 'But not at once. I cannot leave until I have told you how much I grieve for you.' He motioned to Eleanor and they both drew up chairs to the table, Frank sitting close to Dick, Eleanor opposite them. Frank put his hand on Dick's arm, and Dick did not shake it off, as he had done with Eleanor, but allowed it to remain.

'Words cannot express the sorrow I feel for you,' Frank began. 'I have only known you through my wife, but her

friends are mine and I wou'
your friends to share your

Eleanor stayed quiet, liste
the depth of his sympathy an
and he allowed long silences i
the ticking of the clock on the
silences, afraid that Dick would go
that in the end nothing would be
last she saw Dick raise his head
realised that she had been wrong. F
time, was wiser than she.

'It's good of you to come,' Dick said
I don't appreciate it. I'm sorry I told y
you can't do anything for me.'

'Perhaps not,' Frank acquiesced. 'In th
to you. But we can be here for a little wh
keeping you from your work. I wonder . . .
we might have a cup of tea? I usually do in t
the morning and one gets used to things. Ther
for you to move. I'm sure Eleanor can make

Dick nodded assent and Frank waved Eleanor
didn't want to leave the table, she wanted to hear ev
that was said, but Frank had made his wishes quit
She was not wanted.

She filled the kettle, then busied herself at the sink.
was plenty to do. She doubted if anything had been touc
in the last fortnight. To her amazement she realised th
Dick, as well as Frank, was talking, but they spoke to
quietly for her to hear the words over the sound of the
crockery she was washing, and now the singing of the kettle.
She longed to know what they were saying. For an instant
she caught Frank's eye, but his look clearly said 'keep off'.
She mashed the tea, left it to brew for five minutes. Then
she rooted around and found a few biscuits in a tin. They
were oatmeal biscuits, and she realised that they must have
been made by Jane, perhaps one of the last things she did
before the baby started. She ached at the thought –
nevertheless she put a few on a clean plate.

'I have an option on a parcel of land in Hebghyll,' he said. 'Twenty acres. And I still have the money my father left me. In time I want to produce and sell only seed, but for a while I would have to grow other things also, keep up the markets. Seed is a long-term business.'

It was the longest speech he had made since the lifeblood had, literally, poured out of his wife. The previous night had brought him his most coherent thoughts since then, and now, because of the presence of these two people, he was able to put them into words.

Hebghyll, Eleanor thought. It was no more than a dozen miles from Akersfield. But she could not visit him.

'What will you do about the children?' she asked. 'I suppose little Emily can stay with her aunt for a while, but what about the baby?' She tried to keep the eagerness out of her voice. She must go slowly, tread carefully.

Dick felt his whole body tighten. He could not and would not think about the baby. Not now, not yet. No-one could make him.

'The baby is all right where it is,' he replied sharply. 'I can pay the woman to look after it.'

'That's not the point,' Eleanor said gently. 'It's not a suitable place. Mrs Laycock isn't a suitable person. In any case she can't keep the baby for long. She has too many children of her own.'

'My wife went to see your baby yesterday,' Frank said. 'She was distressed by the conditions. Clearly you can't be expected to care for the baby yet, but we have an idea to put to you . . .'

Eleanor sighed with relief. At last. But with a great effort she kept quiet and allowed Frank to do the talking. He put forward the idea calmly, quietly and with skill. He made it sound the most sensible thing in the world.

'And although we would delight to have the child as our own, to give him our name and to bring him up as our son, we would not press this on you,' he concluded. 'We are willing, if you will agree, to take him for a year — two years if you wish — and simply look after him for you. He will

195

be your child during that time. You will be a welcome visitor whenever you wish. But later on, for Peter's own sake, a more permanent decision should be made. When it reaches the age of understanding, every child must know where it belongs.'

'Peter?' Dick said.

'The name the vicar chose,' Eleanor told him.

'We shan't ask you to decide here and now,' Frank said. 'That wouldn't be fair. But we have to leave Felldale tomorrow afternoon. If you do agree, then there will be arrangements to be made.'

'I would look after the child as if he were my own. I make a solemn promise,' Eleanor declared. 'For your sake, for Jane's sake, most of all for the baby's sake.'

'Think about it,' Frank said. 'If we may we'll call again this evening. If you haven't decided by then we can call tomorrow morning.'

Dick stood up, walked to the window, turning his back on them, staring out at his land. But instead of the land he saw Jane's face, pale, pleading. To his heightened imagination it seemed to him that there was no condemnation in her face, no blame, but that she was pleading for her baby; that she would not rest, and he would not rest, until he had fulfilled that responsibility. He turned back into the room.

'I don't need time to think,' he said. 'You can take the baby whenever you think the time seems suitable.'

'We can keep him?' Eleanor asked eagerly.

'No!' Frank's voice was sharp. 'We shall not do that. We shall have him in our care for two years, and after that Dick will decide.'

'There is just one thing,' Dick said. 'Against my own feelings, I've decided I shall go to see him before you take him away.'

'That's a wise decision,' Frank told him. 'You'll sleep more easily in the future because of it. Eleanor and I are going to Mrs Laycock's now. Shall you come with us or would you prefer to go alone?'

196

'I would be glad of your support,' Dick said.

The same pandemonium reigned in Mrs Laycock's house as on Eleanor's previous visit, the same smell pervaded the room. Perhaps the inhabitants had ceased to notice it. Mrs Laycock looked on, mystified, while the unexpected visitors stood around the cradle, though she was pleased to see that the child's father had put in an appearance – none too soon either. The baby lay on his back, his fists waving, making patterns in the air.

'Put your finger against his hand,' Eleanor whispered to Dick.

He did so, and the baby took it in his grasp, as he had done Eleanor's. As his son clung to him, looked at him from deep blue eyes, Dick felt the first faint stirrings of – not yet love, perhaps, but responsibility, an acknowledgement that the child was his. Well, if he cared about the baby, and of that he was not yet sure, he could do no better for him than let him go to the two people standing here beside him. They would look after him well, and that would be a small step in his atonement to Jane.

'Peter,' he said, then disengaged his finger and turned away.

It was more than a month before the arrangements were completed and Eleanor and Frank went to Felldale to collect the baby. Everything in Akersfield had been ready for some time. A small room had been furnished as a nursery, a cot installed, a baby bath bought, every drawer in the new white-painted chest filled with baby clothes, and the baby carriage which Ben had made so long ago was brought out of the attic, as strong and sturdy as ever, and refurbished. It was weaning the child which took time. He was slow in taking to the substitute milk and failed to gain weight. When Eleanor first held him in her arms she was shocked at the lightness of him. His arms and legs were like sticks.

'But he's taking the bottle now,' Mrs Laycock said. 'You'll have no more trouble with him!'

When they went down to see Dick at the garden he was

no longer there. Instead a young man was hoeing while a young woman pegged clothes out on a line across the orchard.

'Nay, he went three weeks ago!' the man said. 'Me and my wife have taken over.'

'Why ever didn't he tell us?' Eleanor asked Frank as they walked back. 'Why didn't he let us know?'

'It doesn't matter,' Frank said. 'Hebghyll's not a big place. We can find him if we need to. And he knows where we are. Perhaps he'll find his place in the world more quickly if he's left alone.'

It was a fine September Sunday evening when they arrived back in Akersfield with the baby. Mrs Foster and the three girls, hearing the car, dashed out of the house to greet them. Mrs Foster took the baby gently in her arms and held him to her breast.

'The little lamb,' she said softly. 'The poor little lamb! Come on then, my pretty one. Grandma will give you a nice bottle!'

CHAPTER TWELVE

Eleanor stood on the platform of the tram as it slowed down towards Ashfield Road, wondering if she could jump off before it actually stopped. A year ago she would have done so without thinking. It was not ladylike, not done at all, but that small leap was enjoyable and adventurous. Now she decided, it would be quite dangerous. She might well find herself rolling in the road. Skirts, though they were shorter, reaching only to the instep instead of to the ground, had become so narrow that it was a matter of some difficulty to stride at all. She was not so stupid, or quite fashionable enough, to wear the new hobble fetter, which would fasten around her legs just below the knee and prevent her entirely from lengthening her stride, but she did follow fashion enough to have a strong, confining band of material stitched around her tubular skirt just below the knee, and another at the ankles. So she waited until the tram came to a full stop before climbing down. Then she walked with quick short steps, up Ashfield Road towards home.

She usually hurried home these days, the reason being, though it wasn't one she admitted, even to herself, that she was always anxious to see Baby Peter. Well, eager rather than anxious. He was a child who never caused a moment's anxiety, except perhaps that of growing too fond of him, loving him too much. And really she should stop thinking of him as Baby Peter. He would be two years old next month and had been walking and talking for almost a year.

But today she had another reason for hurrying. They were to give a musical evening in their own home. Not many people – a neighbour or two and a few of the friends she and Frank had made by going to the concerts in Akersfield town hall. Nothing elaborate, either, though she wanted everything to be just right. She wasn't used to entertaining – she and Frank were usually too busy – and she was a little nervous.

She went into the house and called out a greeting, which brought Mrs Foster to the hall, her finger to her lips.

'Hush! The little fellow's having his nap!'

'I'll go up and see him,' Eleanor said.

'Don't do that,' Mrs Foster advised. 'He's only just gone off. Come into the kitchen. I've made a cup of tea. Why isn't Frank with you?'

'A commercial traveller came just as he was getting ready to leave,' Eleanor said. 'He needed to see him or he wouldn't have stayed behind on a Wednesday. He won't be long.'

She followed her mother into the kitchen. When they'd first brought the baby from Felldale she herself had stayed at home with him for several weeks, only paying evening visits to the cafe when he was tucked up in his cot. But business had continued to boom, and she was needed there. Frank would have engaged someone in her place in the cafe but she didn't want that. And to be truthful, dearly though she loved Peter she missed the stimulation of work. Also, her mother enjoyed caring for the baby above everything else. There was quite a rivalry between them as to who should serve him.

In the end Frank had intervened.

'If you really want to come back to work, my love, then you may. I admit you are missed there. So come as much or as little as you wish, but only on one condition. We must have extra help in the house. I insist on that for your mother's sake also.'

So now, in addition to Mrs Pollack three days a week, they had Brenda. Brenda did everything that was required of her from morning until night, was paid fifteen shillings a month, all found, and slept in the back attic. It was a good position. Food was plentiful and Mrs Kramer didn't expect her to provide her own uniform out of the fifteen shillings. Also, Mrs Foster was kind and considerate. This was because (though it would not do for Brenda to know it) she had once been a servant herself and knew what it was like.

'We should have asked Brenda to change her afternoon off,' Eleanor said as she sipped her tea. 'In view of all there is to do.' It still surprised her sometimes that she actually employed a servant. Who would have thought of it only a few years ago?

'No need,' Mrs Foster replied. 'She's not taking more than a couple of hours, and it's given me a bit of space to myself in the kitchen to prepare a few things.'

'What about your afternoon rest?'

'I don't need the rest. It's just an excuse to read,' Mrs Foster said.

After the children, reading was her greatest pleasure. Not only did she read the newspapers, she had joined the public library and now devoured whole books, mainly novels. It had been an eye-opener to her to discover all those books in the library; more than a person could read in a lifetime.

'In any case, I don't much like what I'm reading now. *Ann Veronica*, by that clever Mr Wells. The librarian gave me a funny look when I asked for it! "Not quite nice," he said. Well, he's right, and I've kept it well hidden from that young minx Becky. I shall take it back tomorrow.'

The author she really liked was Marie Corelli. She had read *Barabbas* twice, and cried buckets over it – she, who never cried in real life!

Eleanor put her cup down.

'I think I *will* just go and take a look at Peter.'

Eleanor was far too fond of the child, Mrs Foster thought. Well, they all were, bless his little heart. Who could help it, with his taking ways? But with Eleanor, it seemed to go deeper. She didn't care to think why. And it would be Eleanor who would suffer most if the child's father took him away, as he was well within his rights to do. She sighed, and began to prepare the girls' tea. They'd be in from school before long.

In the nursery, Eleanor stood beside Peter's cot and gazed down at him, steeling herself not to waken him for the sheer delight of seeing his face break into a smile at the sight of her – which was his usual greeting. He lay on his back, his arms wide, his small hands gently curled. In the warmth of the June afternoon he had kicked his bedclothes away so that his chubby legs were bare. His dark curly hair, so like his father's, was damp with the heat. Fine, dark eyebrows – well marked for one so young – were crescents above his closed eyes and long silky lashes lay against his cheeks. He was so beautiful, and she knew that when he wakened he would look at her with eyes which were heart-stopping in their likeness to his father's.

She wished he did not look so like Dick. It would be easier if he favoured his mother, but there was nothing of Jane in him. Since the day they had brought him back to Akersfield she had kept the promise she had made to herself, had tried with all her might to be a good loving wife to Frank, and to put Dick Fletcher out of her mind. She had accomplished the first – it was not difficult to love Frank – but the second was less easy, especially with this small replica of Dick always in front of her. But she had promised, and would keep her promise, no matter how often she fell, and had to pick herself up again.

They had not set eyes on Dick since he had gone with them to see his baby, for the first and last time. On Peter's first birthday a parcel had arrived, postmarked Hebghyll, containing a woolly rabbit for him and a packet of seeds and a short note for herself and Frank.

'I hope all goes well (he wrote). Business is thriving and I keep busy. Will come and see you one day. Plant the seeds in autumn and they'll flower next summer.'

There was no address. More than once she had wanted them to get into the motor car and go to Hebghyll to find him, but Frank had disagreed.

'It's better for him – and for us – that we leave him alone for the present. He says he'll come one day, and I'm sure he will when the two years are up. I trust him.'

202

As Peter's second birthday drew near, she could never decide whether she wanted Dick to come or not. However hard she tried she couldn't help but long to see him, but what if he wanted to take Peter away? Could she bear it? And who, most of all his own father, setting eyes on the child, so lovely, so winning in his ways, would *not* want to snatch him up and take him away? While looking down at Peter, thinking these thoughts, she heard the front door, and then Frank's step as he ran up the stairs. He was like herself in that the moment he came into the house he wanted to see Peter.

As he bounced into the room she put up her hand to silence him. He came and stood quietly by her at the side of the cot. As they watched, the child stretched his limbs and then opened his eyes. He focused on their familiar faces, these faces which spelt warmth and security to him.

'Mama! Papa!'

He put out his arms and Eleanor lifted him and held him against her. He was so warm and cuddly, fresh from sleep. She felt the tears sting her eyes as she laid her cheek against his hair. 'Oh Frank!' she exclaimed. 'What are we going to do? It's almost two years. What if we have to part with him? Frank, we should have taken him for good, right from the beginning.'

'No we should not,' Frank said gently. 'We both know that would have been wrong. We've known all along that he doesn't belong to us, not yet.'

'And perhaps never will.' The tears were running down her cheeks now and the child looked at her, perplexed. His mouth turned down at the corners and his lower lip began to tremble.

'And perhaps never will,' she repeated.

'We don't know that, but it's a possibility we have to face,' Frank said. No-one could know what the thought did to him. Deep down inside him he felt as though the child was flesh of his flesh. It was the nearest he would ever come to being a father, but surely even a father couldn't love his child more?

'I should never have let him call me "Mama",' Eleanor said. 'Nor you "Papa".' But it was something neither of them had been able to resist.

Frank put his arm around Eleanor and the child.

'Cheer up!' he said. 'See, you're going to make Peter cry!'

As they walked down the stairs, Jenny came in at the front door. Peter gave a cry of delight and almost leapt out of Eleanor's arms at the sight of her. When Eleanor put him down at the bottom of the stairs he ran to Jenny, flinging his arms around her legs, calling her name. Of all the dear, familiar people who surrounded him, his action said, she was the best. Eleanor felt a small stab of jealousy, which she immediately stifled.

'Do you have any homework?' she asked, after greeting her daughter. 'If so, you could do it before tea, while you're waiting for the others.' Jenny still went to the same small school, but Selina was at the grammar school now, with Becky.

'I don't have any,' Jenny said. 'May I take Peter out in the pram?'

Eleanor shook her head doubtfully. 'You're too small. It's a big pram,' she said.

'I'm ten years old,' Jenny protested. 'I can manage the pram quite well. I promise to keep just to Ashfield Road and Warley Villas. I won't go near the main road.'

'Why not wait until the others come?' Frank suggested. 'Then you can all go.'

'It's always the same,' Jenny grumbled. 'I always have to wait for the others. Why can't I ever do anything on my own? Becky won't want to go anyway.'

'True!' Eleanor agreed. Becky was fond enough of Peter, and would often play with him or help to bath him, but she drew the line at pushing his pram in public. 'But Selina might,' Eleanor added.

Jenny asked Selina the minute she and Becky came in from school.

'Yes, all right,' Selina agreed. Selina would do anything for anyone. She loved the whole world, and most of all her own dear family.

204

'You can count me out,' Becky said. 'As we're having guests this evening I simply do *not* have the time.'

'But they won't be here for another three hours!' Selina pointed out.

Becky gave her a withering look. 'Some of us will have more than a lick and a promise,' she said. 'Some of us actually *care* how we look.'

'Some of us care a sight too much,' Mrs Foster put in. 'Anyway, you'll all have your tea afore you do anything or go anywhere. I want to get cleared away.'

'Mother, please, *please* may I put my hair up?' Becky entreated. 'Just for this evening?'

'You may not,' Eleanor said. 'And you know it.'

'Why not?' Becky persisted. 'I'm fifteen now.'

'Precisely because you *are* fifteen, and therefore too young. As I've told you a hundred times, you can put up your hair when you're sixteen and not a minute sooner.'

'I do think when we have guests . . . I feel so childish with my hair down my back.'

'You *are* a child,' Eleanor said. 'And you show it in your behaviour. Count yourself very lucky that you're to be allowed to stay up for the first part of the evening.'

'Me and Selina aren't,' Jenny said. 'It's not a bit fair. Just because you play the piano best.'

'May we sit on the top step and listen?' Selina asked.

Eleanor smiled. Selina was so open. 'Only if I don't catch you at it,' she said.

While Selina and Jenny ate heartily of the tea their grandmother put out for them, Becky picked and pecked. Some of the girls at school were horribly plump and spotty and she lived in dread that it might happen to her. In vain her mother assured her that it never would. She was not built that way. She was tall, already almost as tall as Eleanor, and she had grown so fast that there was no question of her putting on a spare ounce. She was pretty, too – very pretty. It was a pity, Eleanor thought, that she was so aware of it.

'How can she not be?' Frank had said once, when Eleanor mentioned it. 'She sees what faces her in the mirror. Before

205

we know where we are she will be a beautiful young woman. But don't worry,' he'd added. 'None of your daughters will be lovelier than you!'

That thought had not been in Eleanor's mind. She was simply a little dismayed that they were growing up so quickly, and in Becky's case, growing beyond her understanding. She had never been an easy child, but now there seemed to be this great distance between them. They had no meeting place.

When Becky had gone upstairs and Selina and Jenny had taken Peter out in the perambulaor, Eleanor said, 'Am I too harsh with Becky, Ma?'

'She needs a firm hand,' Mrs Foster replied. 'But if you draw a thread too tight, it snaps. She reminds me for all the world of you.'

'Me?' Eleanor was astonished.

'You were always wilful, wanted everything your way. I wasn't firm enough.' If I had been, she thought, you wouldn't have gone off and married that Ben Heaton. You'd have been there when Dick Fletcher asked for you. But would Dick Fletcher have been a better husband than Frank? She was quite sure he wouldn't, but that didn't stop the expression she sometimes saw on her daughter's face, in her eyes, when she thought no-one was looking. There were times when Mrs Foster blamed herself bitterly for not having been a different kind of parent.

'But we're all amateurs,' she concluded. 'We think we know best and children don't know anything, but that's not always true.'

The guests arrived promptly at seven o'clock, carrying their music. Evening entertainments started early in Akersfield and there was nothing polite about arriving a little late. It only inconvenienced everyone. So they more or less congregated together on the doorstep. Mr and Mrs Henry Marks and Mr Austen Bulmer, acquaintances Frank and Eleanor had made at the town hall concerts; Mr and Mrs Arthur Layton – he was on a charity committee with Frank – and their son Roland. Roland, who was seventeen, was

206

there totally against his will. He clutched his violin case nervously and hoped he wouldn't be asked to perform. Miss Hermione Green and Mrs Hannah Clifton, the latter a widow, who kept house together at thirteen, Ashfield Road, and Frank and Eleanor, Mrs Foster and Becky, made up the round dozen. It was just the right number to fit comfortably into the drawing-room, and to offer all those who wished to do so a chance to perform, and enough listeners to give a nice round of applause.

Eleanor took the ladies up to the bedroom. Having travelled, Mrs Marks and Mrs Layton, as much as two miles in cabs, and Miss Green and Mrs Clifton all of a couple of hundred yards up the road, it was natural that they should want to titivate their hair, adjust their dresses – and in Miss Green's case wickedly, and in front of everyone, dab at her face with a sheet of *papier poudre*. Hair, thank goodness, was less elaborately dressed than a few years ago, not so many curls; but it was necessary to have as much width as possible, which meant inserting pads in the right places and drawing the hair skilfully over them. It was the security of these pads which now occupied the ladies' attention. How awful if a toss of the head in a passionate rendering of a piece of music should cause one to fall to the ground!

When all the guests were safely gathered in the drawing-room, Mrs Foster came in with Becky. Mrs Foster wasn't used to such affairs. She would have been happier to absent herself, go to her room and read, but Frank and Eleanor had been adamant.

'Put on your best dress and join us. It will do you good,' Eleanor said. 'You need do nothing more than sit and listen. You know you like listening to music.'

Frank's face lit up at the sight of Becky coming into the room. She had prevailed on her mother to lend her a narrow skirt, in place of her schoolgirlish flared one. It was of deep blue fine linen, and with it she wore a blouse of cream silk which, though full, clung a little to her high, rounded breasts. Her hair, gleaming like gold in the evening sunlight which streamed in through the big window, was caught in

207

a large black bow at the nape of her neck, from which it fell to below her waist in a shining cascade. Her skin glowed with youth and health, her eyes sparkled. Frank and Eleanor smiled at each other in pleasure at the sight of her, and Frank brought her forward to introduce her to the guests.

To Roland Layton, seeing her standing there in the doorway, she was a vision beyond his imagining. He thanked heaven that his parents had made him come.

'Good evening, Miss Kramer,' he said, shaking her hand. 'How very nice to meet you!' His hand trembled; hers was cool and firm. Her smile turned his insides to water; and seeing the effect she had on him she mischievously let her hand lie in his for a fraction of a second too long before she moved away.

'There you are!' Mrs Layton said when Roland rejoined her. 'Didn't I tell you it would be all right?'

They got down to business almost immediately. In Akersfield a musical evening was just what it said it was. No chit-chat until the refreshment interval. Mr Marks, a powerful bass, started off with 'Rocked in the Cradle of the Deep', with 'Sailors Beware' as an encore. As he descended, struggling, to the final low notes, Becky caught Roland's eye and bit her lip in an effort not to giggle. Mr and Mrs Layton then lightened the proceedings with a merry duet from Gilbert and Sullivan. Miss Hermione Green protested that she neither played nor sang.

'I suppose I must confess to being here on false pretences,' she chirped. 'I think Mrs Kramer invited me to make sure that my friend Mrs Clifton would come. *She* is a simply splendid singer and will more than make up for little me!'

Mrs Clifton obliged, though protesting heartily, and would have obliged further except that, as the applause died away, Roland Layton spoke up.

'What about Miss Kramer? With what is she going to delight us?'

'I thought Chopin,' Becky replied. There was no point in mock modesty. She'd been practising it all day.

'Marvellous!' Roland enthused. 'My favourite composer!

Perhaps you will allow me to turn the pages?'

'Why certainly,' Becky agreed.

She played a nocturne and an *étude* – her long, mobile fingers moving over the keyboard like butterflies, her shoulders swaying to the music. As she played, a lock of hair escaped, falling over her face. Roland longed to touch the errant lock, to stroke it back into place. She was a corker this one, and no mistake!

'And now for some refreshments,' Eleanor said. 'Becky, you can give Brenda a hand.'

'Oh do let me help too,' Roland offered.

'You're very kind,' Becky said, smiling. How nice to have someone so attentive!

'When you've had something to eat,' Eleanor said quietly to Becky, 'it's time for you to retire.'

'Oh Mother, how *can* you?' Becky protested. Why did her mother have to say such a thing in front of Roland Layton, making her out to be no more than a child?

'A little longer, *please* Mrs Kramer,' Roland begged. 'Actually I did wonder . . .'

'Yes?' Becky's voice was eager.

'I wondered if you and I might play a duet? If you would be so kind. If I am good enough. I brought my violin, as I expect you saw.'

Frank had joined them.

'Why not?' he said. 'I'm sure we'd all enjoy that. Becky, my love, why not try the Schubert if Roland can manage it?'

'I'll show it to you,' Becky offered. They moved away to the music cabinet at the other side of the room.

'I say, your father's a capital fellow!' Roland said. 'Your mother too, of course – I mean lady, that is.'

'I adore my father,' Becky admitted. 'And my mother is really quite clever.'

'I suppose any male creature would have to compete with your father, then?'

'Oh, absolutely!'

But he was encouraged by the look she gave him. He thought he might at least be allowed to try. They bent their heads together as they pored over the music. The scent of her mother's lavender water, which Becky had used lavishly, gave Roland the greatest pleasure as it assailed his nostrils.

In the rest of the room the talk was all of the Coronation, due to take place in a week or two. Even Mrs Foster found something to say.

'Just fancy, all those years without a coronation, and now two in nine years. What a pity King Teddy couldn't have lived a bit longer to enjoy himself!'

'I'm afraid His late Majesty dug his grave with his teeth,' Mrs Clifton said gravely, biting into a cream puff.

'But the new king is a good man,' Mr Marks said. 'We must all stand by him.'

'He's a sailor king,' Mr Layton observed. 'He'll be glad that Lloyd George is building up the navy, even though it *is* costing a mint of money.'

'We need a strong navy,' Mr Marks said. 'A bulwark against our enemies.'

'I'm sure we don't have an enemy in the world!' Miss Green trilled. 'But that's you men all over. Always talking about armies and navies, wars and enemies!'

'Don't you worry your pretty head about it, my dear,' Mr Marks said, smiling.

'Shall you be going to the Coronation Ball at the town hall?' Roland asked Becky as they joined the others.

'I don't know. I'd like to, but it depends on my parents.'

'I hope you do,' Roland said. 'I shall claim several dances,' he added quietly.

Becky smiled at him. He was really quite nice – but who knew who else she might meet at the Coronation Ball? Oh, she would just *die* if she wasn't allowed to go!

After the refreshments were cleared, Roland and Becky performed their duet. She was agreeably surprised by how well he played the fiddle. But the crowning point of the evening was Eleanor's own singing, though it had never been her intention to perform. She did so at the request of the company, and of her husband.

'I'll sing Kathleen Mavourneen,' she told them.

Eleanor's voice rang out sweet, true, powerful – filling the room with beautiful sound. Her voice had, if anything, improved with maturity. She sang naturally, without affectation, and from her heart.

'Oh hast thou forgotten how soon we must sever?
Oh hast thou forgotten how soon we must part?
It may be for years and it may be forever,
Oh why art thou silent, the voice of my heart?'

When the last note died away there was a moment of complete silence before the applause broke out. Frank turned around from the piano, his eyes shining with love as he looked at his wife. He took her hand in his and kissed her fingers.

'Thank you, my dear one,' he said.

It was after half-past ten when Becky was packed off to bed.

'I'm not the least bit sleepy,' she protested to her grandmother who accompanied her upstairs. 'Really, Grandma, it shows what a dull life I do lead when a musical evening with a lot of old fogies counts as excitement!'

'Not so much of your old fogies!' Mrs Foster reprimanded. 'And what about Roland Layton? He was all right, wasn't he?'

'Yes,' Becky conceded. 'But Mr Marks must be almost forty, and Mrs Clifton has a voice like a mill buzzer. If a buzzer broke down they could employ Mrs Clifton to get people to work.'

'You're too critical, miss!' Mrs Foster tried not to smile. 'I suppose you'll allow your mother sang well?'

'Why yes, she did.'

She looked nice too. In a way, she supposed, she was rather proud of her mother; except that she doesn't understand me in the least, she thought. She has no idea what it's like to be me, to be young. Eleanor was thirty-two; she probably couldn't remember. But sometimes Grandma could – and her father understood best of all. She never remembered now that he wasn't her real father.

When her grandmother had left the room Becky surveyed

herself in the mirror; then she drew up her hair and fastened it on the top of her head, turning this way and that to get the view from all angles. Yes, it suited her, showed off her long slender neck, made her look at least eighteen. She let it down again and began the one hundred brush strokes which she must give her hair each night.

Oh well, not long to go now. Another year, and not only would she be able to put her hair up, she would leave school. She longed for the time to pass, to be out in the world. Her parents fondly imagined she was going to stay at home then, help her grandmother in the house, intensify her music studies. Well, they had a shock coming to them. She had her own plans.

Eleanor and Frank, getting ready for bed, talked over the evening and were pleased with it.

'It went well,' Frank said. 'And I thought Becky conducted herself nicely. She seemed to enjoy it.'

'In part,' Eleanor replied dryly.

She had seen the expression on Becky's face as she listened to the guests. But she said nothing to Frank. He loved all the girls, but Becky was his blue-eyed one.

'Shall we close the cafe for the Coronation?' she asked. 'There are no bookings for the rooms that night. Everyone seems to be otherwise engaged.'

'And so shall we be,' Frank said. 'Nothing will prevent me taking you to the Coronation Ball! It will be out own special celebration. Much grander than the last one – but no sweeter!' He bent over her where she sat at the dressing-table and smiled at her reflection in the mirror. 'How lovely you were then, in your black dress, and the hat you had trimmed with paper flowers from the cafe.'

And how her life had changed in King Edward's short reign, Eleanor thought, plaiting her hair. At the point where he became king she had been down and out, no food in the house, no money in her purse, her husband dead, no future. And now look at all she had! She was the most fortunate woman in the world – and if she was not the happiest it could only be her own fault.

'Let's take Becky to the ball!' Frank suggested.

'But she's too young!'

'She will pass easily for seventeen,' Frank said. 'And it would be a night she would never forget. Let's take her!'

It was exactly as Frank had predicted. A night, Becky thought, as she was waltzed around the floor in the arms of Roland Layton, she would remember when she was an old, old lady. Everything about it was wonderful, from her very first evening gown of white tulle (though she had lost the argument with her mother about how low-cut the neckline might be), to the splendour of the town hall, lavishly decorated with every floral display that the Akersfield Parks Department could provide. Roland looked very handsome in his white tie and tails and she had to admit that he was a good dancer. All the same, she had not allowed him to fill in too many dances on her card. Her father had claimed two and she kept several blank in the hope that some of the attractive young men she saw all around her would request the pleasure. She was not disappointed.

'I'd like to fill in my name against every dance,' Roland said, taking the card from her.

She snatched it back, but with a smile.

'You can't do that! Whatever would people say?'

'That I'm keen on you,' he sighed. 'Which would be true. But you seem to have a dozen on a string!'

'Nonsense!' Becky protested.

'Well, at least I must have the supper dance and the last waltz.'

'Very well,' Becky said prettily. Then she looked up with a welcoming smile as she saw her next partner approaching. Oh, she was having a wonderful time!'

'Our daughter is enjoying herself,' Frank remarked, watching her.

'She certainly is,' Eleanor agreed. 'I hope it doesn't put ideas into her head. She's still a schoolgirl, remember.'

'But for now she's a princess,' Frank said. 'And you

213

are my queen. Come along, let's you and I dance again!'

Dick Fletcher sat in the train between Hebghyll and
Akersfield. It was another hot day and the compartment
was stifling, the more so because the lady opposite had
requested that the window be closed against the smuts
blowing in from the engine.

Being a Sunday, the train stopped at every station on the
line. He was impatient to reach Akersfield, yet he was
apprehensive. He had sent a card to say he was coming,
but had revealed nothing of his purpose. Now he looked
out of the window at the green, hilly landscape and gave
himself up to his thoughts.

He had made a good move when he went from Felldale
to Hebghyll. The land was more fertile and his stretch
of it flatter. True, it was close to the river, but there
had been no floods along that part in living memory. He
had had to work hard in the first year: from dawn until dusk
every day, and sometimes after dark by the light of a
hurricane lamp. Hard work, and its consequent fatigue,
leaving him no time to brood or think, had been his
salvation.

He had set aside a portion of his land for the new seed
beds, and as time went on he would take more, until his
whole business was in seeds. But seeds took time. The
money would come, not quickly, but once it started it would
snowball. He had faith in himself, and this faith he had
transmitted to his bank manager, who had lent him the
money to invest in one of the new motor lorries and to hire
an assistant so that he could work more markets. His
assistant couldn't understand why Dick had ruled out
Akersfield market.

'It's one of the best around,' he protested.

'I don't want Akersfield, and that's a fact,' Dick stated.

'Well I don't understand – but you're the boss,' the
man said.

How could you, Dick thought. How could you understand that the only woman I've ever loved is there. He knew

214

that if ever he set foot in Akersfield again he wouldn't be able to keep away from her. And there was his son. The pain which had surrounded Jane's death had healed in the last two years, but the guilt of his son never left him. That was what he now had to repair. That was why he was going to Akersfield now.

'Shipley!' the woman opposite observed. 'We'll soon be in Akersfield.'

She wondered if he lived there, if some lucky woman would be at the station to meet him. He was so handsome, and the look of sadness in his strong face, the set of his sensitive mouth, the dark, heavy-lidded eyes all added to his attraction.

'Will your wife be meeting you?' she ventured.

'I'm not married.'

It was because there was no woman in his house that his daughter Emily still lived – happily, it seemed – with her aunt in Skipton. He had never had the degree of guilt over his daughter that he had about his son. The memory of the only occasion when he had seen the boy, the moment when the frail baby had taken his finger in its grip, had never left him, never dimmed.

The train drew into Akersfield station, stopped with a tremendous hiss of escaping steam. He left the station and began to walk towards Ashfield Road.

At number seventeen there was a tension in the air. It was Peter's second birthday. There had been presents in the morning and now there was to be a special tea – the new season's strawberries, and a birthday cake with two candles. But only for Peter was the day filled with unqualified pleasure. Over everyone else hung the shadow of the little boy's future. The fact that none of them knew what it was to be made it almost more difficult to bear. They swung, each one of them, between periods of wild hope and of dark fear. The only thing certain was that Dick Fletcher was coming. They had had his card to say so.

'If only he had given a hint,' Eleanor said to Frank in

the privacy of their bedroom – in front of her mother and the children she tried to keep cheerful. 'I think if I knew the worst I would find it easier to bear!'

'I know, my dearest,' Frank agreed. 'Don't think that I feel any differently. But we have known all along that this day must come. If the worst happens, and we have both faced the fact that it might, then we must be thankful for the happiness Peter has given us over the last two years. Nothing can take that away.'

When he took her in his arms it was more than she could bear. She buried her face in his shoulder and sobbed without control. She was still crying when the doorbell rang.

'Dry your eyes,' Frank said. 'Be brave, my love.'

He went to answer the door, and she followed him downstairs. She wanted Peter to be in her arms when Dick set eyes on them. When Frank showed Dick into the drawing-room, where the whole family had congregated, grouped close together as if for comfort, he was met by five pairs of wary, apprehensive eyes. Only his son looked at him with fearless curiosity, the way he looked at all strangers. Secure in Eleanor's arms, everyone he knew around him, why should he be afraid?

Mrs Foster was the first to find her voice.

'You'll be wanting a cup of tea after your journey,' she told Dick. 'I'll go and make one.' She was glad of the excuse.

'Sit down. Make yourself at home,' Frank said. He had cautioned everyone beforehand to behave as naturally as possible, not to make their guest uncomfortable. 'He has a right to come,' he explained. Nevertheless, he found it as difficult as everyone else appeared to. 'Tell us the worst,' he longed to say. 'Get it over with!'

He was sure that Dick Fletcher would want to take his son. Why else would he come? And how could he resist him, seeing him there in Eleanor's arms? And if he did take him, Frank knew that something in him would die. He would try to be strong for Eleanor's sake, but he had allowed Peter to take the place of the child he had hoped for so much.

We pay for love with pain, he thought. And the pain would be great.

Peter wriggled in Eleanor's arms. He wanted to be free. She put him down on the floor and at once he walked across to Dick and stood looking up at him, smiling. Then he held out his arms to be picked up. Dick bent down and lifted the child in his arms. He was so light, so soft and warm, clinging as if they had known each other all their lives. A feeling he had never known before swept through him.

He looked at Eleanor, and from her to Frank.

'Can we talk?' he asked quietly.

'Children, go into the kitchen. Tell Grandma not to serve tea just yet,' Eleanor said at once.

'I think we *should* talk,' he said as soon as they had left the room. 'It will be easier for all of us to get it over.'

Dick was still holding Peter. Eleanor watched the two of them with anguished eyes, watched the picture they made, dark heads close together, faces so alike. If only, if only . . . She pushed the thought away from her. It could never happen now. Frank, who was the only innocent adult here, needed her. Without Peter he would need her more.

The silence seemed to go on forever, until it was broken by Dick.

'I have to tell you,' he began, 'that I came to say that I want to take my son. I'm about to engage a housekeeper, a young widow with a child of her own. She is more than willing to look after Peter, and to have Emily too . . .'

'Oh no! No!' Eleanor cried out, swayed; would have fallen had not Frank at once supported her.

Dick shook his head. 'That is what I came to say. I am no longer saying it. I've seen Peter with you – with all of you. He belongs here. I don't know much about children but I guess it's because he's secure with you, knows you will always be there, that he can let me, a stranger, hold him like this. I could never take him away from you – not just for your sake, but for his.'

Eleanor made no attempt to hide her tears now, and there were tears in Frank's eyes too.

217

'If you'll excuse me, I won't stay for tea,' Dick said. 'I'll leave now. I'm sure you understand.'

'You must visit often,' Frank told him. 'You will be Peter's most welcome uncle!'

Dick shook his head. 'Thank you, but I think not. And I'll be in touch with you about the legal arrangements.'

He handed the child to Eleanor. For one brief moment as their eyes met Eleanor knew that he was thinking what she had thought a few moments ago. Then he looked away, went to shake hands with Frank.

'I'm off then,' he said.

His last sight, as, having left the house he turned back to look again, was of Eleanor holding his son in her arms.

CHAPTER THIRTEEN

It had been such splendid weather, this summer of 1914, Eleanor thought. She was glad she had persuaded Frank that it would be reasonable to close the cafe for Akersfield Feast week and bring the children to the seaside for a holiday. 'Most places here will shut down,' she'd pointed out. 'Akersfield will be dead as a doornail.' Anyone who could scrape up the money would make for the sea, and those who couldn't would be off to Shipley Glen or Baildon Moor for the day. 'So we'll miss nothing in the way of trade,' she said.

Besides, they were now so well-established – you might say they were Akersfield's premier cafe and assembly rooms – that there wasn't the slightest doubt their customers would quickly come back to them.

'Peter, put your hat on again,' she called out. 'The sun's hot. We don't want you getting sunstroke, do we?'

It was unlikely, given his thick dark curly hair – but then she was more careful with Peter than she had ever been with the girls. Sometimes she still felt, as she had in the first two years of his life, that he was on loan to them, that at any minute cruel fate might snatch him away. It was a ridiculous notion really. And no scene could look more permanent, more settled, than the one in front of her at this moment: Peter building his sandcastle with Frank industriously digging the moat around the perimeter, both totally absorbed in their tasks.

At the water's edge Selina and Jenny, their skirts pinned up around their waists, their long bloomers showing, paddled in the sea. Selina held Jenny's hand as they jumped

219

the incoming waves, the pair of them shrieking with delight whenever the tide caught them unawares. Though there were only two years between them, and at thirteen Jenny didn't need it, Selina was always protective of her younger sister. But Selina was protective of everyone; she was a kind and thoughtful person.

'The tide's coming in fast now!' Eleanor shouted. 'We'll have to move back soon. Anyway, it's almost dinnertime. Does anyone know where Becky is?'

She sighed. Becky was a law unto herself. And at eighteen there wasn't much anyone could do about it. She had no interest in being with the younger ones, except that sometimes she would decide to amuse Peter.

'She said she would take a walk on the pier,' Frank reminded his wife. 'But don't worry, she'll turn up at the lodgings for dinner. She's not one to miss her food!' All the same, he was not totally happy that his attractive stepdaughter should be walking around Sandcombe on her own. But one had to trust one's children.

On the pier was exactly where Becky was, walking sedately, her parasol – parasols were so fashionable this summer – held at an angle which would keep the sun from spoiling her complexion and at the same time not hide her pretty face. Who knew whether or not Max Anderton himself might, just by chance, pass by? Since he appeared in the twice-nightly show in the pavilion at the end of the pier (matinees Tuesday, Thursday and Saturday) he must sometimes walk this way. Perhaps he might even recognize her? He might have noticed her, every night for the last five nights sitting in the second row of the stalls? She had spent almost all the money she had earned in paying for the seats. Not that she begrudged a penny of it. In fact, she was pretty sure he had seen her, that the words of some of his songs had been addressed directly to her.

She shuddered when she thought how nearly she had missed seeing him altogether. She hadn't wanted to come to Sandcombe. It wasn't smart. But her mother and father had been set on it. It was the nearest seaside resort to Akersfield, and they could drop Grandma off for her promised visit to Felldale and pick her up again on the way back.

Fate had been kind, however. On the very first evening, on the landlady's recommendation, her father had booked seats in the stalls for the first house of the 'Frolics'. And when Max Anderton had walked on to the stage, so tall, so suave, so elegant as he leaned against the piano, his evening dress immaculate, his blue-black hair plastered down and shining, she had recognized at once that he was the aristocrat of the show, a cut above all the others. There was nothing like him in Akersfield.

But alas, there was no sign of him amongst the holiday-makers who thronged the pier this morning, and it was high time she was back at the lodgings or she'd miss her dinner. She sighed again at the thought of *lodgings*. Why couldn't they have stayed in a proper hotel? But since they were paying for full board, not buying their food and taking it in for the landlady to cook, perhaps she could (if asked) describe it as a private hotel?

'Just in time!' Eleanor remarked as Becky slid into her seat. The fried haddock and parsley sauce was already on the table. 'Where have you been?'

'Just walking,' Becky said vaguely.

She was praying hard that she would be allowed to go free this evening, and that, above all, the rest of the family wouldn't decide to pay another visit to the 'Frolics'. She had to go alone. Tonight, as every Friday, was 'talent' night. She had spent the whole week screwing up her courage to step up there on to the stage and play the piano. It was not that she had any qualms about her ability. She knew she was good enough; she might even win. But if she went on to the stage she would be certain to meet *him*, since it was he who encouraged people from the audience, asked their names, introduced them. In the circumstances he couldn't fail to notice her. And who could say what might happen then?

221

'So what are we all going to do this afternoon?' Frank asked. 'We must make the most of it. We go home tomorrow.'

I can't bear it, Becky thought. I can't leave now! Could she perhaps find a job in Sandcombe, live away from home? For the last year she had worked, unwillingly, in her parents' business, so she wasn't without experience. But she doubted she'd be allowed. No young woman of her aquaintance left home before she was married. The despair she felt at her situation almost took away her appetite.

'The beach, the beach!' Peter shouted. 'I want to go on the beach!'

'The pleasure gardens!' Selina and Jenny cried simultaneously.

'Well, we can't go on the beach until the tide turns,' Eleanor said. 'So we could go to the pleasure gardens first. But what about you, Becky?'

'I think I shall go for a walk,' Becky replied. 'I'm too old for the beach and the pleasure gardens. Perhaps I shall walk on the pier.'

'Very well then,' Frank said doubtfully. 'But take care. Don't speak to strangers!'

'Oh Father, don't fuss!' Becky answered. 'In any case I shall be back early. I want to wash my hair.'

'But you washed it only two days ago,' Eleanor remonstrated.

'It's the salt in the air,' Becky said. 'It makes it sticky.' How could she explain that it was imperative that she should look her very best this evening?

So when the meal was over they all set off again.

'I must say, Becky is a strange girl,' Eleanor said, 'She never wants to do the same as the rest of us.'

'She's growing up, wanting to spread her wings.' Frank told her.

'When I was her age I was married and had a baby,' Eleanor said. She didn't altogether hold with early marriages, but perhaps it would be the best thing for Becky, settle her down. Roland Layton had proposed to her, she knew that from Mrs Layton, who was in favour of the match; but Becky had turned him down, and she had said nothing of the proposal to her family.

They enjoyed the pleasure gardens – swings, round-abouts, the water chute, and a glass of cool lemonade in the little cafe. Then it was time for the beach. The girls took Peter down to the water's edge to paddle while Frank and Eleanor sat side by side on the firm sand.

'This has been a wonderful summer,' Eleanor said. Though there was seldom a day when she didn't think of Dick Fletcher, her prayer that she would grow to love Frank more had been answered. Though she would never have the overwhelming passion for him of which she knew she was capable, she did truly love him. Thinking thus, she stretched out her hand and took her husband's. He smiled and drew closer to her. He never failed to respond, day or night.

'What a perfect day this is,' she sighed happily.

She felt Frank stiffen against her, as if her words had touched a nerve.

'What is it, Frank?'

'Don't you know, Eleanor? Don't you know what's going to happen?'

'I know you're on about war again,' she said after a pause. 'But I still believe it won't happen. Why would the murder of some foreign archduke bring us into a war?'

' It's not as simple as that, and you know it isn't, my love. I've explained it to you before but you go on believing what you want to believe. Wiser people than you and me have seen this war coming for a long time. And now Germany will line up with Austria, and Russia with Serbia, and the French have a treaty with Russia.'

'But none of that involves us,' Eleanor protested.

'If Germany marches through Belgium, as she surely will, then we have an old treaty to come to Belgium's aid. Though treaty or no treaty, honour wouldn't allow us to stand aside. You must see that.'

'Then thank God we have no son old enough to fight,'

223

Eleanor said. 'And let's not spoil this lovely afternoon by talking about it.'

'We must talk about it sometime, dearest. We can't ignore it, and you know why. I am not a fighting man, but if the war comes — when it comes — I shall fight. It will be agony for me to leave you all, but I must go.'

She pulled away from him, faced him with blazing eyes.

'You can't!' she cried. 'Why should you? You're too old!'

'I'm thirty-five, Frank said. 'Older men than I will fight. What sort of a man would I be if I refused to defend my wife and children, or to come to the aid of my country?'

It was what she had dreaded hearing. She knew that this was the very reason why she refused to discuss the possibility of war. She had never had any doubt that he would enlist, and at the first opportunity. And his motives would be of the highest. He had a deep love for England.

'But what about Germany?' she cried. 'It's your parents' country! How can you fight the Germans?'

'Do you think I haven't considered that?' he asked quietly. 'Do you think it will be easy for me?'

Peter was running towards them, bucket in hand, his face alight with pleasure.

'Father, look what I've got! I've found a starfish! Is it lucky to find a starfish?'

'Lucky for you, less lucky for the fish,' Frank answered. 'Let's have a look at it.' Heads together, they peered into the tin bucket. Frank felt the warmth of his son's body, smelled the childish cleanness of his skin and his hair. Dear God, how would he bear to leave him? He felt as though he was flesh of his flesh; he bore his name. He wanted to take him in his arms and never let him go.

'It's beautiful,' he said. 'Show it to your mother, and then you must take it back and put it near the water's edge. It won't be happy in your bucket.'

When Peter had run off again Frank smiled at Eleanor. 'We'll talk no more of war today. And as a special treat, and because it's our last night here, I'm going to book for the "Frolics" again. You wait here while I walk along to the booking office by the pier. I shan't be long.'

'Everyone will enjoy that,' Eleanor said. 'Especially Becky. She can't get enough of the show. I just hope it's not re-awakening her ideas of going on the stage. I thought we'd got over that.'

Frank had always hoped that Becky would be talented enough to train as a concert pianist, but he had faced the fact, and so had she, that though she was a good musician she was not quite gifted enough. Nor did she have the dedication. What she hankered after was musical comedy, or to be a member of a professional concert party. Both he and Eleanor were guiltily relieved that so far no opportunity had come her way.

They had done what they could to compensate. When, last year, he and Eleanor had acquired the premises next door and had thereby enlarged the cafe, he had installed a good piano. Three or four times a day, mercifully released from the clerical work of the business which Eleanor was trying to teach her reluctant daughter, Becky was allowed to play the piano to customers as they drank their tea and ate their toasted teacakes. She played popular pieces, light classical, musical comedy. She enjoyed it and it brought people in. But for how long would she stick to it, Frank asked himself as he walked along the promenade towards the pier. He hoped she would stay there, be near to her mother, when he had to go away.

It would be very soon now, his departure. He was sure of it. And though he didn't want to leave his family, yet a *frisson* of excitement ran through him when he thought about it. He had been happy in his steady, uneventful life, but now he experienced a certain tension, almost a feeling of welcome for what might come. There was something in the air in that summer of 1914.

He bought the tickets, glanced around in the hope that he might see Becky, but did not – so he went back to the beach.

When, at teatime, he told everyone about the tickets,

225

Becky was mortified, fuming! Why did she have to have her family always around her?

'Are you sure you want to go?' she ventured. 'I don't mind going on my own if there's something else you'd rather do.'

'Of course there isn't,' Eleanor replied, puzzled. It was not like Becky to be sacrificial.

'We're all looking forward to it,' Frank said. 'It's going to be a splendid night.'

But not for me, Becky thought. Nevertheless she refused to let the presence of her family spoil her plan. She was determined to take part in the talent contest. She would say nothing about it beforehand but when the moment came she would simply rise from her seat and go up to the stage.

The seats were good ones, only three rows back. But for the first half of the evening – the talent contest didn't take place until after the interval – Becky saw and heard very little of what went on. She felt sick with apprehension. It wasn't until Max Anderton came on to do his solo spot – he was always the last item before the interval – that she began to calm down a little. How could she not, once he began to sing?

'By special request,' he announced in his silky voice, 'I shall render that ever-popular favourite, "Come Ye Back to Sorrento".'

By whose special request, she wondered jealously. But it didn't matter. As the notes soared upwards she knew he was singing to her.

'Now I hear that thou must leave me
Thou and I will soon be parted.
Canst thou leave me broken-hearted?
Wilt thou nevermore return?

Oh I will, I will, she vowed silently.

Becky looks rather flushed, Eleanor thought. I hope she's not sickening for something.

After the interval the talent contest was announced.

'Don't be shy, ladies and gentleman, boys and girls.' Max Anderton persuaded the audience. 'Step forward and show us what you can do. Who knows what it may lead to?'

Becky had managed to take the seat nearest to the aisle so that she was up and away before her family knew what was happening. Though her legs trembled and her insides churned, she went forward bravely. When Max Anderton held out his hand to help her up the steps at the side of the stage she thought she would swoon.

'A brave little lady,' he smiled. 'And as beautiful as she's brave. Now who is going to keep her company?'

There was no lack of contestants now that she had made the first move. Max Anderton spoke to them in turn, then lined them up at the side of the stage. Seen closed to he was not . . . well, he was not *quite* as good-looking as he had seemed from the auditorium. Under his make-up his skin looked rather coarse, and he was a little bit baggy around the eyes. There was no denying, either, that he had a double chin and a bit of a stomach. In fact, Becky realised with a sharp stab of disappointment, he was as old as her father! But his manners were good. He introduced every contestant with courtesy and was the first to lead the applause when they had performed. Becky he left until last. Something told him she was out of the ordinary run, as well as being quite a looker.

'And what do you intend to play?' he enquired.

When he leant over to hear her reply his breath smelt strongly of spirits. But perhaps for medicinal purposes, she thought charitably.

'The Bees' Wedding, by Mendelssohn.'

'Ah! A touch of class!'

She performed well. She had lost all her nervousness, partly because, in a disappointing way, it no longer mattered. The applause when she had played the last note was sweet to her ears.

'You are a discerning audience,' Max Anderton announced. 'You yourselves have chosen the winner!'

She was applauded all the way back to her seat and her family beamed with pleasure as she joined them. Her parents seemed not the least bit annoyed.

'A delightful show,' Frank said as they walked back in the soft, warm darkness. 'You gave us a pleasant surprise for our last evening, Becky.'

'Thank you, Father.' But for Becky, winning the contest was not what the evening had been about. She felt deflated, and as though something had escaped her.

'It will be so sad to leave Sandcombe tomorrow,' Selina sighed. 'Can we come back again next year?'

'Certainly,' Frank said. There was no doubt in his mind that by next year the war would have been fought and won and everything would be back to normal.

Felldale, as they approached it next day in the summer sun, looked more beautiful than ever. Not much corn was grown hereabouts, but what there was already showed golden, almost ripe for an early harvest. Frank had a sudden vision of all England, all Europe, as a vast golden cornfield. He wondered if the harvest would be gathered before it was trampled down by armies.

Mrs Foster welcomed them warmly.

'I'm packed and ready,' she said eagerly.

She hasn't enjoyed herself, Eleanor thought. We should have persuaded her to come to Sandcombe.

'Is Flo on duty?' Becky asked. Her cousin was training to be a nurse, in Keighley.

'Yes. She'll be home tomorrow, her day off,' Clara said. 'She'll be sorry to have missed you.'

'And what about Jimmy?' Frank enquired. 'How is he faring?'

'Very well,' Clara replied. 'He's still on the *Lusitania* – England to America and back again. Very high-class passengers they get. If there's a war coming I'm thankful our Jimmy chose the Merchant Navy. He'll not be involved, not like his cousin David, in the army.'

On the way home Eleanor spoke suddenly to Frank.

'I want you to teach me to drive the motor car.'

He almost swerved in surprise at her words.

'*You* learn to drive the car? But my dear, women don't drive cars!'

'Since I shan't have a man to drive me,' she said tersely, 'this woman will! I'm trying hard to understand why you want to enlist, but if you do so, then I must keep life as normal as possible for the children. If we still have our jaunts in the motor car it will pass some of the time until you come home again.'

He was silent for a while. He wished he could make her understand that the thought of them being parted was as painful to him as it was to her. Then he said: 'You are quite right, my dear. I will give you your first lesson tomorrow; but you must promise me always to be very careful, exceedingly cautious, and make sure that you never travel faster than twenty miles an hour. Even at that speed the motor car is a lethal weapon.'

By Monday morning Akersfield was itself again. The roundabouts and sideshows had departed from the fairground; the mill buzzers sounded and the millhands hurried to obey them. Shoppers thronged the town centre and then dropped in at Kramer's for refreshments. Becky was back at the piano. When a customer requested that she should play 'Come Back to Sorrento' her eyes misted so that she could hardly see the sheet music. But only for a moment. She quite quickly recovered.

Between dinnertime and teatime, when there was always a lull in the cafe. Frank took Eleanor out for her second driving lesson.

'You are coming on remarkably well, my dear,' he said.

'Don't sound so surprised,' she chided. 'And since we're going to supper with the Laytons this evening, why not let me drive there? It's not far.'

They had struck up quite a friendship with the Laytons in the last year or two, not least because Roland had been in love with Becky since that first musical evening and he let no chance slip of bringing the two families together. He had also persuaded Becky to join the Akersfield Amateur Dramatic and Musical Society, so that he could see her even more often.

Becky was not averse to Roland. She just wished he would

229

occasionally do something exciting. He was persistent in asking her to marry him but, though she longed to escape the confines of home, she couldn't bring herself to accept.

When supper was over Mrs Layton said, 'Why don't you take Becky a turn around the garden, Roland, while it's still light?'

'There's something I've been meaning to say to you, Frank,' Mr Layton began when Roland and Becky had gone. 'I hope you won't take it amiss. It's meant in friendship.

'Then I shan't take it amiss,' Frank said. 'What is it?'

'I'll put it bluntly. There's a war coming any day now, we all know that. Kramer is a German name. It will tell against you; it will tell against you heavily.'

'But it *is* my name. I'm not ashamed of it, though I'm as English as you are. And most people in Akersfield know me. They know I'm a loyal subject of this country.'

'People are different in wartime,' Mr Layton persisted.

'So what do you expect me to do?' Frank was smiling. He could hardly take his friend seriously.

'Change it, of course! And the sooner the better! Change it to Crown. Why not?'

'Because that's not my name. My name is Kramer. It's an honourable name and I'm not ashamed of it.'

'Then if you won't do it for yourself, do it for the sake of your wife and children,' Mr Layton pleaded.

Frank turned to Eleanor. To join or not to join the army, to fight for England, had seemed a clear-cut decision compared to what he was being asked to do now. His eyes questioned her. She crossed from her seat and stood beside his chair, her hand on his shoulder.

'I am proud to be Mrs Frank Kramer,' she declared. 'I don't wish to be known by any other name and I would think the less of my husband if he were to disown his name and that of his parents.'

'Well, there you are,' Mr Layton said. 'I was trying to help. No offence meant.'

'And none taken,' Frank replied.

'So what about a hand of whist?' Mrs Layton suggested. In her opinion a good hand of whist could smooth away the most awkward situation. 'The young people seem to have disappeared. I expect they're up to their own pursuits.'

Roland and Becky were walking around the garden, which was so large that much of it was hidden from the house. In the falling daylight the scents of flowers and shrubs came strongly to Becky's nostrils, and the paler blooms, the tall white Japanese anemones, the white roses, were doubly accentuated against the green of leaves and stems which the coming of the night had turned almost to black.

'They're like lanterns,' she said. 'Like fancy-shaped lanterns in the dark. You could almost see your way by them. And perhaps we should see our way back into the house.'

'Not yet.' Roland stepped. 'There's something I want to say to you.'

'Oh Roland, it's all been said before!' Yet though she protested, she wasn't really averse to hearing it again.

'No it hasn't,' Roland contradicted. 'It's not what you think, Becky. At least not all of it. Stand still and listen to what I have to say.'

She did as she was told. It was so unlike Roland to be the least bit masterful.

'I'm joining the army,' he said. 'I'm going to sign up tomorrow. It'll be war for us any day now and I want to be in it from the beginning. I shall get a commission, I haven't the slightest doubt about that. I shall be in France in no time at all.'

'Oh Roland!'

'I wanted you to be the first to know. I haven't told my parents yet. But there is something else . . .'

'Yes?'

'Oh Becky, if you'd only be engaged to me! I wouldn't ask you to marry me until it was over and I came back . . . and if you'd changed your mind then, well . . . no hard feelings. But you know how much I love you, and to go to war feeling I had you to fight for . . . well, it would make all the difference.'

231

On and on he pleaded with her. It was almost too dark to see him in reality, but in her mind's eye she saw him – tall, undeniably handsome – in his officer's uniform. She saw herself waving him off, writing to him, watching the mail for his letters. As the fiancée of a serving officer – he would probably be a captain in no time at all – she would receive sympathy, commiseration, perhaps even envy. She would have standing. And it was not the final step that marriage would be. She had sense enough to know that she was not yet ready for marriage. That was all in the future. Her thoughts were vague at this point.

'I can't tell you how much it would mean to me,' Roland said.

Her duty was suddenly quite plain. Of course she must say yes. She must do it for *his* sake. And after all she did like him; she liked him very much indeed.

'Oh Roland, I will!' she murmured. 'I shall be honoured to be your fiancée!'

She was astonished by the ardour of his embrace, and by her own passion in returning it. The sky was black and the stars out before they finally broke away from each other and went into the house to announce the news.

CHAPTER FOURTEEN

Frank rose early, leaving the bed quietly so as not to waken Eleanor. It was a wasted effort, had he but known it; she had been lying awake for the last hour, and indeed for most of the night. Now she sat up in bed.

'No call to go creeping around,' she said. 'I'm wide awake. Pass me my dressing-gown and I'll get up and make you some breakfast.'

'I don't want any breakfast,' Frank told her. 'I'll make myself a cup of tea and bring you one. Then you must try to go back to sleep. It's not yet six o'clock.'

'As if I could!' Eleanor said sharply. 'How do you expect me to sleep, with you off to sign your life away?'

'It's not like that, my love. It might be a while before they send for me, and probably I'll be back home again in no time at all. But we've discussed all this, Eleanor. Some women are actually proud of their menfolk who enlist. I don't expect that, but I do wish you'd understand.'

Eleanor got out of bed, took her dressing-gown from the hook, and slipped it on.

'Of course I'm proud of you, silly! But that isn't to say I agree with you. If I live to be a hundred I'll never understand why men have to kill each other just to settle an argument – an argument that isn't even theirs in the first place. Anyway, you're not going without breakfast. I'll have my way about that. I'll make it while you're shaving.'

When she got downstairs she was already too late. Mrs Foster was up and dressed, the kettle was singing and the strips of bacon lay in the frying pan, ready to be cooked.

'What are you doing up, Ma?' Eleanor asked.

'I was awake. I don't need much sleep at my age.'

She took the teapot to the kettle and mashed the tea. She could not tell Eleanor that she had been kept awake by the thought of that other man, her son David, who had gone off to fight in the Boer War and had never come back. She had made him a good breakfast on that last morning but he had eaten none of it. After he had left the house she had fed it to the pig.

'Frank is only going to enlist,' Eleanor said. It was as if she could read her mother's thoughts. 'They might not even take him. They might say he's too old.' They were the same arguments with which she had tried, and failed, to convince herself since that day in Sandcombe.

'So eager!' Mrs Foster sighed. 'Why are they all so eager? Why does he have to be off at the crack of dawn on the first day's recruiting?'

'Don't ask me,' Eleanor said. 'But they're all alike, as if they were joining in a game.'

Since war was declared they had watched the regular soldiers march behind their band from the local barracks to Akersfield station, and from there to who knew where? Straight to France, most people said, but no-one knew for certain. The Territorials had gone, too; eager to the last man.

'Look at Roland,' Eleanor continued.

Jumping the gun, Roland Layton had joined up the very day after his engagement to Becky, pausing only long enough to place a half-hoop of diamonds on his beloved's finger. He was already somewhere in North Yorkshire, training to be an officer.

'Becky seems to have taken it in her stride,' Mrs Foster observed. 'I'd go so far as to say it's done her good.'

'Perhaps.' But Eleanor had her own thoughts about that. She was by no means sure that her daughter loved the man she was engaged to marry, certainly not enough to spend the rest of her life with him. But now was not the time to voice those doubts. Becky was tickled to death with her new status as an engaged woman.

234

'The dining-room table's laid,' Mrs Foster said as Frank came into the kitchen. 'Sit you down and I'll bring your breakfast.'

'I don't want it,' Frank protested. 'But if it will please you both I'll try to eat it.'

The bacon choked him, the egg stuck in his gullet. In the end he pushed his plate away. It was no use. He was too churned-up inside to digest anything. He was excited, he was afraid; he was eager, he was apprehensive. One emotion followed another and sometimes they jostled in him all at the same time. He would be glad when the enlistment was over, the deed done, no going back.

'You're wearing your Sunday suit,' Eleanor said.

'I wanted to look my best.' He had put on a white shirt, heavily starched, and a wing collar so stiff that it cut into his neck.

'Well, you do.' Eleanor rose from the table, went to him and put her arms around his neck.

'One last time, Frank, and then I promise I won't ask you again. Must you do this?'

He stood and took her in his arms, stroked her golden hair, tilted her face so that he looked into her eyes.

'You know I must!'

He was amazed when he reached the drill hall to find a queue, three deep, already stretching along the street. It was not quite seven-thirty and the enlistment wouldn't start until nine. He took his place beside a man he recognized as the assistant in an ironmonger's shop in the town.

'I reckon some of 'em must have been here all night,' the man said. 'Frightened they won't get in, else.'

'Do you think that's likely?' Frank asked.

The man shrugged. 'Who knows? I daresay they might have some sort of quota, else where would they put us all till they could ship us to France?'

'I hadn't thought of that,' Frank said. He hoped that if he was accepted he would be called quickly. The most difficult time was going to be between now and his leaving. Every day would seem like another parting and, in spite

235

of what Eleanor said, it would be easier for both of them if everything happened quickly.

The men in the queue were surprisingly lighthearted, quipping and joking all the time.

'If the Hun could see us lot, he'd give in right away?' a burly youth said. He raised an imaginary gun to his shoulder and fired make-believe bullets into the distance. 'Bang-bang!' The word 'Hun' gave Frank a quick stab of pain, but it was something he would have to get used to. He was going to hear it, and epithets like it, a thousand times from now on.

Halfway down the queue a young man brought out a mouth organ and began to play songs from other wars: 'Dolly Grey', 'Soldiers of the Queen', 'Minstrel Boy'. There would be songs from this war, Frank thought. If it lasted long enough, that was. Most of the men in the queue looked to be in their twenties but there were a few youths who were clearly nowhere near the minimum age of eighteen. Well, if they could worm their way in, maybe he could do the same at the other extreme.

On the stroke of nine the doors opened and there was a cheer from the waiting men as they began to move in.

'Now for it!' Frank said to his neighbour.

When it came to his turn, Frank stood in front of a desk at which sat an officer, with a clerk beside him.

'Name?'

'Frank Kramer.'

The officer looked up sharply.

'Kramer? Where were you born?'

'In Akersfield, sir.'

'I see. Occupation?'

'Café owner.'

'Age?'

'Thirty, sir.'

It was the clerk's turn to look up. He gave Frank a direct stare, but the officer showed no reaction at all.

The medical examination followed, in another part of the building. Frank was pleased to see that the examining doctor was a soldier, a stranger, not one of Akersfield doctors who might have known him. It was all routine: eyes, teeth, feet, lungs.

'You're in good condition,' the doctor said when it was over, 'though I'd put you at about thirty-five, if asked.' He looked keenly at Frank, who stood there without speaking. 'Anyway, you'll do. A.1. Next please!'

It only remained to move to another room, swear the oath, take the shilling, and he emerged as Private Kramer of the West Yorkshire Regiment.

'When . . .?' he began.

'You'll be notified.' the sergeant said shortly.

It was a fortnight before he was called. During that waiting period he spent as much time as he could sorting out the business, making everything as smooth as possible for Eleanor, who would now have to run it on her own. But though it would be hard work, she was more than capable. They both knew that.

'There is nothing you can't do,' Frank said. 'I have total confidence in you. But I would like you to engage another person so that you will physically not have so much to do.'

'I could help,' Selina put in eagerly. 'I could leave school. I'm almost sixteen. Oh Father, do say I may? I so want to help!'

Frank looked at Eleanor, raised his eyebrows in a question.

'I don't see why not,' Eleanor said. Selina, young as she was, would be a great help; better than a stranger, better perhaps than Becky. Becky, at the moment, had her mind elsewhere, and who could blame her? There was talk of her going to spend a few days in Richmond to be near to Frank before he was sent to France.

'Very well then,' Frank agreed. 'I would like to think of you helping your mother,

'What about me?' Jenny cried. 'I want to help too!'

'Well, you're too young to leave school,' Frank said. 'But I'm sure there are lots of things you can do. Perhaps you might be allowed to help in the café on a Saturday.'

237

'You can always give me a hand, too,' Mrs Foster told her. 'I shouldn't be surprised if Brenda goes off on munitions the minute she gets the chance. There'll be more money in munitions.'

There were always those who'd make money in wartime, she supposed. Factory owners, mill owners. Some of the mills in Akersfield had already gone over to weaving khaki cloth – the finest worsted for officers' uniforms. If the war went on long enough, and she wasn't one who thought it would all be over by Christmas, there'd be a new crop of millionaires in Akersfield when it ended.

Frank was sent to a camp in Lincolnshire to train. It was a pitifully short training and at the beginning they had neither uniforms nor real weapons. But eventually both came, and they learnt the rudiments of how to fire a gun, how to use a bayonet, how to march while bowed down by a back pack, and since they were now in uniform it was somehow easier to do these things. Above everything else Frank hated bayonet practice, but the uniform gave him a sort of protection, another identity, as if it was someone else doing it.

When they were sent home, at the end of September, on a forty-eight-hour pass, they knew without being told that it was embarkation leave.

'Two nights,' Frank told his family. 'I have to report back on Monday morning.'

Eleanor took a deep breath. She must not, by a single word or action, spoil any moment of this time they would have together. It must be a happy time, with no murmur of complaint. The memory of these last two days would have to sustain them both until he came home again.

'What shall we do?' she asked. 'The choice is yours. We could go to Sandcombe for the day, or Felldale. Whatever you want,' For a moment, just for a moment, her thoughts turned to Hebghyll. What was happening to Dick in all this? Perhaps . . . She put the thought from her at once. The time was for Frank, and for no-one else.

'I don't want to do either of those things,' Frank said.

'I would like to spend the time close to home. Perhaps take the tram to Saltaire, walk up Shipley Glen, as we used to before we had the car. Spend time on Baildon moor. I think that's what I'd like to do.' Those were the places he would remember, scenes he had known all his life. 'And in the evening Becky can play to us, and we'll sing, just as we've always done. I don't want anything new or different.'

'But Father, Roland has sent for me to go to Ripon!' Becky cried. 'He seems to think that he also is going to France. What shall I do? You know I want to be with you, but I want to be with Roland too.'

Frank smiled at her. 'There isn't any doubt what you should do, Becky. Since Roland can't come home, you should go to him. Tomorrow morning I shall take you to the station myself. We shall all miss you in the next day or two, but it's right that you should go, so don't worry about it.'

When he had seen Becky off at the station he insisted on spending the rest of Saturday with Eleanor in the cafe. She had offered to find someone to take her place, even to close down for a day, but he wouldn't hear of it.

'I want things to be as they always are,' he said firmly.

On the Sunday they packed a picnic and went to the moors. It was a warm September day. The purple heather was still in bloom, but here and there the bracken was turning to its autumn gold, and when the evening came there was a coolness in the air. Eleanor shivered.

'We must make for home, my dear,' Frank said. 'We can't do with you catching cold!'

When they went to bed, and it was earlier than usual because they were longing for each other, had been longing all day, there was no coolness. They made love with an almost frightening passion, not once but several times. And when they were physically exhausted they lay awake in each others' arms and waited for the morning. When the day came they made love again, and then it was time for Frank to leave.

'You must let me go with you to the station,' Eleanor

said. 'But only me. The children must say goodbye to you here.'

'I'll be back soon,' he promised Selina and Jenny. 'While I'm gone, look after your mother – and Grandma too.'

They walked to the station. On the platform they stood close together, hands touching, until the last moment. Not until the guard had blown his whistle and the train had started to move did Frank jump into the nearest carriage. He leaned out of the window and Eleanor watched him until the train rounded the curve just outside Akersfield station, taking him out of her sight. Then she turned and went home.

She should have gone straight to the café. There was work for her to do there, especially since neither Becky nor Frank were there to help. But she felt a deep need to go back to her own home, to reassure herself by the sight of her children and her mother, by the familiar surroundings, that something remained, that some sort of normality could prevail even though Frank was gone.

Her mother and Peter were waiting for her, Peter his usual sunny self, not aware that his father had gone anywhere other than to his daily work. Mrs Foster touched Eleanor's hand. It was the equivalent of the embrace she wanted to give, but such a demonstration was not in her character. Yet I know how you feel, she thought. I've watched my son go. I want to comfort you.

She did it in the only way she knew.

'The kettle's on, love. In the meantime, look at this.'

She went to a drawer, took out a large paper bag, and emptied the contents on the table. Hank upon hank of khaki wool, which she had bought earlier and saved for this moment.

'Jenny can help me wind it if Selina's going to the café with you. Then this evening we'll all make a start. Socks, balaclava helmets, gloves. They'll all be needed, and not only by Frank.'

'I'm not very good at knitting, Grandma,' Jenny said.

'Then you can make a scarf. That's quite easy, and your dad'll be glad of it when the winter comes.'

It was Christmas before Eleanor faced the fact that she was pregnant. The signs had been there all along but she had refused to acknowledge them. The absence of menstruation she had attributed to worry, to the responsibilities which Frank's absence placed on her; her occasional sickness she dismissed as due to something she had eaten, or perhaps a germ she had picked up. But when on three successive mornings she couldn't fasten her skirt at the waist, she allowed herself to consider what had been at the back of her mind for several weeks. A visit to her doctor on the day before Christmas Eve confirmed that she was, indeed, pregnant.

'I can't believe it!' she said to her mother. 'After all these years when we've wanted a baby! What will Frank say, I wonder?'

'He'll be thrilled,' Mrs Foster replied. 'If he needed another reason for coming safely out of this lot – which he doesn't – this will certainly be it.'

Eleanor told the children on Christmas Eve. Selina and Jenny were delighted at the thought of a new brother or sister – 'though I shan't love it more than Peter,' Jenny said. Becky reddened with disgust at the news.

'It's terrible!' she grumbled. 'Whatever will people think? I'm almost glad that Roland's in France so's I don't have to tell him. But *what* will Mr and Mrs Layton say?'

'Well, we'll soon know,' Eleanor said briskly. 'You can break the news to them any time you like.'

'Oh I couldn't!' Becky declared.

'In that case, don't. It will announce itself before too long.'

She sounded calmer than she felt. Though she was annoyed by Becky's attitude, she had some sympathy with it since she was by no means sure of her own feelings. How would she cope? There was the business to consider. But then there were woman all over England in the same sort of situation. They would all, somehow, manage. And her

241

mother was right, Frank would be delighted. When everyone else had gone to bed she sat down to write to him.

Whenever there was a lull in the fighting, and sometimes, though the German front line was only a hundred yards away, nothing more than a few stray shots came over for hours on end, Frank took the letter out of his pocket and read it again. All Eleanor's other letters – she wrote often – he kept back in his billet, but this one he carried with him whenever he came into the forward trenches. He had had it four months now, so there was no wonder it was wearing thin along the folds. He didn't need to open it, he knew it by heart, but he liked to see her handwiting – large, open, the lines sloping upwards across the page. She was keeping very well, her subsequent letters had said. The girls and her mother were all of them towers of strength and Peter was as darling as ever. Only a few weeks now and the new baby would be born. He could still scarcely believe it. He wanted above all to be with her, to see her in the beauty of her pregnancy, for he was sure she would be beautiful.

On a sparkling May morning, Eleanor, with Selina and Becky, caught the tram to the centre of Akersfield. The beauty of the weather did nothing to compensate them for the sorrow in their hearts. The *Lusitania* had been torpedoed and sunk, four hundred miles from Liverpool. Fourteen hundred people had been drowned in the cold Atlantic, and one of them was Jimmy Foster.

'Poor Auntie Clara,' Selina said, her eyes brimming with tears again. 'She was so pleased Jimmy was in the Merchant Navy, hadn't joined the Royal Navy.'

'I didn't like leaving your grandma this morning,' Eleanor said. 'She's very upset.'

'Nor I,' Selina agreed. 'I wanted to stay and comfort her.'

But the café had to be run. It was like that for so many people nowadays. Each week the casualty lists grew longer, more families were in mourning, but those who were left had to keep going.

'I wonder how Father is?' Eleanor said. She thought of him a hundred times a day. She missed him so much, and now she hadn't heard from him for two weeks. Sometimes she also wondered about Dick Fletcher. There had been neither sight nor sound of him for a long time. Hebghyll was no more than ten miles from Akersfield but he might just as well be in a far country. Perhaps he was? Perhaps he too was fighting in France? Once or twice she had thought she would get into the car and drive herself to Hebghyll, pay him a visit as a friend might. But she had resisted the temptation. She knew very well that friendship alone was impossible between them. And by now she was so cumbersome that she could no longer drive the car, except with difficulty.

They alighted from the tram in the town centre, Eleanor with some difficulty, for the step was high and she was so big. Sometimes she wondered if she might be carrying twins.

There were not many customers in the cafe this morning; just a few women who had interrupted their shopping to indulge in a pot of tea and one of Kramer's pastries, which Eleanor still made herself.

'You and Selina might as well make up the order for the wholesaler,' she told Becky. She wanted them to learn as much as possible of the routine so that when she had the baby they would be able to carry on in her absence.

'Oh must we?' Becky moaned. 'I would so like to do some *real* war work. Especially since Roland's in France.' In the absence of her fiancée she grew fonder of him all the time. His letters and field postcards were the only excitement in her otherwise dull life. Except for the Bluebirds.

'You are doing war work,' Eleanor said. 'You're helping to carry on the business while your father fights in France.'

Becky sighed. 'I know. But it's not the same. Oh Mother, *why* won't you let me join the Bluebirds?'

The Bluebirds was the name of a concert party made up

243

of such members of the Akersfield Amateur Dramatic & Musical Society as were still available – which meant a good many women and a few middle-aged men. They went around the hospitals and convalescent homes in the West Riding and entertained the wounded soldiers. On the few Sundays Becky had been able to go with them she had been much appreciated for her accompaniments and piano solos. She could sing, too – though not as well as her mother. Now the Bluebirds were to become a full-time concert party; professional, ready to go anywhere, perhaps even out of the country. How she would enjoy that – as well as bringing cheer to the wounded, of course.

'You know why you can't join,' Eleanor said. 'We've been over it again and again. I need you to be here when I take a fortnight off to have the baby. Selina is too young for such a responsibilty, and with the war on I can't get experienced staff who would fill in for me. If I could I would take three months off. But afterwards, when I get back to work, we'll discuss it again.'

She thought she would let her go then. Becky wasn't happy in the cafe and she was already prepared to dislike the baby. To be fair, it was the kind of thing Becky had always wanted to do, and she was good at it. But Frank wouldn't approve, Eleanor thought with a sigh.

She left the office and was walking towards the front of the cafe to deal with the menus when the first stone came through the window. It was immediately followed by a hail of stones, some of them large. Glass flew everywhere and a sliver caught Eleanor on the temple. She put her hand to her face and felt the blood running down.

'What is it? What's happening?'

Becky and Selina came running from the office, the staff from the kitchen. The customers jumped to their feet, screaming hysterically, and made for the door – but they were driven back into the cafe by the gang of stone-throwing youths who marched in, brandishing sticks and shouting. The whole cafe was a cacophony of horrible sound, everything happening at once, and so quickly.

'Bloody Huns! Bloody murderers!' the youths cried.

They were so young, Eleanor thought: schoolboys, too young to enlist so they were waging their own war. But the hate in their faces aged them.

In the cafe they threw everything from the tables – crockery, cutlery, jugs of milk, pots of tea – on to the floor. The customers flattened themselves against the wall until the youths made for the kitchen; then they ran for the door. It was not until afterwards that Eleanor realized that not one of them had come to her aid, though her head was bleeding profusely and she was obviously very pregnant.

'Run and fetch the police!' she called to Becky and Selina.

'I can't leave you, Mother,' Selina protested. 'Becky can go.'

'No, you must both go,' Eleanor said firmly. She was no longer afraid for herself. Anger at what the youths had done had taken the place of fear. But she could not risk harm coming to her daughters.

When they had left she went into the kitchen. The boys had taken everything they could lay hands on – food, crockery, fat – and had hurled it to the floor, or against the wall. They were still at it, still at their terrible shouting.

'Bloody Huns! Bloody murderers!'

She summoned all her strength and shouted at the top of her voice, trying to make herself heard above the din. The blood was still running down her face.

'There are no Huns here! We are Yorkshire born and bred! And my husband is fighting on the Western Front for the likes of you! He's the man whose livelihood you're destroying!'

The leader of the gang, taller and broader than the rest, paused with a plate in his hand and took a step towards her. His dark eyes burned with hatred in his pale face. She felt herself submerged by an ice-cold wave of fear. Shivering, she instinctively placed her hands over her abdomen as if by doing so she cold protect her baby. The youth's eyes followed the movement.

'So we're going to have another little Hun in the world,

are we? Well we'll soon see about that, *Frau* Kramer!'

'Don't, Jackie! Don't touch her! Let's get out of it!'

It was one of the younger boys shouting. He made for the back exit and the others, except for Jackie, followed him. Jackie came a step nearer to Eleanor, his hand raised. As she tried to back away she slipped in a pool of grease, lost her footing and fell to the floor, striking her head against the door frame as she went down. The last thing she saw was the boy's white face close to her own.

She was unconscious only for seconds. When she came to, lying on the kitchen floor, she looked around her at the chaos. It was as she tried to get to her feet that the pain struck her. It started in her back and then seared the whole of her abdomen. It struck with such intensity, taking over all of her senses, that she thought she must faint. Fighting it, trying to stay conscious, she didn't hear Becky and Selina, with a policeman, run into the cafe. The policeman dropped to his knees beside her.

'My word, that's a nasty cut, missus!' he exclaimed. 'We shall have to see to that!'

'Never mind the cut,' Eleanor gasped. 'Get me to hospital. I'm having my baby!'

When Eleanor's baby, a son, was three days old she opened her eyes after a short daytime sleep to find Dick Fletcher standing by her hospital bed. He was dressed in an officer's uniform, one pip on his shoulder, looking incredibly handsome. She thought she was dreaming, and closed her eyes again, but when she reopened them he was still there.

'Hello, Eleanor! How are you?'

The deep voice convinced her. He was standing there.

'I'm very well!' It was true, or soon would be. She was weak after the difficult birth, but there was nothing wrong with her, and the baby was fine.

'You had a nasty experience,' Dick said. 'I'm sorry.'

'It's over. No harm done.' She wasn't sure that she would ever forget the youth, Jackie, but she would try to. From what she had heard from the other patients in the ward,

246

his was only one of several gangs going around the West Riding in what they saw as just revenge for the sinking of the *Lusitania*.

'And now you and Frank have a son. Congratulations!'

'Thank you. How did you know I was here?'

'I went to your home. Your mother told me.'

'I see.' But why had he gone there in the first place?

'I had to see you,' he said. 'I wanted you to know that I'm going to France tomorrow. I couldn't leave without telling you, Eleanor. You understand?'

We might never see each other again, she thought. She understood only too well. The thought stabbed her like a rapier. This might be the very last time; you standing there, me lying in a hospital bed.

'I'm glad – glad you came, I mean.'

'Glad'! What sort of word was that to express her feelings? But there were no words in the language for what she felt.

'And I wanted to see Peter before I went.'

'Did you see him?'

'Yes. He's a fine boy. You've done a wonderful job there, you and Frank. But now that you have a son of your own . . .'

'You needn't worry. Peter will always be as dear to us as our own son. There will no difference between them.'

'I should have known better than to think it,' he said.

They both fell silent. What had always been between them was still there, but it was not to be exposed, even with the knowledge that they might not see each other again. Eleanor was the first to break the silence. She felt that if she didn't do so, she would cry out with the pain of it.

'What about your business?'

'I've left it in good hands. Herbert Crowther, my assistant, will take good care of it. He won't be called up, even if conscription comes. He's over age. But he won't be able to keep up the seed business. I shall have to start that again when . . .' He had almost said 'if', but had caught the word back in time '. . . when I return.'

Though he had not used the word, in his almost imper-

247

ceptible pause she had sensed it. Officers in France, especially junior officers, had lives almost as short as that of the mayfly, often no more than a few days. Everyone knew that.

'Does Frank know about the baby?' Dick asked.

'I've written to him. He'll be thrilled. Dick . . .'

'Yes?'

'I want you to know . . . I've been happy with Frank, he's the best of husbands, But . . .'

'Sister said I mustn't stay long.' He interrupted, but his eyes told her that he knew what she wanted to say. 'You're not fit. She only let me in because I'm in uniform and I said I was your cousin.'

He leaned over her and kissed her on the cheek, then he turned swiftly, almost as if he was on parade, and left. She watched him down the length of the ward, her hand touching the place on her cheek. When he had gone she closed her eyes again.

'Your cousin's a very handsome young man,' the lady in the next bed said.

They had been in the forward trench for a week now. The rule was no more than three nights in this sector of the front line, but the relief company had not come. Rumour said that they would move in tonight, under cover of darkness. Then, thank God, we can get back to the billet for some sleep, Frank thought. There had been little enough of that for the last few nights, though some men literally fell asleep on their feet, or dropped in the mud of the trench and let their fellows walk into them and rats run over them where they lay, without feeling a thing. It was the rats which got him down most, even more than the lice and the everlasting mud. Some of the men fed the rats from their hand, but the mere sight of them horrified him.

The billet to which he looked forward to returning was in a ruined house. It was cold and hard, but compared to the trenches it was like the Ritz Hotel. There'd be rest, and better food. All the same, they couldn't grumble much

248

about the food in the front line. Men risked their lives every time they brought the rations. There was no communication trench here and they had to come over the top. That was why the relief party hadn't come, no doubt. The firing had been so fierce. It would have meant wholesale slaughter of the men visibly moving overland. Not that they had escaped in the trench. The casualties had been heavy, and there were dead bodies still around. You grew used to that, but you tried not to become callous. It was a matter of luck, not skill, whether you survived. A yard to the left, a few inches to the right, could make the difference.

If it was humanly possible, the post would be brought up today. That was another group of men who risked their lives, knowing how important letters from home were. He was one of the lucky ones. There was almost always a letter for him. And an hour later, so it proved again on this day.

Some men tore open their letters, but he opened his carefully to prolong the pleasure. In a few weeks now he could expect to hear that Eleanor had had the baby. In the meantime, waiting every bit as anxiously as she, he knew that his luck would hold. He felt it in his bones.

'Dearest Frank (he read)

A line to let you know that we have a son. Six pounds at birth because a month premature. We are both well. Shall we name him Robert?'

He read no further. He leapt to his feet, waving the letter in the air.

'I've got a son!' he cried. 'I've got a son!'

He never heard the bullet which killed him. When his mate, who had been standing a few feet away, bent over him, Frank was still clutching the letter in his hand, a smile still on his face.

CHAPTER FIFTEEN

'It's six o'clock,' Selina said. 'Time we were closing, Mother.' They closed earlier now because, two years into the war, food was running short. They could never get enough sugar to bake all the cakes the café customers expected to be served with their pots of tea, let alone to fill the sugar bowls on the tables. Eleanor, however, was glad of the earlier closing time. It meant that, two or three days a week at least, she could get home in time to bath Robert and put him to bed herself. It was a great pleasure to her to do so. She felt, too, that for the sake of her mother she must try to get home at a reasonable hour. It was a long day for a woman of sixty-five with a seven-year-old and a baby of just over a year to look after. Jenny helped when she came in from school, and there was Hepzibah, who had taken Brenda's place when the latter went on munitions. Even so, her mother bore the responsibility, and much of the actual work, and she wasn't getting any younger.

'We still have a customer,' Eleanor said. 'Actually I'm sure he finished ages ago. Wouldn't you think a soldier on leave would have better things to do than linger over an empty teacup? Have you given him his bill?'

'Ages ago,' Selina replied.

Something in Selina's tone of voice made Eleanor look up from the bookings diary she was consulting. Her daughter was unusually pink in the cheeks.

'Oh! I understand. He's waiting for you. Do you know him?'

'Not really,' Selina confessed. 'He was in the canteen

last night. Didn't you notice him?'

'Since it's chock-a-block with young men in uniform, I'm afraid I didn't,' Eleanor admitted. 'Did he speak to you then?'

'Yes. He asked me where I worked in the daytime.'

The canteen was in a large basement room in Akersfield town hall. It was open every night for the benefit of soldiers, sailors, and members of the Royal Flying Corps, though very few of the last-named found themselves in Akersfield. Kramer's cafe, in spite of its German name, had for the last nine months had the catering contract, supplying cakes, biscuits, tea and coffee.

'I'm amazed that with a name like Kramer we should get such a contract,' Eleanor had said to her mother at the time.

'I'm not,' Mrs Foster had replied. 'There's a great deal of respect for the name of Frank Kramer in this town. His death was felt by a lot of people.'

'And by me every day of my life; every day since the telegram came,' Eleanor said. 'What did I do to deserve a man as good as Frank?' And had she ever loved him enough, she asked herself?

'You made him happy,' her mother told her. 'I wasn't sure you would, but I have to hand it to you. I fancy he was a happy man till the minute he died.'

There had been a lot of sympathy for Eleanor after the raid on the cafe, and with the announcement in the casualty lists of Frank's death, so soon after the birth of the son he would never see, it increased a hundredfold. She had cut out, and would always keep, a letter which had appeared in the *Akersfield Record* soon after Frank's death.

'We should be bitterly ashamed of what has been done to this brave woman, whose husband gave his life. It is up to all of us to do what we can to compensate her for the actions of these hooligans.'

It was simply signed 'Well-wisher'. She thought it might be partly responsible for the increase in her trade which had continued to this day.

She smiled now at Selina. 'I see! Well, I suggest you put your hat on, ready to leave. That should bring him out of his corner.'

Selina quickly disappeared in the direction of the office and emerged shortly afterwards, her straw hat perched on her pale gold hair, tilted provocatively over her pretty face. Her hair had never darkened, never lost its sheen. My second daughter is very attractive, Eleanor thought. She supposed she would have to get used to young men queuing up for her. But with the thought came the sadness that Frank wasn't here to see it. He would never experience the womanhood of this daughter or the maturity of any of his children.

Selina's ruse worked. As she stood by the cafe counter, clearly ready to leave, the soldier quickly left his seat and hurried to pay his bill.

'Haven't I seen you before?' he asked Eleanor shyly as he handed her a shilling. 'In the canteen? You two must be sisters?'

'Selina is my daughter,' Eleanor replied dryly.

'I don't believe it!' he said gallantly. 'Well, since you two ladies are obviously leaving, perhaps I may walk with you part of the way? I'm sure we go in the same direction.'

I'm sure you'll see to it that you do, Eleanor thought. Out loud she said, 'I cannot leave just yet, so you must ask my daughter. Selina, tell Grandma I hope not to be late. If he isn't too sleepy I'd like it if she'd keep Robert up until I get home.'

'Then if I may?' the soldier asked Selina.

Eleanor watched them leave. It was, in fact, too casual an introduction. They knew nothing of the young man. But in wartime things were so different. There was no time to get to know people slowly. Always at the back of the mind lurked the thought that there might never be another chance. 'Here today and gone tomorrow' had taken on a new and dreadful significance.

She locked the door, pulled down the cafe blind and went into the office. There were two meetings upstairs this evening, one of the Akersfield Comforts Fund Committee, the other of such members as were left of the Akersfield Debating Society, mostly middle-aged or elderly men. Even when, as this evening, one of her staff would be left on duty, she liked to welcome people herself, offer them some small personal attention.

She was not kept long. Evening meetings in Akersfield began early. She stayed only long enough to greet the first arrivals for each event and to make sure that Ruby, whose turn it was to see to the light refreshments which still accompanied such affairs, had everything in hand.

'Well, Ruby, I'll say goodnight,' Eleanor said. 'Try to get them off the premises by ten o'clock.'

'I will that,' Ruby promised. 'Never fear!'

Eleanor decided to walk home. She could have taken the tram, but it was a fine evening and she felt in need of fresh air. It was the kind of summer evening when she and Frank would have taken the children for a walk, but for a long time now she had been too tired for that. The streets were quite busy. Now that conscription was in force, most of the men she saw were in uniform, some of them in hospital blue. A whole wing of Akersfield General Hospital was constantly filled with the wounded and many of the rich woolmen of the town, enriched even further by the war, had made room in their sumptuous homes for convalescent soldiers. Officers preferably.

The sight of khaki-clad men turned her mind to Dick Fletcher, though it took little to do that. She had heard nothing of him since the visit he had paid to the hospital after Robert was born. He wouldn't know that Frank was dead. But who was to say that Dick wasn't dead? The fighting was fiercer than ever now, all along the Somme.

Sometimes not knowing about people was the most difficult part to bear. After Frank's death, though she mourned him deeply, she had somehow managed to pull herself together, to face the future. It was up to her now to look after them all, to shoulder the double burden – though she couldn't really think of her children, her

253

mother, the business, as burdens. They gave a purpose to her life.

She longed to have news of Dick. Sometimes she felt that if anything terrible happened to him she would know it in her heart; but countless women tried to comfort themselves with that kind of thought. Had it any foundation?

She turned into Ashfield Road, walking a little more briskly now that she was nearing home. She hoped her mother had kept Robert up. When she opened the door of number seventeen Peter rushed into the hall, followed by her mother carrying the baby. Eleanor took Peter in her arms and gave him a hug.

'Now watch this!' Mrs Foster said. 'No, stay right where you are. Kneel down and hold out your arms' She set the baby down to stand on the floor.

'Now walk to your ma!' she said.

He stood there, hesitant, swaying a little on his feet, until he saw his mother's outstretched arms, her smiling face. Then with short, ungainly steps he tottered the three yards which separated them, and was gathered up by her.

'You're walking!' Eleanor cried. 'What a clever boy! You're walking?'

'He did it the first time, not an hour ago,' Mrs Foster said. 'I told you he wouldn't be long getting off. There was you, thinking he was never going to walk just because he was a bit later than the others!'

'It was foolish of me,' Eleanor admitted. But sometimes she *was* foolish about Robert, more anxious about him than she had been about the girls. And yet his life and Peter's were far more secure than theirs had been. She never forgot the time just after Jenny was born, when they had no food in the house and she didn't know which way to turn – nor the way they had ridden on Dick's cart to Felldale. It was a world away, but she hoped she never *would* forget it.

'There'll be no stopping him from now on,' Mrs Foster said. She led the way back into the parlour, Eleanor and the two children following.

'Where's Jenny?' Eleanor asked.

'Gone to the library to change my books for me.'

'And Selina? She left long before me.'

'Up in her room, getting ready to go to the canteen. I thought it wasn't her night, but she said she was doing an extra turn. There's a letter from Becky, by the way.'

'Oh good!' Eleanor said. 'All the same, I'd better see to Robert and Peter first. It's time they were both in bed.'

'You see to the little one, I'll do Peter,' Mrs Foster offered.

'I want Mother to put me to bed!' Peter complained.

'So I shall then,' Eleanor told him. 'But first you can help me to bath Robert.'

It was a task she enjoyed. As she soaped and sponged his small body it seemed to cleanse her too; to wash away the cares of her business day, to set her firmly in the home. She was drying Robert when Selina came into the room, dressed for going out.

'So what's his name?' Eleanor asked. 'This soldier who's persuaded you to do an extra evening's duty?'

'Bob Harwell. He's very nice, Mother. You'd like him. He goes back to France tomorrow.'

'Well, take care,' Eleanor said. She trusted Selina, but she was afraid of this most tender-hearted of her daughters getting emotionally involved with something that was too big for her. A man going back to the war could touch the heart of most women, let alone Selina. And her daughter was a very young seventeen.

'I will, Mother,' Selina assured her. 'But you don't need to worry. I'm not the least bit serious. However nice he is, I don't want to get serious about love and marriage for ages yet. I want to stay with you.'

'But not forever.' She was cut out to be a wife and mother.

'For a long time yet,' Selina said.

'Well, if Private Bob Harwell offers to walk you home, invite him in for a cup of cocoa,' Eleanor suggested.

By the time Eleanor had put Robert and Peter to bed, she was exhausted. She sank into a chair, refusing the meal which Mrs Foster had prepared for her.

'I couldn't at the moment,' she said., 'Perhaps later.'

Mrs Foster looked at her daughter with concern. She was too often dog-tired these days.

'You work too hard,' she said.

'Look who's talking!' Eleanor replied. 'You're sixty-five, Ma, and you're working like a woman half your age. I feel ashamed that I allow it, yet what can I do? There's no more help to be had. Everyone's on munitions.'

'There's nothing wrong with me,' Mrs Foster said. 'I'm as strong as a horse and you know it. Anyway, I'm not used to help.'

'You're a wonder,' Eleanor told her. 'And you look about twenty years younger than you are.' Apart from a single inch-wide streak, which grew from the front and had been there as long as Eleanor could remember, there was no grey in her mother's hair. She was thinner than she had been, but they all were because of the wartime food. That was no bad thing. All the same, she felt guilty that her mother had to work so hard at an age when she should be taking it easy.

What no-one understood, Mrs Foster thought, was that although she *did* feel tired from time to time, and would have been glad of a chance to put her feet up in the afternoon, inside herself she was still a young woman. She felt no different from when she had been twenty. She had no difficulty at all in identifying with the heroines of those novels Jenny brought her from the public library. No difficulty at all – though no-one would believe her, so she kept quiet about it.

'It's you I'm worried about,' she said to Eleanor. 'I might have work but I don't carry the responsibility. What you need is a break, a holiday.'

Eleanor laughed. 'Fat chance! Will you pass me Becky's letter?'

Becky was doing a month's tour of northern counties with the Bluebirds, playing, as usual, mostly to soldiers in hospital, and sometimes in barracks.

'If anyone can be said to be enjoying the war, I'd say Becky is,' Eleanor commented as she read the letter. 'She

256

says that Roland is fit and well and that she hears from him regularly, but that she longs to see him again.'

'How does she get the letters?' Mrs Foster asked. 'She's never in one place long.'

'He sends them to his parents. They know the details of her tour, really more than we do. They send them on to her.'

'He seems to live a charmed life, that young man,' Mrs Foster said. 'When you think that he's been in France eighteen months and most officers don't last more than a week once they get to the Front! Well, good luck to the lad, I say!'

'Me too,' Eleanor agreed. But Becky had always been the lucky one.

She handed the letter to her mother, then leaned back in her chair and closed her eyes.

'I still say you need a break,' Mrs Foster declared. 'And if you put your mind to it, you could take one.'

'Mother, how could I?' But it was what she would like most in the world. 'Besides, by the time I'd organized the children to go with me, I'd be more exhausted than ever!'

'I didn't mean with the children,' Mrs Foster said. 'I meant just you on your own. I could manage quite well for a day or two. Jenny and Hepzibah would help me. Selina too if you went at a weekend.'

It was a heavenly thought. Just to be alone, with nothing to do. If she left after an early finish on Saturday . . .

'You could take Monday off,' Mrs Foster said, picking up her daughter's thoughts. 'You're never that busy on a Monday.'

'Where would I go?' Eleanor mused. 'I'd feel more free if I could take the car, but I don't have much petrol.'

'Lots of places. Harrogate, Ilkley, Skipton.'

Eleanor lay back in her chair and gave herself up to the idea. If she could get away, just for a couple of nights, she'd be a new person, better for everyone.

'I think you're right,' she said, sitting up. 'I'll do it, Ma! I'll go late Saturday afternoon and get back Monday evening. Are you sure you'll be all right?'

'Of course I will,' Mrs Foster smiled. 'What do you think I'm made of?'

'Gold,' Eleanor replied. 'Pure gold!'

It was quite late that evening when Eleanor answered Selina's ring at the door. Behind her daughter, on the step, stood the young soldier she had seen earlier in the cafe.

'I've brought Private Harwell back for cocoa,' Selina said shyly. 'You said to do so.'

'Of course! Come in, Private Harwell.'

'Bob, please?' Eleanor thought again how musical his Welsh accent was, how attractive his dark, celtic looks.

'Why don't we go into the kitchen,' she suggested. 'I'll put the cocoa on at once.'

'I think the kitchen is the bit of home I miss most,' Bob said.

'Where do you come from?'

'Carmarthen.'

'So you're a long way from home?'

'Most of us in my lot are,' he said. 'But we'll be further before we've done.'

'Bob goes to France tomorrow,' Selina said.

Eleanor heard the sadness in her daughter's voice, and at the same time saw the stars in her eyes.

They chatted over the cups of cocoa. Bob Harwell spoke with fondness of his family.

'I'm the eldest of five,' he told them. 'My dad's a farmer.'

'They must miss you,' Eleanor sympathised.

'Not more than I do them. I was glad to hear Selina's one of five. I'd like to have been around long enough to meet the others.'

'I'll write and tell you all about them,' Selina said. 'Didn't I promise I would?'

'You did. And it's what I'll look forward to most.' He turned to Eleanor. 'I hope you don't mind?'

'Not at all.' He seemed a nice young man. As things were going they might never see him again. This evening might be the start of heartache for her daughter, but she could give her no protection. When he had drunk his cocoa and gone, Eleanor had it in mind to warn Selina not to build up her hopes, but one look at the girl's radiant face as she came back into the room after seeing him off, made her think again. Not for anything would she spoil this moment.

'I'm going to bed. Goodnight, Mother.'

'Goodnight. Sweet dreams, my love!'

Selina turned at the door.

'You do like him, Mother, don't you?'

'Of course I do,' Eleanor assured her. 'He seems very nice indeed.'

The cafe was so busy on Saturday afternoon that Eleanor almost changed her mind about her weekend trip.

'Oh do get off, Mother!' Selina urged her. 'We can manage perfectly well without you, though I know you don't think so.'

'Very well then, if you're sure. I'll telephone home to let you know where I'm staying, and I'll be back Monday evening.'

It had been another fine, warm day and she had the car hood down as she drove. She had tucked her hair under her hat as far as she could, for it was abundant, and had tied her hat on with a scarf. She didn't want to arrive at the hotel looking a fright. Which hotel it would be she truly didn't know. 'I'll give the car its head,' she'd said. 'Go where it takes me!'

Yet in her heart she knew she was going to Hebghyll. It was not the car which took her on the right road, but her own inner desire. And though, even as she drove along the quiet roads, she told herself she had no further plans once she got there, she knew this wasn't true. She knew she intended to find Dick Fletcher's market garden.

When she turned into the wide main street of Hebghyll she was struck at once by its air of prosperity. well-dressed people sauntered along the pavements, stopping to gaze into the windows of high-class shops. It was a clean-looking town too. The high moors at its back not only sheltered it, but kept off the prevailing, soot-laden wind which blew from the manufacturing towns a few miles distant. She drove slowly along the street before stopping outside an hotel at the far end. This would do nicely.

'I'd like a room at the back,' she told the receptionist. 'That should look towards the moors, I think.'

'That's right, madam,' the woman said. 'You wouldn't get one at such short notice, only we've had backword on a single room.' She wasn't sure that she approved of women who travelled alone, especially driving a motor car, and booked into hotels. But that was the war for you. It changed everything.

It was a pleasant room to which Eleanor was shown: well-furnished, scrupulously clean, with a view of the hotel grounds and beyond them the moor; green now, but in another month the heather would be out and the ground would be sheeted in brilliant purple. She opened the window and stood by it, filling her lungs with the clear moorland air. She felt better already.

When she had washed and changed she went downstairs and asked the receptionist if she might telephone. Her mother answered the phone.

'I'm in Hebghyll,' Eleanor said. 'At the Plume of Feathers. Is everything all right there?'

There was a pause before her mother replied. There usually was. Mrs Foster had not grown accustomed to the telephone and avoided using it whenever she could.

'Hello Ma!' Eleanor repeated.

'Everything's all right,' Mrs Foster shouted. 'Goodbye!'

Eleanor smiled as she went in to dinner. Her mother would see straight through her reason for being in Hebghyll. But it didn't matter. Nothing mattered except that she was here. When she had finished her meal she would go for a walk. The newly-introduced Summer time Act, though the farmers complained that the cows didn't like it, certainly made for long light evenings. Now, as a rare treat, she lingered over her meal, savouring the well-cooked food, watching the other guests. The room was full. There were several men in uniform and she observed, not for the first time, that you could easily tell the soldiers on leave from

260

France from the ones who had yet to go. The former, however brightly they acted, had a deep weariness in their faces, a haunted look, as if they had seen things they could never talk about. They said that men home from France all refused to talk about the war.

By the time she had finished her coffee it was too late to walk up to the moor. It would be deserted. Instead she strolled along the length of the main street, looking in the windows of closed shops, observing the passers-by. She was taken by the ambience of the place. It was the kind of little town she had always wanted Frank to move to, but she had never been able to dent his loyalty to Akersfield. Perhaps if he had lived he would have changed his mind. It was a better place for his son – for all their children – to grow up in. It took her no more than five minutes to make up her mind.

By the time she was back at the hotel she had decided to call on the estate agent first thing on Monday morning. Making enquiries would in no way commit her, but it would be interesting to see what was available. The fact that, when he came back, Dick Fletcher would be working in the town need no longer be a bar.

The next morning she found Dick's market garden without difficulty. There was no sign to say that it was his, but she didn't need one. The signs were all there in the way it was laid out, in the rows and beds of healthy-looking produce. She hadn't expected to find anyone working on a Sunday but there was a young woman in Land Army uniform, hoeing.

'Are you looking for someone?' she asked Eleanor.

'I'm looking for whoever's in charge,' Eleanor said. 'Is that you?'

'Heavens, no!' the girl replied. 'The owner is off at the war, but Mr Crowther is in charge. He lives in the cottage just up the lane there.'

Herbert Crowther was as Eleanor had imagined him, a big burly man in his fifties with the tanned skin of someone who had spent all his working life in the open air.

261

'I'm a friend of Mr Fletcher's,' Eleanor began. 'I happened to be passing . . .'

He looked at her with suspicion. 'It's not many people as pass by here,' he said.

'No, well, I thought I'd call . . .' Eleanor said. 'I grew up with Mr Fletcher in Felldale. I worked for him there one time, a few years back.'

He relaxed at that.

'Aye well, I daresay you'll know he's off to the war, then?'

'I do,' Eleanor said. 'He came to see me before he left. I was in hospital. He forgot to leave me details of how to get in touch with him, and now I'd like to write. I expect you could tell me.'

'I could,' he admitted. 'The question is, should I?'

'I'm quite genuine,' Eleanor told him. 'I've known him all my life.'

He relented. She looked genuine enough. A very well-favoured young lady, in fact.

'Come in a minute,' he said. 'I'll write it down for you.' Eleanor watched him while he searched in a drawer for a piece of paper.

'Is everything going well here?' she asked.

'Very well. We've got right good crops this season. You can tell Mr Fletcher that when you write to him.'

'What about the seed business?'

'Nay, that's had to be put aside till t'war's over. There's nobbut Mr Fletcher hisself understands that. But he'll start it up again, I don't doubt for a minute. He's an ambitious young man – but when war comes you have to put ambition aside, don't you?'

'I suppose so.'

'Well here's the address, miss. give him all the best from me. I'm not much of a writer meself.'

That afternoon she climbed up to the moor, and walked and walked through the tufty, springing grass, the breeze, which never left these high places, cool on her face. Her thoughts whirled around in her head.

Was it wise to open up a correspondence with Dick?

Might it already be too late? She thought of the pretty land girl. How do I know he hasn't met some other woman, she asked herself? Yet in her heart she didn't believe that was so. She believed that she and Dick were meant to come together. Unless – it was a thought which could never be dismissed – he was destined, like Frank, never to return from France. In the end, as she had always known she would, she made up her mind to write to him that evening. If a cruel fate decided to separate them, that was one thing; but she would not be a party to it.

After dinner, pen in hand, the blank sheet of white paper in front of her, she found it difficult to know what to say. In the end, she decided to keep it just a letter from a friend, to take the gamble on life giving them a further chance and to stifle, for now, the things she longed to say.

'. . . You will be surprised to see,' she wrote, 'that I am at the Plume of Feathers in Hebghyll. I'm here on my own, just for the weekend, since I've been working rather hard lately; but so have we all . . .I am sorry to tell you that Frank was killed in the fighting at Ypres, more than a year ago now. His officer wrote that he didn't suffer, and that he knew about the baby just before he died. Poor Frank! I was on the moor this afternoon and it was quite beautiful . . .'

She added that she had seen Herbert Crowther and that all was well there, and in the last sentence she wrote. 'I would be glad to hear from you if ever you have the time.'

That done, she sealed the envelope and dropped it in the hotel post box in case she should lose her courage, change her mind.

On Monday morning, straight after breakfast, she went to see the estate agent.

'I suppose a little teashop is the kind of thing you'd be wanting?' he said.

'Not at all. I haven't made myself clear. I already have a fair-sized cafe, with rooms for functions over. I want to expand, not contract.'

She didn't in the least look the hard-headed business-woman, he thought. She was far too attractive, her voice, though firm enough, was soft. She looked the sort of woman made to please a man.

'I thought something in the nature of a guest house, large enough to take several visitors, plus my own family, with a good-sized cafe for passing trade. I daresay there's a lot of passing trade in Hebghyll?'

'You're right about that,' he agreed. 'Especially since the *charabancs* started coming. But running such a business in wartime isn't easy, what with food short and staff difficult to come by.'

What am I saying, he asked himself suddenly. I'm here to sell businesses, not to put people off. But this woman appealed to his better nature. He wanted to protect her.

'The war won't last forever,' Eleanor said briskly. 'Do you think you have anything on your books?'

'Well, not right now,' he admitted reluctantly. 'People wanting to sell their businesses wait until the season's over. Something might come towards the end of the year.'

'Then I'll give you my address and perhaps you'll let me know. I want a *good* business, mind. In a prime position.'

'It won't be cheap,' the estate agent said doubtfully.

'I don't want anything cheap,' Eleanor replied. 'Just at a fair price.'

By selling the Akersfield business as a going concern, selling the house in Ashfield Road which Frank's parents had prudently bought so many years ago, and by adding the money from the insurance policies which Frank had taken out on his life when they were first married, she was sure she could manage the money.

'So I look forward to hearing from you,' she said, taking her leave. 'I'm sorry you have nothing now.'

It was a pity, she would have liked to look something over while she was here. Now that the idea was in her mind she wanted to get going. She wondered what her mother would say, not to mention the children. They might hate to leave Akersfield.

'My word, you look a deal better,' Mrs Foster greeted her when Eleanor arrived home that evening. 'You look as if it's done you as much good as a week at Blackpool!'

'So it has, and I can't thank you enough, Ma. Now sit down and listen. I've something I want to tell you.'

She felt as if her life was about to change. Perhaps in more ways than one, she thought, remembering the letter she had posted last night. But she would say nothing about that for the moment.

The heather had bloomed, and died again, and still she had not heard from Dick. Perhaps he had never had her letter. Perhaps he'd decided not to reply. Perhaps – the ultimate possibility, from which she shied away but could never overcome – perhaps he was no longer alive to reply to her. She thought sometimes of going back to Hebghyll to find out if Herbert Crowther had any news. There had been nothing from the estate agent, but now that thought loomed less in her mind than the absence of any word from Dick.

Then one day, late into the autumn, the letter came. When she picked it up from the hall mat, saw the writing on the envelope, her head spun and she had to lean against the wall for support. She ran upstairs, to open it in the privacy of her bedroom. As she started to tear at the envelope she saw that the postmark was Surrey. What was Dick doing in Surrey?'

'. . . I am in hospital here,' he wrote. 'Apart from the fact that your letter took a long time to follow me here, I am wounded in the right arm and so couldn't write for a while. One of the nurses would have written for me but I wanted to do it myself.'

'Eleanor, please come and see me if you can! I know it's a long way and that you're busy, but I can't tell you what it would mean to me. There's so much I want to say to you that can't be put into a letter . . .'

'Oh I will, I will!' she cried out loud.

She ran downstairs, tears of joy and relief pouring down her face. When she burst in on her mother, waving the letter in her hand, Mrs Foster thought her daughter looked as though she had been given the world. Even before Eleanor spoke a word, her mother knew the reason for that look.

CHAPTER SIXTEEN

Sitting in the buffet at King's Cross station, Eleanor sipped at a reviving cup of tea. Even at this early hour the place was crowded, and she shared the small marble-topped table with three others, two soldiers and a civilian. She had travelled from Akersfield on the sleeper, but for her the word was a misnomer; in spite of the soothing motion of the train, rocking her in the narrow bunk, she had hardly slept a wink. All night long, thoughts of the day to come had chased around in her head. She wondered if it was the same for Dick? She had written to tell him she was coming, but after that she had acted so quickly that he might not yet have had the letter. But she couldn't have borne any delay, she longed so much to see him.

London, or at least the bit of it which she passed through on her way to Waterloo station to get the train for Guildford, disappointed her. She hadn't expected the streets to be paved with gold, but nor had she thought they would be so dirty, so noisy, so crowded with traffic and pedestrians. The railway stations too, with their vast high roofs echoing the hiss of steam, the whistles of the trains, the voices of hundreds of people, were confusing. She was glad when the Guildford train pulled out and they eventually left the city behind. She settled back in her seat and tried to calm her mind by looking out on the countryside as they passed through it. It was so different from the northern landscapes, the only ones she knew. More trees, magnificent trees, and they were in their full autumn glory of red and gold and yellow, whereas in Akersfield the leaves had already fallen and the air was cold.

Outside Guildford station she stopped a woman shopper and asked the way to the hospital.

'It's five miles out,' the woman said. 'Too far to walk. There's a bus goes on the hour, so you've not long to wait.'

The bus deposited her at the hospital gates. She walked up the long drive with a fast-beating heart. By the time she found Livingstone Ward she was breathless.

'My name is Mrs Kramer. I'm here to visit . . .' Eleanor began.

'Lieutenant Fletcher is expecting you,' Sister interrupted. 'You can go right in. He's in the fourth bed on the right.'

So this was the lady whose letter had restored her favourite patient's appetite, brought a smile to his face and excitement to his eyes. Well, she was a good-looker all right. And she must think something of him to have travelled all the way from Yorkshire.

Dick had closed his eyes, trying to catnap to make the time pass more quickly. When he opened them she was walking towards him.

'Eleanor!'

'Dick!'

So many times during the journey she had wondered how they would greet each other, what their first words would be. Now they had no words, but it didn't matter. She leaned over and kissed his cheek, but with his uninjured hand he reached up and turned her cheek so that his lips met hers. All these years, all this longing.

He put his arms around her and held her close. Neither of them knew how long they embraced, nor were they the least aware of the interest of the other patients. They were alone with each other. It was not until Dick felt Eleanor's tears on his face that he released her – and at the same time felt the tears pricking in his own eyes.

She took a handkerchief from her bag and dabbed at her face.

'I'm sorry! I didn't mean to cry.'

She looked at him now for the first time. He was the same, yet different. He was thinner in the face, and around his mouth and across his forehead there were lines which had not been there before; lines of suffering, she thought. It showed in his eyes too. There was a sadness in them not entirely erased by his joy at seeing her. But he was as handsome as ever. His skin was still tanned, as if he spent every waking hour in the open air. It was not until she had looked for a long time at his dear face that she noticed his injuries. And then she was surprised. His right arm, as she had expected, was heavily bandaged and in a sling: what she had not expected to see was the mound in the bed where a cradle kept the bedclothes off one foot.

'Yes,' he said. 'How many people do you suppose could stop a bullet in the arm and another in the foot at the same time?'

'Why didn't you tell me, in the letter?'

'I didn't want you to worry,' he said.

'How bad is it? Does it hurt?'

'I'll recover,' he assured her. 'Given time I'll be as good as new! Actually it's the kind of thing some of the lads out there used to pray for. A "Blighty" wound – bad enough to get you home without being too serious.'

'I don't believe you! Praying to be wounded!'

Why should she, he thought? No-one who hadn't been there could believe what went on. But he had seen one man in his own company deliberately shoot himself in the hand so as to be sent back out of the front line. There were limits to what some men could stand, and times when he had come near to those limits himself. It was because he understood that that he had not reported the man.

'Well, never mind about that,' he told Eleanor. 'I want to hear about you.'

'Where to begin?'

'I was sorry to hear about Frank,' Dick said.

'Yes. He was a good husband. The best in the world. I loved Frank – I want you to know that, Dick. I mourn his death.'

He took her hand and held it in his.

'I understand. I mourn him too. He was a good man.'

269

It was Frank's goodness, Eleanor thought, which kept you and me going in an otherwise unbearable situation.

'You'll want to know about Peter,' she said. 'Well, all I can tell you is that he's a wonderfuil little boy, a joy to be with. We all love him dearly and I think he loves us.' She delved into her handbag. 'Here, I've brought you a photograph, taken on his seventh birthday.'

He gazed at the photograph with a quiet smile on his face. If he remembered the pain of Peter's birth, and the months which followed, he showed no sign of it now.

'I should have put it in a frame,' Eleanor said. 'I'll send you one as soon as I'm home. Then you can put it on your locker.'

'No,' he said. 'I would like to keep the photograph, but I shall keep it to myself. He's your son now.'

She told him what the other members of her family were doing. 'My mother doesn't change at all,' she said. 'She's a rock. I sometimes think that constancy is the best thing about a mother.'

'And what about you?' Dick asked. 'You've told me nothing about yourself. You must have a life apart from your family.'

Have I, she wondered. If she had it was an internal one. For several years now she seemed to have lived only in other people's lives: Frank's, her children's. But if she started a business in Hebghyll it would be something of her very own. She started to tell Dick about it.

'If the right place comes up,' she concluded, 'I just know I can make a success of it!'

'It isn't what *I* want you to do,' Dick said slowly.

'What do you mean?'

'You don't need to ask that, Eleanor. You know what I mean. I love you. I want you to marry me. You can't pretend to be surprised.'

'No,' she said. 'I'm not. You see, I love you too, Dick. You must know how long I've loved you. And what you've just said is what I've wanted to hear. But I don't know . . .'

'We love each other,' he said 'What's to come between us?'

'If it were just you and me,' she said, 'nothing. As it is . . . well, I have the children . . .'

'One of whom is mine,' he interrupted.

'And my mother. I can't bring all my responsibilities to you.'

'Why can't you?' he demanded. 'I know what your responsibilities are. I don't expect you to ditch them. I want to share them with you.'

'If I set up in Hebghyll we shall be near each other. We can see each other as often as we like.'

'Oh no!' Dick said. 'That's not what I want at all! I want to live the whole of my life, for the rest of my life, with you. When the war's over and I'm back home, I want to wake up in the morning and find you lying beside me. I want you to marry me, live with me. Tell the truth, Eleanor. Isn't that what you want?'

'Yes,' she admitted. 'Yes, it is! Oh Dick, it's what I want above everything else in the world!'

'And I,' he said. 'It's what I've dreamed of. I wish it could happen right away. As it is . . .'

'Yes,' she broke in suddenly. 'Oh yes, Dick! You're so right – and I was wrong to hesitate. As soon as you're out of here . . . the minute you're home again! Oh Dick, I can hardly wait!'

She bent over to kiss him again, then drew back when she saw the wariness come into his eyes.

'What is it? What's wrong?'

'You realise, my darling, that I shall probably be sent back to France?'

She stared at him in horror.

'Oh no! I don't believe it! They can't do that to you!'

'They can. And if I heal up completely and the war's still on, they will. We have to face that.'

'I can't face it,' Eleanor said. 'It's too cruel!'

'You can and you will, my love. You'll be strong, as you always have been. That's why I think it might be a good idea for you to go ahead with starting a new business in

271

Hebghyll. It will give you a lot to think about while I'm away . . .'

'What you mean is . . .' she said slowly '. . . in case you don't come back.'

'I *shall* come back,' Dick insisted. 'You must never let yourself think otherwise.'

There was a silence between them, broken in the end by Dick.

'I'm due to go for convalescence in a few weeks' time.'

'Where will they send you?' Eleanor asked.

'I don't know. A lot of convalescents get sent up north. I'm asking to be one of them.'

'Oh, if only you could be!' Eleanor cried. 'There are several convalescent homes in the West Riding. I think there's one in Hebghyll.'

'There is,' Dick confirmed. 'I know the matron. Miss Betty Yorke.'

'Then why don't I go and see her?' Eleanor said quickly. 'Why don't I ask her to use her influence? These things often go by who you know in the right place. Oh Dick, it would be marvellous!'

'It would be,' he agreed. 'But it's a long shot.'

'Well, I shall try,' Eleanor said. 'The minute I get back. I could mention it to Sister here.'

'No, leave that to me,' Dick advised. 'But just think, if I could get to Hebghyll I could talk to Herbert Crowther. I might be able to go down to the garden, even if I were on crutches.'

'I can see you're dying to get back to work,' Eleanor said.

'Yes. There's a lot of developing to do; a good future to look forward to if I work hard. Eleanor, you must hang on to the thought of that future. I want us to be married the minute the war's over.'

'Why not earlier? Why not . . . if you have to go back . . . Why not before then?'

The ward sister came and interrupted them.

'I'm afraid you must leave now, Mrs Kramer. It's been quite a long visit. Shall you be here tomorrow?'

272

'No. I have to catch the sleeper back to Yorkshire.'

'Then I'll leave you to make your farewells,' Sister said. 'Only a minute, mind!'

'Let's not waste the minute, my love,' Eleanor said when Sister had gone. She leant over Dick and kissed him on the lips while he held her in the circle of his arm. Feeling his closeness, his body against hers, a wave of strong sexual passion swept over her, so that she began to tremble. She knew, by the tightening of his arm, the hardness of his lips against hers, that his feelings were akin to her own. Was he remembering then, as she was, that afternoon all those years ago? When she had control of herself again she eased away from him.

'Blast!' he said savagely. Then, more gently, 'I love you, Ellie. Never forget I love you!'

'I love you too.'

In the doorway of the ward she turned around, and they waved to each other.

Afterwards, Eleanor remembered little of the journey back to Akersfield. In a cafe close to King's Cross station she ordered a meal which she hardly touched, though she hadn't eaten since morning. After that she sat in the ladies' waiting room until it was time to board the train. She didn't sleep. All night long the thoughts came and went: longing thoughts for Dick's presence, which made her want to get off the train and go straight back to the hospital. Thoughts of what the future might hold – good and bad thoughts, these were.

She knew that her love for Dick was deeper and stronger than ever. She knew, too, that somehow Frank, with the strength and unselfishness of his own love, had made her understand what real love was. She would bring what Frank had taught her into her marriage to Dick.

Looming above all others, like a cloud as black as the night she was travelling through, was the thought that Dick might have to return to the war. She could not put it out of her mind for long.

But when Eleanor walked into the house in Ashfield

273

Road, early on Sunday morning, Mrs Foster found herself looking into the face of a woman who was in love, and who was equally beloved. When you were older people never believed that you knew about love, that you had known its raptures and remembered them. And now it was not only in Eleanor's face that she saw the effects of love, in the shining softness of her eyes and the curve of her lips; it seemed to pervade her whole body, was part of every movement she made. Silently, Mrs Foster prayed that nothing would ever come to take this away from Eleanor. She had waited a long time. She had been a good girl,

'There's a cup of tea ready,' she said.

'I could do with it,' Eleanor replied, following her mother into the parlour. 'Are the children still asleep?'

'Yes. And Becky's here.'

There was something in her mother's voice which made Eleanor look up sharply.

'Becky? This is a surprise, isn't it? She wasn't due to come home?'

'She's had bad news.'

'Roland! He's . . .?'

Mrs Foster shook her head. 'No, not killed. He's been taken prisoner on the Somme. The Laytons sent her a telegram and she came home yesterday. Very upset she was.'

'My poor little Becky!' Eleanor exclaimed. 'I must go to her at once!'

'I hope she'll not have wakened yet,' Mrs Foster said. 'I dosed her with camomile tea to make her sleep.'

'I won't wake her,' Eleanor promised. 'But I must go to her.'

As Eleanor looked down at her sleeping daughter she saw the tears wet on her lashes, as if she might have been crying in her sleep. She looked so young, so vulnerable. Eleanor was filled with tenderness towards this daughter who had never been her favourite, though she had tried not to show it; with whom she had never got along. Now all she wanted was to take Becky in her arms, hold her close and comfort her.

Becky stirred in her sleep, opened her eyes and saw her mother standing there. It was the compassion on her mother's face which brought reality back to her too quickly. She cried out, and turned away, burying her face in the pillow. Eleanor put her arm around Becky's shoulders, stroked her shining hair.

'I'm sorry, my darling. I'm truly sorry. But try to tell yourself that he'll be safe now. He's out of the war.'

Becky sat upright.

'How do you know he's safe? How do we know he isn't wounded? Do you think he'd have let them take him prisoner if he wasn't? And how do we know what the Germans will do to him? They might torture him. They're capable of anything!'

'I don't believe that to be true,' Eleanor said. German blood alone had run in Frank's veins, and he had been the gentlest of men.

'Why didn't I marry him on his last leave?' Becky cried. 'Oh, why didn't I marry him when he wanted me to? It would be so much easier for both of us to bear if we were married!'

She broke into a paroxysm of sobs and allowed Eleanor to take her into her arms. 'Why didn't I marry him?' she kept on crying. She was right, Eleanor thought, holding her close. She has taught me something. If you love a man who is going to the war, you should marry him. She knew at that moment that if Dick had to return to France, she would persuade him to marry her at once.

'Let me bring you a breakfast tray,' she suggested to Becky when her crying had subsided. 'It will do you good to eat.'

'I can't eat,' Becky said. 'Besides, I must get up and go over to the Laytons. They'll need me. Tomorrow I have to be back with the Bluebirds. We have an engagement in Knaresborough.' She gave a wan smile. 'The show must go on, you know!' Then she broke down into a fresh storm of tears.

275

It was Christmas before Becky heard from Roland. When the letter came from Germany it was to tell her that he was fit and well, that he was not injured, and that his captors were treating him well.

'He'd have to say that, wouldn't he?' she said scornfully. 'His letter is censored.'

He had gone on to say that all he looked forward to now was the end of the war, when he could come home and they'd be married.

'That's just how I feel,' she told her mother. 'I'll marry him the day after he gets here, see if I don't!' How could she once have thought that she didn't really want to marry Roland? How true it was that absence made the heart grow fonder.

It was Christmas, too, before the news came that Dick was now fit enough to go convalescent. There had been complications over his foot; it hadn't healed as well as it should. But now he was on the mend, he wrote in his weekly letter, and since his arm was all right again he could use the crutches and it was amazing how fast he could move.

'With any luck I'll be in Hebghyll in the New Year,' he wrote.

Thanks to string-pulling from Matron Betty Yorke, who remembered Dick and liked him, and to pleas from Eleanor and repeated requests from Dick himself, it had been agreed that it would not materially affect the outcome of the war if he were to be allowed to convalesce in the nursing home for officers in Hebghyll. 'Thank God!' Eleanor wrote back. 'With any luck I shall be able to see you every weekend.'

But for how long, she asked herself. In a few days it would be 1917, and the war, which at first everyone had predicted would be over in a few weeks, showed no sign of ending. There were thousands of men spending their third successive Christmas in the mud of France – and thousands more, the less lucky, who had not lived to do so. With every week that Dick had spent in hospital, not well enough for convalescence, Eleanor had comforted herself with the thought that, at any rate, he could not be sent back to France. Now, with his foot improving so rapidly, and the war dragging on, who could tell?

On the last day of the year details of a property in Hebghyll arrived in the post. Eleanor had taken no further steps to find one since that first visit. She had been in a mood to let the future, aside from Dick, take its course, at any rate for a while. Her thoughts were full of him. Also, they had been inordinately busy in the cafe and in the letting rooms for the last few months. But now as she read the details from the estate agent her interest was stirred again.

'I must say, it sounds exactly what I'm looking for,' she said to her mother. 'Five bedrooms for letting, with enough left for us, and a cafe seating seventy. Situated at the far end of the Drive, which is a good position. What do you think, Ma?'

'But you'll be marrying Dick the minute the war's over,' Mrs Foster objected. 'He won't want you to be saddled with a business. And you mustn't worry about me. I'd not want to be a bar to your happiness . . .'

'You've never been a bar to anything I've wanted, not for a minute of my life,' Eleanor replied. 'On the contrary, it's always been you who's helped me. But you would stay with me if I married Dick?'

'Yes. Since you say you discussed it with him and he agreed.'

Mrs Foster supposed she'd be reasonably happy, happier than if she went back to Felldale. She wouldn't be separated from the children – and she had always liked Dick Fletcher. Most of all, though, what choice had she? You had to learn to live with what was inevitable.

'It would be more in the country than Akersfield,' she said. 'I'd like that.'

'Dick thought it would be a good idea for me to start the new business in Hebghyll,' Eleanor said. 'If he has to go back to France . . .'

Neither woman expressed the thought which those words brought. There was no need to. It was always there.

'Anyway,' Eleanor went on after a pause, 'I'll go and look at this place on Sunday. Would you like to come with me? Selina could look after the little ones for the day.'

'You'll be best on your own,' Mrs Foster said.

The snow came down during Saturday night, and when Eleanor left for Hebghyll next morning everything was white. Even Akersfield, with its mills and warehouses, its soot-blackened stone, was transformed into a town of strange, silent beauty. There was little traffic on the roads and it was difficult going, but from the moment Frank had taught her, Eleanor had proved herself a skilled driver. By the time she reached Hebghyll children were sledging down the lower slopes of the moor. She drove slowly along the main street. The property – 'The Beeches' – was at the far end.

She knew as soon as she stepped inside that it was exactly what she wanted – yet not so exactly that there wouldn't be scope for her to change things around, make small improvements as she had always delighted to do in Kramer's. The guests' rooms were well furnished, though she would lighten them with different draperies; the living quarters were spacious. The cafe was well proportioned and the layout of the kitchens was especially good. It would be altogether pleasant and easy to run, and its position – on the level, close to the shops, and at the bottom of one of the roads which led up to the moor – was first-rate.

All her business acumen rose up and told her she had to have it, though she tried hard not to seem too eager. She felt as she went from room to room that this would be a happy place. She thought that Dick, when they were married, wouldn't necessarily require her to give it up. That was something they would discuss when the time came – but she never wanted anything to come between herself and Dick, ever again.

Within minutes of finishing her inspection of the place she had struck a bargain with the owners.

'You realise, of course, that I have to sell my own business first? But I don't expect any difficulty there.'

'That suits us,' the owner replied. 'As I told you, me and the wife are retiring, going to live near our daughter in Thirsk. We don't particularly want to move until the spring.'

'Then I'll be in touch very soon,' Eleanor said.

That night she wrote to Dick.

'You'll be in Hebghyll within the week now. As soon as you let me know you're installed I shall come over, and if Matron will let me I'll take you to see The Beeches. But more than anything, I just long to see you. I can hardly wait . . .'

'But where will you live when you're married?' Mrs Foster asked next day when they were discussing it. 'You can't rightly expect your husband to live in your place. He has his own home. It's one of the things he's been fighting for.'

'I fully intend to live in Dick's home,' Eleanor told her. 'I've never thought otherwise.' She longed for the day. 'I shall just come to some arrangement about The Beeches when the time's ripe.'

'I've already thought of an arrangement,' Mrs Foster said. 'If your mind hadn't been too full of other things I daresay you'd have done so by now.'

'What do you mean, Ma?'

'I mean you can live with Dick – you can take the two little ones with you. I think that would be only right. Then me and Selina and Jenny – and Becky when she's at home – can live in The Beeches.'

'Live in two separate houses?'

'Not more than ten minutes apart. I know the girls will be agreeable. Don't forget that Selina's nineteen, Jenny seventeen. They'll be wanting to spread their wings, fly the nest, before long. But both of them working in the business, you'll see plenty of them until they do.'

'But what about you?' Eleanor asked. 'You haven't said how you'd feel. I think I'd feel I was deserting you.'

'Rubbish!' Mrs Foster said forcefully. 'Doesn't it occur to you, lass, that I might like a bit of independence? I'd be more or less mistress in my own quarters. And you could give me some proper duties, pay me a bit of a wage. I'm quite capable, you know. I'm not too old and I'm as strong as a horse.'

Eleanor stared at her mother in amazement.

'Oh Ma! All these years and I've never given a thought to how you felt about being dependent! I've enjoyed my own measure of independence and never thought about yours. I feel ashamed!'

'Well, don't be,' Mrs Foster replied. 'The time wasn't right. But now it is.'

'Well, if you're sure,' Eleanor said slowly, 'we'll discuss it with the girls.'

'I'm quite sure,' Mrs Foster said.

On Saturday Eleanor had a telephone call to say that Dick had arrived in Hebghyll. On Sunday morning she drove out and presented herself at the convalescent home.

'I'm afraid there's no question of you taking Lieutenant Fletcher out for a walk,' Matron said. 'He couldn't manage on the snow. Also he's very tired after his journey from Guildford. But you can stay with him here for a little while.'

'Couldn't I take him in my car?' Eleanor pleaded. 'Just for a short trip?'

Matron relented. They were so much in love, these two. She hoped things would work out for them.

'Very well then – but only for an hour!'

'Where would you like to go?' Eleanor asked Dick when they were in the car. 'As if I didn't know!'

'Right,' Dick said. 'I want to look at my land, even if it is under snow. I can't tell you how often I've thought about it, dreamed about it!'

'More than me?'

'Never more than you! Never!'

Eleanor drove slowly along the lane which bordered Dick's land. At the end of the lane, in front of a small house which was set back from the road, Dick said, 'Stop the car, please! This is my house!' There was pride in his voice.

It was a low, stone-built house, with deep-set windows. Snow lay heavily on the roof and there was no smoke from the chimneys. It was a house awaiting its owner.

Eleanor looked at it, found it entirely to her liking.

'So this is where we shall live?'

'Yes,' he said. 'And I have something else to tell you. You remember we decided, soon after your visit to Guildford, that if I had to go back to France we'd get married at once . . .?'

A chill as icy as the weather around them gripped Eleanor. It couldn't be true! She couldn't lose him again, not so soon! She leaned across and clutched at him, her fingers digging into his arms.

'It's not true! You're not going back! Dick, say it's not true!'

'It's not true!'

She was so beside herself, so frantic, that she didn't hear him.

'It's not true,' he repeated. 'You didn't hear me out. I'm not going back to France at all. My foot's going to be fine – a slight limp, nothing more – but not equal to route marches. So they won't have me. The army might find me a desk job in England, but as my business is food production it's much more likely that they'll release me to go back to it!'

'Oh Dick! Oh Dick, I can't believe it! It's like a dream come true!'

'For us it is,' he said. 'I wish it would come true for a lot of others. Even at a time like this I can't forget them.'

'Any more than I shall ever forget Frank,' she said. 'But they wouldn't begrudge us our happiness, would they?'

'No. And you still didn't hear me out. The question is, as I'm not about to depart for France, will you still marry me at once? Please, Eleanor! I can't wait!'

'Nor I,' she answered. 'I'll marry you as soon as you like.'

In each other's arms the minutes passed without words.

They scarcely felt the cold. In the end it was Eleanor who spoke.

'I promised Matron not to keep you out too long, my love. We must go.'

'Are you going to take me to see The Beeches, then?' Dick asked.

'No,' Eleanor said. 'Today is for you and me. Nothing else matters.'

PART TWO

CHAPTER SEVENTEEN

'Mother, I'm glad there were no bookings for The Beeches for Christmas,' Selina said. 'It will be so nice to spend it together here, at Whinbank.'

She was trimming the Christmas tree which stood in the bay window of the sitting-room. They had saved all the baubles and glass balls, brought them with them when they moved from Akersfield to Hebghyll last year.

'It's just as well we *did* save these trimmings,' she continued. 'There are none to be had in the shops.'

'That's to be expected after four years of war,' her mother told her. 'Most of them came from abroad anyway.'

'In any case, I prefer these,' Selina said. 'I've known them most of my life.' She liked familiar things. 'I love this dear little robin which bobs up and down on the branch just as if it were alive!'

'That's one your step-grandmother Kramer brought with her when she left Germany more than forty years ago now,' her mother reminded her. 'And this red and silver one, like a bugle. And the two little lanterns. There aren't many of hers left, so they're rather precious.'

'I know they are. I'll hang them near the top of the tree so they won't get knocked by the children.'

She stepped back to view her work. She was really pleased with it. 'And when all these tiny candles are lit this evening it will look even better!' she said.

'In fact,' Eleanor said, 'there *were* one or two requests for rooms, but I turned them down.'

Selina looked around in surprise. It was unliker her mother to turn away business.

Eleanor smiled, catching her daughter's look. 'I do sometimes think about things other than business,' she said wryly. 'My family, for instance.'

'Oh I know you do, Mother! You don't have to tell me that!'

'And like you, I wanted us all to be together. I think it's what most people want, the first Christmas of the peace, to spend it in their own homes, with their loved ones. Four years of fighting. It's a long time.'

'It's a pity that it's taking such ages to get the soldiers home,' Selina said. 'Some say it will be more than a year before they're all back from France.' She wondered how she would bear another year, waiting for Bob Harwell. They had known each other only a few days, more than two years ago, before he went off to France. Since then it had been nothing except letters. Bob was a good letter writer, she felt she had learned a lot about him from his letters, but she wasn't so fluent. She expressed herself best in the actual presence of those she loved, by word and touch and in doing things for them.

'But at least he's alive, and in one piece,' she said out loud. 'All the way through the Somme, and since, without a scratch. It's a miracle.'

'It certainly is!' Eleanor didn't need to be told that her daughter was speaking of Bob Harwell. She so often was, especially since the Armistice. It seemed as though the thought that he might soon be back, that he was safe, had released the words which had been penned up inside her for so long. 'Perhaps he'll be demobilised quickly. If his father applies, says he needs him on the farm . . . Agricultural workers should have a high priority.'

'You'd think so,' Selina agreed. 'But miners, and men in industry come first. And what they call "pivotal" men.'

'Pivotal men?'

'It means somebody who's needed before somebody else can start work. Like in shipbuilding you'd need the riveters before the rest could start. But Mr Harwell has applied for Bob's release, and that will help.'

'He means to go back into farming?' Eleanor queried.

'He's not sure. But for the time being, yes.'

And if he does, Eleanor thought, if he goes back to work on his father's farm in Carmarthen, I shall lose my daughter. Wales seemed a world away from the West Riding of Yorkshire. Though nothing definite had been said, she was sure they would marry, Selina and this young man she had known for so short a time. She herself had met him for no more than an hour or two, when Selina had brought him home from the canteen in Akersfield. She had liked him, she had nothing at all against him, but what could you know of a man in a few hours?

Selina laid her hand lightly on her mother's shoulder. She knew what was behind her question but she could give no reassurance. She loved her family deeply. Once she had thought she could never leave them, or leave Yorkshire itself, but now she knew that if he asked her to do so, she would follow Bob Harwell to the ends of the earth.

'What time will Becky be home?' she asked.

'Who knows? The trains will be at sixes and sevens on Christmas Eve, especially with so many of them commandeered to get soldiers home in time for Christmas. But knowing Becky, if she's decided to come home tonight, she'll do so. Becky usually manages to get what she wants!'

Eleanor's smile did not quite counteract the dryness of her tone. Never since the day her eldest daughter was born had she found her easy. She was beautiful, talented – but not easy. Even when Becky was a child, she had not felt totally comfortable with her.

'She'll be tired,' Selina said. 'She works so hard – all that travelling. Playing and singing.'

Since they were formed in 1915 the Bluebirds had travelled all over Yorkshire, entertaining soldiers in camps and in hospital. Becky, a dedicated Bluebird, was seldom at home.

'I think she enjoys it,' Eleanor replied. There was no point in telling Selina that her elder sister thrived on the gadding about that would have been anathema to her.

'Since prisoners of war are being brought back as fast as they can find ships and trains to carry them, I daresay Roland will be home pretty soon,' Selina said. 'And then he and Becky will be married. And live happily ever after!' She sighed, wishing her future was so settled.

'I'd have thought he'd have been home already,' Eleanor said.

But will they be happy ever after, Eleanor wondered? Will Roland Layton and my daughter get on together after all this time? At the beginning of the war, when Roland had taken a commission in the West Yorkshire Regiment and they had become engaged, Becky had been an immature eighteen and Roland only twenty, and it had all seemed a great adventure, a bit of a lark. Eleanor was afraid that, in a way, it was still that to Becky.

'I think Becky has almost enjoyed the war,' she remarked.

'Mother, how can you say such a thing!' Selina spoke with unusual sharpness. 'How could she enjoy it with Roland a prisoner of war for the last two years? She must have been dreadfully anxious, wondering how he was being treated. I know I would have been.'

But you and Becky are made of different stuff, Eleanor thought. At first Becky had enjoyed being the fiancée of a serving officer, but as the war went on it seemed, at any rate to Eleanor, that Becky had almost forgotten Roland. It had been *she* who had reminded her of the importance of sending regular letters and parcels to the prison camp in Germany. Sometimes it had even been she who had made up the parcels of comforts and sent them off in Becky's name.

'You judge Becky too harshly,' Selina said.

'Perhaps you're right.' Selina saw the best in people. 'I wonder how Roland will have changed? Prison camp must surely leave its mark.'

Before Selina could answer there was a commotion at the front door.

'That means Jenny's back with Peter,' Selina said.

Jenny never moved quietly, but wherever she went she

288

brought sunshine with her, as she did now, coming into the room on this darkening December day. Even her appearance was sunny, with her yellow hair escaping from under her tam-o'-shanter, her skin glowing from the cold.

'It's *freezing* out there!' she exclaimed. 'Wouldn't it be heaven if it snowed for Christmas! Where's Robert?'

'I put him down for a nap,' Eleanor said. 'Otherwise he won't be fit to stay up this evening.' At three and a half she still guarded his every moment.

'And where's Grandma and where's Uncle Dick?' Jenny demanded. She always like to account for the whole family.

'Grandma is presumably on her way home from The Beeches,' Eleanor replied. 'She said she had some clearing up to do. If she doesn't arrive soon, one of you had better go and meet her. Uncle Dick should be home any minute.' He had always been 'Uncle Dick' to the girls and there seemed nothing else they could conveniently call him. The man they thought of as their father, Frank Kramer, was still deeply mourned and much missed. Not one of the girls could ever call anyone else 'Father'.

'I've spent up?' Peter announced. 'Christmas presents cost far too much and there are too many people in this house!'

'I daresay you won't think that when you're opening *your* presents!' Selina teased.

'But you all have more money than me,' he protested.

'Then you should try saving,' Jenny said. She didn't add that she had slipped him two shillings of her own savings when his money wouldn't stretch to seven presents. She had suspected from the first that that was why he wanted her to go shopping with him.

In some way Peter was the odd one out in this family, though he was equally loved by all of them. Perhaps not equally. Dick Fletcher had reason to love him more. Peter was flesh of his flesh, though he might never know it.

'We're having supper early,' Eleanor said. 'I promised both Peter and Robert they could stay up for it, as its Christmas Eve.'

'What about Becky?' Jenny asked.

'Let's hope she'll be here,' Eleanor said.

But when they sat down at the big oval table in the dining-room, both Eleanor's mother and Dick having arrived, Becky's place was still empty.

'Shouldn't we wait supper for her?' Selina suggested. 'She might be disappointed.'

'It isn't practical,' Eleanor answered. 'She's given us no idea what time she'll arrive. And if we leave it too late, then Peter and Robert will be past enjoying anything.'

'Anyway, I'm starving!' Peter said. 'I could eat a horse. They say the soldiers in France ate horses. Did you eat horsemeat in the olden days, Grandma?'

'No I did not,' Mrs Foster replied. 'And not so much of the olden days, neither. A bit of nice cold chicken is what you're getting, and see you go easy on the pickles, my lad. They lie heavy on young stomachs at bedtime.'

She only half believed what she was saying. All her life she'd eaten with gusto whatever was in front of her and the only time she'd suffered discomfort was when there hadn't been enough of it, like those first awful days in Akersfield, when they'd lived on whatever leftovers they'd been given by Frank Kramer or his mother.

Now she looked at the laden table and thought how different everything was. Her daughter had come a long way, and she with her. But it didn't do to forget your origins.

'I wish Becky *would* come,' she said. 'I don't like to think of her traipsing around after dark on Christmas Eve.'

'I'm sure she'll be all right, Mrs Foster,' Dick Fletcher reassured her. 'She's a young woman who can look after herself. But straight after supper I'll go down to the railway station and see if there's any sign of her.'

'I really don't see why you should, Dick!' Eleanor broke in. 'There's a wicked wind blowing off the moors. I don't want you standing about in it just because Becky hasn't seen fit to let us know what time she's arriving.'

'Jenny and I will go,' Selina said. 'I don't mind the cold.'

'Nor me,' Jenny agreed.

They had been brought up to it. Everyone around the table, and their ancestors before them, had lived all their lives in the long northern winters, the short summers and the incredibly beautiful weeks of spring and autumn. Strong winds and rain from the Pennine hills, fog brought from the industrial towns, frost and snow, were the normal pattern of weather. Only Eleanor, though she never took a cold and was never ill, seemed ultra-sensitive to it – which was surprising since she had been reared in Felldale, where almost every winter they were cut off by the depth of the snow.

'I don't see that anyone need go out on a night like this,' Eleanor persisted. 'Mr Tomkins will have his cab outside the station. There'll be no need for her to walk home. Not that it's far.'

They let the matter drop. Everyone knew that Selina and Jenny would go to meet their sister if they wished to. Eleanor got up from the table and went to fetch the mince pies and cheese from the sideboard, with a dish of jelly for Robert.

'Why aren't we having trifle?' Peter asked.

'Trifle is for Boxing Day,' his grandmother said. 'Mince pies and cheese Christmas Eve, goose and plum pudding Christmas Day, with spice cake at teatime; trifle on Boxing Day.'

'Why?'

'Because that's the way it is,' Mrs Foster replied patiently.

Peter was about to say more when he was interrupted by the ringing of the telephone in the hall.

'I'll answer,' Jenny said. 'It'll be Becky.'

She was back in seconds, her eyes wide.

'It isn't Becky. It's for you, Selina!'

'Me? Who can be telephoning me?' Selina said, rising. And then she caught her breath, felt the strength drain out of her, clutched at the edge of the table.

'It isn't! It can't be . . .!'

She rushed out of the room. Everyone at the table looked towards Jenny.

'I don't know! There was a lot of noise. I couldn't hear what he said, except he wanted Selina.'

Eleanor was half out of her seat but Dick motioned her to sit down again.

'No, Ellie! If it is him, let her be on her own.'

She sat down. He was right, of course. When had she ever wanted to share Dick with anyone else? But it seemed an age before they heard the faint tinkle as Selina replaced the receiver and came back into the room.

It was as if she walked in a cloud of sunbeams and moonbeams. Everything about her shone, radiated. Even the tears in her eyes were like diamonds.

'It's Bob!' she whispered. 'It's Bob! He's home in Carmarthen. He's coming here on Boxing Day!'

Eleanor was around the table, taking her daughter in her arms. She felt Selina's tears, now overflowing, and her own mingled with them.

'Oh Selina!'

'That's grand news, love. Just grand!' Mrs Foster said. 'Now sit down and finish your supper, doy.'

'Oh I couldn't, Grandma!' Selina cried. 'I'm far to happy to eat!'

'How was he?' Dick asked. He looked forward to meeting this young man who brought such radiance to his stepdaughter's face. He had just better be good enough, that was all!

'All right. He was phoning from the nearest public house. His parents don't have a telephone yet. There was a lot of singing in the background, so it was difficult to hear.'

But she had heard what she needed, that he was safely home and soon he would be with her. She started calculating the hours until his arrival on Boxing Day. There was no telling what time he would come; it was a long journey and the trains were any old way. But forty-eight hours at the most and she would see him, talk to him, touch him. Happy tears overwhelmed her again and she was still drying her eyes when Becky made her entrance.

Becky did not simply come into a room, she made an

entrance, every bit as dramatically as if she was stepping on to the stage. It was second nature to her. Now she stood in the doorway, her face framed by the deep fur collar, her red lips stretched in a wide smile, a fringe of copper-coloured hair escaping from under her hat. She flung her arms wide in a gesture which seemed to embrace everyone in the room.

'Here I am! At last! Merry Christmas everyone! Did you think I was never going to arrive? Well I did, and I'm starving! So is Jimmy! I hope you've saved us some supper?'

'Jimmy?'

'Jimmy Austin, Mother. He's our new stage manager. He brought me in his motor car because he knew how much I hated the thought of those horrible crowded trains. *Wasn't* it kind of him!'

'Very kind,' Eleanor said. 'Where is he?'

'Getting the cases in. He wasn't sure whether you'd welcome him, being Christmas Eve and all that, but I assured him you'd be delighted to meet him.' She turned, and called over her shoulder. 'Jimmy, don't stand there in the hall! Do come in!'

He came and stood behind Becky. I have not heard of this one, Eleanor thought. And he was not at all what she expected. What men there were in the Bluebirds were either too old for active service, or unfit. Here was as fit and handsome a man as she had ever set eyes on. He was tall, topping Becky by at least six inches, broad-shouldered, fair-haired, and certainly not a day over twenty-five.

'This is Jimmy,' Becky said. 'And this . . .' she waved a hand around the circle of faces all turned in his direction, 'is my family. I'll introduce them separately later. Much too much all at once!'

Dick moved forward to greet the visitor, his hand outstretched.

'Pleased to meet you! Let me take your greatcoat. And I'll make the introductions. First of all I'm Dick Fletcher and this is my wife.'

His wife! He never used those words without a warm thrill

293

of pleasure coursing through him. He loved her so much, and he had loved her so long. Sometimes it seemed to him that he had loved her and waited for her for the whole of his life. His caring extended now to all the family in this room because they were, in one way or another, part of Eleanor; but his real happiness would be when the evening was over and the two of them were alone in their bedroom, the rest of the world shut out.

'You must have some supper with us before you go,' Eleanor said. She spoke politely, though somehow she felt wary of this good-looking stranger. 'But if you'll excuse me, I'll just see my two youngest off to bed first. It's very late for them.'

'You take the children up,' Mrs Foster told her. 'I'll lay a place for Mr Austin and see to him and Becky.'

She could see through her daughter's politeness, knew she wasn't happy, and understood why. It was to have been just a family occasion, the first, and with the girls grown up, perhaps the last for a long time. But if a stranger came at Christmas you had to welcome him, choose how. There was no gainsaying that.

'Come over to the fire, both of you,' Selina said. 'You must be frozen!'

'We are a bit,' Becky admitted.

They stood in front of the fire, two beautiful women and the handsome man, smiling at each other, their faces glowing in the light from the flames.

'You've already been demobilized, then, Mr Austin?' Selina asked.

'Some time ago,' he said. 'Dicky heart, as a matter of fact.'

'Oh, I'm sorry!' He looked so strong and virile.

'I *must* tell you, Becky!' Selina went on excitedly. 'The most wonderful thing! I had a telephone call from Bob – just before you came. He's home! And he's coming up to Hebghyll on Boxing Day!'

Becky shrieked with delight. 'That's wonderful! Marvellous! Now I know why you look as though you've been given a thousand pounds!'

'Oh I do so hope for your sake that Roland will be home soon,' Selina said impulsively. 'I want you to be as happy as I am! I know you can't be until you have him back.'

'Roland?' She heard the question in Jimmy Austin's voice, saw the way Becky bit her lower lip – a trick she always had when something wasn't quite right. Had she said something wrong? Was it possible that Becky hadn't told Mr Austin about Roland – but what did it matter anyway? Perhaps there hadn't been time, perhaps she hadn't known him long, or didn't even know him well? That must be it. It was none of his business.

'Roland?' Jimmy Austin insisted. There was more than a hint of possessiveness in his voice. He sounded like a man sure of his ownership. Becky was saved from replying by the reappearance of Dick Fletcher, who had been with Eleanor, seeing the young ones to bed.

'I'm sorry, Mr Austin,' he said. 'I should have shown you where to wash your hands. If you'd like to follow me. . .'

Jimmy Austin's look was fixed on Becky.

'I'll explain later,' she said quietly. 'Do go with Uncle Dick. I'm sure supper's almost ready.'

'Why is he upset about Roland?' Selina asked when the two men had left the room.

'He's not. Don't be silly! He's just surprised, that's all. I haven't had the opportunity to tell him.'

'But you are going to tell him, Becky?'

'Of course I am! But things are never as simple as they seem to you, Selina. You're so *naive*!'

'I'm not a fool!' Selina said sharply. 'It seems quite straightforward to me. But oh, Becky, I do so want you to be happy. I'm so happy myself, I want everyone else to feel the same.'

'I know. You always do. I just hope for your sake that everything will be all right when you see your beloved Bob. I really do hope that.'

A shiver of fear went through Selina.

'What do you mean, Becky? Why shouldn't everything be all right?'

Becky shrugged.

'No reason! Just that people change when they don't see each other for a long time. It's to be expected.'

'I haven't changed,' Selina said. 'I don't think Bob has. I don't believe it.'

'I daresay you're right, little sister. Stop worrying. Listen, will you do me a favour – since you want to make everyone happy?'

'What is it?'

'Will you persuade Mother to invite Jimmy to stay the night? I more or less promised him she would, but by the look on her face I don't think it's going to happen unless you persuade her. It's far too late and too nasty for him to go back to Thirsk.'

'He could stay at the Shoulder of Mutton,' Selina suggested.

'He wouldn't get in,' Becky said evasively. 'Far better for him to stay here – *please* Selina!'

'Oh very well,' Selina agreed.

'A camp bed in the drawing-room,' Becky said. 'That will do quite well. You're an angel, Selina, and you're not to take any notice of what I said – I mean about people changing. You never change.'

I know that, Selina thought. I feel pretty sure Bob is just the same, too. But *supposing*? There was a small cold lump of fear in her heart as she left the dining-room in search of her mother.

When everyone had eaten they moved into the drawing-room.

'The tree looks splendid!' Dick said. 'You did a good job there, Selina. And now we're all going to have a glass of port wine.'

He handed round the glasses, wondering, as he gave one to Jimmy Austin, just where this man fitted into Becky's life. He himself knew nothing of Roland – except that Becky was engaged to him. He had never met him. But he

296

knew that Eleanor was disquieted and he resented anything which troubled his wife. And now the fellow had somehow been invited to stay the night. But for the time being, no matter. Nothing must be allowed to spoil this very special evening.

'Before anything else,' he announced, 'I want us all to join in a toast. Let's drink to absent friends – to those still far from home, to the ones we shall see again, and those we shall never see in this world.'

He reached for Eleanor's hand and held it tightly in his own, turning to look into her eyes. He knew she was thinking, because so was he, of Frank Kramer, that good and kind man who had been her husband; that man who, though of German blood and parentage, had given his life for England. He nodded his head, showing her that he shared her thoughts, and understood. The shadow of Frank Kramer would never come between himself and Eleanor.

He thought too of his dead wife, Jane, whom he should never have married; and of Emily, the daughter of that marriage, who was lost to him because he had let her go when she was a small child. He had wronged Jane and he had wronged Emily; how could he deserve the wonderful happiness which was now his?

Becky, Selina and Jenny also thought of the man they had called Father. But it was more than three years now since his death, and the hurt was beginning to heal. Selina wouldn't forget him, but there was Bob. It was to Bob she was now raising her glass. For Becky the hurt would last longer. She had been his favourite. She had felt secure, admired, loved in his presence. And now she had to think of Roland. What was she going to do?

Susannah Foster thought of her son and daughter-in-law in Felldale, and of Jimmy, her young grandson, who had gone down with the *Lusitania*. But most of all she thought of her youngest son, David: the apple of her eye, the light of her life. He had died in the Boer War. No-one would ever understand that to her it felt like only yesterday.

'Let's sing some carols!' Jenny cried. 'Let's choose one each

297

in turn. Bags me "In the Bleak Midwinter". What about you, Selina?'

In the background, when Bob had telephoned from the public house, they had been singing a carol, their Welsh voices rising in beautiful harmony. 'I choose "Once in Royal David's City",' Selina said. It would bring her nearer to Bob.

'Are you going to accompany us, Becky?' Dick asked.

'If you wish.'

'Then I shall turn the pages,' Jimmy Austin said.

His offer brought Becky a twinge of discomfort. She had first met Roland when he had turned the pages for her at a small musical evening her parents had given in Akersfield. But once she was playing, with everyone gathered around, the feeling passed. They were a music-loving family. For each one of them, while the music lasted they could forget whatever troubled them and live only in the moment.

'Come on, Grandma,' Becky said. 'What's it to be?'

'Well I suppose since I've spent most of my life in sheep country, it'll have to be "While Shepherds Watched".'

When it came to Eleanor's turn she said, 'Dick and I have chosen one between us. We want "Silent Night".'

'Is it for a special reason?' Selina asked. She had detected something in her mother's voice.

'Yes. We want it because it's German, and because for the first time in four years we're at peace with Germany. We think they might be singing it too.'

'Then you must sing the first verse as a solo, Mother,' Jenny insisted. 'None of us can sing like you.'

It was true. And her voice goes on improving, Becky thought as she listened to the rich, round, soaring notes. It was the carol she herself would have chosen, because it had been the favourite of the man who had been a father to her. Tears filled her eyes as she thought of him, so that she could no longer see the music; but it didn't matter, she knew it by heart.

'Now Becky, your turn,' Eleanor said when the last note had died.

'I'll share that with you and Dick if I may? There's nothing better.'

Eleanor rested her hand on Becky's shoulder, gave her a gentle squeeze. She knew what her daughter was thinking.

'Of course you may, love.'

Shortly after midnight everyone went to bed.

'I hope you won't be too uncomfortable on your camp bed, Mr Austin,' Eleanor said. 'I've given you plenty of blankets.'

'I'm sure he's slept in worse places,' Dick smiled. 'And it's only for the one night!'

In the bedroom they shared, Selina and Jenny were quickly between the sheets.

'I shall be eighteen in the New Year,' Jenny said. 'I long to be eighteen. Mother can't stop me from training to be a nurse then, can she?'

'She can until you're twenty-one, but she won't,' Selina replied. She didn't want the usual conversation she had with Jenny before they settled down to sleep. Tonight she wanted to think only of Bob. Before she blew out her candle she looked, as she did every night, at his photograph on her bedside table. He looked so wonderful in his uniform. She had never seen him in civilian clothes. Would he be very different?

For a long time she lay awake, hearing her sister's deep breathing; and when she fell asleep it was to dream that she and Bob had arranged to meet in a railway station. The train arrived, but they passed each other by, neither of them recognising the other.

Mrs Foster looked out of the window before she got into bed. The snow was lying. It would be deeper still in Felldale, covering everything in a thick blanket, like as not blocking the lanes. Though she would never tell anyone, at Christmas time she was always homesick for Felldale. It was to be expected. She had been born there, lived there for the first fifty years of her life; married there, had her children. However happy she was anywhere else, Felldale would always be the place first in her heart.

299

Eleanor was brushing her hair. Dick came behind her and looked at her in the mirror.

'Don't ever have it cut, will you?'

He bent over, buried his face in her hair. It was like silk, delicately perfumed silk. She turned around and drew his head down to hers, her mouth finding his in a kiss which grew more passionate as they clung to each other.

'Come to bed,' Dick said.

They never grew tired of their lovemaking. It was deeply satisfying to both of them. When they came together as they did now, it was perfection. They were the only two people in the world. Eleanor wondered, so good was it, why she never conceived. Even at forty, she wanted Dick's child, though he did not. He was always afraid that something might go wrong for her, and relieved each month when she told him it wasn't to be, not this time round.

It was half-past one in the mroning, Christmas Day, when the door of Becky's room opened quietly and Jimmy Austin entered. She was sitting up in bed, arms outstretched, waiting for him.

'I thought you were never coming,' she whispered, turning back the bedclothes, drawing him towards her in a fierce, clutching embrace.

CHAPTER EIGHTEEN

Jimmy Austin, propped on one elbow, looked down at Becky as she lay against the pillow. He smoothed a strand of damp hair away from her cheek and she gave a little murmur of appreciation. She was almost asleep.

'I have to go,' he whispered.

Roused, she lifted her arms and clung to him.

'Not yet, Jimmy! Don't go yet!'

'I must. It's almost morning. We can't risk it.'

'Well one more kiss then – and tell me you love me, and you understand about Roland!'

He understood all right. In the preliminaries of making love, he had got it out of her, in spite of her reluctance to talk. He was not particularly surprised. He had first met Becky three weeks ago, and had summed her up in the first three days, though he hadn't suspected there was someone like Roland in the picture. That, he thought, was going a bit far. But she was a hot little piece, and two years was a long time to wait, even though the man *was* languishing in a prison camp. Also he was sure he wasn't the first who'd helped her fill in the time. You could always tell.

'I understand,' he assured her.

'I was so young. He pressed me so hard to be engaged before he was sent to France.'

'Does he know you don't intend to marry him?'

'I thought it would be better to tell him when I saw him.' In any case, she had not decided, not until she had met Jimmy, that was. Now she could think of no-one else. Roland was a pale, distant shadow. She had almost forgotten what he looked like. Jimmy was here; passionate, demanding, his flesh calling out to her flesh. 'It's you I love, Jimmy! You do love me, don't you?'

'Of course I do, sweetheart. As long as you understand we couldn't get married for ages and ages.' Never, in fact, though he knew she'd had wedding bells in her ears, right from the beginning. 'I haven't a bean. No job, no prospects. Not to mention expensive tastes! Perhaps when he comes home your Roland could give me a job. You say his father owns a mill. He must be worth a bob or two.'

'Oh he is,' Becky agreed. 'But if I didn't marry Roland, why would he do that for you? And if I do marry him I'll lose you. I couldn't bear that.'

'Not if he gave me a job, you wouldn't. I'd see you often. Of course we'd have to behave ourselves.'

Or at least be discreet, he thought. And it would have to be the right kind of job – perhaps travelling for the firm; selling. He could do that. Yes, there were real possibilities.

'We're talking too much, my sweet,' he said. 'Someone will hear us. I must get back to my own cold bed!'

He gave her a kiss which melted the marrow in her bones, and left her longing. Longing – and desperately considering ways and means. She had never felt like this about anyone before. She had been fond of Roland; she still was, but it had never been like this, and now she had butterflies in the stomach at the thought of confronting him. He was bound to be home soon. Perhaps he would have grown tired of her, she thought hopefully. She turned over and pulled the bedclothes around her head. Oh well! In the end a way would be found; Roland would be pacified and she and Jimmy would marry.

When she went downstairs next morning Jimmy was up and dressed, sitting in the kitchen eating the substantial breakfast Mrs Foster had cooked for him. Becky was bitterly disappointed. She had made an effort and got up early in the hope of finding him alone. Trust Grandma to be up before the birds!

'Merry Christmas, Becky! Merry Christmas, Mrs Fletcher,' he added as Eleanor came into the kitchen behind Becky.

302

'Merry Christmas, everyone! I trust you slept well, Mr Austin.' Eleanor hoped his early appearance meant an equally early departure. He was pleasant enough, but there was something about him . . . though perhaps it was no more than the fact that he had been foisted on her.

'Like a top, thank you! I hope you'll excuse me invading your kitchen so early, but I have to be away.'

'But why?' Becky couldn't keep back the protest. 'It's not even light yet!'

'It's a family occasion, Christmas, isn't it? So I'm sure you'll understand I have to be with my own folks?' He addressed his remarks to Eleanor and her mother. And well he might, Becky thought! *She* knew that his only family was a sister in Harrogate with whom he didn't get on. So where was he rushing off to?

'Certainly we'll excuse you.' Eleanor hoped the relief didn't sound in her voice. She turned to her mother. 'Peter and Robert are bound to waken any minute. Will you manage if I go back upstairs so that Dick and I can be with them when they open their stockings? We'll have the main presents after breakfast, as usual.'

'Then I'll say goodbye,' Jimmy said. 'Thank you very much for your hospitality, Mrs Fletcher.'

'Thank you for bringing Becky home,' Eleanor replied.

He was quickly ready for off. Becky went out to the car with him. Daylight came late in the north but the sky was lightening now. There was an inch or two of snow on the ground and the air was crisp. It was going to be a fine day. If only she could spend it with Jimmy!

'When shall I see you again?' she asked.

'Soon, my sweet. Don't worry, I'll be in touch!' He cranked the car, and while it still shuddered leapt into the driver's seat, and was away. She watched until he turned the corner of the road and was lost to sight.

'Come and get your breakfast,' Mrs Foster said.

'I'm not hungry, Grandma.' What did he mean by 'soon'? How could she bear to wait?

Selina had come into the room.

'When do you plan to visit the Laytons?' she asked, helping herself to porridge, sitting at the table. 'I'm sure you must have made some arrangements over Christmas.'

'As a matter of fact . . .' Becky looked hesitant. '. . . I had promised to visit them on Boxing Day. But in view of the weather . . .'

'Weather?' Mrs Foster queried. 'You don't call a couple of inches of snow bad weather! The trains will be running to Akersfield as usual.' It was a strange objection, coming from Becky. She was usually only too happy to get away from home again after the briefest of visits.

'And then I didn't know Bob Harwell would be coming on Boxing Day, did I?' Becky said eagerly. 'It would look awfully rude if I wasn't here to greet him! I could telephone the Laytons. They'd understand.'

'No need to do that,' Selina put in quickly. 'I'm sure Bob will excuse you.' She loved her sister dearly, but on this occasion she would just as soon she was absent. Becky would outshine her, as she always did, even without trying. Becky automatically shone, became the glittering centre of attraction. Usually it didn't matter, but tomorrow was different. Selina sent up a swift prayer that Becky would go to Akersfield.

'I think Mr and Mrs Layton would be very disappointed if you didn't go,' Mrs Foster said. 'Especially with not having Roland home for Christmas.'

Becky sighed. 'I suppose so. I'd better go then.'

She liked her prospective in-laws. They had been kind to her from the beginning, treating her as if she were the daughter they had never had, and hoped she would soon become. Mr Layton was quite indulgent, arranging little treats when they saw her, sending her the presents he said Roland would have wanted to give her if he'd been there. It was because they looked forward so much to her becoming one of the family, and because she really did respect them, that she now, for the first time, dreaded facing them.

Upstairs, when Eleanor entered the boys' room, she found Dick already there. He had lifted Robert from his

304

cot on to Peter's bed. Now he put out a welcoming hand to Eleanor.

'Come and sit on the bed, love.'

The two boys had each borrowed a stocking from their grandmother, reckoning it capable of holding more than their own. Peter was carefully feeling the strange bumps and protuberances in his.

'I want to guess what everything is before I take it out,' he explained. 'I can feel the orange and the apple, and maybe these are nuts in the toe — but what's this square thing, very hard?' He hoped it was what he'd been longing for, what he'd seen on display in Thompson's window, and coveted for ages.

Robert didn't wait to explore. He emptied everything on to the counterpane as quickly as possible, his face beaming as he surveyed the treasures spread out around him: a coloured ball, an apple, a golliwog, a rag book of nursery-rhyme characters, nuts and sweets; nothing of value and everything riches.

'For goodness sake, Peter, get on with it!' Dick cried. 'You're keeping us all in suspense!'

'No I'm not,' Peter contradicted. 'You know what's in the stocking, Uncle Dick. You and mother filled it!'

Uncle Dick. If he could call me Dad I'd be the happiest man in the world, Dick thought. But they hadn't judged the time was ripe to tell him, and perhaps it never would be, for it would mean revealing that Eleanor, whom he adored, was not his mother.

Peter was emptying the stocking now, ranging the contents on the bed. There was a pencil box with two compartments and a sliding lid, which would be jolly useful; a notebook, marbles. Then slowly he drew out the hard square object.

'It is! It is!' he shouted. 'It's the printing set!'

He opened the tin box and surveyed the contents — grooves which were filled with rubber letters of the alphabet, and all the figures; a stamping device into which four rows of letters could be fitted at a time; an inked pad. Now he would not only be able to write his own stories, he would be able to print them.

'How did you know?' he cried. 'How did you know it was exactly what I wanted?'

Everyone, it seemed, was equally pleased by the presents exchanged after breakfast.

'Grandma, how *did* you get through all this knitting – socks, gloves, scarves – without anyone seeing it?' Selina asked.

'It wasn't easy,' Mrs Foster admitted. 'I couldn't pretend I was knitting a red scarf or a pair of blue gloves for the troops!'

It had been easier, though, because at The Beeches she had her own room. At first Eleanor had been troubled at the thought of splitting the family, but there wasn't really room for them all at Whinbank.

Eleanor had waited for this third marriage, Mrs Foster thought. Even to her, the thought that Eleanor loved Dick Fletcher had been, at first, no more than a fleeting suspicion which she had at once pushed to the back of her mind. But her daughter had behaved honourably, she felt sure she had. And she'd been a good wife to Frank Kramer while he lived. Now she wanted her to have all the happiness she could, and if there was a man in the world who could give it to her, that man was Dick Fletcher.

'Now I want you to take it easy today, Ma,' Eleanor said. 'With all the girls here I've got loads of help cooking the Christmas dinner. There's no need for you to lift a finger.'

Sometimes she worried about her mother. She was sixty-five and working as hard as ever, but she never had a day's illness, and if she felt tired after a long day in the cafe, she never admitted it.

'Well, if you say so,' Mrs Foster replied. 'Though I'm not used to doing nothing, as you know. But I've got my *Woman's Weekly* magazine to read and two new books from the library to start on.'

She was well aware that Eleanor did all she could to ensure that, in the business, she was allocated the jobs which didn't keep her on her feet too much. She looked after the repair and replacement of the linen, saw to it that the tables had been correctly laid in the cafe, and that in the four guest rooms everything was in apple-pie order. In a way it was no more than an extension of what she had done all her adult life; first in service, then in her own home with her husband and children; after she was widowed, in her son's home, and then with Eleanor. The difference was that now she didn't have the hard graft of washing, cleaning, baking. There were younger bodies to do that. And Eleanor, in spite of being newly married and still having two small children to look after, remained the driving force, the organiser, the maker of decisions.

'You should let Selina take on more,' Mrs Foster sometimes said. 'She's ready and willing for more responsibility.'

But now, at Eleanor's insistence, she took herself off to the sitting-room and settled herself in an armchair in front of the blazing fire, magazine in hand and her books on the side table.

'And I'm pouring you a glass of sherry,' Eleanor said. 'I've decided to spoil you for today!'

For Selina, happy though she was with her family, Christmas Day crawled by. As she prepared the vegetables, spread the big table in the dining-room with the best white damask cloth, laid out the cutlery, her thoughts were entirely on Bob Harwell, her mind wishing away the hours which must elapse between now and the moment when she would set eyes on him.

Becky, on the other hand, would have preferred time to stand still, have wished the ages they spent over preparing, serving, eating the Christmas dinner, and afterwards playing childish games, to have been endless. Anything to stall the hour which would inevitably come when she must walk down to Hebghyll station and take the train for Akersfield. Best of all she would have liked to have turned the clock back to last night, to the moments Jimmy had spent in her bed, she in his arms, concentrating entirely on the present bliss. Why oh why did life have to be so complicated?

307

In spite of the fervent wishes of both sisters Boxing Day dawned at its appointed hour, no sooner, no later. Selina sprang out of bed, and, too eager to go down to the kitchen to draw hot water from the fireside boiler, too anxious to start the day, poured ice-cold water from the ewer into the basin, stripped to the waist and sluiced herself. There was no bathroom yet at Whinbank, though one was due to be installed soon. No matter. This morning she would have washed herself in the snow with no trouble at all. Then she went to waken her elder sister.

'Becky!' she whispered. 'Eight o'clock! Time to get up!'

Becky moaned and turned over, burying her head beneath the sheets. It couldn't be. Not so soon. She was so tired; she didn't feel well. Was she, in fact, fit to *go* to Akersfield? Might she not be sickening for something?

'I feel *awful*!' she groaned. 'Selina, I really don't feel fit!'

'Nonsense!' Selina said briskly. 'Rubbish!'

'No, truly!'

She can't do this to me, Selina thought rebelliously. I won't let her.

'I'll go down and fetch you some hot water,' she offered. 'I'll make a cup of tea. You'll have to get going or you'll miss the train. It's a restricted service on Boxing Day.'

She was downstairs and back again, bearing the enamel jug of hot water, in no time at all. She poured the water into the basin, then shook Becky into life.

'Go away!' Becky grumbled.

'I won't!' With a movement quite unlike herself she tore the bedclothes from Becky and left her shivering in her nightdress.

'Get a move on!' she said firmly. 'By the time you're dressed I'll have breakfast ready. And dress warmly. It's cold outside.'

It would be, Becky thought, reluctantly getting out of bed. It would probably snow again before she got to Akersfield. Where was Jimmy? Was he *really* at his sister's? If only she was going to join him she would get up readily enough. She gave a passing thought to where poor Roland might be and was thankful that today, at any rate, she would not have to face him.

An hour later – Becky had dawdled over her breakfast as long as she could – Eleanor came downstairs.

'Becky is just going for her train,' Selina said. 'I'm going to walk down to the station with her.'

'There's absolutely no need,' Becky protested. 'Anyone would think you wanted to get rid of me!'

'Why in the world should I do that?' Selina queried. But she knew it was true, and she knew why. Deep in her heart she had this fear that if Bob Harwell saw Becky – so much prettier, more lively, more talented – he might fall in love with her. Who could possibly prefer her, Selina, once they had seen Becky? It was this thought which put the steel into her, made her determined to supervise Becky's departure. She would have no security until she had seen the train, with Becky on it, pulling out of Hebghyll station. Becky could have the rest of the world and everything in it, but not Bob Harwell. He is mine, she thought fiercely. He's all I've ever wanted.

'I shall quite enjoy walking you to the station,' she said. 'It's a nice fresh morning and the walk will do me good.'

'Wrap up well, both of you,' Eleanor cautioned. 'Becky, give my regards to Mr and Mrs Layton and tell them I hope Roland will be home soon. I'm quite sure he will be. Then they must all come over and visit us. We shall have a lot to talk about, I'm sure.'

Selina walked with Becky to the station, saw her on to the train. She does look awfully pale, Selina thought, observing Becky's wan face as the train pulled out of the station. Could she really not be well? Have I been unkind, unfair? But she knew she would do it again, though this purposeful, almost ruthless, feeling was new to her, and strange.

It was only as she started to walk back home, the snow crisp and crunching under her boots, the cold air nipping her face, that she thought to ask herself why Becky was behaving so. It was as untypical of her sister as was her own

309

present mood of herself. But since Christmas Eve she had had nothing in her mind except Bob Harwell. Now she recalled the awkwardness when Roland had been mentioned in Jimmy Austin's presence and the way Becky had pushed the subject aside. So was it . . .?

But surely Becky couldn't do that to Roland, not when she was engaged to him, not after all he had gone through? And not for the kind of man Jimmy Austin seemed to be, for Selina didn't care for him at all. All the same, she knew one couldn't fall in and out of love to order. Love had hit her like a thunderbolt and there was nothing she could have done to stop it, even if she'd wanted to. Filled with her own happiness, she found it in her heart to be sorry for Becky, though still pleased that she was safely out of the way. By the time she reached home her thoughts were once again entirely with Bob.

'Selina is in another world,' Eleanor said to her husband. 'I hope everything's going to be all right.'

'Have you any special reason for thinking it won't be?' Dick asked.

'No. I liked what I knew of Bob Harwell. But he's been at war – right through the Somme. War changes men.'

'Sometimes,' Dick admitted. 'But not always.'

'I know. It didn't change you, my love.'

But perhaps it had, and for the better, she thought. He was still the strong, ambitious man she had always known, determined to be successful, but there was a depth of loving, of understanding in him that hadn't been there before. Perhaps it wasn't only what he had gone through in the war – the life in the trenches, the severe wounding and the painful months in hospital from which he had been so slow to recover – but the fact that they had had to wait for each other so long, and had done so without ever telling their love, though they both knew it was there, which had mellowed his nature and enriched every moment of their marriage. It didn't occur to her that the difficulties of her own life, or, rather, the strength with which she had faced them, had brought her also to a gentle maturity.

310

'Will Bill Stead be able to get to the markets if the bad weather continues?' she asked.

'If the snow doesn't get too deep, or drift,' he answered. 'But I'm never convinced that the motor lorry is as reliable as the old horse and cart on a bad surface. The problem will be having enough produce to take. We've got root vegetables stored, but if the frost goes on a long time we shan't be able to get more stuff out of the ground. Snow doesn't matter – snow keeps stuff warm underneath it – but hard frost can damage.'

'You were lucky having Herbert Crowther to keep the garden going for you through the war,' Eleanor said.

'Don't I know it. He was worth his weight in gold – still is. And Stead is good with the markets. I never really liked doing the markets. I preferred growing the stuff.'

'Yet if you hadn't done the markets we might not have met up again,' Eleanor said softly. 'I was at rock bottom when I came to your stall that Friday afternoon.'

He nodded. 'But you'd have pulled through. You always would and always will.'

Selina popped her head around the door.

'I'm going down to the station. He might be on the four-fifteen.' Whichever train he came by he would have had to change at Leeds or Akersfield for Hebghyll. There was just no telling when he'd arrive. He hadn't telephoned again and she had no way of contacting him.

'You really don't need to go, love,' Eleanor told her. 'He'll find his way.' Her daughter had spent the day going to and from the station. It was almost dark, and getting colder.

'I want to be there to meet him when he steps off the train,' Selina said. She wanted to be the first person he saw, to have him to herself for a few minutes before they were surrounded by the family. If it meant meeting every train between now and midnight, she would willingly do it.

He was not on the four-fifteen, nor on the seven o'clock. Just before nine o'clock, wrapping the knitted scarf her grandmother had given her for Christmas more tightly around her neck, pulling her tam-o'-shanter over her brow,

311

she set off again. Supposing, just supposing, he didn't come at all! Supposing he had changed his mind? Supposing something terrible had happened to him, an accident? But she was being stupid. It was a long journey from Carmarthen and everyone knew the trains were impossible. She arrived at the station ten minutes early and stood on the platform. She could have gone into the ladies' waiting room, where a bright fire burned, but her mood was too impatient.

She heard the whistle of the approaching train, saw the steam from the engine rising into the dark sky, watched the lighted windows as it drew nearer. Then with a hiss of steam it came to a standstill at the platform. Two carriage doors opened – there were few passengers for Hebghyll at this time of night – and she didn't know which way to look. While she looked towards the front of the train and saw a stranger approaching her, footsteps sounded at her back. When she turned her head he was standing there.

He dropped his valise to the ground and she was in his arms, held tight against him, her face buried in the heavy cloth of his army greatcoat.

'Oh Bob!'

'Oh Selina, my love!'

'Oh Bob, I thought you were never coming!'

'I know. I thought I'd never get here. I left home before six this morning. Let me look at you, Selina! Let me look at you! It's been so long!'

He held her at arm's length, though not letting go of her, while he gazed hungrily at her remembered face, the face in the photograph which had never left him, right through the fighting.

'You haven't changed,' he said. 'Oh Selina, how wonderful that you haven't changed!' The same golden hair falling from under her cap, the same blue eyes, though now swimming with tears as they looked into his. Sometimes in France he had thought that the whole world had changed, and that this girl he had known for such a short time would have changed with it. But she hadn't.

'Nor have you,' Selina told him. He was as dark as she

312

was fair; Celtic-looking, no more than an inch taller than she, and there was the same Welsh lilt in his soft, almost musical voice which over his long absence she had tried to hear in her mind. It was his voice, requesting a cup of tea and a sandwich, which had first attracted her when she had met him in the army canteen in Akersfield.

'Of course you didn't have three stripes up when I last saw you, Sergeant Harwell,' she reminded him, laughing. 'You were a humble private! But let's get going or we shall freeze to the platform.' There was no-one else around, even the porter had retired to his den. 'Anyway, you must be awfully tired and very hungry.'

'I am both,' he admitted.

'Well, there's a meal waiting for you. And home is only ten minutes' walk away. Oh Bob, I just can't believe it's true!'

'Nor I, Selina. But it is!'

He took her in his arms again and kissed her long and lovingly. In the ice-cold air her lips were warm and pliant against his. Then he picked up his valise and, arms around each other, they left the station. It was snowing heavily; thick wet flakes which clung to their clothes, their hair. They were hardly aware of it. When Mrs Foster came to the door they couldn't think why she shrieked at the sight of them.

'Heavens above! You look like a couple of snowmen! Get inside at once and get those wet clothes off or you'll both catch your deaths!' She allowed no time for leisurely greetings and her cries brought Eleanor and Dick into the hall.

'I'm very pleased to meet you,' Dick said. 'We've been looking forward to it.'

'You must be starving,' Eleanor told Bob. 'You must have something to eat first, and then we'll catch up on the news. It's been a long time.'

'The kitchen is the warmest place in the house and I've got a pan of stew and dumplings on the stove,' Mrs Foster said. 'Come away in, both of you.'

Hardly a word was spoken while they ate. It was enough for Bob and Selina that they were together, side by side. Mrs Foster wondered if they even tasted the food, though Bob

313

put it away as if he hadn't eaten for a week.

'It was a marvellous meal,' Bob said later, when they had all moved into the sitting-room. 'And I was ready for it.'

'How long since you ate?' Eleanor asked.

'Hours and hours! Mam put me up some sandwiches but I ate those ages ago. There was no food to be had on the railway stations.'

'Food's not as plentiful as it was,' Mrs Foster said. 'We're on ration books now. But we manage quite well.'

'I didn't think you'd be in uniform,' Jenny remarked suddenly. She had sat quietly until now, studying this young man about whom Selina was so besotted. Well, he was nice enough. Not exactly her idea of Prince Charming, but nice enough.

'I'm not finally demobbed,' Bob said. 'I've been through the dispersal unit, got all the payments and been measured for a civilian suit, but we have twenty-eight days furlough before we're finally out. We're allowed to keep our khaki. Not the greatcoats though. We have to turn them in at the end of our furlough.'

'Ridiculous in this weather!' Mrs Foster declared.

Bob turned to Selina.

'I still haven't met your elder sister. She was away with a concert party before I went to France. Is she still with them?'

'Becky? Only for a little while, I reckon. Right now she's visiting her future in-laws in Akersfield.' It wouldn't have mattered if Becky had been here, she thought. He's mine. No-one can take him from me!

When the Laytons' maid, Hannah, opened the door in the late morning of Boxing Day and saw Becky standing there, the anxious expression on her face changed to a tremulous smile of relief.

'My word, miss, the master'll be glad to see you, and no mistake. We was hoping you'd come.'

'I said I would,' Becky answered. No matter that she'd done her best to get out of it. 'Where is Mr Layton?' He usually came quickly into the hall to greet her, as did his

314

wife. Now there was no sign of either of them.

'He's upstairs. The mistress isn't a bit well. I don't know whether it's the good news has knocked her over, after all these years, or whether it's something worse.'

'Good news?'

'I know Mr Layton tried to contact you but he couldn't get through on the telephone, and there were no telegrams Christmas Day. Mr Roland is on his way home, miss! Isn't that the best news you ever heard?'

Becky's stomach lurched. She was saved from answering by Mr Layton's appearance. He came down the stairs to greet her, his face heavy with concern.

'By Gow but I'm glad to see thee, lass!' Though he was now, thanks to the miles of khaki cloth he had turned out during the war years, a well-to-do man, with an assured place in Akersfield society, he had not lost, and never would lose, his Yorkshire voice and way of speaking. He reckoned nothing of posh talk, though it was permissible, just, in those who'd been brought up to it.

'Hannah says you've had news of Roland?'

'Aye, we have. He's in England. He's in a reception centre in the south, where they check out the prisoners of war. So we can at least thank the Lord God Almighty for Roland's deliverance.'

'But there's something else?' Becky queried. He didn't have the look of a man whose only son was coming home after long years in a prison camp. 'Is he all right? Is there something wrong with him?'

He shook his head. 'No, no, not as I know of, lass. It's the wife. She's bad. She's real bad. Hot as fire, shivering to shake the bed, weak as a kitten.'

'But you must send for the doctor!' Becky cried. 'Have you not done so?'

'Aye, I have that. He's been. It's the Spanish flu, Becky! That's what it is. The Spanish flu and she's got it real bad! The doctor says we should try to get Roland home quickly, while there's time. I've already telephoned and he's on his way. Please God he won't be too late!' He buried

315

his face in his hands, Becky put her arms around him, held him close.

'Oh Pop, I'm so sorry! But maybe it's not as bad as you think. Maybe she'll take a turn for the better. They say it sometimes goes as suddenly as it comes.'

He shook his head. 'Nay lass, I don't think so. But will you not go up and see her? Next to Roland you'll do her more good than anybody in the world. She's allus thought a lot of you, Becky love.'

For an instant, fear swept through Becky; fear of catching this illness which was spreading like a plague over a country already weakened by war; fear of dying from it before she had begun to live. But she was not a coward and the fear left her as quickly as it came.

'Of course I will,' she said. 'I'll go up at once.'

Standing by the side of the bed, Mr Layton opposite her, Becky took Mrs Layton's hand and held it in her own. The woman's flesh seemed as burning hot as a live coal. Her face was a dusky red, the eyes as bright as glass, her lips blackened and cracked with fever. But it was the look on Mrs Layton's face which shocked Becky. She knew at once — though how could she recognize it since she had never seen it before? — that the look on the face of this woman who had been so kind to her, a woman she truly liked, was that of someone who was going to die.

She bent over Mrs Layton, touched her hot, dry cheek with her own cool fingers. 'I'm sorry to find you so poorly, Mama Layton,' she said quietly.

'Roland is on his way,' Mr Layton told his wife. 'He'll not be long.'

'That's all I want,' Mrs Layton whispered. 'Just to see Roland! I'll be content then.'

She was not to see him, at least not in the flesh, though at one point she lifted her head from the pillow and her face lightened, as if she saw something the others could not. Five minutes later she closed her eyes for the last time.

Mr Layton's cry of anguish rang through the room,

brought the maid running. When he spoke, his words pierced Becky like a sword.

'What am I going to do? What are me and Roland going to do without her? Don't ever leave us, Becky love. You must never leave us! You're all we have now!'

The undertaker was still there when Roland arrived. Becky herself opened the door to him.

CHAPTER NINETEEN

It wasn't him! It couldn't be! This man who stood on the doorstep, valise in hand, his uniform lightly powdered with snow, could not be Roland. He was too thin, his face too bony. He looked smaller, shrunken, almost. And there was nothing of the fire, the excitement, which had been Roland's.

'Becky! Oh Becky!'

The voice was Roland's. Though he was a little hoarse, and his fatigue sounded even through the brief words, there was no mistaking his voice. It was deep, with an almost musical timbre, and the slight lengthening of the vowels which betrayed his West Riding origins. Yes, the voice was his.

He stood for a moment, just looking at her, taking her in, then he stepped inside the house, put down his valise, pulled her into his arms. She felt the dampness of his clothing on her dress as he held her close, the chill of his fingers as he touched her neck, the iciness of his lips against hers. He felt the warmth and softness of her body, smelled her perfume in his nostrils. Sometimes he had wondered if such things as women's perfume still existed.

'Oh Becky, I've lived for this moment! You don't know how I've longed . . .'

He continued to hold her close. Even through his uniform she could feel the thinness of his body, the boniness of him. He had been so strong, so powerful.

'Oh Roland!' She could think of nothing to say – and now he had to be told about his mother.

'I know,' Roland said. 'I understand. You can't find the words and nor can I, though I've rehearsed them a thousand

318

times! But we will, Becky. We will. And now we have all the time in the world.'

She drew away from him. It seemed almost indecent to be embracing while that poor woman lay upstairs. It was almost as if the sight of Becky had driven from Roland's mind why he'd been sent for in such a hurry.

'Roland,' she began. 'Your mother . . .'

'I know,' he said. 'Let me get my wet coat off and I'll go up and see her right away. Is she any better?'

'Roland, you don't understand. She's . . .'

She was saved from saying more by the sight of Mr Layton and the undertaker descending the stairs together. Roland moved quickly towards them, grasping his father's outstretched hands in his own.

'Oh Dad, it's good to see you! And this must be the doctor. How is my mother, sir?'

Fresh tears spurted from Mr Layton's eyes. He took out his handkerchief and blew his nose.

'Nay lad, he's not the doctor. He's the undertaker. Thy mother's dead!'

There was a second's frozen silence, everything turned to stone, then a piercing cry from Roland as he pushed past his father and ran up the stairs. Becky thought she would never forget that cry as long as she lived. It was a wail of anger, frustration, deep desolation; an animal cry of one who had borne everything and could bear no more.

Mr Layton, his face wet with tears now, turned to go after his son, but the undertaker put out a restraining hand.

'Leave him be, Mr Layton. That's my advice. Leave him be for a while. We all have to mourn in our different ways. I'll take my leave of you now, Mr Layton, but if there's the least thing I can do . . .'

At the door he turned to Becky.

'I'm sure you're going to be a great source of strength to this family. You mark my words!'

'She is that,' Mr Layton said fervently. 'She is that!' He put his arm around her shoulders. 'The lass will be our salvation.'

319

'I'm not! I won't! I don't want to be!' But she didn't allow the cry that was in her heart to reach her lips. She couldn't, with this sad man beside her and Roland's terrible shout still ringing in her ears.

She couldn't tell them that she wasn't strong, as they thought. She was weak. She didn't want to be their salvation, she wanted to run away from it all. She wanted to run as fast as she could, and she wanted – dear God how she wanted it – to run straight into the arms of Jimmy Austin. Less than forty-eight hours ago she had been in his arms, their bodies warm against each other. Now the whole world had changed, grown as cold as the icy landscape outside, and, in spite of her outward calm, inside herself she didn't know how to cope with it.

It was a full hour before Roland reappeared. Mr Layton longed to go to him, and it was only with difficulty that Becky dissuaded him.

'The undertaker was right,' she said. 'We must leave him be. He'll come down when he's ready.'

While they waited she sat with Mr Layton in the sitting-room, listening to him talking. He was half-incoherent, not making sense, but it seemed to help him to talk, his grief pouring out with the words.

'I had some happy times with Edith,' he said. 'When we were young and Roland was little. They were the best times. Nobody knows how much I'll miss her!'

While he talked about the past it was bearable, but when, almost in the same breath as if there was no difference, he spoke of the future, Becky wanted to put her hands over her ears, to shout to him to stop.

'It's all up to you and Roland now. I'm a broken reed now, no use to anyone without my Edith. But you mustn't let my grief stop you getting married. I know it's what you both want.'

'We needn't talk about it now,' Becky said. 'Roland might not want it. Not so soon. Not in the circumstances.'

'Of course he will, love! Don't you fret. I'm sure it's what he's been dreaming of. And it's what his mother would have

wanted. My lovely Edith! How can I go on without her?'
He buried his face in his hands and sobbed.

'I understand, Pop,' Becky told him gently. 'But Roland
will look after you. You know that!'

'And you,' he said eagerly, looking up, reaching out and
grabbing her hand. 'You'll not desert us, Becky love! Yes,
she'd have liked to think of you looking after us, would
Edith. She trusted you.'

But it's not what I want, Becky thought desperately. Does
no-one care what I want?

'I don't need to tell you you'll be comfortably off,' he
went on, speaking quickly now. 'I'll see to it you want for
nothing. I'm not without a bob or two and you shall have
a little income of your own, a bit of independence. There's
not many married ladies have that.'

He was begging her, fear in his eyes, anguish in his face.
She wanted to shout to him to stop. It wasn't fair!

'If you don't like the house we'll move somewhere different,' he pleaded. 'But my Edith loved it. She chose every
single thing in it, you know!'

'It's a beautiful house,' Becky said truthfully. It was also
substantially furnished with everything that money could
buy, though Mrs Layton's taste was not necessarily Becky's.
Also, if she were choosing, she would prefer the more
exclusive Halton area of Akersfield, where the nobs lived,
and where Mr Layton could well afford a house. But she
was not choosing, and she had no desire to do so.

'I wouldn't be a nuisance to you,' Mr Layton cried. 'I'd
have my own rooms. I daresay you'd only see me at meal-
times. And Roland can take over from me in the firm
whenever he likes. I've no heart for it any longer. I've no
heart left for anything, Becky love!'

'I'm sure you'll be needed in the business for a long time
yet,' Becky said. 'Besides, perhaps Roland won't want to go
into the firm. Perhaps he'll want to do something different.'

'What? Oh no, I don't think so, lass. It's always been
understood that he'd join me. Becky, love, to start with
you'll stay with us until after the funeral's over? Say you'll

do that! I can't face it, and I daresay Roland can't. I'll get old Aunt Hettie to come, to make it all proper. There'll be a lot to see to that needs a woman's touch – the funeral tea and suchlike. Now if Edith were here . . .' His voice trailed away in confusion.

Becky felt herself being drawn in, trapped, bound hand and foot. It was not the arrangements for the funeral; that was a small matter which, with the help of the undertaker, she could take in her stride. It was all the rest. How could she possibly fight this sad suffering man? There was a terrible strength in his pleading.

'Of course I'll see to the funeral,' she promised. 'But there *is* one thing. The Bluebirds have a concert in Harrogate on Friday, at a home for wounded officers. I have to be there. I can't let them down.' And she had to see Jimmy, she absolutely had to. Wherever he was now, he would turn up for the performance.

'Well if you must, love, you must,' Mr Layton agreed. 'You're not one to let people down. I know that. And you'll not let me and Roland down, will you? But I'll send Briggs with the car to pick you up after the show and you'll be back here the same night.'

'I'll have to call in home to get some clothes,' she pointed out. 'But I'll be back on Saturday, late morning for certain. The funeral won't be until Tuesday, so that gives me plenty of time.' She had no intention of being collected straight after the concert, much as she liked the idea of a chauffeur-driven car calling for her.

'Aye,' Mr Layton said. 'The undertaker apologised for the delay. He said people were dying like flies from this terrible flu. He's never had so many funerals in hand at once. Where will it all end, I wonder?'

I can't bear it, Becky thought suddenly. She was sorry for him, sorry for both of them, but four more days of this gloom would drive her mad. Thank heaven she had an excuse for a break.

When Roland finally joined them he was calm again, but the sorrow in his unhealthily pale face, the grief in his eyes, aroused a deep and unusual pity in Becky. Why must fate be so cruel to him when all his life he had been straightforward and honourable? For one moment, as she watched him embrace his father after their years of being apart, she wished that she had never met Jimmy Austin, or for that matter any of the others, though *they* had not counted for much; that she had been as eager for Roland's return, for the start of their new life together, as Selina had been for Bob Harwell's.

The moment quickly passed. She was not Selina, and never could be. Selina saw things in black and white; she was deep down good. I am my mother's daughter, Becky thought. We see things less clear cut. It should have brought them together, yet she had never been as close to her mother as Selina was.

'I've been telling Becky,' Mr Layton said. 'There's nothing to stop you two getting married. The Lord knows you've waited long enough, and I'll not stand in your way. Because my life's as good as over doesn't mean yours mustn't go on.'

'Pop!' Becky protested. 'You mustn't talk so. And surely that's a subject for Roland to bring up, not anyone else!'

Roland smiled for the first time, and when he smiled he began to look more like himself, the self she remembered.

'Dad was never known for his tact! All the same, Becky, he's right, though I'd rather he'd left it to me to say so. It's what I want. I hope it's what you want.'

'Well, I'll leave you both,' Mr Layton said. 'I'd like to be on my own for a bit.'

Becky watched Mr Layton move, almost stumble, towards the door.

'He's taking it badly,' she said when he had gone.

'They were everything to each other,' Roland said. 'She was a good wife and a wonderful mother. I shall never forget her . . .'

She waited quietly while he overcame his grief.

'But you and I will be everything to each other,' he continued presently. 'Oh Becky, you do want us to be married soon, don't you?'

323

All at once he felt uncertain. He remembered the briefness and paucity of her letters when he had been in the camps; the frequent occasions when the mail arrived and there was nothing from her.

'I was never sure from your letters,' he confessed. He had searched them in vain for an expression of the kind of love he felt for her.

'I'm not good at letters, Roland. Not everyone is.'

'I know, dearest, But I'm here now, in the flesh. Oh Becky, it's been so long.' He made a move towards her but she drew away.

'It was a long time for me, too.' It seemed a lifetime away. He had been so dashing, so full of vitality, so handsome in his officer's uniform.

'Too long? Are you telling me you couldn't wait?' He would try to understand if it was so. He loved her so much; he would forgive her anything.

'Of course not, Roland,' she said hurriedly. 'But I don't think we should talk about marriage until after the funeral. It doesn't seem proper.'

Before then she would see Jimmy. She felt sure that if only she told him how desperately she loved him, he would marry her. Roland would have to let her go then.

'Oh Becky!' Roland said, smiling. 'When did you ever care about being proper? But I'll wait until after the funeral – and not a minute longer!'

When she arrived at the convalescent home on Friday afternoon Jimmy was already there. He was a good and conscientious stage manager. It had been a lucky day for the Bluebirds when he had joined them – could it be only three months ago? And luckier still for me, she thought. At the sight of him her spirits lifted for the first time in days. Oh, he was so handsome, so charming, she had never known anyone to come within a mile of him. He gave her a hug and a quick kiss and she at once felt full of optimism.

'Sorry I'm late,' she apologised. 'Blame the trains!'

She had decided to say nothing, at any rate not at first, about Roland's return or Mrs Layton's death. She couldn't bring herself to talk about it. For the moment she must put it right out of her mind or she would go mad.

'Be a darling and try the piano,' Jimmy said. 'It's probably frightfully out of tune.' They usually were.

She sat down at the piano, ran her fingers expertly up and down the keys, played a few chords.

'It seems reasonably all right,' she told him. 'There are one or two notes which stick, and the pedals are not all they might be. But I've managed with worse.'

She practised numbers from *Chu Chin Chow*, which was sure to remind some of the officers in the audience of the leaves they had spent in London during the war; she played – and sang in her sweet, true, but not very powerful soprano – songs from *Maid of the Mountains*, and the war songs which people everywhere still loved to sing.

'Jimmy,' she said, 'will you take me out for tea in the town when we've finished rehearsing?'

'Why not?' he agreed.

They had tea in a cafe at the top of Parliament Street. Becky waited until they had drunk their second cup and Jimmy had finished his toasted teacake – she couldn't swallow hers – before she could pluck up the courage to say what was in her mind. It was not the ideal place for it – this crowded cafe – but where would they ever get a chance to be entirely alone? And it shouldn't be up to her to say it, but it was now or never and there was no other way. She took a deep breath and came straight out with it, the words tumbling over each other in her effort to get them said.

'Jimmy, will you marry me? I love you with all my heart! Please say you will, Jimmy. Oh, you don't know what it's cost me to speak like this!'

He held up his hand to stop her.

'Whoa! What's brought this on all of a sudden?'

'Oh Jimmy, it's not all of a sudden. You know it isn't. But the truth is, Roland has come home and his mother's died and Mr Layton is pushing me to marry him. And so is Roland.'

Jimmy stared at her.

'Roland is home, his mother's died – and you rehearsed as if nothing had happened!'

'I wanted to speak to you first.' Oh God, she prayed, let him say yes! Please let him say yes!

He reached across the table and took her hand.

'Sweetheart, I can't,' he said gently. 'I've told you, I'm not the marrying type. I've nothing to offer you. I couldn't keep you, Becky, not the way you've been used to. I have to say no for your sake – though God knows it goes against the grain!'

'I don't care about any of that! I'll find a job, I'll work for the two of us!'

'But think what you'd be giving up,' he said. He knew how rich old man Layton was.

'I'd give up everything for you,' she whispered.

It was one of the few occasions in Jimmy Austin's life when he felt very slightly ashamed.

'It's still no go,' he said. 'I'm sorry, love.'

She bit her lip, fought back the tears.

'Then supposing I tell you I'm pregnant!'

She wasn't sure about it. She was only a few days overdue but usually you could set the clock by her, and she had this feeling inside her. She hadn't meant to use this as a weapon, but if there was no other way . . .

'Are you?'

'I might be. If I am, it's yours!'

'If you are,' he said slowly and firmly, 'then I advise you to marry Roland as quickly as possible!' He was certainly not going to tell her that he couldn't marry her, even if he wanted to, because his so-called sister in Harrogate was actually his wife and they had two little brats of their own.

Becky blushed to the roots of her hair.

'You don't mean that, Jimmy! You can't mean it!'

'Every word!' he assured her. 'For your own sake *and* the kid's.'

She drew on her gloves, smoothing down each finger carefully and deliberately, not hurrying in the least, not looking at him. When she felt she could control her voice she said:

'I think I shall take a little walk in the Valley Gardens before I go back to the concert. No – don't get up. I'd rather be alone!'

He watched her weave her way across the crowded cafe. What a pity, he thought. What a bloody pity! She's a spunky little piece! But by God, if he were Roland he'd keep a sharp eye on her.

Sitting in the train between Harrogate and Hebghyll, Becky felt bruised and beaten, and as cold and dark inside as the night outside. For one brief moment, as the train pulled into Hebghyll station, she wondered if she might confide in her mother. But it was a silly thought. How could her mother possibly understand what it was like to be in love with the 'wrong' man? Besides, she was forty – too old. Nor could she tell Selina. Selina would be shocked to the core. Yet she felt so badly in need of comfort, of someone who could understand how she felt. No-one could, of course.

The first person she saw when she went into the house was her grandmother.

'You look frozen, Becky love,' Mrs Foster said. 'Come into the kitchen and I'll make you a cup of hot Bovril. Have you had anything to eat?'

Her grandmother, of course! She would understand. She wouldn't approve, but she'd understand.

She followed Mrs Foster into the kitchen, then she was in her grandmother's arms, crying as if her heart would break – as it surely must! Great sobs tore at her body as grief tore at her heart and mind. Mrs Foster held her, gently removed her hat, stroked her hair.

'There, there, Becky love! Don't take on so!'

'Oh Grandma, I'm so unhappy! I'm so unbearably unhappy!' She could hardly speak for crying.

'I know, love! It was a great shock to all of us, Mrs Layton's death. We all felt it but I know you were especially fond of her.'

All the same, she hadn't expected her granddaughter to show so much grief. You never quite knew where you were with Becky. She wasn't a loving girl, not like Selina and

327

Jenny, but Mrs Foster remembered that Becky had been the one most affected when her stepfather died.

'But she didn't suffer long, poor soul! We must be thankful for that. And now you have Roland home to comfort you.'

Becky lifted a tear-wet face and stared at her grandmother. What *was* she going on about? Oh, Jimmy, Jimmy, Jimmy! She hadn't had a thought in her head except for Jimmy since that terrible moment when she'd walked out of the cafe. Out of his life, for she knew it was all over between them. But how could she expect her grandmother to understand? She knew now there was no point in telling her, none at all.

'You'll feel better after the funeral,' Mrs Foster consoled her. 'Everybody feels better once the funeral's over. Here you are love, dry your eyes and I'll make you that hot Bovril.' She gave Becky a loving pat on the shoulder and handed her a large handkerchief. She was a strange girl and no mistake. She had a suspicion there was more to it than Mrs Layton's death. Something to do with Roland, no doubt.

'Things will sort themselves out,' she said soothingly. 'You'll see. Given time.'

All the time in the world won't sort this out, Becky thought. And supposing she was pregnant? She wished she knew about that, one way or the other.

'Selina'll be in any minute with her young man,' Mrs Foster went on, handing Becky the mug of Bovril. 'They've all gone to a little bit of a do at the Tate's house. Your ma and Uncle Dick as well. You haven't met Bob yet, have you? He's a fine young man. You'll like him.'

'I suppose Selina's in seventh heaven?'

Mrs Foster jerked her head up sharply at the bitter note in Becky's voice.

'Of course she is! And so will you be about Roland, once you get over the shock.' She hoped she was right about that.

'And speak of the devil, that's them at the front door,' Mrs Foster said. 'They'll be surprised to see you. And pleased.'

'I must go upstairs and tidy myself,' Becky said quickly. 'Grandma, please don't tell them I was upset!'

328

'Of course I won't, love. Not a word if that's what you want.'

Becky grabbed her hat and bag and ran out of the kitchen and up the back stairs. In the bedroom she bathed her face in cold water, tidied her hair, took several deep breaths and went downstairs. She couldn't manage a smile, but in the circumstances they wouldn't expect it.

'I'm very pleased to meet you,' Bob Harwell said when they were introduced. 'You were away with your concert party when I was in Akersfield during the war.'

During the war. The words sounded strange in his ears. He couldn't believe that it was all over, all in the past. You couldn't get rid of it just like that; the terrible sights, the smells, the noise. Most nights he wakened, sweating in terror, the sound of the heavy guns, the lighter rattle of the machine guns, in his head; the wounded crying in agony and the men yelling for the stretcher-bearer. It was all there in the night, every detail. But in the daytime you hid it. You didn't want to talk about it to people at home, who could never, ever understand what it was like. Not even Selina. And he supposed he'd get over it one day.

Becky liked the look of Bob, though he wasn't entirely her type. She preferred tall fair-haired men. Like Jimmy. She knew she was going to compare every man she met with Jimmy. She tried to push the thought of him away from her. But Bob was just right for Selina. She was lucky, as usual.

'How long are you here for?' she asked him.

'Another week. Then I must go back home, sort things out.'

Selina came and stood beside him, took his hand, looked at him with love in her eyes.

'We're going to be married in two months' time,' she said. 'Isn't it wonderful, Becky? And now Roland's home and you'll be getting married, won't you?'

Becky ignored the question.

'Where are you going to live?'

'That's what's so marvellous,' Selina said. 'Mother has offered Bob a job at The Beeches. He's to learn everything

329

about it, work with me, and eventually we'll take it over!'

'But not just yet,' Eleanor put in from her armchair. 'I'm not quite worn out yet!'

'I have to discuss it with my parents,' Bob said. 'Dad expected me to help him on the farm. But we're a big family, he'll not lack for help – and I've never thought I was cut out for farming.'

'Bob is taking me back with him to Carmarthen, to meet his family,' Selina said. 'Becky, I want you for a bridesmaid – if you're not married first, that is. I suppose you might have to put it off for a bit, being in mourning. Poor Mrs Layton!' For a moment she felt guilty that other people were sorrowful when she was so blissfully happy. 'Anyway,' she continued, 'if you marry first, you can still be a matron of honour.'

Becky was almost glad, next morning, to leave this house which seemed to be overflowing with happiness. She didn't fit in. But she dreaded the Layton's too; dreaded Mr Layton's entreaties and plans; dreaded the moments of intimacy which must come with Roland. Due to Mr Layton's insensitivity and self-absorption, she and Roland had scarcely been alone, but that couldn't last. She didn't know what to say to him, didn't know what she should do.

'I shall see you on Tuesday then, in Akersfield,' her mother said when Becky was leaving.

'I've told you there's no need for you to come to the funeral, Mother. It will be a very small affair.' She didn't want her there. Her mother was too quick to notice when anything was amiss.

'Nonsense! Of course I shall come,' Eleanor insisted. 'Edith Layton was a good friend of mine. I wouldn't dream of not attending her funeral.'

When Becky arrived in Akersfield her mood had not changed. If anything, she felt worse. What had happened to the bright future she had seen for herself before the war? And even during the war life had been exciting, always something to do, new places to visit with the Bluebirds, new people to meet. Now she could see nothing good ahead.

To her surprise, Roland was waiting at the station. He looked pale and tired, but his face lit up in a smile as she walked towards him.

'I telephoned your mother to ask which train you'd caught,' he explained. 'Oh Becky, it *is* good to see you again. I can't tell you how I've missed you, even though it's only been two days. I don't ever want you out of my sight again.' He tucked his arm through hers and held her close.

'We'll get a cab,' he said as they came out of the station.

'No,' Becky said. 'I'd like to walk.'

The snow in Akersfield had long since turned to grey slush underfoot, and it was unpleasant and treacherous; but she didn't want to hurry back to the house. Anything to put off the moment.

'I have a fancy to walk past Kramer's,' she said. 'Do you mind? It's no more than ten minutes' walk from here.'

'Not a bit,' Roland answered. 'I want to see all the old places I used to know.'

It was Kramer's no more, of course.

'Do you remember I worked here for a time, after I left school?' she asked Roland. 'I hated it. I always wanted to get away. Sometimes now I think I'd like to be back.'

Roland gave her a curious look. 'There are better things in store for you than that,' he said.

The name over the door was Johnson's. It had gone to seed. The cakes in the window looked fly-blown and stale, the paintwork was dirty – even the few people at the tables inside looked older and shabbier.

'We must go,' Roland told her. 'You'll catch cold.'

They lingered a few, sad minutes, then Roland took her arm and led her away, cutting across the side streets of the town towards his father's house.

'When I was in the camps,' he said suddenly, 'I used to go for a walk in my head around the streets of Akersfield. Every night I did that.'

Becky pulled a face.

'I could think of better places to walk! Grimy mills, shabby buildings, chimneys belching smoke!'

331

'It was home,' Roland said.

But she had never grown to like it and thought she never would, though if she felt secure anywhere, which was doubtful, it was here in Akersfield rather than in the smarter Hebghyll.

It was awful entering the house. The curtains were drawn across all the windows, and would remain so until after the funeral, so that the gas lamps had to be lit though it was not yet the middle of the day. Roland's aged Aunt Hettie was in the kitchen. She was dressed in deepest black, which reminded Becky that she had to go into the town that very afternoon to buy mourning.

'Though goodness knows what I shall find ready-to-wear,' she said to Roland.

'Which reminds me that my father left this for you.' Roland handed her an envelope. 'He said you were to get the best possible, whatever you wanted.'

The envelope contained twenty gold sovereigns. Becky gasped at the sight of them.

'I can't possibly accept this!' But even as she said it, she knew she wanted to. She had never had as much money in her life before.

'Please do,' Roland begged. 'It will mean so much to him.'

'But I don't need even half of that to buy an outfit.'

'I told you what he said. You're to get the best. Please!'

'Well, if you're quite sure . . .'

'I am.'

She put the money away carefully in her purse. She would shop at Barnet's. She had never dared to enter Barnet's before, it was so expensive.

Roland took her purse from her and put it on the table, then he drew her down beside him on the sofa.

'Becky, we have to talk. It might be the only chance we have to be alone. Father will be back soon from the solicitor's.'

Becky interrupted him.

'But Roland, we said not until after the funeral. It doesn't seem right with your mother . . . upstairs.'

'You're wrong, Becky. My mother loved you like a daughter. She would have wanted me to say it. Becky, when can we be married? I love you more than anything in the whole world and I want you for my wife.'

'It's so soon, Roland!'

'Soon, Becky? We've been engaged for four years.'

'I know, but . . .'

'Becky, are you saying you don't want to marry me? Oh, my dearest love, tell me that's not what you mean?'

'Of course it isn't.'

'Then what is it? If it's my father, we don't have to live with him for always, though I wouldn't like to leave him just yet.'

'Of course it's not your father, poor man. I'm fond of him, and he's always been so kind and generous to me.' She thought of the twenty pounds reposing in her purse, and of the allowance he had promised her when she married Roland. 'No, of course it's not your father!'

'Then it must be me! Tell me why, Becky! Tell me how you want me different, and I'll *be* different if I can.'

'I don't want you to be different. I like you as you are, Roland.' She *did* like him. He was a kind, good man. It was not his fault that he wasn't Jimmy Austin. He would probably make a far better husband, and in any case, Jimmy was lost to her. That was certain.

'But not enough to marry me? Is that it, Becky? Well, I won't hold you against your will.'

'I didn't say that.'

What should she do? If she didn't marry Roland, what else could she do? She could think of nothing. And if I'm pregnant, she thought, what then? It would be wrong to marry him without telling him. But if she wasn't — and she was by no means sure, so many things had happened which might have upset her rhythm — then it wouldn't be fair to distress him by telling him. She couldn't undo what was past. She didn't want to. Oh, there were so many things to think of and she was so tired of it all!

'Becky, I'm waiting for your answer,' Roland said. There

333

was, for the first time, a hint of steel in his voice. If she refused him now he might never ask her again.

'What's it to be, Becky? I repeat, I love you with all my heart. I will try to be the best husband in the world to you, as long as we live.'

She took a deep breath.

'Oh Roland, of course I'll marry you. I'll marry you as soon as ever you wish!'

'Can you tell me you love me, Becky?'

'Of course I love you, Roland.' She said it with only the slightest hesitation. In her own way, she *did* love him.

When he took her in his arms she was amazed at the strength and passion of his kiss, and at the way his hands moved over her body, arousing feelings in her which she had thought could be awakened only by Jimmy Austin.

CHAPTER TWENTY

Becky and Roland were married, in Akersfield registry
office, three weeks to the day after Mrs Layton's funeral.
Heavy rain all the previous day and throughout the night
had washed away the last traces of snow, leaving the
pavements dark and shining. It was still drizzling, the sky
low and heavy, when the wedding party emerged after the
short ceremony, crowding into the hallway, waiting for the
cars to take them back to the house for the reception.

'I perfectly understand that your wedding has to be a
quiet one,' Selina had said. 'After all, you are in mourning.
But are you positive you want it in a registry office? Surely
a church . . . Hebghyll church is so pretty . . . or even a
nonconformist chapel, because after all, the Laytons are
Wesleyans.'

'Selina, I know what I want,' Becky had replied. She'd
hated those last three weeks in Hebghyll, everyone advising
her what to do. 'You arrange your wedding, I'll arrange
mine. I don't care two hoots about a church wedding. In
fact a registry office suits us very well – and Roland agrees.'
She was in no mood for a church ceremony.

'That's true,' Roland confirmed. 'I don't mind whether
we get married in a cathedral or on the top of a tram, just
so long as we do it, and soon!' He smiled lovingly at Becky.
He was so unbelievably lucky.

'Moreover, it's going to be Akersfield registry office,'
Becky said.

'Well, I shall give you your reception at The Beeches,'
Eleanor said. 'It's not all that far for the cars, and no-one
can say I don't know how to do a wedding reception!' These

days, with everyone rushing to get married after the long war, she was doing two or three a week.

'No,' Becky said. 'Thank you all the same, Mother, but I don't want it. I don't want all the fuss. And Pop is far from well. It's only three weeks, remember. We shall offer a glass of wine and some food back at the house. That's all.'

'But Becky . . .!'

'Selina can have all the fuss! I just don't want it.'

Selina's wedding was not until mid-March, but already she was in a welter of arrangements − dresses, flowers, lists for this and that. She was enjoying every minute of it.

Aside from her family there were to be no more than a handful of guests at Becky's wedding, and those mostly members of the Bluebirds. It had been Roland's suggestion that Becky should invite some of her friends from the concert party, though since that last engagement in Harrogate she had resigned from the company.

'They looked after you, kept you interested and happy all that time when I was away,' he said. 'I feel I owe them something. Besides, I'd like to meet them.'

'Are you sure, Roland? You might not like them.'

'Of course I shall, silly! They're your friends, aren't they?'

In spite of the shock of his mother's death, he seemed happy now. He was still pale and thin, physically not his old self, but since the moment they had fixed the date of the wedding he had had a new confidence. It showed in his voice, and in his eyes.

'Well, don't blame me if they bore you to tears,' Becky warned him.

She didn't want to take up with them again. With all her heart she longed to see Jimmy Austin, yet she dreaded it. She wanted − she was determined − to be a good and faithful wife to Roland. To see Jimmy again, even with the status of a newly-married woman, would not help her resolve. She pushed away from her mind the thought that, since she planned to ask only four members of the company, Jimmy need not even be included.

'Well, get on with it,' Roland urged. 'Write the invitations.'

That was why, waiting in the entrance hall of the registry office on this winter morning, were Percy Moore, baritone and reciter of dramatic monologues, Alicia Scholes, mezzo-soprano and co-duettist with Percy (as well as being Mrs Moore), Fluffy Proctor, charming soubrette – and Jimmy Austin.

'I think the rain's easing off a bit,' Mr Moore said, peering out. 'Ah! The cars are here!'

It came to Becky suddenly that the hired Daimlers were the same ones which had borne them to Mrs Layton's funeral so short a time ago, except that now they were decorated with stiff bows of white ribbon and streamers on the bonnets. She hoped the thought hadn't occurred to Roland or his poor father. Mr Layton was far from well; his usual ruddy complexion was unhealthily pale.

Back at the house Aunt Hettie, who had felt it unwise to take her winter cough out into the inclement Akersfield weather, was in the hallway to meet them. A strong smell of coffee pervaded the house.

'I didn't know we planned to have coffee,' Becky said. Aunt Hettie blushed.

'We didn't! I did it against the infection. I didn't know it would smell so strong, did I?'

'Did what, Aunt Hettie?' Becky queried.

'You throw a good handful of ground coffee on to the fire in each room. It keeps down the infection. It was a hint in the *Akersfield Record*. A lot of people in the house and all this flu going around. You never know. I thought it was a good idea . . .'

Her voice trailed off. Tears came to her eyes. She had done the wrong thing again, reminding them of what the flu had done to this house. And on this day of all days! What a silly old fool she was!

'Really . . .!'

Becky bit back the rest of her retort. It wasn't the time or place. But she would be glad when this foolish old woman had returned to her own home and left her in peace to run the household which was now hers.

337

'I'm sorry!' Aunt Hettie gulped.

'Don't worry, Auntie,' Roland said gently. 'It's all right.'

'Actually, it smells heavenly,' Eleanor remarked. 'And perhaps if we served some coffee to finish off the meal, no-one would think anything of it.'

'The trouble is,' Aunt Hettie confessed, 'we haven't any left. I threw it all on the fire!'

'I'll slip out and get some later,' Dick Fletcher offered. 'No-one will miss me.'

The others were arriving now. Becky and Roland took up their places at the doorway of the sitting-room to greet them.

'You look real lovely,' Mrs Foster said to her grand-daughter. 'Pale mauve is every bit as becoming as a white wedding dress. It suits you.' She had watched Becky since that tearful scene in the kitchen, but there had been no more confidences between them. She was far from certain that the girl was happy. Two brides in one family, and the difference between them was enormous.

'Thank you, Grandma,' Becky replied. 'Go and sit by the fire and keep warm.' She had not had much choice in the colour of her dress. Short of wearing black, and as she certainly didn't want white, mauve was the only permissible colour while she was in mourning.

'I echo what your grandmother says! You look lovely, and I hope your new husband won't mind me saying so!'

The speaker was Jimmy Austin. When he took her hand in his Becky felt that she would catch fire. Everyone must surely notice her panic! How many times had she told herself, tried to convince herself, lying awake, tossing and turning with longing in the night, that once she was married to Roland her feelings towards Jimmy would change, *must* change. She had been wrong, dreadfully wrong. Oh, what a fool she was to have given in, actually to have invited him to her wedding!

'I don't mind at all,' Roland said affably. 'Now that she's really and truly mine! And I'm pleased to meet you. I've been looking forward to meeting Becky's friends.'

With one more openly admiring, lingering look at Becky,

Jimmy moved away. She had not spoken a word. She would avoid talking to him at all. She would make sure that for the next hour or two she stayed close to Roland. But she was still thinking of Jimmy when she became aware that Percy Moore was speaking to her, and by the tone of his voice he was saying something for the second time.

'I said if you want me to do a little turn for the guests, Becky – or should I say Mrs Layton – I'd be willing to oblige with a monologue. If you wish it, that is.'

' "The Green Eye of the little Yellow God",' Becky teased him. 'Well, at least I know the accompaniment by heart!'

'Don't be ridiculous, Percy,' his wife said. 'It's quite unsuitable.'

'Just a thought, Alice,' Percy said. 'Just a thought, love.'

'Now a nice duet would be another matter,' his wife suggested. ' "Love Will Find a Way", for instance. Call on us if you want us, Becky.'

When everyone had been met and briefly welcomed Roland took Becky's hand and began to move around the room with her. She willed him not to go near Jimmy, and whenever he was in the vicinity she concentrated hard on talking to whoever was in front of her, about anything she could think of. Fluffy Proctor was amazed and delighted by Becky's amiability. She had always thought her a mite stuck-up when she was in the Bluebirds. Marriage was certainly softening her.

'Ladies and gentlemen!' Dick Fletcher called. 'Could we have a bit of hush? You've each got a glass of champagne in your hand, and if not just grab one quick because I want to say a few appropriate words.'

Standing beside Roland, Becky was acutely aware of Jimmy, across the room from them, aware that he was watching her with a sardonic smile on his face while Dick Fletcher, in glowing terms, proposed the health of the happy couple.

She felt trapped. She wanted to run away, as fast and as far as she could; to put a thousand miles between herself and the people in this room. She wished they would go home, yet she didn't want them to. All too soon after they left it would be time to depart with Roland on their honeymoon. If only . . .

'. . . And so I ask you to raise your glasses to Roland and Becky!' Dick Fletcher was saying. 'May all their troubles be little ones!'

She never knew why she raised her eyes again and met Jimmy's at that precise moment. It should have been Roland's gaze which held her own, but for what seemed an eternity, it was Jimmy's. His eyes mocked her, twinkled with amusement at her. Only you and I know how apt those words are, they said. She hated him. She hated him!

When the toast had been drunk and people were moving again, Jimmy came over to the newly-married couple.

'I don't know when I've enjoyed anything so much,' he said. 'Thank you for inviting me.'

'You must come again,' Roland replied cordially. 'We shall be pleased to see you any time you are in Akersfield. Don't forget, now!'

'I won't,' Jimmy promised.

A maid came up to them.

'Excuse me, Mr Roland, you're wanted on the telephone,' she said.

'I won't be a minute, my darling,' Roland told Becky. 'I'm sure Mr Austin will look after you.'

As soon as Roland was out of the room she started to move away from Jimmy, but he caught her by the wrist and gently pulled her back.

'Now, now,' he chided. 'You heard what your husband said. I'm to look after you. And wasn't it kind of him to invite me to call?'

'Don't you dare to come here!' Becky said quietly.

'I think I shall call during the day,' he went on, as if she hadn't spoken. 'Yes. In the afternoon!'

'You'll be wasting your time,' she said. 'If my husband isn't in I won't receive you. I don't ever want to see you again.'

'Oh, I don't think I'll be wasting my time,' he replied. 'I'm quite a purposeful man.'

Roland had come back into the room and was walking towards them. Jimmy turned to her with a smile on his face, his glass raised.

'As the gentleman said – may all your troubles be little ones!'

She wanted to tell him that she wasn't pregnant, that if he thought he had any sort of hold over her, he was wrong, but Roland was already with them. Besides, it might not be true. She had had no sign of a period since the end of November and it was now the twenty-first of January.

Jimmy had moved away and Selina was by her side. 'It's been lovely, Becky dear, but Bob and I must go now. We have an appointment with the vicar this evening. You're looking a little pale, love. Never mind. I hope you have a lovely honeymoon in London. Oh Becky, we're all going to be so blissfully happy!'

Mr Layton, though he openly grieved over the fact that Becky and Roland were leaving him, even for a few days, had nevertheless insisted on paying for the very best room in the hotel in London, with further instructions that anything which money could buy to make their honeymoon even better was to be theirs, and the bill sent to him. He had also kept his promise and arranged Becky's allowance.

'You'll find ten pounds paid into the bank for you on the twenty-first of every month,' he said. 'Starting on your wedding day.'

She was staggered by the amount. She flung her arms around Mr Layton's neck and gave him a big hug.

'It's wonderfully generous of you, Pop! Why, it's as much as some men keep a family on!'

He reckoned she was right at that. He had skilled men in the mill who took home no more than two pounds ten for a week's hard graft.

'You're worth it, lass,' he said. 'And it's just for yourself – not to spend on the house, mind. What's more, I've opened an account for you at Barnet's, only don't go mad, will you?'

'Oh, I won't,' she promised. 'Oh, it's so good of you, Pop!'

341

'Nay, I'm only teasing,' he said quietly. 'Get what you want, love. Money's not the same to me without my Edith to spend it on. There's only one thing I ask.'

'What's that, Pop?'

'That you'll be a good wife to our Roland. He's not had an easy time in the war. You must make it up to him.'

'Oh I will, Pop!' Becky said. 'I promise I will!'

'Aye, of course you will, love! He thinks the world of you. It'd break my heart to see him let down.'

'Your father's so kind to us, Roland,' Becky said, looking appreciatively around the hotel room.

'I know,' he agreed. 'But for now let's forget even my father. Let's forget everyone else in the world.'

The hotel gave on to Hyde Park. Becky crossed the room and held back the heavy velvet curtains to look out, but it was too dark to see anything except the traffic on the road below. Everything about the long journey from Akersfield had been exciting to her: dinner on the train as it sped through the darkness; the taxicab from King's Cross, the lights of London – which, though the cab driver said they were not yet back to their pre-war brilliance, were like nothing she had ever seen or imagined. Oh, she was going to love London! It was a dream world!

Roland's words, the frightening eagerness in his voice, jerked her back to reality. Throughout the day she had managed to push aside what was to happen when the night came. It was not that she didn't like the act of sex. So far, at least in the moments when it was taking place, it had brought her pleasure and satisfaction. No, she was afraid because she knew that Jimmy Austin was still in her heart and she couldn't get rid of him, but what worried her even more was that Roland would discover that she was not a virgin. Could men tell? She was too ignorant to know, but she feared it might be true.

But if there was any truth in it, their first coming together, which because of Roland's eager insistence took place within minutes of them being shown to their room, convinced her that it didn't apply to Roland. His need seemed so great, so urgent, that she wondered, as she was often to do, whether he even knew that it was she, Becky, to whom he made such passionate love. It wasn't until it was over that he looked at her, spoke her name.

'Oh my darling Becky, my dearest, it was wonderful! You're marvellous!'

Was it wonderful, she thought as she lay back against the pillows. In the beginning she had been carried away on the tide of his passion, but he had left her high and dry. The fears which had haunted her had gone – there had been no time to think of Jimmy – but in their place was disappointment, a niggling dissatisfaction.

Roland turned to her, buried his face against her shoulder, put his hand on her breast.

'Again, my love! Again!'

'Oh yes, Roland! Yes! But slowly, Roland, slowly! Wait for me!'

It was not in his nature to be patient, she thought afterwards. He had no control over the passion which soared so swift and strong in him. A passion which left her behind, alone, lonely.

But the daytime hours in London left nothing to be desired. They went everywhere, saw everything. Parks and palaces, restaurants and the river – and the shops; the wonderful, marvellous shops!

'I could spend all day in the shops!' Becky enthused.

'Sampling the wares!' Roland teased.

They spent freely, he denied her nothing for which she showed the slightest desire. And every evening it was the theatre – a play or a musical.

'It seems as if every way one turns, there's another theatre,' Becky said. 'Oh, it's all so exciting! Even the people on the streets are exciting. So fashionable, so gay. It's as if the war ended yesterday, instead of two months ago, and they're still celebrating.'

It was only the nights which were wrong. In the end, lying awake unsatisfied after their lovemaking, she plucked up courage to speak to him.

'Roland.'

'Mmmm?' He was lying with his back towards her, almost asleep.

'Roland, please don't go to sleep! I want to talk to you.'

'Talk? Is it important, darling? Too important to wait until morning?'

'It is to me.'

He turned to face her, propped himself up on one elbow. 'I'll turn on the light,' he said.

'No! Don't do that. It's easier in the dark.'

'Whatever can it be, my love, that you have to say to me in the dark, at one o'clock in the morning? You're not ill, are you?' He was mystified.

'No. It's about . . . it's about when we make love, Roland. I make you happy, don't I?'

'Of course, sweetheart! The happiest man in the world! Why do you ask?'

'Because you don't make me happy, Roland.'

'I don't?' He sounded disbelieving.

'No, you don't. It's all right at first, when you first start, but then it's as if you forget me, forget it's me, Becky, I mean. You rush away without me, leave me behind. *You* are satisfied, but I never am!'

'Oh Becky, I didn't know! I didn't realise . . .!' He was all contrition.

'Women have their needs, just as much as men, Roland.'

'Oh my love, I'm sorry! You must tell me what you want me to do.'

'If you could spend more time at the beginning. Caresses mean a lot. If you would have patience and wait for me.'

'Oh I will, I will!' he promised. 'It will be different in future, you'll see.'

He took her in his arms and began to fondle her, but when he made love, in the end it was no different. He seemed driven by something over which he had no control. It doesn't even have to be me, Becky thought. It could be anybody.

So she tried to blot out the emptiness of the nights with

the ceaseless activities of the days, and succeeded until they were back in the hotel room, preparing for bed. It was often after midnight, for they would have supper somewhere after the theatre. She hoped that sheer physical fatigue would ensure a night's sleep after Roland had made love to her — for she never denied him, however often he wanted her. It didn't.

'I wish we didn't have to go back just yet,' she said when the cab came on Saturday morning to take them to King's Cross. 'I wish we could have stayed a little longer.' She dreaded the thought of Akersfield. The days would be empty there.

'I know,' Roland agreed. 'But I promised Dad I'd start work on Monday morning. He's been very patient and he does really need me at the mill.'

January blew itself out with a gale which tore down hoardings in the centre of Akersfield and dislodged roof slates all over the town, and February came in with dark skies and a promise of more snow. Becky had had no sign of a period, and now it seemed certain she must be pregnant.

There was no other indication. She didn't feel in the least sick, and when she surveyed her naked body in the dressing-table mirror after Roland had gone off to work, she could see no change in it. Her waist was still the same twenty-one inches, and since she had always been full-breasted, there was nothing different there. How long before anything showed? She knew nothing about these things and there was no-one she could ask.

It *could* be Roland's, she told herself. Right from the first he had made love to her every night, sometimes two or three times, and he took no precautions. If it was Roland's it would be born in October, but if it was Jimmy's it would make its unwelcome appearance in September. How could she bear to wait so long, not knowing? But she must tell Roland she was pregnant, and the sooner the better.

'Why, that's marvellous!' he cried. 'Wonderful! Oh Becky darling, it's the best news in the world! It will make our marriage complete. But you must take the greatest care. Oughtn't you to see the doctor right away?'

'Certainly not!' Becky said. 'I've no need of a doctor. My mother had all her children without going near a doctor. I shall be the same.' A doctor's opinion was the last thing she wanted.

'Well, promise me you'll take every possible care,' Roland begged.

'Of course I will. Don't fuss!' Roland's solicitude was something else she could do without. It only added to her guilt.

Mr Layton was as delighted as Roland at the news. It did more than anything to lift him out of his misery.

'A grandson! I hope it'll be a lad, Becky. Someone to carry on the name!' He spoke as if he had founded a dynasty. 'Now you must look after yourself, love. Don't go out in this weather, catching cold. And you must have extra help in the house, of course. My word, this is splendid news!'

As it happened it was Roland who took a chill, and took it badly. He came home from the mill in the middle of the afternoon, flushed and shivering, his teeth chattering while his skin burned. Becky helped him to bed and sent for the doctor at once. She had no experience of illness, and hated and feared it. The flu epidemic was on the wane in Akersfield, but just supposing . . . It was too awful to contemplate!

'A nasty bout of bronchitis,' the doctor pronounced. 'No doubt a legacy from the prison camp. He's not had time to build up his strength.'

'What shall I do?' Becky asked. She dreaded Roland mentioning that she was pregnant and mustn't look after him. It would lead to awkward questions. If he did, she decided she would have to lie about the dates of her periods. But Roland said nothing.

'Give him plenty of fluids. Fresh lemonade. I'll give you a linctus for the cough, and if you rub his chest and back with camphorated oil and then cover it with sheets of brown paper, it will help to relieve the congestion.'

She loathed the smell of camphorated oil and tried to turn her head away as she massaged it first into his chest and

346

then into his back. How white his skin was. And how strange that she had not really seen him without clothes before. She had not looked at his body, nor he at hers. What took place between them was swift and passionate, and in the dark.

She rubbed the oil into his skin with a circular motion, from waist to shoulder, side to side, covering the whole area of his lungs. The camphor fumes stung her eyes.

'You have a birthmark on your left shoulder,' she commented. It was a diamond-shaped brown mark, slightly raised.

'All the Laytons have,' he said. 'My father, and his father before him. Our son will have it, you'll see!'

She took her hands off him, fractionally, held them suspended. She was glad she was behind him, his face hidden.

'What's the matter?' he asked. 'Are you all right?'

'Of course I am. I was the slightest bit dizzy, but it's gone. Anyway, I think you've had enough.' She fixed the sheets of brown paper, one on his back, the other on his chest, and helped him on with his pyjama jacket. 'Now get some sleep,' she said.

It was the first week in March before Roland was fit to go back to work. He was up and about before then, but he had a persistent cough and the weather was so bad that Becky hated to see him leave the house every morning, even though Briggs did collect both Roland and his father in the car.

'I hope the weather improves before the fifteenth,' Becky said. 'Selina's planned everything down to the last detail, but even she can't organise the weather. Which reminds me that I simply have to go out and buy some shoes and gloves for the wedding.'

She had yielded, unwillingly, to Selina's desire that she should be her matron of honour, with Jenny and Bob's sister Ethel as bridesmaids. She had acquiesced in Selina's choice of lavender marocain for her dress, but had insisted that it should have the new low hipline.

'When I was in London, all the smartest women had the

347

low hipline. If you walked down Bond Street there wasn't a waist to be seen! Which suits me in my condition!' Actually, it was only her waist which had changed. Her waistbands were getting tight, but as yet there was no swelling of her abdomen, though she looked for it all the time.

'If you must go out on a day like this, I'll tell Briggs to come back and take you,' Mr Layton said. 'In any case I shan't want him again until this afternoon.'

'You're so kind to me, Pop,' Becky said.

'Why shouldn't I be? You're the lass who's going to give me a grandson, remember!'

He – Roland also – always spoke as though the baby was especially for them; she would just carry it and give birth. Well, as far as she was concerned, they could have it. She didn't want this baby at all. How nice if they could do the carrying *and* the birthing! Men got away with everything.

All the same, Pop *was* kind. There was no getting away from it. The trouble was that he was always there. Though he paid lip service to leaving the newly-married couple to themselves, he was just too lonely to do so. When they returned from their honeymoon he showed them the little sitting-room he'd had fixed up for himself.

'So you needn't think I shall get in your way,' he said.

In fact, he scarcely used it. Becky had expected that he would take his meals with them, but not that he would sit with them every evening. The air was thick with his tobacco smoke, which nauseated her, while he droned on about the price of yarn on the Bradford Exchange; about 'tops and noils', 'greasy and scoured' and other strange things. She ought to know the language. She had lived in the area all her life, surrounded by woollen and worsted mills, but she had never taken the slightest interest in such matters. In the evenings now she often played the piano to pass the time, or sang the songs she had heard in London. Life was so boring!

'Why don't we go out somewhere tonight?' she asked Roland as she helped him on with his coat, handed him his thick scarf. 'The theatre perhaps?'

But she knew even as she spoke why they couldn't. It

was filthy weather and Roland was really not well enough.

'No, forget I said it, Roland!'

'I'm sorry, sweetheart. In a few weeks' time we will. When the better weather comes. In any case, I don't want *you* to catch cold.'

'Of course.'

But in a few weeks' time she would be visibly pregnant, and therefore not able to go out in public. It was going to be a dreary spring and an even worse summer.

When Briggs came back for her later in the morning she instructed him to take her to Barnet's.

'And you can call for me at two o'clock,' she told him. 'I shall have some lunch in the restaurant here.'

She bought grey kid shoes, with silk stockings to match, then fine doeskin gloves in a lavender shade which would exactly match her dress, entering everything to the account her father-in-law had opened for her. Then she had a lamb chop, followed by a plate of trifle, in the restaurant, which passed the time until two o'clock. By two-fifteen she was home, with the rest of the day in front of her. The weather was, if anything, worse. She stood in the big bay window and watched the soot-laden rain falling on the square of blackened grass in front of the house. After a few minutes she moved away.

She was relieved, half an hour later, to hear the front door bell. Even if it was only the vicar, come to collect for the missions, it would be a small diversion.

'It's a Mister Austin,' the maid announced a minute later. 'Are you at home, mum?'

Jimmy! She couldn't! She mustn't! She had determined on her wedding day that if ever he carried out his threat and called on her, she would refuse to see him. Yet she longed to see him, only to set eyes on him, no more. And after all, it was Roland himself who had asked Jimmy to call whenever he was in the neighbourhood.

'Show him in, please,' she said.

Her first thought when he came into the room was how incredibly handsome he was. It was not something on which

349

her memory had played her false. When he smiled at her his eyes crinkled at the corners, his mouth curved. He was bareheaded – he had left his damp coat and hat in the hall – and his hair sprang from his head as thick and bright as her own. Though he had doubtless spent the whole of this revolting winter in the West Riding, he somehow managed to look bronzed and fit.

'How are you, Becky? Is marriage agreeing with you? You look well.'

He came towards her and clasped both her hands in his own. She felt life and vigour flowing from him into her like a stream of molten lava – and pulled her hands away.

'I'm very well, thank you. I think I need hardly ask you. You look fighting fit.'

'I am,' he said. 'Aren't you going to ask me to sit down?'

'Please do.' She indicated a chair, and took one herself as far away as she decently could.

'And your husband? I trust he's well?'

'Not terribly, I'm afraid. He's been ill.'

'Ah! Married life!'

The innuendo was not in the words, but in the way he said them, and in the bold look on his face. She was furious to find herself blushing.

'He has had bronchitis,' she said coldly. 'He's much better.'

'So he's not at home?'

Suddenly she wished she could say he was. She wanted Roland right there beside her.

'At the moment, no. But I expect him soon.'

'Ah! Tell me, was he very happy to hear that you were pregnant? And so soon?'

She was shocked by his words, so baldly spoken. 'I'm not!' she lied. 'I'm not pregnant!'

'But you told me . . .'

'I was mistaken. And it's in the past. If you were a gentleman you wouldn't refer to it!'

'But I'm not, am I? You've surely never mistaken me for a gentleman – just as I've never mistaken you for a lady!'

350

'How *dare* you!' She jumped to her feet. She was furious. 'Get out of my house at once! At once, do you hear!'

'Wait a minute,' he said pleasantly. 'Calm down! And let's get something straight. In the first place, I happen to *know* you're pregnant . . .'

'It's not true! How can you possibly . . .?'

'I know you're in the family way,' he said evenly, 'because Fluffy Proctor met Selina, who told her. You surely don't suggest Selina would lie? And Fluffy told me. So you see, it's more or less common knowledge. Now what *isn't* common knowledge is how long . . .' He broke off, stared at her. She felt sick – and hypnotised.

'I suppose your husband's quite delighted about this baby?'

She found her voice. 'He is. And the baby is his.'

He shook his head. 'We can't be sure, my dear, can we? At least, you and I can't. I'd like to think Roland could, though. But these things have a way of leaking out, don't you think?'

'You RAT! You horrible little sewer rat!' How could she ever have thought herself in love with this creature? Yet even as she asked herself the question, she still felt his magnetism. 'What do you want?' she demanded. 'What are you here for?'

'There's my practical girl! Money, of course. Not a lot, I'm not greedy – well, I don't suppose you'll have a lot right now, but little and often will suit me better. A sort of a bank account, if you get my drift.'

She got his drift all right. She seethed with anger – and felt completely powerless. She would have liked to have told him to go to hell, to tell Roland whatever he liked. She knew she couldn't. Roland would hate her, but it would seem like the end of the world to his father. He would certainly cut off her money and most likely turn her out. Roland hadn't enough to live on, not the way she wanted to live. Besides which – and the thought was genuine – she didn't want Roland to be hurt. He didn't deserve it.

'I'll give you three pounds,' she said. She had been to the bank that morning in Akersfield.

'Make it a fiver,' he suggested. 'You can spare it, I'm sure.'

'Very well. But don't waste your time coming back,' she said. 'I shall tell Roland myself.'

'I doubt that. Anyway, I'll be back just to check on it. But don't wait in for me. I'm not sure when.'

She waited until she heard the front door close, then she ran upstairs to the bathroom and was very sick.

CHAPTER TWENTY-ONE

'Well, you're lucky with the weather,' Eleanor said, drawing back the curtains. 'It's going to be a beautiful day. Happy the bride the sun shines on!'

She deposited the breakfast tray carefully on Selina's knees as her daughter sat up in bed. Selina had moved from The Beeches to Whinbank two days ago, so as to be married from her stepfather's home. In any case, Bob, as well as his mother, and one brother, who had come up from Carmarthen for the wedding, was staying at The Beeches; so even if it had been proper for her to remain there, there wouldn't have been room.

'Besides,' Eleanor said when the arrangements were being discussed, 'I want you at home for a day or two. I want to spoil you. It will be my last chance.' Her daughters, she thought regretfully, had not had much spoiling from her. She had always been so busy earning a living; helping to run Kramer's cafe, running it alone when Frank had gone off to war.

'I'd be happy today if it hailed, rained, snowed and thundered,' Selina said. 'And it's no use giving me all this breakfast, Mother. I can't eat a thing!'

'Oh yes you can, and you will,' Eleanor said. 'It's going to be a long day and you'll need all your strength.'

'Well, just one piece of toast and a cup of tea,' Selina conceded.

Her wedding dress was hanging from the picture rail so as not to get crushed in the wardrobe, shrouded in a white sheet against any possible speck of dust. She lay there, remembering its beauty; ivory silk, with panels of cream

353

lace from neck to hem, and the hem high enough to show her feet in the cream satin slippers which now reposed in their box under the dressing-table. Her mother and Uncle Dick between them had paid for her wedding outfit – far more expensive than anything she had dreamed of. She longed to have a quick bath and to put it on, but there was ages to go yet, the wedding wasn't until noon.

Eleanor was holding a match to the fire which was laid in the grate.

'You are not to get out of bed until the room's warmed up,' she ordered.

'What time will Miss Briggs be here?' Selina asked. Miss Briggs was Hebghyll's very best dressmaker.

'Ten-thirty. It won't take her more than a few minutes to put the last stitches in the hem. I don't know why in the world it's considered unlucky to finish the dress before the wedding day.'

'Well, it is,' Selina said seriously. 'And I'm not taking any chances. Oh Mother, I don't know how I shall bear to wait! I would have liked the wedding much earlier in the day. All the same, we were lucky the vicar agreed to marry us in Lent. And he wouldn't have except that Bob had been away so long at the war. Otherwise we'd have had to wait until after Easter. I couldn't have borne it!'

From her bed she could see the stretch of land that was Uncle Dick's market garden, every inch of it under cultivation though there wasn't much showing above the ground at the end of March. Beyond Dick's land a line of trees marked where the river ran, and on the other side of the river the land rose again quite sharply, divided into oddly-shaped fields by stone walls. It was a pleasant view, but she preferred the one from The Beeches, which was on the higher side of Hebghyll and looked straight up to the moor.

'I'll be back in an hour or so to help you to dress,' Eleanor told her. 'In the meantime I'll waken Jenny.' Jenny was sharing a room with the other bridesmaid, Bob's sister Ethel.

'I wish Becky and Roland could have been here overnight,

354

instead of coming from Akersfield this morning,' Selina said.

'I know. But this isn't a large house and it's bursting at the seams. Anyway, they'll come with Mr Layton. Now do try to rest for the next hour, Selina!'

When her mother had left the room Selina set the tray aside and, curbing her impatience to be up and doing, snuggled down again under the bedclothes. Oh, it was going to be so wonderful! In a few hours from now she would be a married woman. Mrs Harwell!

'Oh Bob, I do love you so!' she said out loud.

Hebghyll's parish church clock had hardly finished striking noon before Eleanor, hearing the slight commotion at the back of the church, turned around to see her daughter walking down the aisle on Dick's arm. She smiled. No nonsense about the bride being late in Selina's case. She had never seen anyone so eager to come to their wedding, so confident. She greeted her bridegroom with a glowing smile, and when it was time for her responses her voice was clear and firm.

When Dick had discharged his duty of giving away the bride he joined Eleanor in the pew. She took his hand in hers.

'Remember?' she whispered.

It seemed not so long ago that the two of them had made the same vows to each other. Well, if her daughter's marriage was as happy as hers, she would be all right. She could think of no reason why it wouldn't be. The more she saw of Bob Harwell, the more she liked him.

After the ceremony they walked the short distance to The Beeches for the reception.

'Two of your daughters married now, only one to go!' Mr Layton said to Eleanor at the reception.

'I know. But Jenny doesn't have a thought of marriage. Her head's too full of nursing!' She smiled at her youngest daughter, who stood near.

'Did you know I'd got a job in Akersfield hospital, Mr Layton?' Jenny asked. 'I start next week as a probationer.'

355

'Nay, I didn't. Becky didn't say anything. Well, it'll be very nice to have you so near. We shall be able to keep an eye on you!'

Jenny pulled a face. She would have liked to have gone much further away than Akersfield to start her training, even as far as London, but it had been part of the bargain with her mother that if she was allowed to nurse, it must at first be somewhere near at hand.

'But I will come and see you sometimes, when I'm off duty,' she promised Mr Layton.

'I should jolly well hope so, else you'll be in trouble!'

'She'll change her mind,' he said to Eleanor when Jenny had moved away. 'I mean about getting married. They all do it in the end. It's a woman's natural job – a home and children.'

'Maybe it is,' Eleanor said, 'though a lot of women will have to do without it now – all those young men who didn't come back . . . Perhaps one of them was destined for my Jenny?'

'Aye, that's so. I thank God every night that my son came back. But we mustn't think gloomy thoughts on such a day as this, must we?' Nevertheless, he thought fleetingly of his friend, Frank Kramer, who had been married to this lovely woman. But she seemed all right now.

'You're quite right! This is Selina's day – and Bob's. And if you'll excuse me I must go and have a word with Bob's mother. She doesn't know many people.'

Crossing the room to Mrs Harwell, Eleanor stopped to speak to Becky and Roland. Becky, expensively dressed, elegantly shod, her hair bright as copper, looked lovely. There was no sign of her pregnancy, though there wouldn't be, so early. Eleanor was surprised that Becky *was* pregnant, and surprised that she had announced it so soon. She couldn't imagine her with a child.

'A lovely wedding!' Roland said. 'Everything's going well. But I must take my Becky away before too long. I don't want her to get too tired.'

He was so loving, so protective, Eleanor thought. He

looked so happy. It was more than she could say for Becky, about whom, these days, there was a withdrawn look.

'Are you all right, love?' Eleanor asked her.

'Of course I am! I'm perfectly fit. It's just Roland fussing!' She was not all right. She was in torment. It was only two days since Jimmy Austin had called and every minute since then she had been in dread that he would come again. She could see no way out of her dilemma. No way at all.

'Well, take care of yourself,' Eleanor said, moving away.

'I'm sorry your husband couldn't come,' she said when she reached Mrs Harwell. 'I know Selina's disappointed too.'

'My husband has the farm to run. It's not easy at any time, and now that he won't have Bob's help . . .' Mrs Harwell had a whining voice, a narrow, pinched face. Bob must be like his father, Eleanor thought. It was quite clear that Mrs Harwell resented her son's marriage, especially to a foreigner from Yorkshire, who was taking him so far away.

'I'm sure you'll miss him,' Eleanor said.

'And he'll miss us,' Mrs Harwell nodded her head firmly. 'Welshmen get very homesick. He's not used to being away from home.'

Not used to it? But he had been in the army for the whole of the war! 'Well, I'm sure Selina will do everything she can to make him happy,' Eleanor said gently. 'And you must visit us whenever you can. You'll always be welcome.'

She was still talking to Mrs Harwell when Dick came up to them, breaking into their conversation without apology.

'Eleanor, come with me! It's your mother!'

'Ma? What's happened? Where is she?' She turned instantly sick with alarm at the sight of her husband's grave expression.

'Becky and Roland have taken her to her room. She came over faint and dizzy, luckily while she was talking to them. I haven't told anyone else. We don't want to upset Selina. Please don't tell her, Mrs Harwell!'

Eleanor followed Dick through the crowd of guests, trying to look composed, not to show her feelings. When she reached her mother's room Mrs Foster was lying on the bed.

She was deathly pale, with a film of sweat around her mouth and on her forehead, her breath coming quick and shallow. Eleanor took her hands – they were icy cold – and began to chafe them.

'Oh Ma, what is it? What happened?'

'Nothing to make a fuss about!' Mrs Foster's voice was weak, but she managed a smile. She would never confess how ill and frightened she had felt, sitting there talking to Becky when suddenly everything started to go dark, and the sounds of the room began to fade. Everything had seemed a long way away from her.

Eleanor turned to her husband.

'Dick, I think you should fetch Dr Clare. How lucky that he's a guest! But do it discreetly.'

'I shall be as right as rain in a minute or two,' Mrs Foster declared. 'I'm feeling a bit better already.'

'You'll stay right where you are until Dr Clare's had a look at you,' Eleanor said. 'Oh Ma, you've been doing too much! What am I always telling you?'

The doctor came quietly into the room, following Dick.

'I suggest you and Roland go back into the party,' Eleanor said to Becky. 'You'll be missed.'

'I don't want to leave Grandma,' Becky protested. 'I'd rather stay.' She never had any doubt that she loved her grandmother, though she didn't find it easy to show it.

'It will be better for Mrs Foster if she doesn't have too many people around her,' the doctor said. 'I'll come and find you when I've examined her.'

Only Eleanor remained with her mother while the doctor examined her. She tried to read his thoughts in his face, but from long practice, he showed nothing. It seemed a long time before he looked up and spoke.

'I would say that your mother has had a heart attack.' He held up his hand as Eleanor gasped. 'No, not a serious one, indeed a fairly mild one I'm pleased to say. Nevertheless, she must take care. She should undress and stay in bed now, and I'd like you to get her two hot-water bottles, see she's kept warm and quiet.'

358

'Of course! Should I give her some brandy?'

'A teaspoon or two of brandy in a cup of tea wouldn't be a bad idea,' Dr Clare said. 'Could you drink that, Mrs Foster?'

'I daresay I could. But I don't want any fuss. You get back to the reception, Eleanor love.' She said the words, but in her heart she didn't want her daughter to leave her just yet. She'd been so frightened.

Relief surged through Eleanor as she saw the colour beginning to come back into her mother's ashen face. But she looked old and frail, lying there against the pillows. Why have I never noticed this before, Eleanor asked herself. I've never thought of her as other than strong, and permanent. My prop and stay. Always sticking by me, through thick and thin. Never judging me, no matter what.

'I'm going to look after you, Ma,' she said. 'I haven't looked after you well enough or I'd have seen this coming. I'm going to take you to Whinbank as soon as the doctor says you can go, and I'm going to spoil you, good and proper.'

Mrs Foster smiled. She really was very tired. It would be nice to be spoiled, especially by her lovely Eleanor.

'I'll not say no,' she whispered.

Selina and Bob were in the train which would take them as far as Penrith, there to be met by Mr Barton, owner of The Feathers, the small hotel near to Ullswater where they were to spend their honeymoon. It would be dark by the time they got to Penrith; they had the last of the sun now, turning the tops of the mountains a reddish purple before it disappeared behind them. They had chosen the Lake District for their honeymoon because neither of them had been there before and it sounded the most romantic place in the world – or at any rate the most romantic within their reach.

'I'm still worried about Grandma,' Selina confessed. 'I wasn't happy to leave her.'

'I know,' Bob said. 'But *she* would have been unhappy if we'd stayed. And the doctor said she'd be all right. I'm sure there's no cause for alarm. So you must try not to worry, dearest.'

'I know. I'll try. Oh Bob, isn't it wonderful to be on our honeymoon at last!'

She had no qualms about the great experience which was to be hers in just a few hours from now. She knew next to nothing about the private side of marriage, and when Eleanor had attempted to say something, she had refused to listen. Everything would be all right. What she had to learn, Bob would teach her. She would not be shy because she loved him so much. When two people loved as they did, nothing of that nature, nothing between them, could go wrong.

The hotel was small, cosy, set part way up the hillside overlooking the lake. Everything was quiet except for the noise of the stream, full and slate-grey now from the winter's snows which had melted on the fell tops. It thundered and rushed downhill, over its rock-strewn bed, eager to lose itself in the lake.

'We've not many staying here at the moment,' the proprietor said, showing them to their room. 'But come Easter, we're fully booked. It seems as if people want to get into the countryside, the first spring after the war.'

'That's so,' Bob agreed. 'We . . . I should say my wife's people . . . have a cafe with a few rooms for letting, in Hebghyll. We're expecting to be very busy at Easter.'

It was the very first time he had said 'my wife'. Selina blushed to the roots of her hair with pleased embarrassment, and turned away, pretending to look out at the view so that the proprietor wouldn't notice. They hadn't mentioned on booking the room that they'd be on honeymoon.

'If there's anything you want,' Mr Barton said, 'Just mention it to me or Mrs Barton. Dinner in about an hour, if that suits you.'

'There's a right couple of lovebirds,' he told his wife when he went downstairs. 'I wouldn't mind his job tonight, and that's a fact!'

'You're a dirty old man, and that's another fact,' Mrs Barton said.

After dinner Selina and Bob went for a short time into

the little bar, where Bob insisted that Selina should have a glass of port.

'It will do you good,' he persuaded her. 'You've had a tiring day.'

'Oh Bob, I've had the most marvellous day of my life,' she said. 'Nothing will ever be better!'

But she *was* tired, and she wanted to be fresh for him, to be everything he desired, so she sipped at the port dutifully, though she had never liked the taste. She became conscious as they sat there in the bar that the locals were looking at them; not unkindly, but with frank interest and sly smiles.

'Oh Bob, it must stand out a mile that we're on honeymoon,' she said. 'I think I'll go up to our room now.' She wanted to; she wanted to be alone with him, away from absolutely everyone.

'I won't be long,' he told her.

She was grateful that he had been tactful enough to give her some time to herself. She was not sure that she would ever be able to take off her clothes in front of a man, not even Bob, though perhaps when they'd been married a while it would be different. When she had washed herself, and splashed her skin with lavender water, she put on the new nightgown, silky and lace-trimmed, which had been chosen with such care. By the time Bob came into the room she was in bed. She turned away and faced the wall while he undressed.

When he climbed into bed he turned her towards him and took her in his arms.

'Don't be afraid, my darling. I won't hurt you. I love you too much.'

'Oh Bob, I love you too. I shan't mind whatever you do.'

He did hurt her, though he seemed not to know it; perhaps because, as the pain went through her like a sword, she stifled the cry which rose to her lips and gave no more than a quick gasp, which went unnoticed. But she had not expected this. She'd not expected anything like this. It was too fierce to be believed. She would never grow used

361

to it, let alone enjoy it, as some women were said to.

'Are you all right, my love?' he asked when it was over.

'Yes,' she said. 'Yes I am, dearest.' She would never let him know, she loved him too much; and now she had learnt where a wife's duty lay.

Yet when he turned and began to make love to her again, it was somehow different. When he stroked her back, touched her body in different places, she felt her own body responding, reaching out to his. And when they made love the second time the miracle had been wrought and she was as eager as he was. When the climax came it was a shaft of lightning for her, a shower of incredibly brilliant stars in the blackness of the night.

After that, they went to sleep quickly, locked in each other's arms; and when they wakened in the morning they made love again.

During the following day they walked on the border of the lake, then climbed the hills, trying to follow the fast little stream to its source. It didn't matter that it rained, that they were soaked to the skin and when they returned had to give their wet clothes to Mrs Barton to dry by the kitchen fire. Nothing mattered except that they were together; and when the day was ended they would come to the night, and to their lovemaking.

'One day when we're here in summer I shall make love to you in the open air, lying on the grass,' Bob said.

'On the top of a mountain,' Selina smiled. 'It has to be on the top of a mountain!'

On the second night of their honeymoon they went to bed soon after dinner. In their desire to be alone together they no longer cared what the other visitors might think. Their lovemaking now was free and pleasurable, with no thought of pain or reticence, and afterwards their sleep was deep.

It happened at three o'clock in the morning. Afterwards Selina remembered the sound of a striking clock somewhere in the hotel mingling with Bob's shouts of terror before she finally wakened him from his dream.

'Bob, what is it? Wake up! Wake up!'

362

She had him by the shoulders and was shaking him. She couldn't stop him shouting. She couldn't make out the words. His eyes were wide open, staring in terror, but not at her, at something beyond her.

'Bob darling, what is it? Wake up, *please!*'

She put her arms around him, tried to hold him close. He was stiff with terror. She stroked his back, trying to relax him, and in the end – it was probably a matter of seconds but it felt like an hour – she felt him go slack against her. He dropped his head against her shoulder, and when he raised it again, almost immediately, his eyes were no longer frightened.

'What is it?' he asked. 'Is something wrong?'

'Oh Bob, you were dreaming! Oh, I was so frightened! Don't you remember any of it?'

He frowned with concentration, trying to recall, and then bits of it came back to him, though not in any sequence.

'Please tell me, Bob darling. I'm sure it will be better for you.'

'It's the war,' he said slowly. 'I'm in the trench. In the front line. The battle's on. It's the noise, all the noise. Guns. Shells bursting.'

But it was more than that. Above the guns and the shells it was the noise of the men, his companions.

'They cry out in pain, in agony, until it nearly bursts my eardrums. And then somebody, I think it's me, is yelling for the stretcher-bearer – and he doesn't come. But the rats do. The rats always come before the stretcher-bearer can get there . . .' He was sweating profusely now, remembering.

'Oh, my poor darling! But do you mean you've had this dream before?'

'Yes. But not while I've been in Hebghyll. I thought it had finished, gone away.'

'Why didn't you tell me?'

'I don't want to talk about the war. No-one who was there wants to talk about it. You push it to the back of your mind, try to pretend it didn't happen.'

'And then it comes out in the middle of the night,' Selina said.

'Usually if I've been disturbed about something. Not necessarily something bad – but emotional maybe. That's when it happens. But sometimes for no reason at all.'

How could he tell her that their new marriage, the emotions it had aroused in him, the intensity of their lovemaking – but everything good, nothing bad – had so heightened his feelings that it had probably brought on the dream. He felt sure in his mind that that was it, but if he told her she would blame herself. Certainly it would cloud their new-found happiness, and that he couldn't bear to do.

'I'm going to light the lamp,' Selina said. 'We'll talk for a while – quietly, so as not to disturb anyone – then we'll go to sleep and you won't have the dream again.' She was quite confident that she could settle everything.

'Did I . . . do you think I disturbed people?' He had no real knowledge of how loudly he shouted in his dream, except that his mother had said it was enough to waken the dead.

'Possibly. But it doesn't matter, my love. Anyone can have a nightmare.' She was fairly certain that everyone in the hotel must have heard his cries but she had no intention of telling him so. After a while she turned out the lamp and they both slept until morning.

She knew by Mrs Barton's demeanour at the breakfast table, and the quick looks from the other visitors in the dining-room that they had all heard. She offered no explanation until after breakfast, when she sought out Mrs Barton on her own.

'I'm sorry if you were disturbed during the night. My husband had a bad dream. It's the war. He was on the Somme for a very long time and it comes back to him in his sleep.'

Mrs Barton was sympathetic.

'You don't have to have lost an arm or a leg to suffer for the war. You can pay in other ways, and perhaps for a long time.'

But surely not for a long time in Bob's case, Selina thought. He had her, they had each other now. She would love him and cherish him, make it up to him. They had their whole future before them. He would put the war behind him, she was confident of it.

For most of that day they walked, again in the rain. Bob seemed so much his normal self that Selina forbore to mention the dream.

'I wanted us to climb Helvellyn,' he said. 'But we'll have to wait until the weather clears. Let's hope it does so tomorrow.'

That night the dream came again, only this time it wasn't a dream. It was much, much worse. He was awake, and they were making love. It was when he was approaching his climax that the noises started in his head. There was the heavy gunfire, in the distance, but all the time coming nearer; the sharp rattle of their own machine guns, the whine of the enemy shells. Then against the rhythm of his lovemaking the shouts of his wounded comrades came, loud and insistent. There was no-one but himself to help them and he couldn't find the stretcher-bearer. He had to find the stretcher-bearer before the rats came, and there was very little time now. They would be on him. As he reached the end of his lovemaking his cries rang out in agony. He was fully awake and he heard them, but there was nothing he could do to stop them.

Selina jerked away from him; terrified, horrified.

'No, Bob! No! You can't be dreaming now!'

He lay back exhausted, clammy with cold sweat, his heartbeat loud and fast.

'*Was* I dreaming?' He didn't know. He found it difficult to speak, as if his voice came from a long way off. 'I thought it was happening. It was the same as the dream but I thought it was real. Oh Selina, my love! What have I done to you?'

She was white with anxiety, trembling with shock.

'I don't know. I don't understand!'

When he held out his arms to her she was hesitant for a second, but when she went into them and he held her she felt reassured.

'Hold me close,' she said. 'Everything will be all right.

We mustn't worry. Above all we mustn't worry. It will only make things worse.'

It was nothing, she told herself. It was one bad moment, like the dream itself. Why it had happened when it did she didn't understand. It was to do with marriage, and with men. There were bound to be things to do with marriage which she didn't yet understand. But she would, and so would Bob. Once again she told herself that together they could solve anything.

The next night it happened exactly as before. She felt the agony pouring out of him as the shouts came, and she put a hand across his mouth to stifle the sound which she knew must be heard right through the little hotel. Her own nerves were jangling, but she wrapped him in her arms and tried to soothe him, calm him down, and eventually she did.

'The only thing is, dearest, I think we must go home tomorrow,' she said quietly. 'We can make the weather our excuse – and I'm sure you'll be better once we're home.' She couldn't face the other people in the hotel any longer, not even Mrs Barton, who had been so sympathetic. She knew they looked at the two of them and she felt they didn't quite believe that it was all due to bad dreams.

While Bob asked for the bill immediately after breakfast, Selina telephoned her mother.

'The weather's terrible,' she told her. 'And I've got a bit of a cold. Also I'm anxious about Grandma. So we'll be back later today.'

'There's no need, unless you really want to,' Eleanor replied. 'Grandma's doing fine.'

'It will be quite nice to have a few days at home before we start work,' Selina said. Then she rang off before her mother could answer.

'Oh Selina, I'm desperately sorry!' Bob said.

'It's all right,' she assured him. 'It will be nice to be home. And you *will* get better, never fear. We must give it time, that's all. It's less than six months since you were at the front.'

'We'll come back here again,' he said. 'We'll stay in

this same hotel, and we'll climb Helvellyn.'

She smiled. She never wanted to set foot here again, but not for the world would she say so.

'May I say something?' she asked.

'Of course, love! Anything.'

'Well . . . I want you to be . . . all right . . . not only for your sake, though that's the most important, but because I want to have a baby. I want a baby as soon as possible.'

There was no need to say that she wanted a child conceived in love and harmony and peace, not one born out of the sounds of battle. Bob would understand that without being told.

'I envy Becky being pregnant,' she said. 'I envy her from the bottom of my heart!'

It was almost the end of May before Jimmy Austin visited Becky again. The long interval since that first visit had lulled her into the belief that he had given up, decided to leave her alone. It was even more of a shock, therefore, when she answered the door – it was the maid's afternoon off – and found him standing on the step. Instinctively she moved to shut the door, but he had his foot in.

'That's not very polite,' he said. 'Aren't you going to ask me in?'

'I am not,' she retorted. 'Please go away at once.!'

'Well, if I do that I might well find myself walking in the direction of Layton's mill! You can take your choice, my dear Becky.'

She held the door wider, let him in.

'I'll give you five minutes only!'

'My word!' he said. 'Not very hospitable, are we? But I daresay five minutes will do. It's up to you, really. You know what I've come for.'

'You're not getting it!' she snapped.

'Really?' He looked her over from top to toe, his eyes deliberately lingering on her figure, her thickening waist, the slight but perceptible curve of her stomach. 'I would say you are . . . let me see . . . about five months pregnant.

367

Of course I don't pretend to be an expert, but I'd say that was about it. And you've been married . . . how long? Four months, is it?'

She picked up her handbag from the chair, took out five sovereigns and thrust them at him.

'Here you are! Take it and get out!'

'How crude!' he chided her. 'Besides, you've got it wrong. I want ten pounds this time. For one thing it's a while since I came; for another I've had an awful lot of expense just lately.'

'I'm not giving you ten pounds,' she protested.

'Look at it this way, Becky dear. You give me ten pounds now and I won't be back as quickly. It all lessens my chances of running into Roland, doesn't it?'

'How do I know you won't be back soon?'

'Well, you don't,' he conceded. 'You'll just have to trust me, won't you?'

'I'd as soon trust a boa constrictor!' She spat the words at him. 'You are utterly foul!'

'I know!' he sympathised. 'That's why if I were you I'd pay up and get rid of me!'

She delved in her purse and handed him five more sovereigns. 'I wish I knew how to get rid of you permanently. If I knew of a way, I'd use it, believe me.'

'Oh I do believe you,' Jimmy said. 'But you didn't always think like that, did you?'

'I must have been crazy! I must have been completely mad!'

'I don't think Roland would take that as an excuse, do you? Well, I know when I'm not wanted, so ta-ta! Or perhaps au revoir!'

She was frantic after he left. What am I going to do, she asked herself. How long will this go on? Am I to go on paying for the rest of my life?

CHAPTER TWENTY-TWO

'If only you had stayed on,' Eleanor said to Selina. 'The weather is perfect now!'

In fact, from the moment Selina and Bob had boarded the train to return to Hebghyll, the sun had shone. It was a pale, spring sunshine, but the air was clear and dry; perfect, as Bob had said, looking out of the train window, for climbing Helvellyn. But Selina had been glad to leave. She felt confused, not a little frightened, anxious for home and everything familiar.

'But you must take the rest of your honeymoon,' Eleanor continued. 'There's no need whatever for you to pitch into work right away.'

She wouldn't put her anxiety into words, it was too private an area, but she was dismayed by Selina's appearance – though not so much her appearance as her nervous manner, the anxiety in her eyes. Gone was the confidence which had radiated from her daughter, turned every day into a sunny one, ever since Bob had returned on Boxing Day. Her gentle, loving manner hadn't changed; it was a delight to see the care the newly-married couple had for each other in look, in word and in gesture; but the easy curves of Selina's mouth were now straightened into firmer, more resolute, lines. And Bob himself, Eleanor thought (though her chief concern was for her daughter) seemed hesitant, unsure of himself. Well, whatever it was that had gone wrong on the honeymoon, she was powerless to do anything about it.

'I can cope perfectly well with the café,' she said. 'And you know there are no room bookings here until Easter.'

'But with Grandma not well, I thought you might need help,' Selina said. She was sticking to this as their reason for returning.

'I have help,' Eleanor informed her. 'I've engaged a Mrs Olive Feather – a war widow. I'll introduce you when you're ready.'

'Is she to live in?' Selina asked quickly.

'No. I think she might like to, but I left that to you. She rents a little house in Hebghyll. She has a small daughter who'll be looked after by the grandmother during the day. I would have waited until you came back to set her on, because after all she concerns you every bit as much as me – but she'd also had another job offered.'

'That's all right,' Selina said. 'If she suits you I'm sure she'll suit us.'

Eleanor nodded. 'I think you'll both like her. And she's agreed to a month's trial, either side. And of course Jenny is helping until she starts her nurse's training in a week or two. But naturally, since your grandma's still at Whinbank, Jenny's sleeping there too. I didn't want her alone in The Beeches so I've been locking it up at night until you came back.'

'You seem to have everything well organised,' Selina said.

She hoped she didn't show her immense relief at the knowledge that they were to have the guest house to themselves at nights, at least for a while. A little time together, she told herself, was all it would take to make everything right with Bob. A little time, and a great deal of love. Love for her husband she had in abundance, spilling over – and now her mother was offering them a little time.

'So you see, you can easily take a few more days,' Eleanor urged.

Selina turned to Bob, touched his arm.

'I'd like that, darling, wouldn't you? We needn't go away. We could just take ourselves off in the daytime, go for walks.'

We could talk, she thought. We could talk all day and all night if we wanted to. There'd be no pressure on them.

They'd be completely alone, as they had not been for a minute since leaving the hotel. On the train the compartment had been full, and here at Whinbank they'd been surrounded by family.

Meeting his wife's anxious blue eyes, Bob read the message behind the casually spoken words.

'Why not, if we're not too badly needed,' he agreed. 'We won't get many such chances once we start work.'

'That's true,' Eleanor said. 'In fact, I intend to opt out of The Beeches quite a bit before long. I want to help Dick – take over most of the paperwork, even some of the other jobs, so that he can spend time developing the seed part of the business.'

If only I could tell her, Selina thought! She had a deep need to confide in her mother, but it would be disloyal to Bob and she could never do it. For a moment she felt isolated, terribly alone; and then she chided herself, for she wasn't alone. She had Bob, they had each other. Everything *must* work out.

'Well, I'll get back to work,' Eleanor said. 'There's still an hour before closing time. Would you like me to pack your wedding presents in the car and bring them over this evening, so you can begin to sort things out?'

'Not this evening, thank you,' Selina replied swiftly. 'I'll come over myself before too long and help pack them.'

They had chosen for their bedroom a room at the farthest end of the house, facing southwest towards the moor. It was already furnished, mostly with second-hand pieces which Eleanor had bought quickly when she first moved from Akersfield. It was pleasant enough, but in time they would have their own things, things they had chosen together; and what was there now would be distributed around the other rooms.

'We could start by changing the curtains,' Selina said. 'I'd like something quite light, patterned with flowers. Wouldn't you, darling?'

'I'm sure I would. But I daresay I'd like anything you

371

happened to choose. I don't know a lot about colours and furnishings.'

He came over to where she stood by the window, putting his arms around her shoulders, drawing her close. They stood looking out at the fading daylight. With the sun gone the moors were dark, almost forbidding, against the sky.

'Bob?' She spoke in a whisper, hesitant.

'Yes, my love?'

'I want to ask you something. Promise you won't be cross with me.'

He held her closer. 'Cross with you? Why ever should I be?'

'Promise!'

'All right, I promise then!'

She took a deep breath. He had promised not to be cross, but he wouldn't like what she was going to say. She was sure he wouldn't.

'I want us to go to the doctor. We'd go together. I want us to tell him about your dream . . .'

She felt his arm around her slacken.

'Tell the doctor my dream . . .?'

'Yes. But not just that. I want us to tell him when it happens. That it happens when we . . . when we're making love . . . at the moment . . .' She didn't know how to go on. It was all too new to her, she was too shy. But it was important, she was sure of that.

He had let go of her now.

'But darling . . . what can the doctor do? I'm not ill. A bottle of medicine isn't going to do the trick!'

'You promised not to be cross!' she reminded him.

'I'm not cross. I just don't think it makes sense, that's all. A doctor is to cure someone who's ill. I repeat, I'm not ill!'

'Perhaps you are,' she said quietly. 'They say a lot of soldiers are ill, even if not physically. Especially those who served in the front line a long time, as you did so bravely, my love. It's nothing to be ashamed of.'

'I'm not ashamed,' Bob said. 'I just don't think it's a problem for a doctor.'

'Dr Clare is very understanding,' Selina persisted. 'Needless to say he'd treat it all in the strictest confidence. No-one else would know.'

He walked away from her, sat on the edge of the bed, looked down at his hands.

'I don't think it's a good idea at all,' he said. 'I think it will all work itself out, and talking to Dr Clare won't help one bit.'

She left the window and went and sat beside him. She put her arms around him and drew him down until they were lying on the bed, then she took his hands and placed them on her breasts.

'Love me!' she invited.

'Now? Love you now?'

'Now!' she said urgently. 'We're alone. Everyone has left the house. There's only you and me. Make love to me now!'

When his climax came, the dream came with it, though with part of him he knew that he was still awake. Across the room and through the window he could see the line of the moors, now almost black in a darkening sky; and it wasn't the moors, but the top of the trench. He heard the sounds of the heavy guns, then felt the thud as they came nearer. The whine of the shells, the loud explosions as they burst inside his head, the rattle of the machine guns came, and then went again as they were overlaid by the agonised shrieks of the wounded. And then the familiar cry – 'Stretcher-bearer! Stretcher-bearer!' – and it was his own voice he heard calling, though it was still inside his head. And then as the rats came, eyes gleaming in the darkness, so did the shout which heralded his climax. And as he cried out, Selina jerked away from him, out of his embrace, and turned towards the wall, sobbing.

Later – it was the middle of the night, they had not made love again and had hardly spoken – he turned to her in the bed.

'Are you awake?'

'Yes.' She had not slept at all. She wondered if she would ever sleep.

'Selina, I'll go with you to see Dr Clare in the morning.'

They telephoned and made an appointment to see the doctor quite early, before his normal surgery time, and he came to the door to greet them himself. He had offered to come to The Beeches but Selina turned the offer down. Everyone in Hebghyll knew Dr Clare's car and speculated why it should be standing outside a particular door. He seated them in his rather dark, heavily furnished surgery, observing the signs of nervousness which were so familiar to him in his patients: both of them sitting on the edge of their chairs, Selina twisting her gloved hands, a muscle twitching in Bob's cheek. Why had they come? They'd been married less than a week, and in any case husbands and wives seldom came together. He often wished they would.

'Well,' he said. 'I'm glad your grandmother is better, Selina — or would you like me to call you Mrs Harwell now that you're a married lady?'

'Of course not, Dr Clare! So you're pleased with my grandma, then?'

'Delighted. She's nearly as good as new, except she's not getting any younger and she'll have to take a certain amount of care.'

'Good! I'm pleased,' Selina said.

They all fell silent. Across his desk, Dr Clare observed the couple, waited in vain for them to speak.

'Well, I'm sure you didn't come to see me about your grandmother,' he said. 'So what is it I can do for you?'

Selina and Bob exchanged looks, each willing the other to speak first.

'Why don't *you* tell me, Selina?' Dr Clare suggested. 'You know me well enough to trust me.'

She told him. As the words came out, hesitantly at first, and then gathering speed, she felt her face flame with embarrassment. It was not fair that Bob should have left this to her. It was *his* dream, *his* problem. Yet that wasn't quite true. They were man and wife now, it was a problem they must share.

374

Dr Clare listened patiently, asking no questions, making no comment until Selina had finished.

'First of all, you did the right thing in coming to me,' he said. 'Especially in coming together. That was a brave and sensible thing to do. You'll feel better for having told someone else your trouble, even though I'm not sure I can do anything about it.' He turned to Bob. 'You saw a lot of fighting?'

'Yes. Before the Somme and right through it. But not more than many other men.'

Dr Clare nodded. His only son had been one of those others, but Alan hadn't come through. One day, if it could be found, he and his wife would visit the grave in France. It was all that was left to them. He himself was the third generation of Clares to practise as a physician in the West Riding. There would now not be a fourth. But of all this he said nothing.

'I came through it all without a scratch,' Bob said. 'Not even the smallest flesh wound.' Sometimes he had felt a great burden of guilt that while his friends were wounded or killed around him, he remained unscathed. 'Lucky Harwell' they'd called him, and the name had hurt.

'There are wounds other than those of the flesh,' Dr Clare said gently. 'They can go deeper and hurt more. We don't understand them yet, we doctors. We're trained to heal the body, but we've seen in this war – and we'll go on seeing – that the mind and the spirit need healing too.'

'Are you telling me I've got some sort of madness?' Bob's voice was truculent. He had seen men gone crazy from the fighting. He wasn't one of those. He half rose from his chair, as if he would like to escape.

'Emphatically not!' Dr Clare said. 'What I'm telling you is that, in my opinion, you've been wounded as surely as if you'd been shot in the leg, and that that wound, just as if it were a leg wound, will take time to heal.' But we don't know the treatment, he thought to himself. We know what to do with arms and legs, but very little about the mind and the spirit.

'But he will be better, he will, won't he?' Selina insisted.

'I'm sure of it,' Dr Clare said. 'And you'll help him.'

'Then tell me how?' she demanded.

He shook his head.

'I'm not a psychiatrist. There are very few psychiatrists, and thousands of severe cases of shellshock still in the hospitals. We're only just beginning to understand it and it's going to be impossible for everyone to get treatment quickly. So I think what we have to do in the meantime – and especially as yours is not the worst of cases, Bob – is to use common sense.'

'In what way?' Bob asked.

'First of all, face the problem – which you've both done by coming to me. In the second place, talk about it. Talk to each other. You, Bob, tell Selina what it was like there. Don't hold back, even on the worst bits – especially on the worst bits. Selina, you must encourage him, ask him questions. Always have it out in the open. We've already noticed, those of us who weren't there, that the men who went through the worst of it just won't talk. I think that's a mistake.'

'It's difficult to talk about it,' Bob said hesitantly. 'It's too much like living it again. What you want is to put it behind you.' The noise, he thought; the sights and smells, the blood and the vermin – but most of all the incessant noise which chiselled into your brain. Who wanted to talk about it? You just wanted to forget.

'But you don't put it behind you,' Dr Clare told him. 'You push it down inside and then it erupts.'

He knew the problem. He and his wife never talked about their dead son now. Each of them bore their pain separately, deep inside. Physician heal thyself.

'Live as normal a life as possible,' he advised. 'Have children as soon as possible. From what you tell me, there's no physical bar to that. A good family life is a great healer.' And pray that there'll never be another war to rob you of them, he thought.

But how can I, Selina asked herself. How can I conceive

376

a child in such circumstances? How can I bear to? But she would try. She would try in every possible way. She leaned across and touched Bob's hand, smiled at him with all the confidence she could muster.

'Thank you, Dr Clare,' she said. 'I'm sure we both feel better for coming. We'll remember all you've said.'

Dr Clare rose to his feet and held out his hand. 'Come again whenever you wish; whenever it would help just to talk. And you, Selina – I look forward to you walking into my surgery to tell me you're pregnant!'

They had been at home no more than a few minutes before Eleanor, who had come with Jenny to open up the cafe, knocked on the door of their room.

'I don't want to disturb you,' she said. 'I just thought you might like to come down and meet Mrs Feather before you went off for the day – that is, if you're going to go out. It's a beautiful day.'

'We are,' Selina replied. 'We're going for a long walk over the moors.' She hadn't had time to discuss it with Bob, but she was determined to make him agree. She wanted to put Dr Clare's suggestions into practice as quickly as possible. 'But I would like to meet Mrs Feather. We should both meet her, don't you think so, Bob?'

What he thought was that things were moving too quickly for him today. He had never thought of Selina as being the kind of woman who would try to organise him, but this was what she was doing, even if it was for his own good. He was upset by what the doctor had said. He had tried until now not to think about his dreams – or 'the' dream, for it was always the same. He had believed that by ignoring it, it would go away. Now Dr Clare had said the very opposite of that. He hadn't talked to anyone about the war and he wasn't sure he could do so – not even his lovely Selina.

'I suppose we should,' he said.

'I told you she was a widow. Her husband was killed at Amiens,' Eleanor explained.

Selina took Bob's hand and squeezed it hard. How lucky I am, the gesture said, not to be a widow before I was even a wife. How lucky we both are to be here, together. He understood the touch of her hand and held hers tightly in return. She was right. They had everything before them. They would make a go of it.

Mrs Feather was tall, plumpish. The cheerful expression on her face didn't reach her eyes, which were brown and sad. She wore an immaculately clean white coat overall, and her rich brown hair was tucked under a white cap.

'I'm pleased to meet you,' she said. 'I hope you don't mind that I brought my daughter with me today. My mother goes into Akersfield on a Thursday, to see a friend in hospital, so there was no-one to look after Lucy. Say good morning to the lady and gentleman, Lucy!'

'I'm sure my mother won't mind,' Selina told her. 'And my husband and I are just off for the day.'

'She goes to school after Easter,' Mrs Feather said. 'So it will be easier.'

'She'll be no trouble,' Selina assured her. 'In the meantime, do you think we might have a few sandwiches to take with us? Anything will do.'

'I'll have them ready in two shakes of a lamb's tail,' Mrs Feather promised. 'And a flask of tea if you like.'

'She seems a very nice woman,' Selina said to Bob as half an hour later they took the steep path to the top of the moor. At the back of her mind she had the germ of an idea about Mrs Feather, but she would wait just a little while before mentioning it.

There was a stiff breeze as they climbed higher. She took off her tam-o'-shanter and stuffed it in her coat pocket. 'I like the wind to blow through my hair,' she smiled, tucking her arm through Bob's.

'Such beautiful hair!' Bob said. 'As I believe I've told you a thousand times before! It was your hair I first noticed when you were in the canteen in Akersfield.'

'Then it's a good thing you didn't see Becky first,' Selina answered. 'She has the most striking hair of all of us.'

'Becky's is nice,' he agreed. 'But I prefer yours. It's pale and delicate – and it smells delicious! In fact, I'm

378

going to kiss your beautiful hair, right here and now!'

'Bob! Someone might see us!'

'There's no-one around to see us, not for miles. Only a few skylarks, and they won't tell.'

It was suddenly as if all their troubles had left them; everything was new again and perfect. There had been no real need to go to the doctor, Bob thought. It would be all right; it would all come out in the wash. They set off again, still climbing steadily, for they hadn't reached the top of the moor, saving their breath by not speaking. When they reached the crest they stopped to look back.

'It's like being on top of the world,' Selina said. 'Oh Bob, I'm so glad you decided we'd live here! I don't know how I would have borne to leave it!'

'Wales is beautiful,' he said defensively.

'Oh I know! But different. See how far away Hebghyll looks from this height. The houses are like toys, quite unreal.'

Like the trouble which lay between them, she thought. Small, far away, not quite real. But almost at once she recognised the danger of that thought. It was real, it existed, just as Hebghyll did. They would have to go back to it as they would to Hebghyll.

'Bob, we mustn't forget what the doctor advised,' she ventured. 'We must talk. We won't get many opportunities like this. Let's sit down, and you tell me about the war. Everything – all the little things as well. What you ate, where you slept, what you laughed at – and about the times when you were afraid.'

'Oh Selina, who wants to hear about the war on a day like this? It's over. Let it rest.'

'*I* want to hear,' she persisted. 'It's a part of your life. There isn't any part of your life I don't want to hear about.'

'It *was* a part of my life. It's over.'

She shook her head firmly. Then she sat on the ground and pulled him down beside her. 'No, it's not over. Not until your nightmares about it go away. And I'm going to see that they do, my darling. Now tell me about just one day. Any day, good or bad, it doesn't matter just so long as you were there.'

'Well, it's true there were some good days – a few,' Bob said thoughtfully. 'Mostly when we were back at base, when the food was better; you could delouse your clothing, get some kip, and the mail came from home, with a letter from you. But I remember another day, and it wasn't a good one. We were up front.'

'Tell me.'

'It was in July. I had a mate called Taffy Williams and it was his birthday, his twentieth. They said that every gun on a twenty-five-mile front was firing on that morning, and Taffy made a joke of it – said it was a salute for his birthday . . .' He paused. Did he really want all this?

'What sort of place was it?' Selina prompted.

'A hill. Well, a steep slope – and Jerry on the opposite slope.' He looked down to where Hebghyll lay, saw the river winding along the floor of the valley.

'There was a brook ran along the bottom of the valley there, through No Man's Land. It looked a peaceful sort of stream, as though it had nothing whatever to do with the war, or all the stuff that was shooting over it. We sent up a lot of smoke screens that morning, but it didn't fool Jerry. He'd got his targets carefully marked and he went for them . . .'

His hesitancy had vanished now. He was talking fluently; remembering. Selina encouraged him with an occasional word, but otherwise she sat back and listened – listened with a sick horror which she tried not to show as his story unfolded.

How little they'd suffered as civilians, she thought. The shortages of food, the tightness of money – they were pinpricks in comparison. But she remembered the day the gang of youths had broken into the cafe in Akersfield, destroyed everything in sight, knocked her pregnant mother to the ground so that she'd almost lost the baby she was carrying – and all because of their German name. And she remembered the dear man who bore that name, and was killed fighting for England. Yes, those at home had had their own kind of suffering, a different kind. And for thousands like Dr Clare (for she knew about Alan) and Mrs Feather, it would go on.

'I think of all the artillery it was the machine guns I hated most,' Bob said. 'They had a nasty, mean sort of sound – and it went on and on . . . Then there was the mud. You wouldn't think we'd be up to the knees in it in July, would you? But we were. We'd had heavy rain that week, and the spring rains hadn't really dried up.'

What surprised Selina was the flat calm of his voice as he described the events. She wondered if he was still holding in his real feelings. She had no idea how long or how much he should go on talking about it all. She felt ignorant and helpless. So when he paused again she didn't encourage him to continue.

'Tell me one last thing you remember about the day, then we'll walk a bit further before we eat our sandwiches.'

'Taffy Williams didn't make it,' he said.

She realised by the look on her husband's face that the whole of the story had been leading up to this.

'He was standing right beside me when he caught it. It could have been me. I was an inch away. Except that I was "Lucky Harwell". I couldn't raise a stretcher-bearer – they were all too busy – so he bled to death.'

Selina shivered. The wind had turned cold on the top of the moor. She turned to Bob and took him in her arms.

'I love you, Bob Harwell,' she said. 'I love you so much!'

They walked all the rest of that day, speaking no more of the past, only of the present and the future. At teatime they called at a farmhouse and were given thick slices of succulent ham and two fried eggs each. 'No shortage of food on the farms,' Bob observed. It was dark by the time they were back at The Beeches.

'I have an idea about Mrs Feather,' Selina said as they sat in front of the fire that lady had left for them. 'I'm sure she would like to live in – it would be easier for her with the little girl – and I know we'd like to live out. Why don't we give her the chance, and if she agrees we could rent her cottage. What do you think, love?'

'What would your mother say? Would she agree to us living out? I wouldn't want her to know . . . well, the real reason . . .' He broke off.

'She wouldn't. I wouldn't tell her. And we could put a telephone in the cottage so that Mrs Feather could get in touch with us quickly if she needed to. It would be so much better for us, Bob. You must see that.'

'My poor Selina,' Bob said quietly. 'Is it so unbearable, then?'

'Not if we're alone,' she told him. 'I can stand anything if it's just the two of us!' But if not, she thought, will the time come when we can't even bear to make love any longer?

They made love again that night. The desire was still fierce between them, and for that she was grateful. But the dream came as usual – only this time the difference was that she did not turn away. Though it was almost unendurable, she stayed with him until it was all over and he was calm again. It was her contribution, her assurance that she would always be there. And who knows, she thought, perhaps I'll have a baby!

Eleanor, when Selina suggested the plan for Mrs Feather, was puzzled, but acquiescent.

'I had thought you'd like to be here,' she said. 'Mrs Feather's cottage is quite small, you know – and a bit isolated.'

'It will suit us beautifully.'

Eleanor noted the stubborn look on her daughter's face but forbore to question her further.

'Well, if it's what you want . . .'

'It is, Mother.'

'And if Mrs Feather is agreeable. I don't have any fears about her competence. I'm quite impressed by her so far. And as you say, she can get us on the telephone if she needs us.'

Mrs Feather was delighted.

'It'll make life that much easier for me,' she said.

382

'Especially as regards Lucy. I'll be able to keep an eye on her and spare my mother the job most of the time. And I don't think there'll be any difficulty about you and your husband renting the cottage, Mrs Harwell. I'm sure the landlord will be pleased to have you for tenants.'

The days were dragging by for Becky. Never had time gone so slowly as in that long, hot summer in the year after the war. If she had to choose the time of a year to have a baby (though she would most likely choose not to have one at all), then she would not be pregnant in the summer. The house was stifling, and now that her condition was so apparent it was unthinkable for her to go out during the daytime. She had to wait until dusk was falling, when Roland would take her for a short walk.

'I've had a pig of a day,' she said when he came home one evening at the beginning of September. 'I've been hot and sweating all day, I've been sick, my ankles are swollen and I look a fright!'

Roland took her in his arms.

'You do not look a fright, my sweet. You look quite beautiful to me!'

'Oh to you, maybe – but I know what I look like. I can see myself in the mirror. I can't think why any woman has a baby after the first. No man would. We'd all be one-child families if men had to bear them!'

'I'm sorry you've had a beastly day, darling,' Roland said. 'Did no-one call?'

'Who would call?'

'I thought Jenny might have.'

'Her off-duty was changed. She telephoned.' That had been a disappointment too. She had never been on the closest of terms with her youngest sister, but her visits made a welcome break in the tedium, even though she did talk about nothing but hospital and her boring old patients.

'So you've seen no-one all day, my pet?'

'No.'

She turned away, feeling her face redden as she told the

383

lie. Jimmy Austin had been. He had telephoned first to check that Jenny wouldn't be visiting and then told her that he was on his way.

'Have the money ready, sweetie,' he said over the phone. 'I shan't have time to stay.'

'I haven't any money,' she told him. 'I can't get to the bank in my condition.'

'Then you'll just have to send someone for it, won't you?' he said. 'What do you have a maid for?'

In fact she had the money. Roland had collected her monthly allowance from the bank for her on the previous day.

'I can't think what you do with it all,' he teased her.

She'd smiled, and said nothing. His father gave her the money, it was hers to do as she liked with. Roland wouldn't dream of taking her to account, just as long as she didn't get into debt, or keep asking him for more – which she never did. But now Jimmy had taken it all and her purse was empty again.

'Well, as soon as we've finished supper you must put on your hat and we'll go for a stroll,' Roland said.

'Where can we go except around the streets?' she demanded. 'I hate the streets around here. I thought when we married we were going to move to Halton. That's what your father said.'

'So we shall, my love. And would have done sooner had you not been pregnant. We don't want to take the slightest risk, do we? But once you've got over the baby . . . And not long now. Only six more weeks! I don't know about you, but I can hardly wait.'

Panic rose in her every time the date was mentioned. She was so big that she was convinced she would have the baby any day now. And if she did, it would be Jimmy's, as she felt more and more sure it *was*. And if it was, even if Roland never knew, would Jimmy ever stop blackmailing her?

'You might not have to wait so long,' she told Roland. 'My mother says she thinks it might come early. Babies sometimes do, you know.'

384

'It will be welcome,' Roland said. 'No matter when.'

He made her feel worse because he was so unfailingly kind, so considerate. Everything he did was for her good and the baby's. He had even stopped making love to her in case it did harm.

She was in the bedroom, putting on her hat, when the ring came at the door. She heard Roland answer it — it was the maid's night off — and then he came running upstairs. He crossed the bedroom and picked up her handbag.

'I'm borrowing half-a-crown, my dear. There's a lady at the door collecting for the missions.'

She turned around quickly, to take the handbag from him, but he had already opened it.

'I . . . don't have any money!' Why had she said that? Why hadn't she said she'd left it downstairs? But it wouldn't have washed. He had the purse in his hand.

'Of course you do, dear. I brought you ten pounds from the bank only yesterday. I put it in your purse myself.' He was staring into the purse. 'But there's nothing here! It's empty!'

'I know,' Becky said. 'I can explain. But hadn't you better go to the door and ask the lady to call back?'

It gave her a short breathing space. What should she tell him? Should she tell him the truth, throw herself on his mercy? But she couldn't, she would never have the courage. If she hadn't said that she could explain things, then she might have let him think that it had just disappeared, that the whole thing was as much a surprise to her as it was to him. But that would have thrown suspicion on the maid and, wicked though she felt herself to be, she couldn't sink to those depths.

He was back in the bedroom within two minutes.

'My dear, this is very strange. How do you account for it? You had the ten pounds yesterday evening and you haven't been out of the house today!' He was mystified.

She took a deep breath.

'I . . . I gave it away!'

'*Gave it away?*'

385

'Yes.'

'But how? You were never out?'

Inspiration came to her.

'Someone came to the door. You know, just like a minute ago when they came to collect for the missions.'

'You gave away *ten pounds* to someone who came to the door?'

'Yes.' It was somewhere near the truth. It was easier if you stuck as close as you could to the truth.

'But who, my love? Which charity was it?'

'It wasn't a charity. It was . . . an ex-soldier. He was down on his luck, no job and no pension. He . . . he said ten pounds would help him to start up in business.'

'Take him to the nearest bookmaker, more like!'

And you don't know how close you are to the truth with that, Becky thought.

'I was sorry for him. We have so much. He had nothing.' By now the tears were brimming her eyes, spilling down her cheeks. It was all so awful, so complicated. She was even a little confused as to whether the tears were for herself or for the mythical ex-soldier. Roland held out his arms to her and she ran to him.

'Oh Roland, I'm so sorry! I'm truly sorry!'

'There, there, my love,' he said, stroking her hair. 'Don't upset yourself. You did it out of the kindness of your heart and it was a very generous gesture. What's more, I rather think it wasn't the first time you gave your allowance away to someone in need. Now was it?'

'No.'

'And to think I accused you of extravagance! Oh my darling, I'm the one who should be sorry. But I beg of you not to do it again. It's right and good to give to charity, but in future you should make quite sure that it's a proper charity. There are plenty of them in need.'

'Oh I will, Roland! I will!'

'And now dry your eyes and put your hat on and we'll go for that walk I promised you.'

But she could not drive the incident from her mind. She

lay awake all night, worrying. And perhaps it was that which brought on her labour the very next day, or perhaps it was that the time had come for the baby to be born.

She was in labour all day, screaming with the pain of it, bathed in sweat on the warm September day. Roland came home from the mill but the midwife wouldn't have him in the room and sent him off to be with his equally distracted father. It was seven in the evening when, with a pain that Becky thought must tear her body in half, and a scream which turned Roland's blood to water, the baby was born.

'It's a grand little boy!' the midwife said. 'And a strong one. Listen to those lungs!'

'Let me look at him!' Becky demanded. There was only one thing she wanted to look for, and if it wasn't there she would just turn her face to the wall and die.

'Here you are then. He's just perfect – except he's got a little mole on his left shoulder blade. A little diamond-shaped mole!'

'My husband said he would have,' Becky said weakly. 'Please tell him!'

So everything was going to be all right. Jimmy Austin would have no further hold on her. In a few weeks from now they would buy a house in Halton. He wouldn't even know where she was. He was out of her life forever.

Later – she had just wakened from sleep and it was dark – Roland came into the room.

'I telephoned your mother,' he said. 'And Selina rang. She said I was to give you a message. She sent her love and I'm to tell you that she's pregnant.'

CHAPTER TWENTY-THREE

Becky surveyed her sitting-room with satisfaction. It was just as she wanted it, everything in it chosen by herself; all the latest, as well as the best. Of course she had asked Roland if he had any special fancies, but almost from the beginning he had left it entirely to her.

'You're a much better judge of these things,' he said. 'If it's as you want it, I'm sure I shall like it.'

So in their own rooms in the new house in Halton she had almost nothing left of Roland's mother's effects, with the exception of the piano, which was a Bechstein. Some of the old furniture had been kept by her father-in-law, so that now his bedroom and small sitting-room were grossly overcrowded with heavy furniture, ornaments, oil paintings in gilded frames, knickknacks – and were a nightmare to clean and dust, though thank goodness Mrs Flynn came in to do that.

'Why not send the things to Briggs's auction rooms?' Mr Layton had suggested. 'It's solid stuff, first-class workmanship. You'd get good prices.'

'I don't think so, Pop!' Becky said.

It was 1924. Who in their right mind would want that old Victorian furniture? Everything now was getting lighter, simpler, and so much more elegant.

'Aye, well, your stuff looks quite nice, love,' he conceded. 'And this three-piece suite is quite comfortable once you get used to it. But it's all a bit austere-looking for me. I can't quite take to it.'

Then why don't you stay in your own room, Becky thought furiously. He still spent far too much time with herself and Roland and she had little hope of changing him. But she would never say as much to him, though she protested frequently to Roland.

'He's lonely,' Roland pointed out. 'The top and bottom of it is, he still misses Mother. And he *has* been very generous to us.'

There was no denying that. Without a single protest he had bought this lovely house in Halton, overlooking the park, and had allowed her whatever money she needed to furnish it. Early in 1920, when they moved, there had been no shortage of money. It was boom time then, though all too soon to be over, worse luck. And her father-in-law was so pleased with her for giving him a grandson that he could deny her nothing. So now Becky stifled her feelings and tried to smile at him.

'It's the fashion, Pop.'

She thought she probably had one of the most fashionable sitting-rooms in Halton. Their neighbours tended to be older people, who hadn't moved with the times as quickly as she had. But there was plenty of money in Halton. It was populated by mill-owners, bankers, solicitors and the like – though some of the really rich, those who had made a killing in the war, were beginning to move out to places like Ilkley, Harrogate, Hebghyll. Unfortunately, the rest of Akersfield wasn't so prosperous. Roland worried about the poverty in the town, and he seemed to want her to worry about it too.

'What good would that do?' Becky said whenever he mentioned it. 'It's not my fault that the textile trade has slumped and that people are out of work. Anyway, they say it's the same all over the north, not just in Akersfield.'

'But Akersfield is on our doorstep,' he insisted. 'We mustn't ignore what's on our doorstep, my dear.'

Mr Layton took out his watch and consulted it.

'How long do you reckon young Christopher will be, then?'

'Not long. They've only gone to the park. Hannah usually keeps him out about an hour.'

Until recently Christopher had had a nanny, but Roland

389

had insisted that at almost five years old, and going to school in September, his son no longer needed her.

'It's not good for Christopher, and it's also ostentatious,' he said firmly. 'I'm really quite determined about this, Becky darling.'

So Nanny Price had departed, and now Hannah took the little boy for his walk when Becky didn't want to do so.

The years since Christopher's birth had been good ones for Becky; moving into the new house, making new friends. Best of all she had been free of Jimmy Austin. She had strongly expected him to turn up again after her baby was born and, though apprehensive, she had been ready for him, ready to confront him with the fact that Christopher was indisputably Roland's son. But Jimmy Austin had not shown his face, and for almost a year she had wondered why.

She might never have known had she not been lining a blanket chest with newspaper against the moths. It was a copy of the *Leeds Mercury*. They never took that paper and she had no idea how it had got into the house, unless a workman had left it when they'd moved in, not long ago. But she could still see in her mind's eye the words which had sprung up at her from the printed page.

GAOLED FOR FORGERY
FOUR YEARS FOR LEEDS MAN

She might not have read it even then – she had not known of him living in Leeds – had she not seen his name. James Thomas Austin. It even mentioned that, though working until the time of his arrest as a chauffeur-gardener, he had at one time been stage manager of the Bluebirds concert party. It also gave a list of his previous convictions.

'When pronouncing sentence (she read) Mr Justice Stephens remarked, "You are a menace to society and in sentencing you to four years' hard labour I am giving you no more than you deserve." '

Yes, you're a menace all right, she thought. I'm glad you're behind bars.

She had screwed up the sheet of newspaper and thrown it in the fire. She didn't want to tell Roland. She just prayed that he would never hear of it and that Jimmy Austin was out of her life forever.

'I'd like to have taken Christopher out this afternoon. I'm teaching him to play cricket, you know. Hold a straight bat, bowl for the middle stump. One day he might well play for Yorkshire, be another Wilfred Rhodes!'

Her father-in-law's words jerked Becky back to the present. She had almost ceased to think of Jimmy Austin, yet once or twice recently the thought had darted into her mind that he must now be out of prison. It was a thought she put away from her as quickly as it came. Surely he would never trouble her again?

'Did you hear what I said?' Mr Layton asked.

'I'm sorry, Pop. I was miles away. You could have taken him. If I'd known you were coming home early he could have waited for you.'

She had been arranging her collection of Wedgwood in the new china cabinet. Now she locked the door of the cabinet and placed the key on top. It was strictly forbidden to Christopher. Then she crossed the room and looked out of the window. She never grew tired of the view. Once the park had formed part of Lord Halton's estate, and when he had departed, with the immense fortune he had made in the West Riding, for sunnier climes, he had given it to the grateful citizens of Akersfield.

Being rather out of the way, the park wasn't much frequented during the week, but on Sundays in summer there was a band, and Becky, though she refused to join the crowds of ordinary people who promenaded up and down the broad walks, threw open all the windows and listened, humming the tunes which wafted in. She could never resist music. No-one would ever know how much she missed the Bluebirds.

'Here they come!' she said. 'Christopher looks awfully flushed. I hope Hannah hasn't let him race about too much.' She sighed. 'But there you are! She's just a servant. Nanny Price would have known better.'

391

Mr Layton gave Becky a doubtful look. He thought the world of her, but sometimes she got a bit above herself. He knew her humble beginnings. There was nothing wrong in humble beginnings, they were true of a lot of Akersfield folk who were now very comfortable, thank you; but it wasn't the thing to forget them, disown them. Her own mother would never do that. Still, she was a good daughter-in-law, and a good wife to his son. She was perhaps less of a good mother, he thought, a trifle uneasily. It was a role she didn't take to.

Christopher burst in, ran to his mother, clutching at her skirts.

'There were some boys sailing paper boats on the pond! I could have played with them but Hannah wouldn't let me. Hannah is an old meanie!'

Becky gently disengaged herself from her son, smoothed down her skirt.

'No, Hannah was quite right. She knows you are not to play with boys in the park.'

'Why not?'

'You might pick things up.'

'No I wouldn't. Daddy told me I mustn't pick flowers, so I wouldn't.'

'I don't mean flowers,' Becky said. 'Now stop arguing. You can ring the bell and we'll ask Hannah to bring us some tea.'

'I never have any *fun*,' Christopher complained.

'You'll have fun when you go to school,' his grandfather promised. 'You'll have other boys and girls to play with. You'll enjoy that.' It was what the lad needed. He hardly ever mixed with other children, and there was still no sign of a brother or sister of his own, more the pity!

'When can I go to school?' Christopher demanded.

'I've explained all that to you,' Becky said. 'You go to school in September. It's July now. At the end of this month, a very few days from now, we go away on holiday for two weeks, then only a few weeks after we return home you'll go to school.'

'In the meantime, as soon as we've had a bit of tea, you and me'll have a game of cricket in the garden. Just think of it,' his grandfather said, 'you'll be playing cricket on the sands this time next week!'

Becky sighed. She wasn't looking forward to two weeks in Bridlington. It wasn't a bad place if you liked that sort of thing, but she would have preferred somewhere smarter, more sophisticated. London, for instance. They hadn't been back to London since their honeymoon and she longed to go.

She broached the subject to Roland that evening. They were sitting on either side of the fire grate which was filled with flowers, for the evenings were warm. For once, Mr Layton wasn't with them.

'It's out of the question, my love,' Roland said. 'London wouldn't be at all suitable for Christopher. When he's older, yes. But not now.'

'But why can't we take a holiday without Christopher?' Becky suggested. 'Say when we get back from Bridlington? Just for a few days. My mother would look after him. Or Selina would.'

'I daresay they would – though Selina has plenty on her plate with two children of her own and a third on the way, not to mention The Beeches. But the fact is – and you know it – I really can't afford to take time away from the mill. Things are not easy these days.'

'It wouldn't be as bad if you were going to be in Bridlington the whole fortnight instead of only the first week, Roland.'

'Now you're being really awkward, Becky,' Roland said. 'You've known all your life that the mills in Akersfield close down for one week at the end of July, and you know that that's the only time I can be away. When the hands go back, I must go back.'

'The way you work, anyone would think you were a millhand yourself, instead of a mill-owner!' Becky said angrily.

'If I were,' he retorted, 'you'd find a difference in your

life! You don't know a foot of the way, my lady! There's very few of my hands will know the luxury of a single day at the seaside, let alone a fortnight!'

'Then what a pity you can't take them with you! I daresay you'd like that!'

She had no patience with him in this mood – and it was the mood he was in all too often these days – almost as if he was ashamed of the gap between himself and those who worked for him. But such gaps were the way of the world and anyone in their right mind recognised that. Sometimes Roland talked like a Bolshevik.

'I *would* like it!' he cried. 'I'd like to pack them all in *charabancs*, and their wives and children with them, and take them to the seaside, or up into the Dales, for just one day. One day away from their poverty and worries. And I can't because the money isn't there, and the trade isn't there, and every month I have to face the fact that I might have to lay a few more men off.'

'All right. Don't go on about it,' Becky said wearily. She had heard it all before, a hundred times. 'And I still say I'm not looking forward to the second week in Bridlington, stuck with Christopher.'

'Stuck with him? For God's sake, Becky, he's your son! And you'll be stuck – as you call it – in a first-class hotel, with money in your purse, your every whim satisfied!'

'It wouldn't be so bad if I still had Nanny Price,' she persisted. 'She would . . .'

Roland brought his fist down so hard on to the arm of his chair that the china in the cabinet rattled.

'Becky, I will not continue to argue about Nanny Price. You know my feelings about a five-year-old boy having a nanny, especially in Akersfield where most people can't afford enough to eat. It's sheer, unwarranted extravagance.'

'We live in Halton, not Akersfield,' Becky said sullenly. 'It's different.'

'Halton *is* Akersfield. And people are people. Akersfield gives us our living – as far as you're concerned a more than comfortable one. The fact that you can no longer see

Layton's mill chimney out of your window doesn't mean that it's not there. We're part of Akersfield, whether you like it or not.'

She rose to her feet, shrugged her shoulders.

'There's no talking to you, is there? I'm going to bed.'

She stormed out of the room and charged up the stairs, rushing past Mr Layton on his leisurely way down.

'Whoa there!' he cried. 'Where are you off to, then?'

'I'm going to bed,' she snapped. 'Good night!'

'Then I won't keep Roland,' he said.

He had been going to have a leisurely nightcap with his son, a bit of a chat about this and that. But now he wouldn't. He knew the signs of a quarrel when he saw one and he also knew that the best place for making up a quarrel between man and wife was in the marriage bed. He wasn't too old to remember that.

'You can keep him as long as you like!' Becky called down from the landing. Then she went into the bedroom and slammed the door behind her.

For two pins she would lock the door against Roland: except that she wanted him, physically and sexually, she wanted him, here and now. Losing her temper always heightened her sexual appetite, so that now she could hardly bear to wait. She undressed quickly and got into bed, held her arms tightly around her body as if to hold in her mounting desire. He knew how she would be feeling, he must know, since it was nothing new – so where was he, why didn't he come?

It had been daylight when she came to bed, the sun still shining into the west-facing room; but while she lay there waiting for him the sun dipped in the sky, and vanished. She was desperate with longing. There was a moment when, but for her father-in-law's presence, she would have gone downstairs to fetch him. But at long last – it was quite dark now – she heard his footstep on the stairs.

She turned over and buried her face in the pillow, pretending to be asleep. He deserved to be punished for keeping her waiting so long, and punish him she would. She lay there with eyes closed, hearing him move about the room, going into the bathroom, coming back into the bedroom. How in the world could he take so much time? But when he finally climbed into bed she could contain herself no longer. She flung her arms around him, almost clawing at him in her desire.

'Love me!' she demanded. 'Love me! Now!'

Over the years their lovemaking, which had started off so badly, had grown to perfection. It was the one perfect thing in their marriage, which was why, she thought, it was the answer to all the other things which went wrong. Roland, while no less ardent than in the early days, had learned patience; to remember her and to wait for her; and with time and practice her climax came more quickly, matching itself to his. Oh, it was the most wonderful feeling in the world! She wanted it never to stop!

Presently they lay back on the pillows, satisfied.

'I think,' Roland said quietly, 'you might have another baby. I did nothing to prevent it. You wouldn't wait, my sweet!'

'Oh no!' she protested. 'No! I couldn't go through that again! Oh Roland, you know I rely on you!' She was so sleepy now, dying just to let go and fall asleep.

'Would it really be that bad?' he asked gently. 'You kept reasonably well when you were pregnant. Other women go through it again and again. It would be wonderful to have a sister or a brother for Christopher.'

She sat up. She was wide awake now.

'It would be nothing of the kind,' she contradicted him. 'And I am not other women. And now since you haven't taken the trouble, I must do something about it.' She would have to use that foul douche contraption. Oh, men were so lucky! They had the best of everything. None of the messing about. None of that awful business every month. No getting pregnant, losing their figure. And then the agony of the birth, and being tied down for years and years. Oh, they had the best of it all right. But if she

396

had the chance, she asked herself, would she want to be a man? The answer was 'No'.

'Come on with you, Billy-boy,' Selina said. 'It's high time you were in bed. Charlotte's been asleep for the past hour.'

'Charlotte's only two, *and* she's a girl. I'm four years and three months old. I ought to stay up later.'

He was sitting on the hearthrug, looking at a book. Already he could read, and no-one quite knew who had taught him; possibly Selina, maybe Bob, but mostly himself. Selina had first been aware of it a month or two ago, when he had read out the advertisements on the billboards in Hebghyll as they walked back from The Beeches to their own cottage. But then, he was bright in every way. He had walked before he was a year old, talked fluently only a few months later, and for some time now he had enjoyed working out complicated sums on his counting frame.

'Well, you've done so,' Selina pointed out. 'It's half-past seven. Other children of your age will have been in bed for ages.'

The fact was, he didn't seem to need much sleep, never had, even as a baby, which had made him an exhausting child. But she loved him so much. He was the child conceived against all odds in the very worst days of her husband's waking nightmares. He had been conceived, she knew it couldn't have been otherwise, at the very moment when Bob screamed in terror as he relived in his mind the experiences of the battlefield. For this reason, though she badly wanted a child, she had been apprehensive throughout her pregnancy, wondering what he would be like (she had always known it would be a son), whether he would be marked either physically or mentally by what had happened in the first moment of his existence.

He had been perfect. From the first hour he had been beautiful to look at, with his father's dark hair and eyes as blue as her own and the regularity of features which was a direct inheritance from his maternal grandmother. He had been totally healthy and invariably happy: he was much loved and very loving, even to people outside his own family. Auntie Olive Feather, for instance, adored him, and he her.

'Then give me a piggy-back up the stairs?' he demanded.

'I can't. You're too heavy for me!' She was four months pregnant and Dr Clare had told her she must be careful. 'But I daresay Daddy will.'

'Come on then, old son!' Bob said. He swung the little boy up on to his back as if he weighed no more than a feather. 'Keep your head down as we go up the stairs or you'll knock it on the beam.'

Selina followed close behind them, and together she and Bob tucked their son into his bed, heard his prayers, kissed him goodnight.

'As it's so light you can look at your book for a little longer,' Selina said.

She took a peep at two-year-old Charlotte, still fast asleep with her thumb in her mouth, and then went downstairs again, following Bob into the small, crowded sitting-room, where she at once began to put away Billy's toys.

'Where we're going to put everything when we have a third child, I just don't know!' she said. 'But I've no doubt we'll find a way. And I wouldn't swop for Buckingham Palace. I love being in our own little cottage, coming back here every evening.'

The arrangements they had made for The Beeches had worked beautifully over the last five years, she thought. Bob worked there full-time during the day, and more often than not she took the children and worked with him. Olive Feather had proved a treasure, hardworking and capable, pleased to have a regular wage, and a rent-free home for herself and her daughter. Almost immediately after Selina and Bob had taken over the cottage, Mrs Foster had moved back into The Beeches, so that there was company for Mrs Feather at night and another pair of hands to see to the guests if need be. There were never many guests. That side of the business hadn't expanded as Eleanor had hoped it would when she'd bought the place, but the cafe and the outside catering thrived and prospered, and made money.

Eleanor left most of the management to Bob and Selina now. She was busier than ever with the success of Dick's seed business.

'Sit down and rest,' Bob said. 'You've been on your feet all day. I didn't want you to have another baby yet. It's too soon.'

'Of course it's not!' Selina contradicted him happily. 'Charlotte's gone two. And I'm as fit as a fiddle! I want lots more children yet. Just as long as we can give them what they need – enough to eat, warm clothing in the winter, and lots and lots of love. And they bring love with them. Some people think there's only so much love and you have to share it out amongst whoever has a claim – but that's not true. The more you give love, the more you have to give.'

Bob laughed, gave her a gentle push to make her sit in the armchair. 'What a little philosopher you are!' he teased.

She blushed. 'Well, it's true! You can laugh at me, but it's true.'

'I'm not really laughing at you. Of course it's true. And Billy takes after you. He loves everyone – and everyone loves him. You both make it seem so easy – but it isn't easy for everyone.'

He loved his wife and his children dearly, but he found it increasingly difficult to come to terms with the life he was living. It was not of his choosing. He had drifted into it because it was where Selina was, and because when he came out of the army it seemed the only alternative to working on his father's farm, which at the time he hadn't wanted. Or perhaps Selina's desire to stay in Yorkshire had been too strong? Anyway, if he wanted it now, and he wasn't sure about that either, it was too late. His younger brother had taken what would have been his place and there was no room for him in Carmarthen. He had drifted away from his own family and now he felt himself hemmed in by Selina's. Hers was a loving, caring family and they had taken him to their hearts, made him one of their own; but there were times when he felt himself smothered by them.

'Do you mean it's not easy for *you*, love?'

'I suppose I do.'

'In what way?'

She had suspected for some weeks now that something was bothering him, and her suspicions had been confirmed, recently, by the fact that his bad dreams had returned. However he tried, he couldn't hide those from her. After the first year of their marriage the dreams had become less frequent, less severe; indeed the improvement seemed to date from the time of Billy's birth, almost as if he had brought a blessing into the world with him. Since then the problem, though it had not entirely gone away, had been bearable. Only when he was worried, or under stress, did some part of his mind return to that awful period in the trenches. She had judged that his recent worry was related to her pregnancy, especially because Dr Clare had warned her that she must take more care, get more rest. But perhaps it wasn't that at all?

'In what way?' she repeated.

'Oh nothing! Nothing of any importance. It's not worth talking about.'

There was no point in talking about it. Nothing he could do or say could change his position, his way of life. He was lucky, when so many men better qualified than himself had no work to go to, to have a safe job, money coming in, a steady living.

'Anything's important to me which causes you the least bit of unhappiness,' Selina said. 'You know that. And you can't deceive me. I know there's something. As for it not being worth talking about – I reckon the best bit of advice we ever had was when Dr Clare told us always to talk things over. It worked for us then and it would now. So come on!'

He rose from his chair and walked towards the window, stood with his back to her, looking down over the long garden which led to the riverside meadows. It was a pretty place, Hebghyll. It was a place which seemed almost untouched by what was going on in the world. Was that why it seemed unreal, why he felt sometimes that it confined him?

400

'If you must know – but don't take too much notice of me, I daresay it's only a mood – I feel as though my life doesn't have much purpose. Oh, I don't mean you and the children – I wouldn't want that any different; but I don't feel as if I'm doing anything that matters, I don't feel I'm getting anywhere.'

'Where do you want to get to?' Selina asked quietly.

'That's just it, I don't know. I'm not yet thirty, and I seem to have reached wherever I'm going, landed there for good. Yet it's not where I want to be. It's as if everything's been levelled out for me, whereas inside me I know I want a few hills to climb, a few challenges to meet.'

Selina came and stood beside him, put her arm through his.

'You mean there's no excitement?'

'Perhaps that's part of what I mean.'

'Well, I admit that running The Beeches isn't the most thrilling job in the world, but I would have thought that the war would have given you enough excitement to last a lifetime; that now you'd be glad of a quiet existence.'

'In a way I'm grateful for that,' Bob agreed. 'But excitement isn't something you take in one dose and that does you for the rest of your life. Anyway, even in the army I spent most of my time obeying orders from on high. Even as a sergeant I wasn't encouraged to use my initiative overmuch.'

'And you don't want to use it running a tearoom?' Selina put in. 'Well, I understand that.'

'Do you know the kind of man I envy, Selina? I envy the man who goes out and breaks new territory, maybe goes somewhere unknown, fights to make a living for himself and for his family. In a way, your mother has done more fighting than I ever shall. All I'm doing is stepping into what she's fought for.'

'She was trying to be helpful,' Selina said.

'Oh I know, and I'm grateful. Your mother's a grand woman, Selina – but I don't want to live the life she's carved out. And *she's* not standing still, is she? She's still

401

building; she and Dick are still climbing mountains.'

'She always will,' Selina said. 'It's the way she's made.'

'And I've begun to think it's the way I'm made. Do you understand, Selina?'

He turned her towards him, took her face in his hands and looked into her eyes. How beautiful she was. And now she had that extra bloom of beauty which pregnancy brought her each time; her skin glowing, her eyes gentler and softer. With Selina for his wife what right had he to complain about anything?

'Of course I understand,' she said softly. 'It's something I should have seen for myself. Perhaps I haven't felt restless, not because I love the job I'm doing, but because the height of my ambition is to be with you and our children. But there's one thing you can be certain of. Whatever you want to do, wherever you want to go, I shall go with you. Not follow you, my love, but be right there beside you. I'd go with you to the ends of the earth, Bob.'

He kissed her long and lovingly, then released her, holding her at arm's length, just looking at this woman he loved so much.

'I hadn't thought of going that far,' he said, smiling. 'But wherever I go – and *if* indeed I go anywhere – I shall always want you with me.'

They turned away from the window.

'I'll go up and see if Billy's asleep,' Selina said. 'Tuck him in.'

She was on her way downstairs again when there was a knock on the door and Eleanor and Dick entered.

'We were out for a walk,' Eleanor said. 'It's such a lovely evening, we decided we'd steal an hour. And I thought we might just be in time to see Billy before he went to bed. Am I too late?'

'He's just fallen asleep,' Selina told her.

'Then I shan't disturb him.' Eleanor doted on all three of her grandchildren, but there was something about Billy which made it difficult not to love him most. Perhaps it was partly because he was more accessible; Becky didn't often come to Hebghyll with Christopher.

'You'll stay for a cup of tea?' Selina invited.

Eleanor glanced at her husband.

'Do we have time, love? Dick's so busy at the moment,' she explained. 'We both are. But a quick cup would be nice.'

'So business is doing well?' Bob asked when Selina had gone into the kitchen.

'Better than I ever expected – or hoped,' Dick said. 'Since we started to put coloured illustrations of what the plant's going to look like on the seed packet, sales have gone up by leaps and bounds. Actually, I need more land. I'm looking around in Hebghyll. Either that, or I'd have to give up the market produce, and I don't want to do that. It's profitable.'

'Have you thought any further about opening shops?' Bob asked. Last time they'd met Dick had put out the idea of opening permanent shops in the towns where he now sent produce to market.

'Not only thought about it. I'm negotiating for one in Otley. It would be a good place to start, and then we'll see how it goes from there.'

Bob envied him. He spoke with such enthusiasm, he had so much to look forward to. What will I be looking forward to when I'm middle-aged, Bob asked himself? Unless he changed his direction, he could think of nothing.

'What I do want to talk to you about,' Eleanor said as Selina returned with the tea, 'is Ma's birthday. She'll be seventy on the twenty-eighth of September, which is luckily a Sunday. I want to give her a splendid party, invite everyone in the family – Albert, Clara, Madge and John; the lot.'

She had no particular wish herself to see Clara or Madge; her memories of them were not happy ones and they had met very seldom over the last few years; but it would please her mother, especially if all the grandchildren could be persuaded to come. Mary and David Brookfield were both married now and had children of their own. Flo had gone back to Felldale soon after Jimmy's death, and helped her parents to run the store.

403

'I think that's a splendid idea,' Selina agreed. 'Some of them would have to stay overnight, though. Have you thought of that?'

'Yes. We shan't take any bookings for The Beeches that weekend – just save it for family. That's why I want to settle it in good time. So I'll send out the invitations and then we'll get together at a later date and sort out the details. Only I don't want Ma to know anything about it. I want it to be a big surprise.'

'I must say, Grandma chose a pretty convenient time of the year to be born,' Selina remarked. 'The busiest part of our season will be over, and John Brookfield will have gathered his harvest in, otherwise they wouldn't be able to leave the farm. It should be a splendid affair.'

'Yes. Well, we'd better be going,' Eleanor said. 'There are some accounts I have to finish before I go to bed.'

'You work too hard,' Selina told her. 'You both do, you and Uncle Dick.'

'But they work hard at something they want to do,' Bob said later, as he and Selina stood at the door of the cottage, watching the older couple walk away down the road. 'They're getting somewhere, making something of their lives!'

Selina gave one last wave to her mother and then took Bob's arm and walked back into the house with him.

'And so will we, my love. So will we. I don't know what we'll do – that's to decide, and we'll talk about it – but we'll do something. Whatever seems right for you.'

'For both of us, and for the children,' Bob said.

CHAPTER TWENTY-FOUR

'But where shall we go? What *shall* we do?' Selina asked.

'What do you *want*, dearest?'

It was the latest of several conversations they had had in the last few days, since Bob had told her that he wanted to get away from Hebghyll. Each day they went off with the children to The Beeches, in the evening they came home and put the children to bed, and afterwards, until it was time to take themselves wearily to bed, they discussed what they might do. But so far all they had done was strengthen their resolve that they *would* make a move.

'What I want is simple,' Bob said. 'I want to build a new life for all of us, I want to work for myself, not for a master; I want to choose what I shall do. Or rather, I want us, you and me, to choose together.'

'It sounds simple, put like that,' Selina agreed. 'But we've already discovered that it isn't. We don't have much money, for one thing.'

'We have my gratuity from the army,' Bob reminded her. 'We never touched that. And there's what we've saved.'

Eating most of their meals at The Beeches, renting the cottage cheaply, they had never needed to spend much. Bob had put the spare money away in the bank, sensing, though never quite knowing why, that one day it might be needed.

'But will it be enough?' Selina questioned. 'And that we don't know until we settle on something. Whatever we do, if you're to start up on your own it will take money. I daresay if it came to it Mother would lend us something.'

'In spite of the fact that we're deserting her?'

Bob felt bad about that, they both did. His mother-in-law had been good to him and it wasn't her fault that he was so restless. Or was it, at least partly? If she hadn't made things so easy for them when they'd first married maybe he'd have struck out on his own from the beginning. But whatever she'd done, it had been in good faith.

'In spite of that, I think she would,' Selina said. 'And really, Bob, we must tell her before long. It's not fair to keep her in the dark, however much the news is going to upset her. There is one thing, though – when we tell her that we considered going to Australia, then decided against it, it will lighten the blow. Oh Bob, I'm so glad you did not choose to go to Australia!'

It was what a lot of young people like themselves were doing, because they felt that since the war there was nothing for them in England. Such promises there'd been. Everything was going to be different, better. There would be houses for all, 'homes fit for heroes to live in', and work for everyone. It hadn't turned out at all like that. Except that the fighting had stopped, for a great many people it seemed as bad as ever. But Australia was so far away, the break so final, Selina thought with a shudder. How could she have borne it?

'You would have gone, though, if I'd chosen it?' Bob said tenderly.

'You know I would. I'm just thankful you didn't.'

'Well, there's still part of that idea left. If we'd gone to Australia it would have been to work on a sheep farm, and perhaps that's what we should settle on here.' It was by no means the first time the idea had been mooted in the past few days, and since he kept coming back to it, perhaps it was the right one.

'Only not to work on someone else's farm,' he stipulated. 'I don't want that. I want us to set up on our own. It'll be hard work, and perhaps not much profit for a long time to come. But we'd be working for our future together. And it would be a healthy life.'

'But we come back to the same question – what do you know about sheep?' Selina asked.

406

It wasn't that she was against the notion, and if it was *his* choice she would back him all the way; but sometimes she worried that he was closing his eyes to the difficulties of this tempting new life he saw before him.

'And as I've said before – nothing. But I can learn. I'd have to find out what it would cost to set up. We'd have to start in a modest way, just a small flock. Enough land to grow our food; hens, a pig, a house cow; but mainly sheep.'

'I've never grown so much as a spring onion,' Selina said. 'Though there's no reason why I shouldn't. So just where would we do all this?'

'I don't know yet. Scotland, the Lake District, North Yorkshire, Wales. There's plenty of sheep country to choose from. It would depend on what was available. Oh, Selina love, shall we think about it seriously, instead of just talking? Find out more? What do you think?'

She heard the mounting enthusiasm in his voice and was glad of it, even though she was not sure about the idea. It was a long time now since he had been enthusiastic about anything.

'Well . . . why not? I agree it would be hard work; we'd be out in all weathers, every day of the year. And it would be a lonely life. I'd have to get used to that. But we'd have each other, and the children.'

'Well then . . .?'

'We absolutely must tell my mother,' Selina insisted. 'It's only fair, even though at the moment we're only thinking about it.'

If Eleanor was dismayed, she didn't show it in front of her daughter and son-in-law when they told her next day.

'It's not that we want to leave you,' Selina said anxiously. 'You do understand?'

'Of course I do,' Eleanor replied. 'Bob wants to strike out on his own. There's nothing strange in that. Dick did it. To a certain extent I did it when I came to Hebghyll. I just hope you're choosing the right thing, that's all. And about that I'm the last person to advise you. I've lived within sight of sheep half my life without ever giving them a thought! And remember that you were born and brought up in a town. You've never lived in the country.'

'I know. But everyone who came before me, in our family, came from the country. I must have some roots there. You were the first to come to Akersfield, and it's not all that long ago.'

'It seems a lifetime away,' Eleanor said.

'Well, nothing's decided,' Selina told her. 'But it seems the best idea so far. With any luck it wouldn't take us too far away from Hebghyll to visit. And of course there's no thought of going until after the baby's born.'

Eleanor smiled with relief. 'I'm glad about that, anyway. And there's another thing – if you need a little more money I could make you a loan. We put most of our money back into the businesses, here and at Whinbank, but I can always manage something.'

'That's very good of you, Ma; and more than we deserve in the circumstances,' Bob said.

'Perhaps Uncle John Brookfield will be able to advise you about sheep,' Eleanor suggested. 'He's farmed in the Dales for a good many years now, though not specifically sheep. I daresay he'll be here for Grandma's birthday. You could talk to him then.'

She would have to consider what to do about The Beeches. Clearly Olive Feather would run it well, given the chance, but she wouldn't compensate for both Selina and Bob. Oh, how she would miss them, and not only in the business! With her mother retired, and these days living a more leisurely life at Whinbank, there would be no-one in the family working full-time at The Beeches any longer.

Becky surveyed her image in the long mirror set into the wardrobe door with a certain amount of satisfaction. The emerald green sleeveless dress, in heavy marocain, and intricately beaded around the low neck, suited her even better than it had in the shop. So it ought; it had cost a pretty penny. The colour matched her eyes, acted as a foil to the clear, creamy skin of her neck and arms and provided a pleasing contrast to her hair. It was certainly very short, daringly so for Akersfield. A couple of inches more and she'd be showing her knees. Not that she minded, for her legs were good. Why hide them? She had kept her figure too, though she wished her bosom was not so curvaceous. Even the tight bust bodice she wore could not quite flatten its shape.

She raised her arm and smoothed her hair. It had taken the Marcel wave well. She had been one of the first in Akersfield to have it cut off. Selina had waited two years longer before taking the plunge. Yes, I look quite smart, Becky thought. She was probably too smart for Bridlington – though the Marlborough was the best hotel there. How suitably she could have graced the London scene!

'Are you almost ready, darling?' Roland asked. 'Christopher is fast asleep and the dinner gong went some time ago.'

'Mmmm,' she murmured. She was at the dressing-table now, adding just the teeniest bit more lipstick to her cupid's bow of a mouth.

'Will I do? Do you like my new shingle?'

'You look beautiful – and I do like your shingled hair, but I hope you won't have an Eton crop. Your hair is so lovely it seems a shame to get rid of most of it.'

'It's the fashion,' Becky said shortly. Men could never understand how awful a woman could feel if she was out of fashion.

She walked beside Roland down the wide, curving staircase and followed the head waiter into the dining-room. Several male heads, sleekly brilliantined, turned; several pairs of male eyes swerved to watch her progress across the room; several women watched their men watching Becky. She was aware of it all, and enjoyed it. Before the evening was over she hoped to have picked out anyone who was the least bit eligible. She might, she just might, find someone of interest. Oh, nothing wrong! She wouldn't step far out of line. All she desired was someone who would help her pass the time more agreeably in this place to which she had not wanted to come. In the meantime she tucked into her food. It was really quite passable and she had an unfashionably hearty appetite. No banting for her!

'What would you like to do after dinner?' Roland asked. 'If you'd like to take a stroll down to the jetty I'm sure the chambermaid would give an eye to Christopher. He never wakens anyway.'

'Oh, I don't think I'd like to do that,' Becky said, frowning. 'Why don't we sit in the lounge, have some coffee, or a cocktail?'

She hated jetties, was bored by boats and loathed the smell of fish. She'd have more than enough of jetties before the week was out. Besides, she wanted to take a look at the other guests.

'Won't there be some dancing? Saturday night?' she asked.

'I expect there will. You'd like that?'

'It would pass the time,' she said.

There was dancing to a four-piece band. She danced a two-step, with Roland, and then another. He was not a good dancer. After that a young man – he couldn't have been a day over eighteen, she thought, and he was several inches shorter than she – asked her for the waltz. She could have killed Roland when he gave his smiling permission, and murdered him twice over when she took to the floor with the youth. He was a worse dancer than Roland. He had no sense of rhythm and she was aware that he was counting out the beats beneath his breath – one-two-three, one-two-three. Also, he had sweaty hands. She was intensely relieved to be delivered back to her husband.

'That was *not* enjoyable!' she muttered. 'I did *not* come here to be pushed around the floor by callow youths with sweaty palms!'

It was soon clear that, although there were many admiring glances in her direction, no woman was going to let her man go in pursuit of Becky. Well, no matter. She didn't like the look of any of the men, anyway!

'We can't sit here like pumpkins all evening,' she snapped. 'We might as well go to bed.' It was going to be a disastrous holiday, every bit as bad as she had expected.

The next day, though it was warm and sunny in the extreme, brought little improvement as far as Becky was concerned. To Christopher it was one delight after another, starting from the moment he walked into the dining-room with his parents and saw so many children. At almost every table there was a family group with two or three, sometimes more, offspring. Some of them were clearly his own age. And everyone looking so bright in summer clothes.

'Do you think I'll make friends, Daddy?' he whispered.

Roland smiled and nodded.

'I'm pretty sure you will, Chris. I suppose most of the children here will be going on the beach with their parents, and that's what we'll do this morning, if the tide is out. We'll buy you a bucket and spade immediately after breakfast.'

He had been up very early, taken a brisk walk along the promenade, breathing deeply, filling his lungs with the strong sea air; had bought a newspaper and read the headlines, all before Becky had put a foot out of bed. It was the way to get value from a seaside holiday, and so good to get away from the smoke of Akersfield for a while, even though he loved his home town.

'Must we?' Becky asked languidly. 'Go on the beach, I mean?' She had slept badly, wakened with a headache, and was not in the mood for anything, least of all the beach.

'Of course we must!' Roland's voice was sharp. 'Why, it's one of the things we've come for, to take Chris on the beach. It's his first seaside holiday, don't forget.'

'I'm not likely to,' Becky retorted. 'And please don't call him Chris. His name is Christopher.'

Christopher looked anxiously at his mother. It was clearly going to be one of her cross days. He wished she wouldn't be cross. He loved her so much, and she was so pretty. She was easily the prettiest lady in the room.

'I think you look the prettiest of anyone in the hotel,' he said.

411

Becky couldn't help but smile at him. 'Well, you certainly know the right things to say!'

'I agree with him,' Roland said. 'You look particularly lovely in that dress. So fresh and charming!'

'What, this old thing?' It was of Macclesfield silk, striped in cream and pale pink, and she had had it more than a year and now found it dull. She had been in a perverse mood this morning when she dressed, and had deliberately picked out the thing she liked least, wondering why she had brought it in the first place.

'You don't see yourself as others see you,' Roland said. 'Christopher is right, you are the prettiest here – and by the expression on people's faces as we came into the room, I can tell we're not the only ones who think so.'

Oh, he could be so nice! Christopher too. Why did she have to be horrid? It seemed sometimes as if she just couldn't help it. There was some devil inside her.

'I'm sorry I was cranky,' she apologised. 'I have a bit of a headache.'

'Then I shall get you a deckchair, you must wear a big hat to keep the sun off, and you can sit and read your magazines while Christopher and I build the largest sandcastle on the beach.'

'With turrets and flags?' Christopher asked.

'Certainly. We'll buy the flags when we buy the bucket and spade. I saw a shop very near to the hotel where they have just the thing.'

The morning didn't turn out as badly as Becky had expected. She sat in her deckchair and glanced idly at *Vogue* and *Queen* which Roland had bought for her, breaking off from time to time to admire the sandcastle. She soon realised that it didn't matter whether she admired it or not. Her husband and son were totally engrossed in the building of it, Roland constructing a moat as if his life depended on it; Christopher fetching bucket after bucket of water from the edge of the sea.

When she saw a man and a woman, with two small girls, approaching, she closed her eyes and feigned sleep. She had

412

seen them in the hotel but she wasn't sure she wanted to make their acquaintance. The man looked quite attractive, with his navy blue blazer and fashionably wide Oxford bags, but the woman seemed the teeniest bit dowdy. If she was the kind of woman who talked about recipes for puddings, or children's ailments, Becky would have nothing to do with her. On the other hand, if they sounded interesting, she could open her eyes and wake up.

Actually, she thought, they sounded quite nice. All four of them spoke perfect English with no Yorkshire accent at all. And when she peered through eyes opened the merest slit she saw that the woman's clothes, though plain, were undoubtedly expensive. You had only to look at her shoes. When they had talked with Roland about the weather, and the hotel, they began to exchange information about the children. The little girls, it seemed, didn't go to school, but had a governess. The family didn't live locally, but had come up to Yorkshire to visit relatives. It was when she heard them say that they lived in London that Becky decided to open her eyes.

'Oh!' she cried. 'I'm so sorry! I must have fallen asleep!'

'And we must apologise for disturbing you,' the man said pleasantly. 'What a shame! But since you are awake, I'm Tim Holgate and this is my wife, Frieda.'

'We noticed you at breakfast,' Mrs Holgate told her. 'Our daughters were very taken by your little boy. When we saw you all on the beach I'm afraid they insisted on stopping to speak.'

'Well, how nice,' Becky said. 'And the feeling seems mutual between our children. Just look at them!'

All three of them were racing across the sands, down to the sea.

'You'd think they'd known each other all their lives instead of for five minutes,' Roland observed. 'Children don't stand on ceremony, do they? But let me find you a deckchair, Mrs Holgate!'

He set up the chair beside Becky's and Mrs Holgate seated herself.

'I've been looking at *Vogue*,' Becky said. 'Such pretty fashions – though too daring, too extreme for the poor old north. When my husband and I were in London I was just crazy about the fashions!'

'You like London?' Mrs Holgate asked.

'Oh I adore it! I absolutely adore it! How could you bear to leave it with the season still in swing?'

'We don't really bother with the season,' Mrs Holgate said. 'We might have to when our daughters are older, but not for a long time yet. And next month everyone will be coming up here, or going to Scotland.'

It was inevitable, since by this time the children could not be separated, that they should all walk back to the hotel together for lunch. Really, they were quite pleasant people, Becky thought. Perhaps the holiday wouldn't be as bad as she'd expected.

'We planned to take the children on the steamer this evening,' Mrs Holgate said. 'It goes up the coast to Flamborough and I believe it's most interesting. Lots of birds. Is it possible that you might be going?'

Oh dear! It was the one thing Becky knew she could not do. She had only to set foot on board . . . She would be sick before they left the harbour! The knowledge humiliated her, she was sure it was common to be seasick, but there was no getting away from the fact and she couldn't risk the awful consequences.

'I'm not sure . . .' she began.

'I'm afraid it will be impossible, much as we'd like to. You see, I've booked seats at the summer show for my wife and myself for this evening.'

Becky tried not to look surprised. How good he was to come to her rescue.

'And what about Christopher?' Mrs Holgate asked.

'Mrs Gibbs the chambermaid will look after him. She's a very motherly soul and he's already fond of her.'

'Then why not let him come with us?' Mrs Holgate proposed. 'You can see how much the girls would love to have him, and he'd be no trouble at all. You won't be back

414

when we return, but I would see him to bed and leave him in Mrs Gibbs' care. Please do let him come!'

'Well, if you're really sure . . .' Becky said.

'Of course I am.'

'Then it's most kind of you, and we accept,' Roland smiled. 'I know he'll just love it.'

'Roland, that was very tactful of you,' Becky said when they were back in their room. 'You haven't really booked seats, have you?'

'No, but I shall nip out after lunch and do so.' He was delighted to see that Becky had shed her black mood. In her present frame of mind she was the most charming person in the world, and he was the most fortunate man.

While she was getting ready to go to the theatre that evening – Christopher, in a high state of excitement, had already left with the Holgates – Becky suddenly remembered that other evening, on the holiday in Sandcombe, when her stepfather had taken them all to the show on the pier, and she had entered the talent contest.

'Did I ever tell you how I won the talent contest?' she asked Roland.

'No! When was this?'

'In the summer of 1914, at Sandcombe. I played The Bees' Wedding.'

'I remember that summer,' Roland said. 'I was always asking you to marry me. When you finally said yes it made it the best summer ever for me.'

'For at least a fortnight I was in love with this man in the concert party. What was his name – oh yes, Max Anderton. Really he was quite awful – or more likely, pathetic. I think it was the fact that he was on the stage that attracted me.'

If only her parents hadn't refused to let her go on the stage, she mused, life might have been so different. Why, at this very moment she might have been putting on her make-up to take the lead in a musical comedy in the West End, instead of powdering her nose to go and see a seaside show on the Yorkshire coast.

'Time we were off,' Roland said.

At the theatre they stood in a short queue, waiting to be admitted. As they edged forward Becky glanced at the man taking the tickets. When she saw him her hand shot up to her mouth to stifle her scream. Jimmy Austin!

Roland had not recognised him and would have walked on, but at that moment – it all happened so quickly – Jimmy looked up.

'Why, Becky! Mr Layton! What a wonderful surprise!'

Roland looked uncertainly at him.

'You don't remember me? Jimmy Austin. I was at your wedding.'

'Why of course! I didn't recognise you.' He shook Jimmy warmly by the hand. 'Darling, isn't this a surprise?' he said, turning to Becky.

Becky found her voice.

'It certainly is!' It was one she could have done without, and she was grateful that at that moment the house lights went down and they had to be hurried to their seats.

'We'll see you in the interval,' Roland whispered to Jimmy. 'Perhaps you'll have time to join us for a drink?'

Becky was glad of the darkness of the theatre, and the fact that Roland was soon taken up with the show. She was sure that her face must reveal the turmoil of her thoughts. Why had she been stupid enough to think that Jimmy had gone out of her life forever? She should have known it was too good to be true. But why was she feeling so panicky, so afraid? There was nothing he could do to her now. She would just put him out of her mind. But she couldn't do so. The singing, the dancing, the sketches, were no more than a noisy blur to her. Around her everyone was laughing, and she wanted to cry.

When the interval came they moved to the bar where a smiling Jimmy Austin was waiting for them. He was thinner. His rather shabby dinner jacket hung on him. He looked unhealthily pale, as if he seldom saw daylight. Seedy – that was the word. 'I'm afraid it will have to be one quick drink,' he apologised. 'I'm not really supposed

416

to leave the door in the interval. A Scotch, if you please.'

And it won't be the first of the evening, Becky thought. But though she disliked him intensely, and resented the fact that he had come back into her life, if only for a brief moment, there was still something about him. He had a charm which couldn't either be defined or denied – and not only for the opposite sex. It was clear that Roland was happy enough in his company.

'So what are you doing here?' Roland enquired.

'Trying to earn a living. But without much success. Unfortunately the job finishes at the end of this week. I'm filling in for someone who's off sick. God knows where I'll get another job. They're not easy to come by.'

In other company he could have pleaded the cause of his wife and children – never mind that he had left them years ago – but it wouldn't work here. Still, there might be a few pickings if he played his cards right. He doubted from their demeanour if they knew anything about his prison sentence. And they both looked pretty prosperous, so why shouldn't he have a share? It was simply a question of how to work it.

'A pity I have to leave you now,' he said, finishing his drink. 'Duty calls! I'd like to have spent an hour or two, talked over old times.'

'Then you must come and have lunch with us at our hotel,' Roland said warmly. 'You're free during the day, I take it?' He turned to Becky. 'Any day will suit us, won't it, my dear?'

So far she had sipped her drink in silence, and all she could manage now was a cool nod. Oh, how could he? How could he?

'Then why not tomorrow,' Roland suggested. 'We're staying at the Marlborough.'

They're prosperous all right, Jimmy thought. You couldn't stay at the Marlborough on twopence a week!

'I wish you hadn't asked him to lunch,' Becky said when they were back in their hotel room.

Roland looked at her in surprise.

417

'Why ever not?'

'Because I don't like him.' She wondered, afterwards, why she hadn't told him about the prison sentence. But it might have made no difference. It would be just like Roland to befriend a reformed criminal.

'But he's a friend of yours. He was a guest at our wedding. And now he's down on his luck.'

'He *was* a friend. It's all a long time ago,' Becky said.

'But you can't ditch your friends when they're down,' Roland protested. 'And he was kind to you when I was in the prison camp.'

If only you knew how kind, you wouldn't be asking him to lunch, Becky thought bitterly. But she wouldn't say any more. She didn't want to be asked questions. She would be civil to Jimmy at lunch and that would be the end of it.

They spent the following morning on the beach with the Holgates, but Becky couldn't concentrate on anything that was said and she was sure that they must have thought her stupid. Back at the hotel, Jimmy was waiting in the foyer. To Becky's chagrin he came forward to greet them in such a way that he had to be introduced to the Holgates. His manner towards them was perfectly correct, and naturally they were courteous to him; but anyone could see that he wasn't a gentleman, she thought. It wasn't only that his suit was shabby and shiny, his shoes down at heel, his hair in need of cutting – it was that in spite of his surface good manners, he had a bogus quality about him. Why had she not noticed this when she'd first met him?

'So this is young Christopher,' Jimmy said when the Holgates had left them. 'My, do you realise that I haven't seen you, Becky, since before Christopher was born? But I remember seeing the announcement of your son's birth in the newspaper.'

Becky knew perfectly well that he was reminding her of his last visit, the visit which had been the cause of Christopher's premature birth.

'He came six weeks early,' she said deliberately.

'A true son of his father!' Roland put in. 'My dad told

418

me that I'd done exactly the same thing. And do you know, he has exactly the same birthmark on his shoulder that my father and I – and my grandfather before us – have. Isn't heredity surprising?'

Becky could have kissed him! And the fact that he said it in innocence made it all the more telling. She was finally released. There was nothing with which Jimmy could threaten her now. Indeed, with the knowledge of his crime, the boot was on the other foot. She allowed herself to smile at him, a smile of pure triumph.

'Amazing!' Jimmy agreed.

He had not missed the triumphant smile, but she was wrong if she thought she was in the clear. He had other plans, foolproof plans. By the time the meal was half over he had brought the conversation around to his lack of a job.

'I'm getting quite desperate,' he said. 'If I don't find a regular job soon, I don't know what I shall do.' There was a smile on his face, his words seemed to be spoken lightly, but there was steel behind them.

'I'm really sorry, old chap,' Roland told him. 'I'd like to help, I really would – but I'm laying men off rather than setting them on. And I'm not sure, even if I had one, that my kind of jobs would suit you.'

You can bet your life they wouldn't, Jimmy thought. He had no intention of working on the factory floor. But there were other jobs in mills.

'Well, it's true I wouldn't be much use to you, spinning or weaving or any of those things. But I could do an office job. Accounts, wages. Or a sales job. I've often thought I might be quite good at selling.'

'I'm sure you would be,' Roland agreed. 'But at the moment there's nothing. Trade is in the doldrums. But tell me where I can get in touch with you and if anything comes up I shall let you know at once.'

'That's very civil of you,' Jimmy said.

Roland handed his card to Jimmy, who pocketed it, and then turned his attention to Christopher.

419

'And are you enjoying yourself in Bridlington, young man?'

'Yes thank you,' Christopher replied. 'Daddy's going home on Saturday but I'm glad I'm not because I have two new friends!'

'So you and Mummy are staying on?' Jimmy queried.

'For a further week,' Roland said. He would have suggested that Jimmy Austin might come to the hotel again, give Becky a little company, but since she seemed to have taken an unreasonable dislike to the poor man, he kept quiet.

'We shall be spending our time with the Holgate family,' Becky put in quickly. 'They're such nice people, so friendly. I don't expect we'll have a minute alone!'

'Well, I mustn't take up any more of your time,' Jimmy said. 'It was kind of you both to invite me and I've enjoyed myself.'

His eyes met Becky's across the table. I wouldn't have invited you in a thousand years, hers said. You haven't seen the last of me, my lady, his said.

'Roland, take us home with you at the weekend,' Becky said that night.

'Take you home? Why? I thought you were enjoying yourself now that we'd met the Holgates.' He was staring at her in amazement.

'I was. I am. But I'm sure my place is with you. Who will look after you when I'm not there?'

'Well, Hannah will, of course. It's very kind of you to worry, dearest, but I wouldn't dream of you sacrificing any part of your holiday. Besides, look how Christopher is enjoying himself! This holiday is doing him a world of good. We really mustn't cut it short, for his sake. No, I shall come and fetch you the following weekend, just as we planned.'

Amid many regrets from Christopher, from their new friends, but a thousand times more from his wife, Roland left to drive himself back to Akersfield on Sunday evening. On Monday morning, soon after breakfast, Becky was called to the telephone. She went to answer it with a sinking heart. She knew, she was quite certain, who it would be.

'Meet me at the shore end of the jetty at eleven o'clock this morning,' Jimmy said.

'I can't! I've made other arrangements. What's more to the point, I don't want to. Just stay away from me, Jimmy Austin!'

'Now that's not very friendly,' he rebuked her. 'I won't keep you long. Surely you can spare me half an hour?'

'I've no intention of doing so,' Becky said. 'I don't ever want to see you again – and I don't have to. You've no hold over me now, and you know it!'

'I'm afraid you're wrong about that,' Jimmy replied smoothly. 'And let me tell you that if you don't turn up I'll have no alternative but to seek you out. It shouldn't be difficult to find you on the beach, or wait for you in the hotel. I hadn't wanted to inconvenience your smart friends . . . but if there's no other way . . .'

'You pig! You foul, ignorant pig!'

He hung up on her. She would come, all right.

She *would* go, she decided in the end, if only to prevent an embarrassing situation with the Holgates. And she would tell Jimmy Austin just what she knew about *him*.

She arrived at the jetty at five past eleven. To the Holgates she had pleaded a headache and a need to return to the hotel. They had been all solicitude and promised to look after Christopher. Jimmy was waiting for her.

'You're a bit late,' he greeted her. 'But no matter – a lady's privilege. And I knew where to find you. I shall always know where to find you now. Well now, how much have you brought for me in that expensive handbag? I think we'll say twenty pounds this time.'

'Are you mad?' she said with contempt. 'You've nothing on me. You heard what Roland said about the baby. It's his.'

'Of course it is,' Jimmy agreed. 'I wasn't thinking about the baby. I was thinking about the fact that you paid me money all those months when you were pregnant. Roland's going to be very interested in that.'

421

She stared at him in horror while the dreadful truth dawned on her. She remembered suddenly, and all too clearly, the occasion when Roland had discovered her empty purse. He had accepted her explanation then, though he'd been puzzled, but if Jimmy went to him now, what would he believe? And her attitude to Jimmy since they had met him again had seemed out of character to Roland. Would he put two and two together? She saw her whole life, everything she loved and valued, falling to pieces before her.

'What about you?' she cried. 'Don't think I don't know you've served four years for forgery! I wouldn't hesitate to tell Roland. He'd never give you a job then.'

Jimmy shook his head.

'Wouldn't do any good, old dear! Two wrongs don't make a right. He wouldn't like me any better for it, maybe he wouldn't give me a job. But it wouldn't let you off, my love. I don't doubt he's a just man. He'll acknowledge I've paid for my mistake. You still have to pay for yours!'

'I won't, I won't! It's blackmail! I shall go to the police!'

'Keep your voice down, love. We don't want everyone to hear, do we? Of course it's blackmail, but you won't go to the police, any more than you'll tell your husband. And by the way, what a nice man *he* is. No, Becky, you know which side your bread's buttered!'

She turned sharply, made as if to escape. She wanted to run and run. She wanted to put the whole world between herself and this loathsome man. But before she could take a second step he caught her by the wrist and spun her around to face him.

'I haven't finished yet,' he rebuked her. 'And it's no use your running away because I'll follow you. Now just listen. Believe it or not, it isn't money I'm really after this time. The twenty pounds is just to see me through for a bit. No, as I told your husband, what I want is a job. I'm sick of living on the breadline, not having enough to eat, nothing in my pocket, while people like you live off the fat of the land. You're no better than I am, even though you have high ideas about yourself. So I'm sure when you put it to

Roland that I have to have a job, he'll give me one. He'd do anything for you, I can tell that.'

'You heard what he said, you slimy toad. He has no jobs!'

Jimmy sighed.

'Well, I'm sure between you, you'll think of something. Tell him I came and talked to you, tell him you suddenly feel sorry for me . . .'

'I don't feel sorry for you. I hate you! I wish you were dead!'

'Well, tell him what you like. I'm telling *you* that, quite by chance of course, I shall meet you at the jetty next Saturday morning, and you'd better be there with some good news for me. Bring Roland and your little boy with you, by all means, but don't fail to turn up or I shall come to find you.'

'But that's not enough time!' Becky protested. 'Roland doesn't get back here until Friday night.'

'I'm sure it's long enough. I can't believe you don't know how to get round him. Ways and means, ways and means! Anyway, just give me the twenty pounds and we'll say ta ta for now. I shan't trouble you for the rest of the week, so enjoy your holiday!'

She pulled the notes out of her purse and flung them at him. When she saw him pick them up from the ground she realised she had made a big mistake.

Though she tried to give the impression of doing so, it was impossible to enjoy herself in the remaining days. She could not get Jimmy Austin out of her mind. She and Christopher spent most of their waking hours with the Holgates, who put her abstraction down to the fact that she was missing her husband. They were due to leave on the Thursday, and did so with lamentations at parting and promises to meet again, sometime, somewhere.

'When you come to London, you must visit us,' Frieda Holgate told her. 'We should enjoy that so much.'

'Thank you,' Becky said. In normal circumstances it was an invitation she would have jumped at, but now she could think of little but the fact that Roland was due tomorrow and she had to get him to promise Jimmy Austin a job. She had to. It was imperative.

It was ten o'clock on Friday night when Roland arrived at the Marlborough. Christopher was fast asleep and Becky ready for bed. She was wearing the nightdress and negligee, of apricot satin trimmed with coffee lace, which Roland had given her as a holiday present. To his eyes she looked utterly charming, overwhelmingly desirable. He took her in his arms and kissed her. He wanted to take her to bed there and then.

'Did you have a good journey? Have you had anything to eat?' Becky asked. Her voice sounded nervous in her ears. She hoped Roland didn't notice it.

'Tolerable. I didn't have anything to eat. I came straight from the mill. But I'm not hungry — not for food!'

'Oh, but you must eat something. Let me ring for some sandwiches and coffee.'

She walked across the room and pressed the bell. She knew what was in Roland's mind and, because she knew that she was deliberately going to use their lovemaking as a prelude to asking him about a job for Jimmy Austin, she had never felt more reluctant. She felt, as she never had before, that she was selling herself. But she had to do it; there was no escape. Sandwiches and coffee were no more than a stalling device.

Their lovemaking was perfect, so much so that after the first few minutes in her husband's arms, she forgot Jimmy Austin. But when they lay quietly afterwards, for the moment satisfied, he was there at the front of her thoughts again. Roland himself made it easy for her to introduce the subject.

'I missed you so much, my darling. Did you miss me? And did you have a pleasant week?'

'Of course I missed you. We spent a lot of time with the Holgates. Oh yes! I saw Jimmy Austin again; I met him by accident down by the jetty. Roland, you were quite right, he *is* in a bad way. I felt so dreadfully sorry for him. Roland, couldn't you possibly give him a job?'

424

He put his arm around her, drew her close against his shoulder.

'That's more like my Becky! I knew you didn't have it in you to be ungenerous, especially to a friend. I haven't forgotten that time you gave your allowance to some poor man at the door!'

Her face flamed. She was glad of the darkness, glad he couldn't see her. She felt false and degraded, and worse than ever because she had to press home her advantage.

'Shall you be able to give him a job? He needs it so desperately.'

'As a matter of fact,' Roland said, 'I can, and I had intended to. But I'm pleased you asked on his behalf. My wages clerk has given in his notice. He's emigrating to Canada. I'll let Jimmy Austin know tomorrow. But for now let's forget him. Let's forget everyone but you and me. Oh, how I missed you! I don't ever want to be apart from you again!'

He wrapped her in his arms and began to caress her again. When he felt her tears against his chest he didn't understand why. It was just another of her vagaries which made her the most enchanting woman in the world.

'Oh Roland, I do love you,' Becky murmured.

The following morning Becky said, 'Above everything Christopher wants to go on the steamer again. Why don't you take him while I do some packing? Later on I'll stroll down to the jetty to meet you both.'

She wished to see Jimmy Austin on her own. She had the whip hand now, and she wanted him to know it. She intended to make her own terms.

'I'll do that,' Roland agreed.

Jimmy was already there when she arrived, leaning nonchalantly over the jetty wall, watching the small boats bobbing in the water.

'I don't have much time,' Becky began briskly. 'So I'll say what I have to say and be done with it. Roland has a job for you.'

'Splendid!' Jimmy said. 'I knew you'd manage it!'

'I shall tell him I met you here by accident this morning and told you to be at the mill at eight-thirty on Monday. But there's one condition, and I mean it. I can stop Roland giving you this job. He would hesitate to give a job in his wages office to a man with your record. Unless you promise never to come near me again, I *shall* stop him. Whether you get the job or not, is in my power.'

The smile Jimmy Austin turned on her was full of confidence.

'Oh no it's not, my dear! The cards are still all in my hand. Work it out for yourself. But you needn't worry. I haven't the slightest desire to see you again, and as long as I have a job I can promise you I won't! Nor will I let him down. I have every intention of going straight from now on. Tell Roland I'll be there – and do thank him for me, won't you?'

CHAPTER TWENTY-FIVE

It was Mary Brookfield, writing from Brighton, where she now lived with her husband and children, who gave away the secret of the party which had been planned for Mrs Foster's seventieth birthday. She wrote directly to her grandmother to apologise for the fact that she couldn't make the journey. 'The baby's due next month,' she explained. 'I expect Mother has told you. But I send you all my love and I'll be thinking of you on the day of the party.'

'What's all this then?' Mrs Foster demanded of Eleanor. 'I don't mean the baby. Our Madge hasn't said a word about that, of course – but then I never see my eldest daughter, do I – and she never writes. You'd think she lived in Timbuctoo instead of in Faverwell. I mean what's all this about a party?'

'I could kill that silly niece of mine,' Eleanor said. 'We were trying to keep it a secret, give you a nice surprise on your birthday. Now she's spoilt it. Why couldn't she just reply to me?'

Mrs Foster was getting the laundry ready, writing out the list in the book. She would willingly have tackled the washing for Whinbank, but Eleanor wouldn't hear of it. She was well and truly cosseted by her daughter these days. She looked up from the list now and smiled.

'Nay lass, it's not spoilt it. Don't fret about that. But you shouldn't have bothered, you know. What's a seventieth birthday, after all?'

'When it's yours, Ma, a very special occasion. There isn't anyone in the family who doesn't want to honour it. Even Clara sounded quite thrilled about it.'

427

'Is Clara coming?'

'Oh yes, they're all coming. Clara, Albert, Flo. Madge and John. David Brookfield's coming from Doncaster with his wife and two children. Apart from Mary and her family, there'll be all your children and grandchildren – and great-grandchildren.'

'Well, it's a lot of fuss about a small matter,' Mrs Foster said. 'But I don't mean I'm ungrateful. It will be nice to see everyone under one roof. Is it to be here, then?'

'No. At The Beeches. It's the only place where there'll be room. Some will have to stay overnight. But that's all you need to know, Ma – and it's all I'm telling you. So ask no more questions and you'll get told no lies.'

'In that case I'll get on with the laundry!' Mrs Foster licked the point of the pencil and began to write.

Eleanor touched her mother lightly on the arm. It was the nearest the two women ever came to a caress.

'I don't know what we'd do without you, Ma,' she said.

Her thoughts turned, as they so often did these days, to Selina. She and Bob were clearly set on going, though a new place hadn't yet been found, and they wouldn't move until after Christmas, when the baby was due. Probably not until the spring, since who would want to take over a sheep farm in the middle of winter? But the time would come all too soon.

'Did Selina tell you they'd written to John Brookfield to see what he thought about setting up on a sheep farm?' Eleanor asked her mother.

'Aye, she did. They're full of it. But you know, lass, Bob was never suited to the job he's doing. And if a man's not happy in his job, his life's a misery. And that touches his family.'

'What about a woman?'

'Women are more adaptable. Come to that, I've always thought women were stronger than men. Perhaps not in their bodies – but in other ways.' You've had to be strong, my lass, she thought. Since you were a slip of a girl you've had to be strong, else where would you be now?

'Well, I daresay John will give them good advice,' Eleanor said.

'Oh yes!' Mrs Foster liked her son-in-law. If the truth were told, she liked him better than her daughter Madge. Madge had always been too bossy by half.

'I shall soon have to think about replacing Selina and Bob. Ma, do you agree with me that Olive Feather would do a good job if I put her in charge and gave her some extra staff? Say one full-time and one part-time?'

'I'm confident of it,' Mrs Foster said. 'And there's something I think you don't know, which might be of interest. I've heard our Olive is doing a bit of courting. I'm quite sure it's serious – they say he's a nice young man – only they can't get married because he's out of work, and that's why they're keeping it a bit quiet.'

'Good heavens! I'd no idea!' But there was no reason to be so surprised. Olive Feather was a very attractive young woman. 'But would that mean she'd leave if he got work and they married?' Was there to be no end to her problems?

'That would all depend, wouldn't it? If you thought he was suitable you might consider offering a job to the lad. His name's Arthur Browning.'

'Well, I'll certainly think about it,' Eleanor promised. 'Ma, you do come up with some surprises!'

Once Mrs Foster knew there was to be a party it became easier for Eleanor and Selina to go ahead with the arrangements.

'We won't tell her anything she doesn't need to know,' Selina said. 'But at least we won't have to whisper together in corners.'

'By the way, Dick will supply the flowers,' Eleanor told her. 'He's got some lovely chrysanthemums, and your grandma likes those. And Peter and Robert have promised to get some nicely coloured leaves from the woods.'

'You care a lot about Grandma, don't you?' Selina asked.

'I do,' Eleanor replied quietly. 'She's been a good mother to me. The best. This party is a very small thank-you.'

'The nice thing about Grandma,' Selina said, 'is that she's always there when you want her. Even Becky loves Grandma.'

'That's not a nice way to talk about your sister,' Eleanor protested.

'I'm sorry!'

All the same, Becky always made her feel less than adequate, and what was worse she made Bob feel the same way, as if the fact that they had so much less than Becky, with her fine house and her expensive clothes, and Christopher going to a private school, was somehow their own fault. Yet I'm happier than Becky, Selina thought. I'm sure of that. And when they had their own place, which might not be too long now, things would be better still.

'Did I tell you that Uncle John is keeping a lookout for a place for us?' she asked.

'Not more than half a dozen times,' Eleanor said, smiling. 'You'll be able to discuss it when he comes to the party.'

Becky spent a long time deciding what she would wear on her grandmother's birthday. She never felt entirely at ease in a family gathering, not like Selina and Jenny did. To know that she looked her best would be a help. In any case, she wanted to look nice for her grandmother. In the end she decided that she had nothing suitable to wear, she would have to have something new. She went into Akersfield and found a dress in deep green silk velvet, with a huge bow low on the hip. It was lower in the neck and shorter in the skirt than the family would approve of, but they didn't know a lot about fashion. She reckoned she'd been lucky to find something so smart in Akersfield.

Sunday the twenty-eighth of September dawned clear and calm, after a week of high winds, with a sky exceptionally blue for the time of the year.

'Weather fit for a queen!' Eleanor said when she took up her mother's breakfast tray. 'And a lot of cards I kept back from yesterday's post. Happy birthday, Ma!'

430

She bent over and kissed her. She didn't remember ever before kissing her mother just because it was her birthday.

'And here's your birthday present from me and Dick. Go on, open it!'

Mrs Foster cried out in delight as she saw the jacket. It was knitted in shades of mauve and blue and softest purple.

'It's beautiful! Why, it's just like the heather!'

'That's why we chose it. I'm glad you like it. Now Ma, will you promise me you'll rest until it's time for the party?'

Mrs Foster looked sternly at her daughter.

'Eleanor Fletcher, will you please stop treating me like an invalid. I've told you, I'm as fit as a flea. And if you think I'm going to have anybody arriving and finding me in bed, then you've got another thought coming! So get on with you!'

All the same, she thought, she would have a nice, leisurely bath, after which she'd get into her best skirt and the new jacket. Why not? And her cameo brooch. Oh, she'd never thought a seventieth birthday would be so enjoyable!

Downstairs Eleanor said to Dick: 'Will you give the boys their breakfast? I want to get off to The Beeches. And will you send Jenny along when she arrives? I've forbidden Selina to come until later. At six months gone she should be getting more rest.'

It was a while since Jenny had spent her off-duty weekend in Hebghyll. If it had been anyone else, Eleanor would have suspected that a boyfriend was taking up her time, but that was probably not the case with Jenny. She was wholly immersed in her career. She had been a staff nurse for two years, and any day now she was due to be made the youngest ward sister in the hospital. She was ambitious as well as dedicated and it was Eleanor's belief that she wouldn't stay for long in Akersfield. Well, her daughters must go their own way. She had always done so herself.

Walking to The Beeches she breathed in the crisp autumn air, with its scent of woodsmoke. The leaves were turning fast but, in spite of the recent winds, they had not yet fallen. Looking across to the moors she could still see patches of heather. She loved this time of the year, never found sadness in it as she knew some people did.

Becky and Roland, with Christopher, arrived at Whinbank in the middle of the morning.

'Come and give me a birthday kiss,' Mrs Foster said to Christopher.

Though Mrs Foster loved all her grandchildren and great-grandchildren, she had an especially soft spot for Becky and Christopher; perhaps because Becky had always been the wayward one whose relationship with Eleanor had never been smooth, and because Christopher seemed such a lonely little boy. He ought to have brothers and sisters, of course. She couldn't think why he hadn't. Becky and Roland seemed happily married. But it was none of her business.

'You're looking very smart, Grandma,' Becky said. 'And far too youthful to have great-grandchildren!'

'I daresay seventy is a bit young for that,' Mrs Foster agreed. 'But I married young, and your ma married even younger − so there it is.'

Often she felt as young inside as when she had married Edward Foster, and the days when her children were small were as clear to her as yesterday. It was simply her body which occasionally let her down, but she didn't believe in taking much notice of that.

'I'd better get along to give Mother a hand now,' Becky said. 'I'll see you later.'

'Now, what do you want me to do?' Becky asked her mother when she joined her at The Beeches.

'Nothing in that beautiful velvet dress,' Eleanor said. 'Put a pinny on at once!'

She thought her eldest daughter looked too thin, and a mite strained and anxious; but she knew better than to remark on it. There wasn't that sort of communication between them, more was the pity.

By the middle of the afternoon everyone had arrived and Dick had brought Mrs Foster over from Whinbank. What struck Mrs Foster, as she entered the large room where they held the receptions, was the silence. You could have heard a pin drop. Then it was suddenly shattered by everyone singing 'Happy Birthday' and shouting and yelling fit to raise the roof. In all her life she had never experienced anything like this. For one short moment she, who never cried in public, wanted to burst into tears, or run away and hide. But the moment was soon over, punctured by her five great-grandchildren who ran towards her as fast as their short legs would carry them to present her with their own gifts.

'Now you're to come and sit down over here,' Eleanor told her. 'In this armchair.'

'You're getting very bossy in your middle age,' Mrs Foster said. Nevertheless, she was glad to sit. She felt just like a queen, just like Queen Victoria whom she'd always admired so much.

Selina and Bob made a beeline for John Brookfield.

'It was good of you to write, Uncle John,' Bob said. 'Have you any news for us?'

'As a matter of fact I have,' John Brookfield replied. 'Though I wonder if you're not wrong in the head even to contemplate farming – let alone hill farming. It's a bad time to start. There's a slump, lad – some say there's a depression which won't be quick to cure – and farmers suffer badly in a depression. Have you thought of that?'

'We have.' Bob nodded. 'We've faced it fair and square, I can assure you. But who's to say when there will be a good time to start? We don't feel we can wait just on the chance of it happening soon.'

'Aye well, that's youth for you,' John Brookfield said. 'Impatient to be off. I suppose I was the same meself.'

'So what *is* the news, Uncle John?' Selina prompted.

'Well, there's a small place up at the top of Longdale. It's run down and neglected; it's out in the wilds at the head of the dale; the farmhouse is halfway up the fell-side and there's hardly enough level land to stand a hen hut on, never mind anything else. The ground is rocky

433

and the soil's thin. Personally I wouldn't touch it with a bargepole.'

'There must be something good about it,' Bob said. 'Else you wouldn't have bothered to tell us.'

'The good side is that it won't cost you much to take over. The owner is an old widower; his wife died two years ago. He's never looked up since then, never been what you might call well, and now he has to go into hospital for an operation. He'll not come back to farming. He plans to live with his married daughter in Hull, when he comes out of hospital.'

'Does that mean he'll want to sell quickly?' Bob asked.

'It does. But for your own sake, never mind his, you'd need to move in pretty soon. He's got a hundred ewes up there – not a large flock, but as far as you'll have a mainstay, they'll be it. You'd have to be there at tupping time or you'd miss next year's lambs.'

'Tupping time?' Selina enquired. 'What's that?'

John Brookfield looked at her in amazement.

'Nay, Selina, you come from a dales family and you don't know what tupping time is? Why, it's when they put the ewes to the ram, that's what it is!'

'And when is it?' Bob said quickly.

'Different times, different parts of the country. But up in Longdale, late October or early November. It takes five months for a lamb to come. You don't want them born before late March or early April. The weather could be too bad up there.'

'But that's only five or six weeks away!' Selina protested. 'We couldn't possibly be there then!'

Bob turned to her, his face alight with enthusiasm. 'We could, Selina! We could if we really tried!'

She stared at him. She couldn't believe what he was saying.

'Bob, haven't you forgotten something?'

'What? What have I forgotten? We can raise the money quickly enough. It's the quiet season coming up here – your mother will manage all right.'

'Bob, have you gone mad? I'm having a baby! It's due at Christmas!'

It was as if all the life suddenly went out of him. She felt guilty, terribly guilty. She felt as if she was robbing him of all he wanted in the world. For the moment he didn't want her, or his children, or the baby – he just wanted that farm. Then as she watched him she saw him pull himself together, take a deep breath, force himself to speak calmly.

'You're right, of course. I'm sorry, Selina, I wasn't thinking straight. It's no go, Uncle John. We shall just have to wait for something else to turn up.' But when would something else turn up which would be as much within their grasp as this was?

'No, wait!' Selina said quickly. 'Don't let's turn it down out of hand. We'll think about it, Uncle, while you're here. We'll try to get a minute to discuss it.'

It was different for Bob, and she must try to understand that. Life, for him, was in his ambition to build for his family. For her, so much was invested in her children, bearing them and rearing them. He could never know what it was like, as she did at this moment, and every day now, to have life moving in you. But her husband was her life, too. Every bit as much as her children, he had his needs and his rights.

'If you can be spared, you could come back with me tomorrow and take a look at it,' John Brookfield suggested. In his own mind he thought that that would be the decider. Seeing the place, who in their right minds would want to take it?

Roland came to join them and after a moment or two John Brookfield moved away.

'Isn't this a splendid do, and isn't Grandma enjoying every minute of it?' Roland said.

'Isn't she?' Selina agreed. 'But if you'll excuse me I have a couple of things to do.' She wanted a few minutes alone with Bob. She hoped he would follow her and they could find some quiet corner where they could talk.

435

In Mrs Foster's corner of the room Clara moved over to sit by her mother-in-law.

'Well, this is a splendid affair!' she said, looking around the room. 'All the family here to do you honour! And here comes Albert.'

'Tea's ready, Ma,' Albert announced. 'I've been told that as your eldest son I'm to take you in. So come on, old girl!'

'Not so much of the "old girl" if you please! I'm your mother and you'll show me a bit of respect!' But she smiled as she spoke, and took his arm and went into the tea party with him.

What a meal it was, she thought! What a spread! Everything she liked best, and she would try a bit of everything even though she'd pay for it with indigestion later. And then the cake! It was such a splendid cake, so beautifully iced and decorated. They'd had a discussion about what to put on it, what name to give her – for she was mother, grandmother, great-grandmother. In the end they had decided to put her own given name: Susannah. When she saw that, her eyes misted over. It was years since anyone had used her name.

When the meal was over, the speeches made and applauded, everyone moved back into the reception room. Becky sat at the piano and began to play.

'Nothing nicer,' Mrs Foster said appreciatively. 'I'm no singer, as you all know, but there's not much I like better than the family gathered round the piano.'

It took her back. They sang the songs she had known as a little girl, songs her mother and even her grandmother had sung to her; there were the songs she had sung to her own children in her not-very-special voice, and the ones her children had taught her. After that it was the turn of her grandchildren, who knew all the latest tunes. Becky played on, Roland turned the pages, everyone sang – and the sound of Eleanor's lovely voice soared over everything.

'One last song!' Dick Fletcher cried eventually. 'What's it to be? Grandma, you must choose!'

436

It was too difficult. She wanted 'Goodbye Dolly Gray' because her son David had sung that when it was all the rage, and David had been very close to her today. But somehow she didn't trust herself to keep smiling through it. This was a joyful occasion and she mustn't do anything to spoil it.

'Well, let's have a rousing chorus of "Ta-ra-ra boom-de-ay",' she suggested. 'The children can join in that.'

After that, the band which had been hired for the dancing began to play. Albert took his mother by the hand and they waltzed gently around the floor, everyone else watching at first, and then joining in.

'I'm a bit puffed, Albert,' Mrs Foster said presently. 'I think I'll sit down.'

Eleanor broke away from the dancing and came over to her mother.

'Are you all right, Ma? You look a bit tired.'

'I am a bit,' Mrs Foster confessed. 'I think I'd like to go upstairs, have a little sit down in my old room, if that's convenient.'

'Of course it is. In fact I had a fire lit in there, just in case you wanted to use it.'

'Well I'll sneak away quietly, while everyone's dancing. No need for you to come.'

There was a wireless set in the room. She turned it on. She would be in time for the Sunday evening service. She'd never been much of a churchgoer but she found the services on the wireless very comforting. And now, with great good fortune, she found a hymnbook on the shelf. She liked to look up the hymns as they were announced, and follow them in the book. It almost made her feel as though she was there.

Such a wonderful day it had been. One of the happiest days of her life. 'St-Martin-in-the-Fields' the service came from. A lovely name, St-Martin-in-the-Fields. She wondered what it looked like? She had never been to London; come to think of it, she'd never been out of the West Riding! A real old stick-in-the-mud she was.

She sat quietly through the service, once or twice almost nodding off. She came to as they were giving out the number of the closing hymn.

'Hymn number twenty-seven,' the announcer said.

She turned to the page and read the text above the hymn.

'Abide with us, for it is toward evening,
and the day is far spent.'

Such lovely words! And her favourite hymn! And now she was so tired, she wasn't sure she could keep awake until the last verse. How beautifully they sang. She closed her eyes.

When Eleanor came into the room a little later she thought at first that her mother was asleep. She bent down to pick up the hymnbook from the floor and then, stretching up again, she looked more closely at her mother's face. She gave a cry of anguish, a cry drawn from the depths of her being. Then, though she knew there was no longer anything he could do for her mother, she ran downstairs to fetch Dr Clare.

It was not possible for Selina and Bob to pay a visit to the farm until after the funeral, though they had made up their minds to do so on the afternoon of the party.

'It can do no harm to take a look,' Selina had said. 'I know you want to.'

She wished so much, now, that she had had a chance to talk to her grandmother about their intention. She would have liked to have had her blessing.

Eleanor, in spite of the feelings which tore at her, offered to look after Billy and Charlotte for the day, and suggested that Bob should borrow her car so that Selina might make the journey in comfort. All the same, she hoped against hope that they wouldn't take the farm. Her mother's death had left her with a terrible emptiness. How could she bear it if Selina went away?

'Yet you do everything to make it easier for them,' Dick pointed out. 'Here you are looking after the children; you've lent them the car, offered them a loan.'

'I know. I admit it. It's what my mother would have done if she'd been able. She did everything for me she possibly could, never mind the cost. That's why I have to act this way.'

Selina and Bob had left Hebghyll soon after breakfast, calling at Brookfield Farm for directions.

'We won't, thank you,' Bob said in answer to Madge's offer of a meal. 'We've brought some sandwiches with us. We'll eat them on the way. But a cup of tea on the way back wouldn't come amiss.'

'They'll need something stronger than tea when they've seen that lot,' John Brookfield remarked to his wife as they waved them off.

Beyond Faverwell, Bob took the left fork over the river bridge, which led into Longdale. It was aptly named. The road was narrow, in parts hardly more than a track, and bound in on both sides by steep fells. It twisted and turned, taking them over precarious-looking bridges, so that the stream, rushing to join the river at Faverwell, was now on their left, now on their right. At the lower end of the dale there were one or two farmhouses, but before long all signs of human habitation petered out.

'Surely it can't be much further?' Selina said. 'We've driven miles!'

'Perhaps it's round the next bend,' Bob said.

It was. And here at the head of the dale the country opened out, the fells were not so close in on them. Halfway up the hill on the left there was a low stone house with a few outbuildings clustered around it.

'That's it!' Bob cried. 'It's got to be. This is the end of the dale; the road goes no further.'

There was no road up to the house, only a narrow uneven track. They parked the car and started to walk. From the valley it had looked like a five-minute walk, but it took fifteen minutes climbing before they reached the farm gate. The house showed no sign of life.

'Are you all right, love?' Bob asked anxiously.

'Just a bit puffed. I'd like to get my breath back before we go in.'

They leaned with their backs to a wall, looking at the opposite fellside. In the October sun the grass was brilliantly green almost to the top. There it gave way to the silver-grey limestone scree, which in its turn bordered on a blue, windswept sky. Lower down, nearer to the stream, there were a few stunted trees, already bare, and patches of autumn-brown bracken. On the near fell, just below where they were standing, sheep grazed.

'I wonder if they're ours?' Selina said.

Bob gave her a sharp look.

'Ours?'

'I like this place, Bob. I'd like to live here. Just look at that view!'

'Selina! We haven't set foot inside yet! It might be awful. And we don't know any of the details.' He felt obliged to speak thus, though his heart had leapt at her words. 'You can't choose a place just for the view!'

'I can,' Selina said calmly. She had never felt so certain of anything in her life. 'Don't tell me you don't like it here.'

'Of course I do, what I've seen of it. But you're the one who's always telling me to be practical. In fact,' he added, 'it does have the best aspect for rearing sheep. Facing east.'

Selina looked at him in astonishment.

'Why is that? And how do you know about it?'

'If the land faces the morning sun, the grass dries more quickly, the sheep can graze all the sooner. It's common sense – though actually I read it in a book from the library.'

'Well, there you are,' Selina said. 'You do know something about sheep farming after all.'

'But what about the baby? How could you have the baby here?'

'The same way as lots of other women must have had babies here. But if you're really worried, I could go back to Hebghyll for the birth. Or down to Brookfield, to Auntie Madge.'

But she wouldn't. She wanted her baby to be born here. This was where she wanted to live and bring up her children. She was totally convinced of it.

'We'd better take a look inside,' Bob said.

'Yes, of course.'

But as far as she was concerned, that was no more than a formality.

CHAPTER TWENTY-SIX

'Here goes!' Bob said. He pushed open the gate and together they crossed the yard to the house. Everything looked so neglected. Hens, which were the only sign of life near the house, clucked around them as if hoping to be fed. There was no smoke from the chimney and the windows were coated with dirt, but as they approached the door a dog barked, and when they knocked a voice called to them to come in.

When they entered the dog, a black and white collie, bounded towards them, then shot past them into the yard to relieve itself. The room they stepped into was cold, cluttered, dirty and unoccupied.

'I'm in here!'

They followed the direction of the voice into the far room. An elderly man lay on the bed, dressed, but with a blanket thrown over him. Selina thought she had never seen anyone looking so ill.

'Mr Henshaw?' Bob enquired.

The man nodded.

'Aye. I'm sorry to be like this. I did expect you, but it's one of my bad days.'

'I must get you something,' Selina said quickly. He looked terrible. 'A cup of tea, something to eat? Have you had anything at all?'

'I'm not bothered,' he replied. 'Not for meself. But I'd take it kindly if you'd put something down for Jess. There's some dog biscuits in a bag in the pantry.'

'I'll do that at once,' Selina told him. 'And I shall make you a hot drink. I daresay milk would be the most nourishing.'

'I got up and milked Belinda this morning,' the man said. 'I've only got the one cow, now – for the house. I don't know why I forgot Jess. I've never done that before. I must be losing my mind as well as my body!'

'Well, she looks all right,' Selina said. 'She's gone out into the yard. But what about you? I'm sure we ought to get a doctor to you, Mr Henshaw?'

'Nay lass, it wouldn't do much good. To tell you the truth, I've got a card from the hospital in Shepton. I'm supposed to go in today – but how can I? I can't leave the stock. The sheep might be all right for a day or two, there's enough pasture for them; and they're hill sheep, not likely to stray, though by rights they need looking at every day. But I can't leave the cow, she has to be milked – and then there's the hens, they haven't been fed today.' Exhaustion overcame him and his voice trailed off.

'Don't worry, Mr Henshaw,' Bob comforted him. 'We'll sort something out between us. What about your neighbours down the dale?'

'I've said nowt to them,' Mr Henshaw replied. 'I've kept meself to meself sin' my wife died. I've been beholden to nobody. Now I've been took bad it's not so easy.'

'Well, I'm sure the first thing is to get you into hospital,' Bob said. He was appalled by the whole set-up, desperately sorry for the old man. 'And don't worry about the stock. I'll have a word with my wife's uncle, John Brookfield. I'm sure he'll arrange something. How did you propose to get to the hospital, then?'

Mr Henshaw leaned back against his pillow, shook his head.

'Nay! I've allus gone down the dale on my bicycle. I'm not sure I could manage it now.'

'I think it might be a bit too much for you,' Bob said kindly. 'Anyway, don't worry about that, either. I can take you.'

Selina came into the bedroom with a mug of warm milk. She had discovered a paraffin stove in the dirty kitchen and had managed to light it. The milk looked rich and creamy,

443

smelled sweet. It was the only thing in the house which did, she thought.

'There, Mr Henshaw! You'll feel better when you've drunk that. And I found a few Marie biscuits. I think you ought to try to eat something.'

He sipped the warm milk, but refused a biscuit. He began to look a little better. The dog came into the house and lay on the floor beside the bed.

'The thing is, Mr Henshaw,' Bob said presently, 'I think we'll have to talk about the sale of the farm. I hate to bother you when you're feeling poorly . . .'

'You're right, lad,' Mr Henshaw interrupted. 'We must come to terms. It's got to be done. Now if we agreed a price, when would you be able to take over?'

Bob looked at Selina.

'I think Bob could come almost at once,' she said. 'I would be just a little later.'

'You see, if somebody doesn't take over quick like, it'll mean the sheep'll have to go for slaughter — and the hens and the cow, well, I don't know what will happen to them. And then there's Jess! What am I going to do about Jess? She's a bit long in the tooth now, but she's served me faithfully, looked after the sheep on yon fellside for many a year.'

He stretched his arm over the side of the bed and stroked the dog. She licked his hand in reply.

'What'll she do without me?' His eyes filled. 'What'll I do without her?' Selina turned away, walked across to the window and looked out, to hide her emotion.

'Don't worry, Jess will be well cared for,' Bob promised. 'Whatever else happens, I'll take her myself and she'll be properly looked after.' He bent down to stroke the dog, who answered with a wag of her tail. 'There you are, you see. We're friends already.'

'Aye, she's taken to you,' Mr Henshaw said. 'I thank you very much, young man. You've taken a load off my mind. And now you and me had better get down to business.'

'Would you like me to go and feed the hens?' Selina

asked. She sensed that the old man didn't want her there. No doubt he thought women had no part in business deals.

'I'd appreciate that,' he said.

Fifteen minutes later Bob joined her outside in the yard.

'It's going to be all right. The price is much less than we thought – and no, I haven't taken advantage of his situation. As he pointed out, it's more than he'd get if he had to sell up, send animals to slaughter. But what about you, love? The house isn't up to much. There's a lot to be done to it. Could you manage?'

'Of course I could! Don't worry about me, Bob.'

'Well, he insists we should take a good look round at everything, and walk up the fell to look at the sheep. He's quite right at that.'

The outhouses were few in number, with all the roofs sadly in need of repair. A fair quantity of hay was stored in the barn; the old man must have managed to get that in before he became too ill. Bob thought how difficult it must have been for him on his own. Every gate needed repairing and as they walked up the hillside they found several parts of the drystone walling which would have to be rebuilt.

'A good thing his sheep aren't inclined to stray,' Bob remarked. 'They'd find plenty of places for getting out.'

The sheep themselves looked in fine fettle.

'Do you see the brand on their backs?' Bob asked. 'Just look!'

Selina wondered why he should sound so pleased about a brand mark, until she looked more closely and saw it was a letter H.

'H for Henshaw, H for Harwell!' Bob exclaimed.

'Oh Bob! It just goes to show. I knew from the minute we got out of the car that this was the place!'

'And you don't mind that it's going to be grinding hard work, and we won't have much money, maybe not much comfort, come to that?'

'Not only do I not mind, I'm looking forward to it,' Selina assured him. 'Our very own place.'

445

'Did you mean it about me coming up here very soon?' he asked.

'Of course! I meant within days, literally. I daresay Uncle John will be able to organise someone to take care of the urgent jobs for a few days, but not longer. You must get here as quickly as possible. I'll follow with the children as soon as I can pack up and arrange the removal.'

'Oh Selina, you are wonderful! Who ever had a wife like you? I swear I'll make it all up to you!' He took her in his arms and kissed her long on the lips.

In his arms, standing on the hillside, she felt that everything here would be good. Hard work, yes, and in plenty – but peace and tranquillity for both of them. No more dreams, no nightmares, no thoughts of war. That was all behind them forever.

'The first thing we must do,' Bob said, releasing her, 'once we've shaken hands on the deal, is get Mr Henshaw into hospital.'

It was all arranged, and the deal was struck.

'Don't you want me to sign something?' Bob queried.

'Your word's as good as your bond,' Mr Henshaw said. 'The signing can wait. You'll find I'll not go back on my word, neither.'

In the end it was decided, for the dog's own sake, that Jess should leave with Bob and Selina. They left the old man alone with the collie for a few minutes while he made his farewells.

'I can't bear to watch,' Selina whispered.

'You can be sure we'll love her and take good care of her,' Bob promised when they were ready to leave. 'And when you come out of hospital, when you're with your daughter, you can have her back.'

'I think not,' Mr Henshaw said. 'My daughter lives in the town. Jess is a country dog, used to working the sheep on these fells. If you'll let her work for you, neither she nor I could ask for anything more.' He gave the dog a final thump on the behind. 'Off you go, old lady!'

'I'll see to it that there's someone to look to the stock,'

446

John Brookfield told them when they called in later. 'Starting this evening with someone going up to milk the cow and shut up the hens for the night. We'll see to things morning and evening until you can get here yourself. Mind you, we'd have done this all along if old Henshaw hadn't been such a stubborn old fool, if he'd let someone know how he was placed. The farmers around here aren't a bad lot, as you'll find out for yourself.'

'Well, I'm sure he'll be glad of help now,' Bob said. 'And I shall try to get up here in two or three days. You will see that he gets into hospital soon, won't you? He looks pretty bad to me.'

'This evening,' John replied. 'I'll telephone the hospital the minute you've left. And Madge will let his daughter know.'

'Then we'll be off,' Bob said. 'Thank you for everything, Uncle John. I'll be back just as soon as I can, two or three days at most.'

'Two or three days!' Eleanor cried. 'Why, it's impossible! Two or three days!'

'It has to be. I told you, Mother – it can't be left. Surely you understand that?' Selina felt deeply upset at the sight of her mother's ravaged face. She had never seen her quite like this before, never realised she was so vulnerable. Her mother had always been the strong one, no matter what.

'I know how hard it must be for you, coming so soon after Grandma's death, but there was no other way, not if we wanted the farm.'

'You must have wanted it pretty badly,' Eleanor said. She must pull herself together, calm down.

'Oh we did, Mother, we did! I can't tell you how much! But it wasn't just that we couldn't wait. If you had seen the old man you would have understood.'

'I do understand,' Eleanor said quietly. 'I see that it's what you have to do. It's just that . . . well, it's a shock, I hadn't expected . . .' She had, of course. It was just that she'd closed her mind to it.

447

'I shan't be going quite as quickly as Bob,' Selina pointed out.

'But not many days after. Couldn't you wait here until you'd had the baby? It doesn't sound as if it's a fit place.'

'No, Mother, I couldn't. Bob's my husband. I want to be with him. Not only that, he's going to need me. You know what that means. You're always there when Dick needs you – and it was the same with Father. You worked alongside him.'

'Yes, you're right,' Eleanor conceded after a moment's silence. 'I can't contradict that. Anyway, I'll do what I can to help. Would it be a good idea if I kept Charlotte while you packed up and moved, and for a week or two after that? She seems very settled here. And perhaps Billy could go to Becky. I'm sure she'd have him, and you know how he dotes on Christopher.'

'That would help,' Selina admitted. 'There's such a lot to do to get straight. The place is a pigsty. I could certainly get through the work more quickly without the children.'

'And I could bring them up when you're ready for them,' Eleanor offered.

'Or I'll fetch them,' Selina said. She had this feeling that she wanted to be thoroughly settled in, have the place looking nice, before her mother saw it.

Becky, when telephoned, agreed to have Billy for a week or two. 'Though you do realise that Christopher goes to school half days?' she reminded her sister. It would be a bit of a nuisance having a small child to look after in the mornings, just when she had been freed from Christopher, but on the other hand she was rather pleased that Selina had actually asked a favour of her. It was a new experience and felt quite nice. And she was sure Hannah could be persuaded to look after Billy when she wanted to go into town, or wherever.

It was not the first time Billy had been to Akersfield, but the fact that his mother was going to leave him there and that he was to stay with Christopher made it different, an adventure. The journey, the sights and sounds of Akersfield itself when they emerged from the railway station into the town centre, the clanging trams, more motor cars than he had ever seen in one place before, and hundreds of people hurrying by, were all exciting.

'It's spiffing!' he cried. 'Can we go on the tram? I want to go on a tram!'

'Certainly,' Selina said. Halton was too far out to walk and she could not possibly afford one of the taxicabs which waited outside the station.

'And can we sit on top, outside at the front?'

'If you wish.'

At the tram terminus they watched while the driver, with a long pole, manoeuvred the trolley from one set of overhead wires to the other, causing showers of sparks in his efforts to connect it. To Billy's disappointment, none of the sparks fell as far as the ground. They boarded the tram, climbed the narrow curved stairs and walked right through to the open section at the front.

'I like it here,' Billy said. 'You can see everything.'

'You're to sit still,' Selina warned. 'No standing, or leaning against the rail. We don't want you falling overboard!'

When they reached the house in Halton Becky was waiting for them, but Christopher was still at school.

'He comes home at noon,' Becky told Billy. 'Perhaps you might like to go to morning school with him from tomorrow. We'll have to see what we can do.' She turned to Selina. 'As it's a private school they can take him though he's not quite five.'

Selina opened her mouth to say that she couldn't afford it, but closed it again, seeing the look of pleasure on Billy's face. It was only for a week or two. They would find the money somehow. But trust Becky not to think of that.

'Roland would see to the fees,' Becky said.

Though she had not uttered a word, Selina blushed for her uncharitable thoughts.

'You'll stay for lunch, won't you?'

It was 'lunch' not dinner, now that they lived in Halton.

449

She needn't put on airs for me, Selina thought. I'm not impressed. But why was she always so peevish where Becky was concerned? She refused to believe that she could be envious. She wanted nothing that Becky had. Indeed, once they were in Longdale, she wouldn't change places with the Queen.

'Thank you, I will. But I must leave soon afterwards. There's so much to do, sorting out and packing.'

'I suppose so. How's Mother?'

'All right, physically. But she seems very strained. She's missing Grandma badly. And now with me going . . .'

'I miss Grandma terribly,' Becky said. 'I never thought of her dying. I knew one day she must, but I never let myself picture it. She'd always been there.'

They both fell silent, a silence broken in the end by Billy.

'I like it here. I'd like to live here, Mummy.'

'But you're going to love the farm,' Selina said, smiling. 'There'll be all kinds of animals. Sheep, a cow, hens – maybe we'll get a goat, and when you're a little bit older I daresay you can have a dog.'

'People have dogs in Akersfield.' Billy's voice was stubborn. 'I'd much rather live here. I'll bet you wouldn't like to live at the farm, Auntie Becky?'

'I most certainly would not!' Becky said firmly. 'I can't think of anything I'd like to do less!'

'Same here!' Billy grumbled. 'I don't know why we have to go.'

Selina turned to her sister.

'Really Becky, did you have to say that? You don't make things any easier.'

Becky raised her eyebrows, replied in a cool voice.

'I was asked a question. I gave a truthful answer.'

'You could have used tact. Was it beyond you to use a bit of tact?'

'Why do you always have to have everybody's approval for what you do?' Becky asked. 'You do exactly what you like, in your sweeter-than-honey manner, and you expect everyone to pat you on the back for it. You always have

450

to be in the right! Dear Selina! Well, I for one think that what you're doing is downright selfish.'

'Selfish? Me?'

'Don't sound so astonished. I know I'm supposed to be the selfish one, but you're just as capable of it as I am — only your methods are different.'

'Putting aside the fact that it has nothing whatever to do with you, how can you say that what I'm doing is selfish?' Selina demanded.

'You're leaving Mother just when she needs you most. You're leaving her with The Beeches, and just when she's fretting about Grandma. You could have waited. Another six months wouldn't have mattered.'

'As it happens it would. We had to grab at the chance. But I'm not going into all that with you. You've made up your mind, though it's none of your business. Anyway, when did you ever fail to grab a chance, and what have *you* ever done for Mother?'

She saw, and ignored, the look of pain in Becky's face.

'When do *you* fit her into your life? Who went off in the war to lark about with a concert party while we were left to carry on as best we could in Akersfield? Who was selfish then?'

'I was,' Becky said. 'All right, I admit it. But it's not the same for me.'

'Oh really? And what makes you so special?'

'Nothing,' Becky said quietly. 'On the contrary, you're the one who's special. Mother would never miss me as she will you. You see, I was never her favourite. Oh, I know she tried to make all three of us equal, but I was never deceived, even as a small child I knew. She didn't love me as she loved you and Jenny. You were the one who mattered. You still are.' Her voice wavered. If she wasn't careful she would cry, and that she had no intention of doing.

'I'm sure that's not true,' Selina protested.

In her heart she knew that it was. She felt now that she had always known it, but she had never realised that Becky

451

was aware, that she minded. Now it was only too clear that she did. Though it was not her fault, the burden of her mother's love made her feel guilty. And not only guilty, but sorry for Becky and in debt to her. She felt closer to her sister at this moment than she had ever done in her life.

'I'm sure that's not true,' she repeated.

'Are you two quarrelling?' Billy asked. 'I don't like it when people quarrel.'

'Not really,' Selina reassured him. 'We just like different things, that's all. Auntie Becky likes Akersfield . . .' She felt safer in bringing the argument back to its original cause.

'But not all that much,' Becky interrupted, her voice now as light as air again. 'It's not nearly as exciting as you think, young Billy!' It could be quite deadly dull. She longed to see London again, and Roland showed no signs of taking her. She had had a letter from the Holgates, formal and polite, but not containing the invitation she had looked for. Oh, if only something would happen!

'Don't you like Akersfield, Mummy?' Billy asked.

'Of course I do. I have a very soft spot for Akersfield because it's where Daddy and I first met. That was in the war.'

In fact her chief memories of Akersfield were of struggling through the war years. Nothing could ever be as bad as that again. Her recent feeling of affection for Becky was strengthened as she remembered the years they had both waited for their men to come home. It was ridiculous ever to quarrel.

'At least, Becky,' she said gently, 'our sons will never have to experience what their fathers went through. They won't have to fight in a war.'

'I'll fight,' Billy interrupted. 'I'll shoot with a big gun!'

'Oh no you won't!' Selina said, smiling at him.

'Roland said he would try to get home to lunch,' Becky told her sister. 'That's because *you* will be here, so count yourself lucky!'

'Oh, I do,' Selina said. She liked her brother-in-law. She had felt sorry for him when he first came back from the war.

452

She was not at all sure that Becky had wanted him back, but everything seemed to be all right now. Then she remembered what Roland had told herself and Bob at Grandma's party. So much had happened since that day that it had gone clean out of her mind.

'Is it true that Jimmy Austin is working at Layton's?' she asked Becky.

'Yes. He turned up in Bridlington. He needed a job, Roland gave him one.'

'How's he getting on?'

'I've no idea,' Becky said shortly. Thank God she had not seen him since he came back to Akersfield. He had kept his promise to leave her alone if she got him a job. She hoped never to see him again, and she didn't want to talk about him.

Roland came home to lunch, as promised, shortly after Christopher arrived from school.

'Now, Selina, tell me all about this new venture?' he said. 'It sounds really exciting.'

'Oh it is!' Selina agreed. 'At first, right at first, I wasn't so sure, but now I'm really thrilled about it.' She launched into a description of the farm, of Longdale, of their plans for the future. There was so much to tell. In the end it was the grin on Roland's face which pulled her up.

'Oh, I'm sorry! I'm talking too much!'

'Not a bit,' Roland said. 'We wanted to hear.'

'Well, I meant it when I said I don't envy you, Selina,' Becky declared. 'But I envy your enthusiasm.'

Yes, you do, Selina thought. I can tell you do. Perhaps my life is better than yours after all, in spite of all you've got.

'Selina always was one for rising to a challenge,' Becky said. 'Now me . . .'

'You don't have any challenges,' Roland teased her. 'Married to me, your life is as smooth as silk, my love. And that's how I want it to be for you.'

'As smooth as silk,' Becky repeated.

'Changing the subject,' Roland said, 'did I tell you that

453

Jimmy Austin came to ask me if he could run a Christmas sweep for the men? So much a week from their wages – I doubt they can spare much – and at Christmas three chances of a lucky win. We've never had anything like that at Layton's. My father's never approved of gambling in any form, and I'm not keen on it. But Jimmy said that it would give the men something to look forward to and I suppose he's right. Anyway, I said he could go ahead.'

He didn't notice – though Selina did, and wondered – the worried look which flashed across Becky's face, and was gone again.

'I really must leave,' Selina said. 'If I go now I'll catch the two o'clock train. Billy, you will be a good boy, won't you? Don't cause any trouble to Auntie Becky.' But her son, she marked with a twinge of sadness, was so immersed in some game with his cousin that, but for a perfunctory kiss, he hardly noticed her departure.

'You will go to see Mother, won't you?' she said to Becky as they made their farewells in the hall.

'Of course I will,' Becky promised. 'I care more about her than you might imagine.'

Bob left Hebghyll the next morning. Eleanor had lent him her car until they could buy a second-hand one, which would have to be soon if they were not to be totally isolated. She would have given it to them, claiming that she didn't often use it in Hebghyll, everything was within walking distance, and in any case it was several years old. Selina had refused to take it. She knew that her mother loved the car and enjoyed driving when she had the chance. She was glad now that she had turned down the offer. Yesterday's scene with Becky still pricked; she felt wary of accepting favours.

She went with Bob to the gate to see him off.

'I hate to see you leave without me,' she told him. 'I so long to go with you. I wanted us both to be together at the start of our new life.'

'I know,' Bob said, kissing her. 'But it won't be long. I'll see you in a week's time. Please try not to work too hard in the meantime. Don't lift any weights. You must remember the baby.'

'I think about it all the time,' Selina said.

Bob stowed his bags into the car, but when he was about to get in himself she stopped him.

'Bob, do you think we're being selfish? Be honest?'

'Selfish?'

'Yes. Not thinking about anyone but ourselves.'

'Of course not! We're doing what we want to do, certainly – but we're thinking about each other and both of us are thinking about our children. We can't live our lives for everyone else.'

He knew what the trouble was. She was upset about leaving her mother, more so now that the time was close.

'Don't worry,' he said. 'Your mother will be all right. She's got Dick and the boys. And The Beeches will be in good hands.' Olive Feather had been delighted by the prospect of taking over and had already announced her engagement to Arthur Browning.

'You're right. I'm being silly.'

She watched as he drove away, waved until he was out of sight, then went back into the house and busied herself packing the ornaments. There was so much to do that the time would pass quickly. In the meantime, though, she would have no contact with Bob because there was no telephone at the farm and they had agreed that he would have no time for letter-writing. The offer to have a telephone put in, as a housewarming present, was one thing she had willingly accepted from her mother, and Bob would ask for it to be installed as soon as possible on the grounds that she was pregnant.

The days passed quickly enough, helped by the fact that there was an unexpected note from Bob, to tell her that everything was going well. She refused an offer to stay at Whinbank, though she saw Charlotte every day.

'It would be much more comfortable for you,' Eleanor pointed out.

'I know. But I want to stay in the cottage until the last minute. Do you understand?'

'I think so,' Eleanor replied. 'I'm not sure.' She had felt, recently, that Selina was moving away from her, not only physically, but in ways she couldn't quite pinpoint. Though she was as loving as ever, she seemed to have wrapped herself in a cocoon of independence.

On the morning of moving day Selina was up early. There was one thing above all others she wanted to do now. She put on her hat and coat, left the cottage as soon as it was daylight, and went down to the parish church: but not into the church; her venue was her grandmother's grave, in the churchyard. She had gathered a few late roses from the cottage garden, and these she placed on the grave. Then she read the inscription on the new white headstone. 'Susannah Foster, aged 70 years. Abide With Me.' She wondered, as she was leaving, if her grandmother would have liked to have been taken back to Felldale to be buried. But did it matter? There was an undefinable feeling in her heart that she and her grandmother had left Hebghyll forever.

When she got back to the cottage the removal van was already waiting. By the time it was packed and the two men had drunk a final cup of tea, Eleanor was there to say goodbye.

'I didn't bring Charlotte,' she explained. 'You were quite right, it wouldn't do for her to see you go off in the van.'

In the privacy of the empty cottage the two women embraced, and it was Selina whose eyes were wet with tears.

'Take care of yourself, Mother. I'll see you again before very long.'

'Of course, love!'

But it will never be quite the same again, Eleanor thought, watching the van move away. All my daughters have left now. But her husband and her sons were waiting for her at home, and it was to them she now returned.

'My word, missus, but you've chosen the back of beyond

up here,' the driver of the van remarked. 'What do you say, Joe?'

They had made good time and were already in Longdale, not more than a mile or two from the farm itself.

'Everyone to his own choice,' Joe said. 'I reckon nowt to the country. An' it's a rough road up here, missus, won't do the springs no good.'

'Or my goods and chattels!' Selina said. 'But it's not much farther. We're nearly there now.'

It was every bit as beautiful as she remembered it; the grass so green, the fells so high, the river rushing and sparkling. And when they reached the end of the road and Bob was there to meet them, she knew that she had come home. She got down from her seat in the van and ran into his arms.

'Oh Bob, I'm here! I'm here at last! I've missed you so!'

The men were unlocking the van. She was glad it had been explained to them earlier that everything would have to be carried the last few hundred yards up the hill. They surveyed the stony path and grimaced at each other.

'Oh well, there it is,' the driver said. 'Why don't you go ahead, missus, and make a cup of tea. We allus work better for a cup of tea. Meanwhile me and Joe'll make a start on this lot.'

'I'll help,' Bob told them. 'And I've found an old hand-cart. We can pile a few things on that as long as we can manhandle it up the track.'

Inside the house Selina went from room to room, at first doing nothing more than look out of the window, revelling in the landscape, and then turning her back on the view, trying to decide where everything would go. There were two rooms downstairs, plus the scullery and pantry, and a small room at the back of the house which Bob had said was the 'drying' room. Upstairs, leading off the square landing, were two good-sized bedrooms and one small one. The trouble was that everywhere there were bits and pieces belonging to Mr Henshaw. Somehow they would have to be got rid of to make room for their own things. When Bob

457

had a minute to spare from carrying furniture up the hill she must ask him if he'd had any report on the old man.

It was late afternoon when the last piece of furniture was carried into the house. In the larder she had found a ham which Bob had acquired from Uncle John, and there was a bowl of fresh eggs from their own hens. She made a meal, and by the time they had eaten it and the men were ready to drive away, the October day had ended.

'Mind how you go,' Bob said.

'If you hear a splash, my mate's driven into the river,' Joe replied. 'Well, I hope you'll be happy here, but I must say I'll be glad to get back to civilisation.'

Arm in arm, Selina and Bob walked back up the track to the house, Bob carrying a small lantern to light the way, for there was no light left in the sky now, and the only sound was an occasional 'Baaaa' from a sheep on the hillside. At the door of the house they turned and looked across the dale, but the darkness was all-enveloping and they could see nothing at all of the opposite fellside.

'But it's a soft darkness,' Selina remarked, 'protective, not menacing.'

'And in time we'll get used to it,' Bob assured her. 'We'll be able to see in the dark, like the animals do.'

When they went into the house the mellow glow from the oil lamp welcomed them.

'I'm so tired!' Selina said. 'Can we go straight to bed?'

'You go up, love. I'm just going to take a last look at the hen house. I fastened up, but I want to make sure, in case there's a fox around.'

She laughed.

'Oh Bob, love, you sound just like a farmer!'

'I am a farmer,' he said happily. 'And from now on you're a farmer's wife. I hope you know how to churn butter. That one cow of ours gives a fair amount of cream.'

Their own bed was ready and waiting – she had seen to that early on. She lay awake, watching the strange shadows cast by the candle, waiting for her husband.

'Make love to me!' she said when he came into the room.

458

'Selina, love, do you think I should? You're very tired and you're seven months pregnant.'

'Don't you want to?' she demanded.

'You know damn well I do. More than anything else in the world.'

'Then blow out the candle, and love me. Here and now, in our own home. Oh Bob, I love you so much!'

There were no bad dreams that night, no memories of the war to spoil their lovemaking. Everything was perfect and she wished it could go on forever, world without end.

CHAPTER TWENTY-SEVEN

'Are we nearly there?' Christopher asked. He felt miserably sick from being in the car so long, but he was determined not to show it, because this was the start of the summer holiday he had begged for.

'I should hope so,' Becky said. 'I was warned it was at the back of beyond. What possessed your Aunt Selina to agree to living here I shall never understand.'

'Perhaps she likes it,' Christopher suggested. 'I would.'

'Oh no you wouldn't! At the end of two weeks you'll be glad to get back to Akersfield. Just you wait!'

His mother was wrong, but he wouldn't argue. He was determined to be as good as gold with everyone, so that he might possibly he allowed to remain longer than the two weeks which had been agreed. How marvellous if he could stay with Billy for the whole month of the school holiday.

In fact, Becky had been delighted by Selina's letter, suggesting that Christopher might like to spend a fortnight on the farm with them. It meant he would be away during Akersfield Feast week.

'With the mill closed and Christopher in Longdale, there isn't the slightest reason why we shouldn't go to London,' she'd pointed out to Roland.

'All right,' he agreed. 'You win!'

At her request they had booked a room in the hotel where they'd spent their honeymoon. Roland grumbled that it was horribly expensive but she knew that underneath he was pleased she had chosen to go back there.

Then, at the moment she'd been planning to take Christopher to Longdale, Jenny had phoned.

'I've got two days off duty,' she said. 'Can I come and stay with you?'

Becky was surprised by the request. Jenny visited from time to time, but never for more than an hour or two.

'Why not go with us to the farm?' she suggested. 'I suppose, like me, you've never been there?'

'I haven't. So why not?' Jenny said.

She saw very little of her family these days. In the beginning, when she had first gone to nurse in Akersfield, she had returned to Hebghyll almost every free weekend, but now she scarcely went there at all. She'd been only once since her grandmother's funeral. She felt herself out of touch with them. Their world wasn't hers; hers would be alien to them.

So now the three of them were on their way to the farm; Becky driving, Christopher, because he was a bad traveller, in the front beside her, Jenny sitting silently in the back. Becky glanced sideways at her son, noting his pallor, hoping he wouldn't be sick before they got there.

He was the first to spot the house, high up on the fellside.

'There it is, Mummy!' he shouted. 'That must be it! Do you think it is, Aunt Jenny?'

She didn't hear him. She seemed to be miles away. He repeated the question.

'I suppose it must be,' she agreed. 'Since we've more or less come to the end of the world!'

'It is!' he cried. 'It is! I can see Billy waving! He's starting to run down the hill! Mummy, can I get out and go to meet him?'

'As it seems we can't get the car any further, you might as well.'

He was away like a shot, his short legs going like pistons as he breasted the hill until he met his cousin at the halfway point.

'Hello!' Billy said.

'Hello!'

They didn't embrace, or even touch each other, but lapsed

at once into a companionable silence as they walked towards the house. Bob passed them on his way down.

'Hello there, young Chris! I'm going down to help your mother with your suitcase.'

'Oh!' Christopher said. 'I forgot that. But Aunt Jenny's with her.'

'Is she? I hadn't realised.'

Becky, though she carried nothing more than her handbag, was totally out of breath when they reached the house.

'However do you do it?' she asked Selina when she had recovered enough breath to speak.

Selina laughed.

'Oh Becky, don't be silly! There are plenty of hills in Akersfield.'

'Not as steep as this!'

'Anyway, come inside and sit yourself down, both of you. I'm so glad you've come, Jenny. It's a pleasant surprise. There'll be a cup of tea in a minute, but in the meantime you must both come and look at your new niece. She's fast asleep at the moment and she's not due to be fed until two o'clock, so we'll get an hour or two's peace.'

Selina's heart was filled, as always, with love and pride as she looked down at her baby daughter in the cot. Her birth had set the seal on the whole family belonging in the dale as nothing else could have done. *She* was a native.

'Susannah,' Selina said quietly. 'After Grandma. But we shall call her Sue. Isn't she just beautiful?'

Jenny turned away as quickly as she decently could. As things were, and she saw no hope of them changing, she would never have a baby. The thought hurt.

'She's rather nice as babies go,' Becky agreed. 'As you know, they're not really my sort of thing. However did you manage, cut off up here? When she was born, I mean.'

'We're not really cut off! Just rather isolated, which is different. Well, I admit we were cut off in January when the heavy snow came – but in December it was all right. Bob fetched the midwife from Faverwell, and after the birth she cycled up each day for ten days, so I was well looked

462

after. Uncle John and Auntie Madge came — and even a couple of farmers' wives from down the dale. She had a real welcome, our little Sue!' She was glad that, in spite of her mother's pleas, she had decided not to go back to Hebghyll for the birth. It had felt so right to have it here.

'Would you like to look round the farm?' she asked. 'When you've drunk your tea.'

Jenny nodded in a disinterested manner. Selina was puzzled by her younger sister. She had always been such a chatterbox, so lively. Now there was an inexplicable sadness about her and she had nothing to say.

'Well, I know you're dying to show us everything,' Becky said. 'and Roland won't forgive me if I can't tell him all about it when I get back. He wanted to come with us but he can't get away from the mill until Saturday, and that's when we're off to London.' Oh it would be marvellous! She could hardly wait.

'I've never been to London,' Selina mused. 'I don't suppose now I ever shall — not that I mind.'

'We're so unalike, all three of us,' Becky remarked. 'I don't know how we came to be sisters. Anyway, if you're going to show us around, let's get on with it. We mustn't set off for home too late.'

'You've only just arrived,' Selina protested. 'I'm not going to let you leave for hours yet. When do you have to be back at the hospital, Jenny?'

'Tomorrow evening.'

It would be better, she thought, it would make life simpler, if she never went back. She'd known that for a long time now, almost from the beginning, she supposed. She should have cut and run from the moment she'd first seen him walk on the ward, the almighty surgeon surrounded by his entourage of students. But she had not known then — how could she? — that he was married. By the time she did know it was too late for both of them. They'd become lovers — and lovers they still were. She could hardly believe that she could ever have taken such a step, let alone continued. But there was no way out, not for them. Akersfield's premier surgeon could not possibly figure in a divorce. It was unthinkable. It was up to her to break the tie, and she didn't have the courage, she loved him too much. He was content to go on as they were rather than lose her, but it was sapping her life away, it was killing her.

'Well, before we start trekking around,' Becky said, 'I need the bathroom!'

Selina laughed out loud.

'Oh Becky, you're in for a disappointment. One day we'll have a bathroom built, though goodness knows when. You wouldn't have to live here long to realise that the comfort of animals comes way before that of humans. Hen houses, cowsheds, barns – they're what counts! Much more important than bathrooms! So in the meantime you'll have to make do with the privy. It's just across the yard.'

Becky grimaced. But she remembered that when they had first come to Akersfield, when her mother had worked in Kramer's and they had lived in the rooms over, they had had an outside privy. She had been small then, and too frightened ever to close the door. Well, that was all in the past, thank goodness. She couldn't possibly live that kind of life now.

'Billy, I want you and Christopher to stay close to the house for a time, while Charlotte and I show your aunties around. If Sue cries you must come and find me at once,' Selina told her son.

It was with tremendous pride that she set off with her sisters.

'Bob would have liked to have shown you things himself,' she said. 'Explain all the improvements he's made. But there's still some hay to bring in from the lower field and he can't leave it to lie. We have to garner every scrap of hay for the winter feeding.'

She introduced them to the small flock of hens pecking around the farmyard, to most of whom she had given names, and waved a hand in the direction of the cow, grazing on the lower slope in front of the house.

'And the goat is Nancy. She's a treasure! And goats are much easier to milk than cows. So not only do we get milk, and therefore cheese, from her, but in the spring we were able to feed her milk to one or two of the lambs whose mothers hadn't much. I hope to get a billy goat and try to breed a small flock. In time, of course. I've discovered that everything has to be done at the right time on a farm. Shall we walk up the hill and look at the sheep?'

'Look at the sheep?' Becky queried. 'But surely if you've seen one sheep you've seen them all?'

'That shows how ignorant you are, you townee! They're all different from each other. By this time Bob can tell most of the ewes apart. They look a bit strange now, because they've been sheared.'

'It's so lovely here. So calm and tranquil,' Jenny said suddenly. They had stopped halfway up the hill to get their breath back and to look at the view. She wondered if she might propose herself to Selina for a visit, wondered if time spent here might bring her peace. But she had little hope. The basic facts of her life would still be the same. She knew what she ought to do, but she couldn't bring herself to do it.

'It's lovely, but quite exhausting,' Becky said. 'If you two want to climb to the top, that's up to you. I shall sit here and wait for you.' The sun was hot, the grass was short and springy. She flopped to the ground, leaned her back against an outcrop of rock, and gave herself up to indolence.

Jenny and Selina climbed the hill in silence. It was an uneasy, not a companionable silence, with Selina strongly sensible of her sister's unhappiness and Jenny unable either to clear her mind, even for a short time, or cover her feelings. Whenever she was working, when she was on the ward with the patients, her professionalism came to the rescue and she gave herself to the job. Away from the ward, all she could think of was him.

At the top of the hill they sat down. The beauty of the landscape – the green fells dotted with sheep, the river like a twist of silver in the bottom of the valley – was all around, but neither of them saw it.

'Is something wrong, Jenny?' Selina ventured. 'You don't seem yourself.'

Jenny didn't answer.

'I don't wish to pry. Don't tell me if you don't want to. But if I could help . . .'

'You can't help,' Jenny said at last. 'No-one can help, and I seem powerless to help myself.'

'I see.' She didn't see at all. She had never known Jenny in this state before, yet when she thought about it, it was a long time since she had seen the old Jenny; the carefree, fun-loving girl. How long has she been feeling bad, Selina thought, and I've been so full of my own affairs that I've never stopped to notice?

'You might feel better if you could talk about it. And no-one but you and me would ever know.'

'Oh, I trust you for that. You could always keep secrets, even when we were quite small.' But this was no childish affair. 'You'll be shocked,' Jenny said.

'I doubt it,' Selina replied. 'Why not try me?'

'You seem so happy here,' Jenny said obliquely.

'Oh we are, Jenny! We are. I just wish everyone could be as happy as we are. I wish you could be, Jenny.'

'That will never happen.'

Selina winced at the fierce finality of her sister's voice.

'I'm in love, Selina. Isn't it ridiculous, I've gone and fallen for a man who's married, with three children. He's in love with me – oh I don't doubt that at all! It happened the minute we set eyes on each other. But I'm not just in love with him, Jenny. There's more to it than that. I'm his mistress. For almost a year now.'

'Oh Jenny!' Selina put a hand on her sister's arm but Jenny shook her off.

'I said you'd be shocked. *Oh Jenny*!'

'I'm not. Not the way you mean.' If Bob had been married when she'd met him, she thought she would still have fallen in love with him. 'Who . . .?'

'Does it matter who? But yes, in this case it does. It makes all the difference. So I shan't tell you his name because if

I did you'd recognise it. He's well known in the West Riding. And don't try to guess, Selina, in case you guess right. If he weren't so well known it would be easier. His wife could divorce him . . .'

'*Divorce*? Oh Jenny!'

Divorce was something you read about in the Sunday papers, all the nasty details. It didn't happen to people one knew, let alone family.

'Now you really are shocked! But it does happen, even, occasionally, in Akersfield. Though you needn't worry, it's not going to happen to us. Divorce would ruin his career, ruin his life. I love him enough not to do that to him. Oh Selina, I love him so much!'

She buried her head in her hands, shut out the bright day. She would have liked to shut out the rest of her life.

'What are you going to do, Jenny love? You can't go on like this!' She felt desperately sorry for her sister — and helpless.

'I know that. I also know what I ought to do — so do you, so would anybody — but it's one thing knowing it and another thing carrying it out. Oh Selina, I'm so desperately unhappy! Sometimes I think I can't go on.'

'Jenny, you wouldn't . . .!'

'If you mean would I kill myself — oh, don't flinch at the word because it is what you mean — the answer is no. Yes, I have the means to hand — a cupboard full of potions in my office. But I'm a nurse. I'm dedicated to saving life, not taking it, even when it's my own. I suppose I'm a nurse — and a good one at that — before anything else in the world.'

'Then there's your answer,' Selina said slowly.

'What?'

'To go on nursing. I'm sure it's not easy. But it *is* the answer.'

It was a long time before either of them spoke again. Selina thought that Jenny was probably already regretting that she'd said anything. 'You're quite right, of course,' Jenny admitted in the end. 'I know it, but I had to hear it said. And I know I can't go on nursing in Akersfield.'

'I think you're right about that. Where would you go?'

'I'm well qualified. I can get a job almost anywhere. As it happens, I've had an offer of a post in Brighton. You can't get much further away than that, so perhaps I'll take it.'

Her voice was flat. She felt unutterably weary, and yet somehow better. Deep down there was a faint stirring of something, not as strong as hope, but more of a knowledge that having voiced her decision she wouldn't now go back on it. She didn't know yet where she would get the strength to carry it out, but somehow it would come.

'Who knows,' Selina said. 'Perhaps in Brighton . . .'

'I might meet someone else? It's too early to think like that. I have to heal.'

She jumped to her feet. 'Come along, we'd better make a move. Becky's waving to us. Please don't say anything. I'll tell Mother as much as she needs to know when the time comes. But I'm glad I told you, Selina. Thanks for listening.'

When she got home tonight she would write the letter, post it at once. She must do so before her resolve weakened, so that by the time she saw him again it would be all cut and dried. Perhaps she might not even see him, since he was on holiday in Devon with his wife and children. That would be best but, oh, how it would hurt!

It was dusk when the two sisters got back to Akersfield.

'I've changed my mind, I won't stay overnight with you,' Jenny told Becky. 'Don't take it amiss. I've remembered something I have to do. Something important. Anyway you're going to be quite busy getting ready for your holiday. Have a good time in London!'

Most of the citizens of Akersfield were looking forward, in one way or another, to the holiday week. Some approached it with dread because it meant a week of no work and therefore no money coming in. A few were well enough off for that not to matter in the least; and there were thrifty ones who had even managed, by denying themselves for a

468

whole year, to save enough for a holiday at the seaside. The workers at Layton's mill were not quite in that category, but since they'd been paying into the holiday club which Mr Jimmy Austin had set up shortly after he'd joined the staff, they'd have enough for a treat or two: a day at Morecambe with the wife and kids, a charabanc trip to Harrogate and Knaresborough, or Wetherby races. They had totted up, on their cards, the contributions they had made each wage day for the last forty-odd weeks, and had made their plans. It only remained to draw the money on Friday morning. There was a feeling of euphoria in the air at Layton's.

'Nearly time for the pay-out, Mr Austin,' one of the men said, passing Jimmy in the mill yard.

'That's right, Joe. Friday noon!'

He sounded cheerful enough – no point in causing anxiety – but he was a worried man. Very worried. It had seemed so easy when he'd started the scheme. Take the money from the men at the point when he paid out the wages, enter it on their cards, take the cash to the bank. It had worked like a dream for several weeks.

'How do we know we can trust him?' someone had asked, half joking, at the outset.

It was Joe Sykes, the man he'd just passed in the yard, who'd answered that one.

'He's a personal friend of Mr Roland, isn't he? That's good enough for me!' And it had been for most of the men.

He hadn't had the slightest intention of defrauding anyone. It was just that, once or twice, he'd had these red-hot tips for York, Doncaster, Ripon. He knew most of the men would give him something for his trouble when he paid out, and you could say he was simply borrowing what he'd be due, anyway. It was an argument he found totally convincing. The trouble was, the horses hadn't always obliged, and now he was eighty pounds short.

He could scarper – in which case he'd have to take the rest of the money with him. He had to live, didn't he? And he'd need to lie low for a bit because the police would be

469

after him. But he didn't really fancy that task. It was like giving in. On the other hand he couldn't possibly face the men eighty pounds short. They'd tear him limb from limb. So there was only one thing for it. Borrow twenty pounds from what money was left, put it on Lucky Lady to win the two-thirty at Doncaster at six to one, and he'd not only have the eighty pounds, he'd have a bit over for himself, to enjoy the holiday week. It was a dead cert anyway. She was a great filly, just look at her form. Really he ought to put more on, but he wouldn't; he'd be prudent.

He popped out at dinnertime, drew the money from the bank and placed the bet himself. The usual bookie's runner was one of the millhands and it wouldn't do to let him know what he was up to. No point in worrying anyone unnecessarily. Later that afternoon, as soon as he knew it would be on the streets, he sent the office boy out for the *Record*. His hand shook a little as he took the newspaper from the boy. Of course Lucky Lady was bound to win, he'd felt it in his bones – but what if . . .?

He read the stop press through, then read it again. Obviously he'd simply missed the name. Easy enough when you were excited. Then as he read the results for the third time he felt the blood drain from his face, felt the beads of cold sweat breaking out on his forehead. He ran his finger inside his collar to stop the choking sensation.

'Are you all right, Mr Austin?' the office boy asked. 'You look awful!'

'Not too well,' Jimmy mumbled. 'Something I ate. Excuse me!' He rushed out of the office and locked himself in the lavatory.

It was some time before he emerged, grey-faced and still shaking. There was only one thing to be done now. It would have to be Becky. He didn't fancy it. He was now a hundred pounds short and she might kick at that amount. But she was his last chance, his only remaining hope. And the sooner the better.

Hannah was out and Mrs Flynn was working upstairs when the doorbell rang. Reluctantly, Becky went to answer

470

it. When she saw Jimmy standing there she gave a sharp cry – then quickly put her hand to her mouth and checked it. In the same moment she moved to slam the door, but he was too quick for her. He shoved her aside and stepped past her into the hall.

'Get out!' she said. 'Get out at once! I don't want you here! You promised you'd never come again.'

'Shut up!' he snapped. 'And unless you want everyone in the house to hear you'd better take me where we can talk privately.' He pushed her, roughly, in the direction of the sitting-room.

She had never seen him like this before. However hateful he was, however nasty his demands, he had always been polite, smooth, urbane. Now he was a different man; menacing. When he closed the sitting-room door behind him and stood facing her she felt cold with fear.

'Listen to me,' he said. 'And don't interrupt. I've no time to waste and I'm dead serious. I want a hundred pounds and I want it tomorrow at twelve-thirty. Not a minute later and the amount in full!'

'How DARE you! I'll do no such thing!'

'Don't waste my time, sweetie-pie! A hundred pounds. In ones – no fivers. And don't pretend you haven't got it because I know better.'

'I won't give it to you!' Becky cried. 'You can't make me!'

'Oh yes I can!' He stepped forward and gripped her by both wrists.

'Let me go, you brute! Let me go!'

She struggled to free herself but he was too strong for her, twisting her wrists until she cried out with the pain.

'Just listen,' he said. 'I want the money. If you don't have it here tomorrow dinnertime then I shall tell Roland a few things. It doesn't matter that the child is his. There's more than that I can tell him. How would he like to know that he has a wife who didn't come pure to the marriage bed? Soiled goods! How would he like to know about the money you've paid out to me over the years? And what about you pushing him into giving me a job when you knew I'd just come out of prison, you not telling him? He's a very upright man, your husband. He won't like any of that.'

'I'll deny it! I'll deny it all!'

'I don't think he'd believe you, love. I can give him time and place. It all fits in. And why would I say it if it wasn't true?'

'You are the lowest . . .'

'I don't like to disillusion a nice man like Roland, but I can and I will, and it'll hurt you far more than the loss of a hundred pounds. Which, in case you're interested, I want for the very good reason that it's for your husband's workmen. Holiday club money. That's another thing: he minds about his workmen.' He let go of her wrists and pushed her away from him.

'I'd like to kill you! It would really be a pleasure to kill you!' Becky stormed.

'I daresay. But you won't. So be a sensible girl and do as you're told. If you don't have the money ready when I call I might just spoil your pretty little face *before* I spill the beans to Roland.'

The whole episode had lasted no more than five minutes. When he left Becky slumped into a chair, trembling from head to foot. She rubbed at her wrists, which were an angry red and would surely show bruised by the time Roland came home.

She had no doubts about what she would do. She would get the money from the bank in the morning and she would give it to him. And she would do this for one reason above all others. She would not do it because she was physically afraid of Jimmy, though she was. She didn't doubt that if he was thwarted he would resort to violence. She had seen the threat in his eyes and it had terrified her. Nor would she pay him because for her own sake she didn't want Roland to know the truth. She had reached a stage where it would be a relief for him to know, so that she would at last be free.

But it was neither of those things which decided her. She would pay the money because she loved Roland. She had never expected to love him so much, but she did. Her love for him had grown slowly, almost imperceptibly, over the years of their marriage, but it was only now that she realised the full strength of it. She would pay every penny she had, make any sacrifice to spare him the hurt which she knew Jimmy Austin could bring. It was the only recompense left to her. She was consumed afresh with hatred for Jimmy Austin. With all her heart she wished him dead. She would feel no more compunction for him than for a fly on the wall.

Next morning at the breakfast table Roland looked at Becky long and hard. Surreptitiously, she checked that the long sleeves of her blouse were covering the bruises on her wrists.

'You don't look at all well, my love,' he said. 'You're so pale, so dark around the eyes. Didn't you sleep well?'

'Not very well,' she admitted. 'But there's nothing wrong with me. It's just the heat.'

'And I daresay the excitement of getting ready for London,' he teased. 'But you must rest today, dear. We want you to be at your best on holiday.'

'I will,' she promised. 'I have to go into town this morning for a few last-minute purchases, but after that I'll rest.'

He was still worried when he left her. She seemed so low-spirited, which was strange when he knew how much she was looking forward to the trip.

'Take care of yourself,' he said as he kissed her. 'I love you.'

She flung her arms around his neck.

'Oh, and I love you, Roland! I love you so much!'

He was filled with pleasure at her words, yet her manner disturbed him. She wasn't usually demonstrative. Was it possible that she was really ill, and not telling him?

'The big pay-out today, Mr Austin,' the office typist said. 'What time are you going to the bank?'

'Late morning. I don't want the money hanging around. Pay-out's at one o'clock.'

In fact, he had already drawn out what money was in the

473

bank, just in case things went awry. He was not entirely sure that Becky was going to play ball. There had been a look in her eyes . . . Perhaps he'd treated her the wrong way, perhaps he shouldn't have threatened the rough stuff. All the same, he thought, clenching his fists, she'd get it if she played him up. He'd have nothing to lose then. Without her hundred pounds he'd be up and away, show Akersfield a clean pair of heels.

It was the doubts in his mind which had caused him to pack his few belongings in a suitcase before he left his lodgings, and bring them with him to the office.

'You going on holiday, then?' the typist asked.

'Just for a few days.'

Later in the morning he quietly cleared his personal belongings from his desk and desk drawers, then at eleven-thirty, when the typist was out of the room, he picked up his case and left, pausing only to collect a macintosh which he kept on the coat stand in case of a sudden shower. It was fine enough today, but you never knew.

It was the absence of the raincoat which the typist first noticed. How strange! It was a dry, sunny day and the bank was no more than ten minutes walk away. But when her sharp eyes also noticed that the heavy lighter was gone from his desk top, together with the brass perpetual calendar by which he set such store, it seemed even stranger.

Without a qualm she opened the top drawer of his desk where she knew he kept his belongings. It was empty. When she opened the other drawers, she realised that not a single thing belonging to Mr Jimmy Austin had been left. Should she go straight to Mr Roland, or tell one of the men first? She had no need to make the decision, since at that moment Joe Sykes came into the office.

'I wondered if Mr Austin would like someone to go with him to the bank,' he said. 'Seeing as how he's carrying a lot of money back.'

'He's gone.'

'Already? He's in good time. Do you think I should go to meet him?'

'I mean he's gone,' she said. 'I reckon he's gone for good. Vamoosed! He's taken his suitcase and his macintosh and all his personal possessions. He went while I was out of the office.'

'Get me the bank on the telephone,' Sykes ordered. 'Quick as you can!'

'Ought you not to tell Mr Roland first?'

'He's out. I met him crossing the mill yard. His wife's not well and he's slipped home to see her. This can't wait.'

When he had spoken with the bank he put the receiver down and turned to the typist, his face purple with fury.

'He collected the money yesterday. Cleared the account! Tell me where he lives. I'm going after him!'

'But he won't be there. He had his suitcase with him.'

'If he's not there, then I shall go to the police. He's got our money and I'm going to find him. He'll not get away with it! Telephone Mr Roland at home and tell him what's happened.'

When Becky opened the door to Jimmy Austin he walked in, hung his hat on the hat stand, and followed her into the sitting-room. He put his case on the floor.

'Where is it?' he demanded. 'Come on, don't keep me waiting!' He had made up his mind that if she came up with the money he'd do the right thing and go back and pay out. He wouldn't lose by it. They'd all give him a bit, and that way he'd still have his job to come back to after the holiday.

Without a word, she opened her handbag and took out an envelope. All she wanted now was to get rid of him as quickly as possible. She felt he contaminated the very air around him. How she could ever have found him desirable she couldn't now imagine. The thought made her feel sick.

'There's no need to count it,' she said as he took the envelope. 'I don't cheat!'

'Except your husband,' he said, laughing.

475

'I'm doing this for my husband. And for no other reason. As far as you're concerned, I wish you were lying dead on the floor. If you were, I'd grind you under my heel.'

He put the envelope away in his inside pocket.

'Temper! Temper! But you always were attractive when you were in a paddy! In fact you're still an attractive lady, so how about a kiss, just to show we're still friends?'

'I'd sooner kiss a toad!' She spat the words at him. Oh, how she hated him!

He stepped forward and took her in his arms, forcing her head back while he fastened his mouth on hers. She tried without success to turn her head away, but her hands were free, and when he ran his hand over her breast and under the neck of her dress, she pummelled him fiercely with her fists.

'You didn't always try so hard to keep me off!' He sounded amused. 'And you can't do anything about it. I'm too strong for you. So why not give in, eh?'

She was fighting furiously with him, raining him with blows from her clenched fists which he seemed not even to feel, when Roland burst in. Her husband didn't wait for an explanation. With a fierceness Becky had never seen in him before he lunged towards Jimmy Austin and grabbed him from behind, taking him completely by surprise. Then he swung him round and hit him with tremendous force on the point of the jaw. Jimmy went down hard, the side of his head banging against the corner of the china cabinet with such impact that everything in it rattled and sang.

Becky screamed as she flung herself into Roland's arms. He was livid with anger but when he spoke to her his voice was under control.

'It's all right, my darling! I'm here now. You're safe. Don't try to talk now.'

For seconds, which seemed like hours, while Roland continued to hold her in his arms, they looked down at Jimmy Austin lying there on the floor. He was unconscious. The contusion where Roland had hit him was the only colour in his chalk-white face. A small trickle of blood ran down from the side of his head, staining the carpet.

'Is he . . . dead?' Becky whispered.

A minute ago she had wished that he was lying dead on the floor.

'I don't think so. I must ring for the doctor at once.'

In the few minutes while they waited for the doctor to arrive, the telephone rang. When Roland had listened he said, 'Wait a minute.'

He went over to Jimmy Austin and carefully felt in his inner pockets. Becky caught her breath as he extracted the envelope with her hundred pounds. Next he opened the suitcase and from beneath the packed clothes he brought out a second envelope, unsealed, stuffed with banknotes. When he went back to the telephone he said, 'The money's here. I can't explain now. Catch Joe Sykes before he goes to the police. Ask him to come to my house to collect the money.'

'Ought you to . . .?' Becky began.

'The money belongs to my men,' he said. 'They've saved all year for this. I'll take the consequences for giving it to them – if there are any.'

As he put the money away in a drawer, the doctor arrived.

'He's not dead,' he pronounced. 'But I don't like the look of him. I'll get the ambulance. I'm not asking for explanations, not my job – but you do realise, Roland, that I'll have to inform the police?'

'I realise that,' Roland said quietly.

The doctor went with the ambulance to the hospital. Less than an hour later he telephoned.

'I'm afraid I have to tell you that Mr Austin is dead. He died without regaining consciousness.'

CHAPTER TWENTY-EIGHT

Roland hung up the receiver and turned to Becky.

'He's dead!'

He had known in his heart, from the moment he had seen Jimmy Austin lying on the floor, that the man would die. He had seen men in France, wounded, dying. He knew how they looked. Yet in the hour while he had waited for the telephone to ring he had refrained from acknowledging his fears to Becky, who had been beside herself with terror.

'We must wait and see, my darling,' he'd said. 'It may not be as bad as we think.'

But while that had comforted Becky a little, he had not deceived himself. The words uttered over the telephone just now, in the doctor's kind but stern tones, had come as no surprise. In a strange way, he felt almost a sense of relief in the confirmation of what he had known was inevitable.

Becky ran into his arms, clung fiercely to him.

'Oh Roland, what will happen? What shall we do? I'm so afraid!'

'Come and sit down, my love,' he said gently. 'We must talk, and we might not have much time. The police will come – they'll ask a lot of questions – and it's possible that they will want to take me away.' It was more than possible, it was highly likely, but he would spare her that thought as long as he could. He was amazed at the calmness he now found in himself, at the steadiness of his voice.

'I can't bear it!' Becky cried. 'I can't bear it if they take you away! Oh Roland, what have I done?'

'*You* have done nothing, my dear. He came to ask you for money because he had been defrauding the men, and from the kindness of your heart you gave it to him. I daresay they'll ask how you came to have so much money . . .'

'I saved it' Becky said quickly. 'Out of the housekeeping and my allowance. Over a long time.'

'I see. And I daresay they'll wonder why he attacked you *after* you'd given him the money.'

'Roland! They surely won't think I encouraged him!'

'Of course not! I know that's the last thing you'd do. Why, you've always disliked him, and how right you were. No, the man's an animal. No matter what happens now, I'm glad I came in when I did.'

With all her heart she longed to tell him, longed to free herself from this burden of guilt, but it was an indulgence she couldn't permit herself. Jimmy Austin was dead. Roland had struck him and he had fallen to the ground. Since Roland had been unaware of it, the admission that she had been blackmailed would not mitigate that, and if it became known it would hurt Roland deeply. In addition to his private grief, it would, without doubt, get into the papers, cause a scandal. Therefore she must bear what was hardest of all for her to bear, Roland's approbation for what he thought of as her generosity. She knew she must swallow the guilt which rose like a tide in her; she must act as if she was what her husband believed her to be.

'It's possible,' Roland said quietly, 'that the police will be here before Joe Sykes comes to collect the money. In that case you must hand it over to him and ask him to pay it out the moment he gets back to the mill. I have no idea whether, in law, I'm doing right or wrong in taking the money from Austin, but morally I'm sure. The money belongs to the men and they must have it. The rest can be sorted out later.'

'I'll see that Joe Sykes gets it,' Becky promised.

'And you had better tell him what has happened. It will get into the *Record* in double quick time and I would rather the men heard it from us first. Tell him the least you can, for the time being.'

479

'How can you keep so calm?' Becky cried. 'Oh Roland, this is terrible!'

'Don't you see, I *must* keep calm,' he said. 'There are things to think of. I know it's a lot to ask, my darling, but it would be for the best if you were also able to compose yourself. Best for you as well as for me.'

In his mind he faced the fact that once the police took him it might be a long time before he saw his wife and his home again. He faced the fact squarely, though it was anguish to do so. To make mundane arrangements for what must be done in his absence was, in a curious way, a help.

'You must let my father know,' he continued. 'And I'm afraid you must telephone the hotel in London and cancel our room. I see no possibility of going to London – but don't worry, we shall go in the end!'

'Oh Roland! As if I cared about that! All I care about is you. I want you to know that, I want you to believe it.'

'I do believe it,' he said. 'It's that knowledge which will see me through whatever happens. And what happens may be very, very hard for both of us to bear. So you must be my own brave Becky.'

'Oh I will, I will! I'll try so hard, Roland! But what will they do? Please try to tell me what they'll do. I want to be prepared.'

'When the police come they'll arrest me, take me to the station.' He kept his voice even, as if he was announcing some unimportant errand he had to do. 'Then tomorrow morning they'll bring me before the court.'

'You mean they'll keep you in a prison cell? You'll sleep in prison?'

'Yes. But don't forget I've been a prisoner of war. It can't be worse than that.'

'What will they charge you with?' Her voice was a whisper. They were words she hardly dared to say.

Suddenly, unexpectedly, he could no longer face her. He turned his back on her and moved towards the window, stood there looking out into the garden. The green of the lawn, the brightness of the summer bedding plants,

480

Christopher's swing, blurred and merged in confusion in front of him. How could it all have happened? How could it be that in so short a time, on this lovely summer's day which had started out as normally as any other, his world had changed?

'Please, Roland?'

He turned and faced her.

'Manslaughter.'

She cried out, and ran into his arms. He held her close, felt her trembling against him. 'Oh Becky, I love you so much!' he murmured.

It was not long before the police came. Under their impassive gaze, Roland and Becky embraced again.

'Be brave, my darling,' Roland repeated.

'Of course!'

Unexpectedly, the presence of the police steadied her. They were kind, matter-of-fact, as if what they were doing was an everyday matter, nothing to worry about too much. Outwardly she remained calm, though her eyes pricked with tears she was determined not to shed until her husband had gone. But she knew that as long as she lived she would never forget seeing him taken, watching him walk out of the house without a backward glance. It was the handcuffs which upset her most. There was no need for handcuffs, she thought bitterly. No need at all.

Joe Sykes arrived ten minutes after they had left.

'Sorry I wasn't here sooner, Mrs Layton. Only I went to Mr Austin's lodgings. I didn't know he lived that far out. Anyway, Miss Fraser caught me before I went to the police station, told me the money was waiting here. I don't quite understand it, but if I could have a word with Mr Roland . . .' He said it all standing on the doorstep, out of breath and flustered.

'Please come in,' Becky interrupted.

As she told him what had happened the high colour in his face deepened further. When she described how Roland had gone for Jimmy she saw him clench his large hands as though he, too, would have used his fists; but when

481

she told him the outcome his eyes widened with horror.

'Dead? And Mr Roland arrested?'

'Yes.'

'I don't know what to say.' He shook his head as if he couldn't believe what he was hearing. 'No more than a couple of hours ago I'd have gone for that man meself if I could have found him – but I'm a man who has a bit of temper, easily roused. Mr Roland is different. He wouldn't hurt anybody. I can't believe it!'

'It was because Mr Austin was molesting me,' Becky told him.

'Aye. I see that. I don't know what to say!'

'You've had a shock,' Becky said. 'You must sit down and I'll give you a tot of brandy. But then you must get back to the mill and pay out the money as quickly as you can. My husband wanted everyone to have what was due to them this afternoon. And will you tell Mr Forsyth what I've just told you?' Mr Forsyth was the mill manager.

'Aye, I will that. It'll be a great shock to him. Mr Forsyth has been with Layton's man and boy for nigh on forty years. He's known Mr Roland since he were a babby.'

'I know. My husband often speaks of him.'

'And the men will be sorry to hear it. Mr Roland's very highly thought of. Very highly thought of. And whatever will it do to the old man? I beg your pardon, I mean Mr Layton.'

'I don't know,' Becky said. 'I have to telephone him now. He's staying with friends in Harrogate. We were going away tomorrow.'

Joe Sykes rose to his feet.

'I'd best be getting off. When you see Mr Roland tell him we'll all be thinking on him. When will you see him?'

The question gave Becky a jolt. When would she see her husband again? And when the time came, would she be near enough to touch him, to comfort him, or would she be at the far side of a courtroom with Roland standing in the dock like a common criminal?

'I don't know. I really don't know what happens next.'

482

She must get the solicitor. Mr Peacock, of Peacock, Peacock, Peacock and Waters. He would know what to do. He would be the person to help Roland. She felt so utterly helpless. She wanted to do everything for him and she could do nothing. In the last twenty minutes her brain seemed to have turned to cotton wool. She hardly noticed Joe Sykes' departure.

'If there's anything at all . . .' he said at the door. 'The mill's closed down for a week after today, as you know, but Mr Forsyth will know where to find us if we're needed. Think on!'

Mr Peacock was at the house within half an hour of her telephone call. In no time at all his concerned, fatherly manner had the whole story out of her – not the blackmail, of course, that was for no-one's ears -- but the episode as Roland had experienced it.

'My dear Mrs Layton! But don't despair. It may not be as bad as you think. I shall do everything in my power.'

'Roland said he'd be charged with manslaughter.' Even the sound of the word frightened her.

Mr Peacock nodded his head.

'I daresay that's true. But even so, none of it may be as bad as we think. In the first place I shall try to get bail for Roland.'

'Bail? For manslaughter?'

'Oh, it's possible, just possible. He's not likely to repeat the crime. He's not going to run away. He has business commitments, responsibilities to his workpeople. It is possible, and that's what I shall try for to start with.'

He didn't tell her, it would be too cruel, that bail or no bail, her husband would eventually have to stand trial at the Assizes – he had no doubt from the description of the events that the charge would be manslaughter – and he would go to prison. For how long or how short a time it was too soon to guess. There was provocation, no doubt; there were mitigating circumstances. But who could tell?

'I'll go at once to the police station,' he assured Becky. 'I daresay they've already sent for me. In the meantime, my advice to you is to keep busy and to get yourself some company. What about your mother? Have you told your mother?'

The suggestion came like balm to Becky. Her mother. Suddenly she felt desperate to see her mother. Her mother would know what to do. She picked up the telephone.

'Hebghyll 237 please.'

Eleanor listened in near-silence to Becky's almost incoherent account, trying not to express her horror as the story unfolded. Then she said, 'I'll be with you very soon. I'll pack a bag and I'll stay as long as you want me. Tell me, have you eaten?'

'Not since breakfast,' Becky said. 'I can't think about eating.'

'Well nor have I, and I'm pretty hungry. So you set about making something for both of us and I'll be with you in about an hour.'

It was not true that she hadn't eaten. She had shared a substantial meal with Dick and the boys less than two hours ago, but it would be best for Becky to have something to occupy her for the next hour. She was appalled at what had happened, and more worried than she would ever admit that the victim had been Jimmy Austin. On the telephone, Becky had been vague about his presence in the house. But no matter. Her daughter needed her, and wild horses wouldn't keep her from giving every bit of support she could.

She spared a moment, as she drove towards Akersfield, to allow herself the pleasure of knowing that Becky, who all her life had seemed to put a distance between them, had turned to her now. She wouldn't easily forget the note in Becky's voice as she had pleaded with her to come. It would never be mentioned, and she would have gone to Becky in any case, but she would never forget it.

Since Hannah had left immediately after breakfast to spend the holiday week with her sister in York, Becky had to prepare the meal herself. Though her mind wasn't on it, and she had no appetite whatsoever, the preparations

484

occupied her physically. She had less time to keep running to the window, scanning the road for the sight of her mother's car. She saw through Eleanor's strategy, but it was a good one. At one point, laying the table, she wondered what, aside from Mr Peacock's suggestion, had made her turn to her mother. They had never been close, yet now, in Roland's absence, she wanted Eleanor with her more than anyone else in the world.

The hour was not quite up when the bell rang. Becky flew to open the door.

'Oh Mother! I'm so glad you're here!'

'I drove much too fast,' Eleanor said. 'But I'm in one piece, and so is the car.'

Then they were in each other's arms, no more trivial words to be said, and for the first time Becky allowed herself to cry. Eleanor gently led her into the sitting-room. On the sofa she held Becky close, making no attempt to quell the sobs which shook her daughter's slender body. She stroked her hair as if she was a small child, asked no questions, simply waited in patience for Becky's weeping to stop in its own good time. Becky felt the love which flowed from her mother into her own mind and body, and was comforted.

'I'm sorry!' she said eventually. 'I didn't mean to go on like this.'

'Don't be sorry,' Eleanor told her. 'Don't be. There are times when to cry is the most healing thing in the world. I feel sorry for men because they don't allow themselves to cry.'

In the midst of all the horror – and she knew there was more horror to come – she felt that in the last few moments she had been given a precious gift. But it was a delicate gift, she must handle it carefully.

'I used to think men had the best of it,' Becky said. 'I don't think so now. Roland lost his temper for a split second, and in my defence. Now he's the one who'll be punished. He'll be sent to prison. No matter what anyone says, I believe he'll be sent to prison.'

'From what you've told me,' Eleanor admitted, 'I daresay that's true. But though prison will be hard and unpleasant, and few people deserve it less than Roland, he's not the only one who'll be punished. You'll have your share, though in different ways.'

There was no doubt that her daughter would be punished, though Eleanor had no intention of spelling it out to her. She'd experience it soon enough. She'd be punished by loneliness, by overheard gossip, by ostracism because her husband had offended. There were plenty of people in Akersfield who were stupid enough for that. And she would be doubly punished through her son, by seeing him endure the same kind of humiliations: the whispers in the play-ground, the former friends who would no longer be allowed to play with him because his father was in gaol. Oh, there was no doubt that society would exact full retribution from her daughter and her grandson. It wouldn't be enough just to put Roland in prison.

'I deserve to be. Roland doesn't.'

The words were clearly and firmly spoken. There is more to come, Eleanor thought. But she must be careful. She mustn't trespass.

'If there's something you want to tell me, then do so. If you don't, then don't. It will make no difference between us. You're my daughter and I love you.'

'Sometimes,' Becky began hesitantly, 'though you long to tell the truth, you can't because it would hurt the other person. Do you understand that?'

'Perfectly. And I agree with it. There are occasions when to tell the truth can be self-indulgence. But I don't think it often applies between mothers and children.'

'I had an affair with Jimmy Austin,' Becky said abruptly. 'Oh, before I was married. Nothing since. I was madly in love with him and I wanted him to marry me, but he wouldn't. So I married Roland without loving him, and for the wrong reason.'

'Christopher?'

'Christopher is Roland's child as well as mine. There's

486

not the slightest doubt of that now. But once there was, and he might not have been. Jimmy Austin blackmailed me from the beginning of my marriage.'

'Oh my poor little girl! My poor, poor Becky! And this is what you never told Roland?'

'At first I didn't tell him because I was afraid to. Then I grew to love him and I couldn't bear to hurt him. Mother, you have to believe that I love Roland with all my heart!'

'I do,' Eleanor assured her. 'At first I thought you didn't. It seems an odd thing to say, but in a way I was more worried about you then than I am now. Whatever happens to you now, I know you'll come through it. You are a stronger person than ever you were – and Roland, though you mayn't have thought so, has always been strong. I sympathise with you now from the bottom of my heart, but I don't fear for you as I once did.'

'The most difficult thing I have to bear is never being able to tell Roland, and the fact that he thinks me better than I am.'

'I understand,' Eleanor said. 'And I think you're right not to rob Roland of that belief. But at some time in the future – though I'm not saying you'll forget it – it won't matter any longer, I assure you.'

'I'd like to believe you,' Becky sighed.

'Then you must, Becky! You must. And now I'm going to be very prosaic and say that you must have something to eat. After that we need to let Selina and Jenny know before they read it in the papers. If you like I'll telephone for you. Then I shall speak to the doctor and ask him to give you something to make you sleep tonight.'

They were just finishing the meal when Mr Peacock telephoned.

'I've seen your husband. I thought you'd like . . .'

'What's happened?' Becky interrupted. 'Please tell me what's happened! And is he all right?'

'Of course he is, my dear. But as we expected, he's been charged with manslaughter . . .'

487

Over the phone he heard Becky's cry, and after that her mother's voice.

'I'm sorry, Mr Peacock. We did expect it, but it's a great shock to my daughter, nevertheless. Perhaps you can tell me the rest?'

'No, Mother!' Becky called out. 'I want to hear for myself.' She took the receiver back from Eleanor. 'I'm sorry, Mr Peacock. Please tell me everything. I want to know everything.'

'There's very little to tell you at the moment, Mrs Layton. Your husband will appear in court in the morning.'

'Then I shall be there!' Becky promised.

'No! He has specifically said he would rather you didn't come. You'll be able to visit him afterwards, and that's what he'd prefer. I assure you he's very well and keeping cheerful. He was pleased to hear that you'd telephoned for your mother. He sent you his love and says you're to try not to worry.'

'How can I help it?' Becky demanded. 'But don't tell him that. When you see him in the morning give him all my love and tell him I shall be thinking of him every minute.'

When Eleanor telephoned the farm, Selina answered.

'Is Christopher in earshot?' Eleanor asked.

'No. Both the boys have gone off up the fell with Bob. Why do you ask?'

Selina listened while her mother told her.

'But Ma, that's terrible! I just can't believe anything like that about Roland! And poor Becky! What can I do to help Becky?'

It was the first time in her life that she had thought Becky in need of help. Becky was the one for whom everything went right, the one who had the easy life, no troubles.

'Very little at the moment,' Eleanor said. 'Except that it might be a good idea if you asked Christopher to stay on for the whole month. He'll like that anyway. And don't tell him anything else. Let him believe his parents have gone to London, as planned. The longer we can keep him in ignorance, the better.'

'I shall tell no-one except Bob,' Selina assured her mother. 'We only get a newspaper when Bob goes to market and I'll see to it that it's not left around.'

Jenny was on duty in the ward when her mother rang. 'It's unbelievable!'

'But true.'

'Poor Becky! Is there anything I can do?'

'Not at the moment,' Eleanor said. 'I wanted you to know before you saw it in the newspaper.'

'I can't talk now. I have a doctor's round any minute. Give Becky my love, and I'll be in touch soon.'

Poor Becky! How would she stand up to this? Becky was the spoilt one, not used to setbacks. But she *was* her sister, and if she could help her she would, though she didn't see how. Not that she was much help to anyone these days, but perhaps things would change for her. She had made her big decision. Today she had posted the letter accepting the ward sister's job in Brighton. It would be a new beginning. Perhaps, when she was settled, Becky would come to stay with her there?

With these thoughts whirling in her head, Jenny went back on the ward and was the greatest possible help and comfort to her patients.

To her surprise Becky, perhaps because of the sleeping draught which the doctor had supplied at her mother's request, slept well. But when she wakened next morning, stretched out her hand to touch Roland and found a cold, empty space where he should have been lying, she remembered. For a moment, she wanted to put her head back under the bedclothes, shut out the day, shut out her entire life: but only for a moment. In the next she thought of Roland. Had he slept on his hard bed? How early had they wakened him in prison? Would he be able to shave – he was so fastidious about his shaving? And when would she see him?

'Why don't we go for a walk in the park?' Eleanor suggested after breakfast. 'Get some fresh air and exercise?'

'You go,' Becky said. 'I don't want to leave the house, just in case.'

489

'In case there's a telephone call? But it can't be yet.'

'All the same . . . And also Pop will be back sometime this morning. I wouldn't like him to come to an empty house . . .'

Not only would she not leave the house, she also refused to take on any of the jobs which her mother invented to pass the time. She could settle to nothing, and in the end she gave in and sat on a chair in the front window bay, from which, beyond the garden, she could see the road. She had been sitting there for two hours, checking the time on her watch almost every ten minutes, comparing her watch to the clock on the mantelpiece, when she saw the taxicab draw up at the gate.

'This must be Pop,' she said to her mother.

Becky rose, and went into the hall to meet him, but when the door opened it was Roland who walked in. For a moment they stared at each other with frightened eyes, but in the next second they were in one another's arms.

'I can't believe it!' Becky cried. 'I don't believe it! It's all over? They've let you go? You're free! Oh Roland, hold me tight, don't ever let me go. Tell me everything's all right again!'

He continued to hold her close against him, but after a while he gently took her arms from around his neck and held her hands while he looked into her face.

'Everything *will* be all right, my love. You have to believe that. But for now . . .'

She stepped back from him. There was something in his manner which frightened her.

'What is it? What are you trying to tell me?'

'I'm out on bail,' Roland said. 'I've been remanded to appear at the Assizes. But for now I'm home with you. Oh Becky, I've been so fortunate! I could so easily have been held in custody – but I wasn't.'

'The Assizes. It sounds so terrible!' In her mind the Assizes meant men tried for murder and treason, men sentenced to death, or to years in prison. 'Oh Roland, whatever will happen to you? What will happen to all of us?'

'Nothing we can't live through,' he said gently. 'Come and sit down, my love, and I'll explain.'

While Roland took Betty into the sitting-room, Eleanor went upstairs and repacked her bag. She wasn't needed here now, it was better for them to be alone. She wished old Mr Layton wasn't on his way home, but that couldn't be helped.

'Come and sit down and listen to me, Becky,' Roland said. 'It's important. Now I shall have to appear at the autumn Assizes, and you must face the fact, my dear, as I already have, that I shall be convicted.'

'But perhaps not!' Becky broke in. 'Perhaps they'll find you not guilty! After all, they've given you bail. That's a good sign, isn't it?'

'My dear little ignoramus, they've given me bail for quite different reasons: because I'm not likely to repeat the crime, or to run away; because I have a business to run and I'm responsible for other people's livelihoods; because certain people in Akersfield, whom I can never thank enough, have vouched for me, given me a good character.'

'But you could still be found not guilty,' Becky persisted. 'You could, couldn't you?' She must cling to that hope.

He hated to kill the eagerness in her voice, to dash her hopes, but he must.

'That will be impossible,' he said quietly. 'I've already pleaded guilty.'

'Guilty? But why, Roland? Why? I don't understand you.'

'Because I *am* guilty. We both know that. If it hadn't been for me, Jimmy Austin would be alive and well at this minute.'

And if it hadn't been for me in the first place, Becky thought. It was she who was the guilty one, not Roland.

'But you didn't mean to kill him,' she said.

'I know. That's why I shall be tried for manslaughter, not murder. And it may not be as bad as we think. Mr Peacock says there's every chance I'll get a light sentence. The fact that I've pleaded guilty might even help that — though that isn't why I did it.'

491

'Oh Roland, it's so awful!' Becky cried. 'Manslaughter, prison, guilty, sentences. I can't bear even to hear the words.'

Roland let go of her hands, rose to his feet, paced across the room, then came back again and stood in front of her, looking down. 'Listen to me, Becky, and don't interrupt.' His expression was stern, his voice almost rough, as if he was tearing the words out of himself. 'If you love me, and I believe you do, then you have to learn to face certain facts. We have to face them together. I can only be strong if you are strong. I can't do it on my own. I can only cope with what's in front of me – in front of both of us – if I know that you're doing likewise. Becky, I'm relying on you as I've never relied on you before in all our married lives. I'm relying on your strength not only to uphold you but to strengthen me, as mine will you. Do you understand that?'

'I do,' she whispered.

They were the two words she had whispered on her wedding day, only then she hadn't given much thought to them and she wasn't sure that she'd have meant them if she had. 'For better, for worse.' She knew now what it meant. It was a promise she'd make now without hesitation. She had never loved him so much.

'I do,' she repeated. 'Oh Roland, I do love you, and I will try to be everything I should. I won't let you down. Only . . . only I'm not as good as you are. It won't always be easy for me.'

He pulled her up from the sofa and took her into his arms again.

'You'll be everything you ought to be, and I'll be proud of you. And now we have three months together, my darling. Except that I have to report to the police regularly, which is a formality and needn't concern you, everything will be as normal. I'll go to the mill, you'll run the home, Christopher will go to school.'

But at the end of three months, what then? The same thought was in both their minds as they looked at each other, though neither of them dared to put it into words.

Mr Layton arrived soon after Eleanor had driven away. How old he looks, Becky thought. He had aged immeasurably since she had seen him less than a week ago. This could kill him, she thought – and with the thought came the realisation that she wanted him with her. She and Christopher both needed him. Next day she said as much to Roland. They had reached the stage now where they could talk to each other, make plans. It cut her to the heart every time the future was discussed, but she would never show it.

'He seems so frail,' Roland said. 'I really can't see him taking my place in the mill. I know he wants to, but I don't think he's up to it any longer.'

'I've been thinking about that,' Becky replied.

Last night they had made love with the same passion they had always had between them, but with a new tenderness. When Roland had first taken her in his arms, begun to caress her, she had stopped him.

'Roland, there's something I want to say.'

'Now, dearest?'

'Especially now. Roland, if you want another child I would be very happy for that to happen. I mean it. I want it too.'

He raised himself on one elbow, looked down at her, traced the outline of her cheeks, her forehead, her lips with his finger.

'Do you really mean that, my darling?'

'Yes.'

'You know it's what I want more than anything in the world. But not now, Becky. I wouldn't want to leave you to go through it without me. I'd want to be there. But there's something more important than you or me. I wouldn't want our child to be born while its father was in prison. Nor would you, my love.'

'Then when you come home again,' Becky said. But when would that be? Would she still be young enough to conceive a child?

Long after Roland had fallen asleep Becky had lain awake,

feeling the weight of his head on her breast, wondering how she would ever bear to sleep in this great bed alone. As she lay there, thoughts of the bleak future milled around in her head. He was right about the baby. She saw that. And then out of the tangled thoughts which followed came one clear one which she must discuss with Roland before the day was much older.

'I've been thinking,' she repeated. 'Why can't I do something to help in the mill?' She held up a hand to stop Roland. 'No, it's my turn to say don't interrupt. After the holidays Christopher will be starting full days at school. I . . . oh, my love, I shan't have you to look after! There'll be so much time to get through.'

'But you don't know anything about the business,' Roland pointed out. 'It takes a long time to learn.'

'I know,' Becky said. 'I'm not thinking I can take your place — I wouldn't be so silly. But there must be lots of things I can do. For a start, I can take on the wages. I'm perfectly capable of that. And there must be all sorts of jobs connected with the men which aren't technical. Things to do with their welfare, with the administration of the mill — things you do now which I *could* learn to do.'

'But my darling . . .'

'Please don't say no right away. Please let's talk about it, Roland.'

'But the men . . . you see, though I know there's a lot you could learn to do, I'm not at all certain that the men would accept you.'

'I think you're wrong. It wouldn't be for ever, only until you came back. We'd make that quite clear. And I have the strong impression that the men will do anything for you. And it *would* be for you, not for me — though heaven knows it would help me. At least let's put it to them when the mill reopens after the holiday.'

'Well, we'll think about it and talk about it in the next few days,' Roland agreed. 'I'm not at all sure about it, but I'll try to keep an open mind.'

* * *

On Monday morning they had an appointment to see Mr Peacock in his office.

'I have to have your account of the unfortunate incident, Mrs Layton,' the solicitor said. 'Though in view of the fact that Roland has pleaded guilty, I doubt if the defence will call you – and of course you can't be called by the prosecution. The law doesn't allow that in the case of a wife.'

When she had confirmed what had happened, Becky said: 'There is something else I would very much like to ask, though I know my husband doesn't approve.'

Mr Peacock looked from one to the other.

'Nevertheless she's going to ask it,' Roland said, managing a smile. 'My dear wife was never one to seek approval for whatever she wanted to do.'

'We would like you to tell us, quite frankly, what length of sentence you think Roland will be given. We know he will go to prison, but if we had even the slightest idea beforehand it would help us in the plans we have to make. I'm sure Roland agrees with that.'

Mr Peacock shook his head.

'It's not easy. Manslaughter is a strange crime – sometimes I wonder if it's correctly described as a crime – and the sentence can be short or long. Your Counsel is certain to mention provocation, and though that's no excuse for the act, it could well be mitigation. And then there's Roland's own responsible attitude in pleading guilty. The judge will take note of that.'

'So what do you think?' Becky interrupted.

He hesitated before replying. He had no intention of telling either of these good people sitting in front of him the worst that could happen – though he believed that Roland knew. On the other hand, for their own sakes he mustn't paint too gentle a picture. It would be no service to them to present too rosy a picture.

'I think . . . possibly three years . . . though it could be more.'

Becky quickly stifled the cry which escaped her.

'From which there will be remission for good conduct. And I'm sure your husband will earn that,' Mr Peacock said. 'And I'm sure I need hardly warn you that you shouldn't quote this part of our conversation. The court wouldn't take kindly to such guesswork.'

The meeting with the workers, which took place on the first day they were back at the mill, went much as Becky had expected, though Roland was amazed and deeply touched by the expressions of sympathy and loyalty which came from so many of them. His suggestion that Becky should take over some of the work in the mill was received at first with a shocked silence, and then there were murmurings, though whether they were for or against the idea it was impossible to tell.

Becky tugged at Roland's sleeve.

'Please let me say a word!'

She stood before them, held up her hand, and waited for them to be quiet. When she spoke it was in calm, even tones.

'I know that you and I care about the same things. We care about our homes and our families, and how we shall provide for them, we care about our friends. I'm sure I'm right in saying that we care about Layton's. Many of you have been here all your working lives, you've known Mr Roland since he was a baby. You've shown him, and his father and grandfather before him, unswerving loyalty. I believe that you'll now show that loyalty to me. There's a lot I have to learn, a lot I rely on you to teach me – every one of you, from the oldest to the youngest, has something to teach me. If you will give me your support so that I may keep this business going until my husband returns, keep your jobs for you, then I will try as hard as I can to do my part. And when my husband returns it will be you and I together who will hand Layton's back to him!'

The outburst of applause gave the answer. And if that wasn't enough, the rush of people who came forward to shake her by the hand, to shake Roland's hand and that of Mr Layton confirmed the verdict.

Mr Forsyth took her hand in a grip which she thought might break her bones.

'We'll do our level best, Mrs Layton. There'll be a few as won't play, and I know who they are so they'd better watch out! As for the rest of us, we'll be yours to a man. I can't say fairer nor that!'

Becky turned with shining eyes to Roland.

'What did I tell you?'

'You were right,' he acknowledged. 'You start work tomorrow!'

And so Becky went to work with Roland every day. When the school holidays ended and Christopher came home again he was put in Hannah's care until his mother returned at the end of the day. Becky and Roland had decided between them – it was an agonising decision – to tell Christopher as much of the truth as they could. 'If we don't,' Roland said, 'someone else surely will. That will hurt him far more.'

'Your father was brave,' Becky told her son. 'He hit a man who was trying to hurt me. Because the man died, the law says your father must be punished.'

'How will they punish him?' Christopher asked. 'Will they hurt him?'

'No. His punishment is that he'll be away from you and me, and from Grandpa, for a time. That's why I shall work in the mill while Daddy's away, to help to keep it running. Do you understand that?'

'Yes,' he replied. 'Can I leave school and come to work in the mill?'

Becky bent down and kissed him.

'Your daddy will be home again long before it's time for you to leave school!'

She was desperately tired every evening now. The days were long and, though she found much of it interesting, she was unaccustomed to the work. Each day she learned a little more; each day brought them nearer to the time when Roland must present himself at court.

When the day came she went with him, though he begged her to stay behind.

'No, Roland. I insist on coming,' she said. 'I want to be with you every minute. Each minute now will shorten the time we're to be apart.'

Since Roland had pleaded guilty, the proceedings were short. Becky held her breath when it came to the moment for the judge to pronounce sentence. Dear God, she prayed, let him be merciful!

'This is a serious crime,' the judge said. 'A man has lost his life, and for that you could receive a long sentence . . .'

I can't bear it, Becky thought. This is the moment I can't bear! Oh, my poor Roland!

'. . . But there is no doubt you were provoked, you came to the defence of your wife. I have taken this into account in mitigation of your deed. I have also taken into account the fact that you showed a responsible attitude in pleading guilty to the crime, and that you have until now been a man of exemplary character, serving your country in time of war. I therefore sentence you to two years' imprisonment in the second division.'

Becky looked towards Roland, and before he was led away he smiled at her. That's a whole year less than we expected, his smile said. It was the thought she made herself carry away with her out of the courtroom, back to Akersfield.

CHAPTER TWENTY-NINE

In the three months Becky had worked with Roland she had shared his office, and it was Mr Forsyth's suggestion that she should now take it over on her own.

'I don't really think so,' Becky demurred. 'I'm certainly not going to pretend I'm running the mill in Roland's absence. I'm just doing whatever small things I can to help out, and we all know it. You are the mill manager, it's you who should take this particular seat.'

'Nay, lass,' he said (it was what he usually called her these days, and to Becky there was a degree of comfort, a feeling of acceptance, in the familiarity). 'Nay, lass, there's been a Layton in that little office ever sin' I came here as a young lad, sweeping the floors for five shillings a week. It seems right for you to sit in that seat until the boss returns.'

Neither of them mentioned old Mr Layton. Though he wanted to help, and came down to the mill perhaps twice a week, it was clear that it was all beyond him. His son's imprisonment seemed to have broken him in body and spirit. In the evenings Becky encouraged him to sit with her rather than alone in his own room and she talked to him about the mill: whom she had spoken to that day, what had been said, telling him only the good things. She brought him no worries. Her own worry, seeing him so frail, and every day a little more removed from reality, was that he wouldn't live until Roland came home. It was her constant prayer that he would.

'And another thing,' Mr Forsyth continued. 'It's right for the hands to realise you have the authority. I know everybody here and I know that to most of 'em it wouldn't matter whether you sat in the boss's chair or in the night watchman's cubby-hole, they'd give you the respect due to you; but there's a few hotheads who need to be reminded.'

'They all know so much more than I do – about the wool, I mean.'

'That's not true,' he contradicted. 'Oh, they know more about their own jobs than you'll ever know. You couldn't walk in here tomorrow and be a carder or a twister, let alone a woolsorter; but very few of 'em know the next man's job; only a few like me who've come through the lot. And you've learned a great deal i' the last three months. I've been surprised at how you've taken to it.'

It was true. While Roland had taken her through the administration, the accounts, the buying and selling, Mr Forsyth had shown her every manufacturing process. Unlike many of the smaller mills, who tended to specialise in one part of the wool manufacture, Layton's did everything from buying the wool to turning out the finished cloth, though on a much smaller scale than the giants like Salts of Saltaire. So words like shuttles, bobbins, warp and weft, burls and slubs, which she had heard without understanding all her life, now had some meaning for her.

'Very well then! I'll sit in Roland's chair. But I don't intend this room to be a little ivory tower.'

'It never has been,' Mr Forsyth said. 'Anyone who wanted it had Mr Roland's ear.'

'Then I hope it will be the same for me, especially where the women are concerned.'

It was amazing how quickly the days passed. They were on full time again at the mill, very busy. It seemed as if the news of Roland's misfortune had brought in the work rather than slackened it. It was a heartening measure of his popularity, and of the loyalty of his friends in the trade. Then towards the end of November she had her first letter from Roland, together with the news that she could now pay the first of the monthly visits he was allowed. He was well, he said. He was settling down and things weren't too bad, though the first few days had been difficult. More than anything in the world he was looking forward to her visit.

Writing that letter had reminded Roland all too vividly of those first days. The journey from the court to the prison, and then the reception; the humiliating transition from free man to prisoner. The 'taking off of the old, the putting on of the new'.

From that moment in reception he had been a number, 4329 Layton. He had emptied his pockets, seen the familiar contents packed away in a cardboard box, signed the inventory. Under watching eyes he had been stripped of his clothes, examined for disease and lice; bathed, had his hair cropped close, donned his prison clothes, been taken to his cell, issued with his chamber pot. In those few minutes he had felt himself more of a criminal than in everything which had gone before. This loss of identity had been, and he thought would remain, the greatest punishment of all. But of all that he would tell Becky nothing. 'Give Christopher a hug and a kiss from his daddy' he added before signing the letter.

When Becky had read the letter at least half a dozen times she telephoned her mother.

'Next Wednesday! Will you be able to come over to stay with Christopher? Hannah and Pop are both willing to look after him, but he might be a little upset when he's left behind while I go off to visit his daddy. Also, Wednesday is his half-holiday. He'll be at a loose end and it would be so good if you could be here.'

'Of course I'll come,' Eleanor assured her. 'We'll have an outing. I'll take him somewhere nice. How is he getting on?'

'Not too badly. I had a long talk with his headmistress. She's a very understanding woman and I'm sure she'll watch out for him.'

'It'll get easier for him as time goes by,' Eleanor said. 'His friends will soon forget about it. He'll be just like any other boy.'

But was that true, she asked herself? After the first few months it might not be so bad at school, but at home, without the father he adored, with whom he had always spent so much time, it would be hard going for a six-year-old.

The night before the visit Becky surveyed the contents of her wardrobe and considered what she would wear. Her desire was to look her very best for Roland, to do credit to him. She wanted to look cheerful, fashionable, pretty. Never, even for Akersfield's most fashionable ball, had she chosen her outfit with more care. The coat she finally decided on, a deep violet wool with a collar of soft grey fur which framed her face, was one of Roland's favourites. The matching cloche hat he liked less. But it had amused him. He'd said it was like a plantpot, and they'd laughed about it, so she'd wear that. She wanted his first sight of her to give him the greatest possible pleasure.

Her reaction, next day, to the first sight of him was one of shock. In little more than a month he was changed almost out of recognition. His hair, normally thick and luxuriant, had been cropped so close that his skin showed through. The well-tailored dark suit, the crisp white shirt, stiff collar, gold cufflinks and striped tie he had worn in court were gone. The coarse prison garb which replaced them was too large. It hung on him, so that he looked as though he had lost even more weight than was the case. Poor Roland! He had been fastidious about his appearance; always so smart, so well turned out.

But this first reaction was over in a second, giving way at once to an overwhelming rush of love for her husband. She wanted to touch him, she longed to hold him, but when she made a move to do so a warder, though in a kindly manner, stopped her.

'Please sit here, madam!'

He indicated a chair, on the opposite side of the bare table from Roland, then he himself took up his place so that the two of them would be always in his sight.

'Oh Roland! Oh my dear Roland!'

She was tongue-tied at the sight of him. She had longed for this moment, there were a thousand things she'd

502

meant to say and now she could manage none of them.

'How . . .?'

'How are . . .?'

They spoke at the same instant, and in laughing at the confusion the ice was broken.

'You look beautiful,' Roland said. 'Quite beautiful! Even that silly hat becomes you.'

'Will he watch us all the time?' Becky glanced in the direction of the warder.

'It's his duty. Don't blame him too much. Try to ignore him. That's best all round.'

At first she found that difficult, but after a few minutes she almost forgot that the man was there.

'I want to know everything,' Roland said eagerly. 'Your letter was marvellous, but I want to hear everything from your own dear lips. And we have so little time to talk. Are you really well? Are you being brave and cheerful? How is little Christopher?'

The questions poured out of him. He stored all her answers in his mind, every word she spoke, that when she was no longer there he would be able to live through the visit again.

'As you can see, I'm very well,' Becky said. 'We're busy at the mill – Mr Forsyth says the amount of business is quite surprising when you consider that trade in the West Riding isn't too good. He sends you his very best, and I can't tell you how many of the men and women said the same thing when they knew I was coming to see you. You have a very loyal workforce, Roland. You can be proud of them.'

'I am. And grateful. In spite of everything, I'm a lucky chap. Becky, can you believe there are men in here who never get a letter from their wives, let alone a visit.'

'I would like to write to you every day,' she told him. 'I write as often and as much as I'm allowed.'

She gave him every bit of news she could remember. He was hungry for even the smallest, most ordinary items.

'It's the ordinary things which remind me that the world

503

is still there, outside,' Roland said. 'It's easy in here to forget that.'

'I had a letter from Jenny,' Becky said. 'She's settled well in Brighton. She sounds much happier. Apparently she's allowed to live out, so she's rented a little house not far from the hospital. She's invited Christopher and me to go and stay with her.'

'And shall you?' Roland asked. 'I'd like to think of you doing so. Christopher would enjoy it.'

'I suppose I might, but not for a while. I wouldn't want to take time off from the mill, so it would have to be at a holiday time. But not at Christmas. I shan't want to spend Christmas away from Yorkshire. At Christmas I want the familiar things . . .'

She stopped, unable to continue for the lump in her throat, terribly afraid that she was going to break down and cry at the sudden thought of Christmas without Roland. He stretched out his hand towards her, then remembered where he was; but the warder was intent on studying his toecaps, so Roland let his hand remain on Becky's for a moment before withdrawing it. His touch was almost more than she could bear.

'I understand,' Roland said quietly. 'We must try not to think too much about it. Just live through it when it comes. Go on with what you were saying, my love. When shall you go to Brighton?'

'Perhaps at Easter,' she said in level tones.

The time flew by. He told her that the prison food was adequate, conditions were reasonable and his cell-mate was compatible. He said nothing of the indignity of the sanitary arrangements, and of slopping out, which he thought he would never get used to if he was there for a lifetime. He mentioned that he was helping one day a week in the prison library, which he enjoyed.

'And in the spring I'm hoping to be allowed to work in the garden,' he said. 'Growing vegetables. I shall like that.'

'Becky,' he added suddenly. 'Please do something for me! Please take off your hat. I want to look at your hair.'

She did so at once, the warder watching her. She's quite a looker, he thought.

'It was your hair I noticed the first time we met. You were sitting at the piano and it streamed down your back like molten gold. Do you remember that musical evening?'

'I do indeed. I wanted to put my hair up and my mother wouldn't let me.'

'She was quite right,' Roland said.

When the time was up Becky said: 'The warder spends an inordinate amount of time looking at his feet. When I stand up to go I'm going to lean across and kiss you. Will you get into trouble if he sees me do it?'

Roland smiled. She didn't know where he got the courage to smile.

'He'll most likely pretend not to see you. But you must be very quick.'

'Then *now*!' she said hurriedly. 'Lean towards me.'

Her lips touched his, her hair fell forward and brushed his face. It was the briefest kiss of their lives, yet in a way the sweetest.

Afterwards, on her way home, it occurred to Becky that she had said so few of the things she'd meant to say. She had wanted to tell him how much she loved him, how much she missed him, how quiet the house seemed, how empty their bed. But she had realised in time that these were the words he wouldn't be able to bear, that it was better for him that she should stick to the mundane, to the little things.

In the end, Becky settled on Hebghyll for Christmas. They had had a pressing invitation to spend it on the farm with Selina and Bob, but Becky decided otherwise.

'Why?' Christopher complained. 'I want to go to the farm. Why can't we?'

'Because I'm afraid that if the bad weather comes we might get snowed up there.'

'But I'd like that! It would be exciting.'

'I daresay. But I have to get back to the mill immediately after Christmas. We could be stuck for a week at the top

505

of Longdale. So stop worrying about it. You'll enjoy yourself at Hebghyll. You'll have Robert and Peter there.'

'They're not the same as Billy.'

For a start, they were a lot older than he was and they didn't always want to be bothered with him. Peter was going on seventeen and Robert would be eleven next birthday.

'I'll tell you what,' Becky offered. 'When Christmas comes, if the weather turns out mild I'll drive you up to the farm on Boxing Day. Since Boxing Day is on a Saturday I can stay over one night. As long as I'm back here on Sunday night, that will do.'

'Do I have to come back?' Christopher pleaded. 'Can't I stay for the rest of the school holiday?'

She supposed he could. Selina was always pleased to have him; he was not a child who gave a lot of trouble.

'We'll see what Aunt Selina says. I daresay she'll agree.'

'Jolly good! Can we write and tell Billy?'

'*You* can,' Becky answered. 'You're quite capable. But you're not to make any promises, mind. It all depends on the weather.'

Eleanor had also invited Pop Layton to Hebghyll, but he had refused. He had a strong desire to stay in his own home, and since Aunt Hettie had promised to come and look after him, Becky thought the arrangement was a good one.

On Christmas Eve, when the workers were paid, Becky added an extra pound to every pay packet, including those of the women. Such a thing had never been done before and when she first mentioned her plan to Mr Forsyth he was not encouraging.

'It's a lot of money,' he demurred. 'It's half a week's wages for some on 'em. I don't know that we can stand it. And it's setting a precedent. They'll expect it every year.'

'I've done the books,' Becky said. 'We can afford it — not easily, but we just can. And it's not my intention to set a precedent — though nothing would please me more than to have it happen every Christmas. I intend to make it clear that this is a small return, not just for the hard work, but for the loyalty they've shown to me and Roland. As for you, Mr Forsyth, all the money in the Bank of England wouldn't repay you for what you've done these last few months!'

'Get away with you, lass!' he muttered. 'It were nowt!' But she could tell that he was pleased.

In the end she put a note into each wage packet, adding, to her seasonal greeting, her grateful thanks for their loyalty. It took her until midnight on the previous evening to pen them all. And then, late on the afternoon of Christmas Eve, she had one of the most pleasant surprises of her life when one of the women workers came to her office and shyly presented her with a Christmas bouquet.

'It's from all of us, Mrs Layton. We took a collection and we had it made up at the florist's. I'm sorry there aren't more flowers out at this time of the year.'

'It's beautiful!' Becky said. 'You couldn't have pleased me more! I shall be certain to tell Mr Roland about it next time I write.'

As soon as the mill closed she collected Christopher from home and they set off for Hebghyll. It was a dark night with a clear sky and a hint of frost, but there was no sign of snow. Christopher fell asleep soon after they'd left the outskirts of Akersfield. As she drove along the almost deserted road, Becky thought of Roland. Every quiet moment of her life now was spent thus, and thoughts of him intruded into even the busiest day.

She wondered what sort of a Christmas he would have. She knew that the prisoners were locked in their cells from early evening until next morning, but would it be the same on Christmas Eve? Her second visit was due at the end of December and for her part she wished Christmas over and done with so that she could see her husband all the sooner. Only for Christopher's sake had she surrendered to her mother's entreaties and agreed to take part in the usual festivities. They would be meaningless for her.

But experiencing the warmth of her family's welcome, from the moment she and Christopher arrived, she was glad she'd agreed. If she couldn't have Roland – and this was

507

only the first of two Christmases when Roland would be absent – then her family was the next best thing.

'Come by the fire,' Eleanor said. 'Get yourselves warmed up. It's bitter out there. Dick, pour Becky a glass of sherry, and then when she and Christopher have thawed out we'll have supper.'

'You shouldn't have waited supper for us,' Becky protested. 'I'm sure Peter and Robert must be starving.'

'Well, not quite,' Peter confessed. 'We've filled up on mince pies!'

Into Becky's mind – she wondered if it had entered her mother's – came the memory of that other Christmas, the first Christmas after the war ended, when her family in the end had not been able to wait supper for her because Peter and Robert were too young. She had arrived disgracefully late, with Jimmy Austin in tow, but even so her welcome had been warm.

It was quite late by the time the three boys had gone to bed. Dick made his excuses and followed soon after, leaving Eleanor and Becky sitting by the fire. He could only guess at how his stepdaughter felt; she put a brave face on everything and he admired her for it. He had known her since that day – it must be almost twenty-five years ago now – when he had picked up Eleanor and her three little daughters from the house in Akersfield and taken them back to Felldale on his cart. Becky had been not quite five. She'd been an obstinate little monkey all her life, though now her obstinacy seemed to have developed into a strength which amazed him. But he was sure she and her mother would benefit from a few minutes alone together, perhaps the last they would get over the holiday.

'Shall I make a cup of cocoa?' Eleanor offered.

'Not for me. I don't want anything more.'

'Nor I,' Eleanor agreed. She was grateful to have these few minutes with her daughter, even though nothing might be said. It had been tactful of Dick to leave them alone, but then he was always the most sensitive of men.

'There was something I remembered when we arrived this

evening,' Becky began. 'I was thinking of the first Christmas after the war. Do you remember?'

'Very well,' Eleanor said. 'I told myself it might be the last time I would have all my daughters together under the one roof – and as it happened I was right.'

'You were cross with me for turning up with Jimmy Austin, foisting him on you. No, don't protest, Mother. I want to mention him. I want to tell you that I've put the whole Jimmy Austin thing behind me – oh, I don't mean the fact that I was keen on him, I got over that long ago. I mean that I've put his death, and what led up to it, out of my life from now on. That might sound hard, but Roland is paying the price for it, and it's a hard price. I don't know what it will do to him in the end. If I can't put it all behind me, both of us start afresh – and I don't mean when Roland comes out of prison, I mean now – then Roland is paying the price for nothing. Do you understand?'

'I think so.'

'I wanted you to know. I wanted you to know that my own healing process is well under way. You don't need to worry about me. Everything now is for Roland.'

'I'm proud of you,' Eleanor said. 'I'm sure Roland is too.'

'Then let's talk about something else,' Becky suggested. 'What about the boys? What are Peter and Robert up to?'

'Peter's mad about flying,' Eleanor said. 'He can hardly wait until he's old enough to take it up.'

'Shall you and Dick let him?'

'Oh, I think so. How can anyone stop young men from doing exactly what they want to do? I don't forget how they all rushed off to enlist in 1914. But it's not as though he's going to be flying in war. Thank goodness we've finished with war.'

'And Robert?'

'Robert wants to do whatever Peter does,' Eleanor replied, smiling. 'If Peter flew to the moon he'd want to go with him!'

'Christopher and Billy are like that,' Becky said. 'I often

wish now that I'd given Christopher a brother or sister. He's not cut out to be an only child.'

'I shall miss Selina and Bob and the children this Christmas.' Eleanor sighed.

'I miss Grandma,' Becky said. 'I loved Grandma more than I ever showed. I just hope she knew.'

The weather held over Christmas Day; cold, but with no sign of snow. In the evening Becky spoke to Selina on the telephone.

'If it's all right with you, then, I'll be up with Christopher about midday. If it keeps fine I'd like to stay over until Sunday, but if it changes I'll need to come straight back.'

'Surely they can manage without you at the mill for a few days?' Selina queried. 'We'd love to have you here.'

'I daresay they can – but I like to think otherwise. Anyway, I shall want to be back.' She had to be there. She had to be there for Roland's sake. In a way, she felt she was living part of Roland's life for him, the part he could not, at the moment, live for himself.

Though the welcome from Selina and Bob was every bit as warm as that given her by her mother and stepfather, Becky did not altogether enjoy staying with them. The sight of their happiness in each other and in their children, their satisfaction with the new life on the farm, was almost more than she could bear.

'You seem very settled here,' she remarked.

'Oh, we are,' Selina agreed. 'Sometimes we feel as though we've been here forever, though we know it's only fifteen months. And we love the life. It's hard, but it's what we want. I'm so glad that Bob persuaded me.'

It was not their way of life which Becky envied. It wouldn't have suited her in a thousand years. She was a town girl. She liked to be where there were people and shops and things happening. She was even beginning to like Akersfield with its mill chimneys and smoke. No, it was that Selina and Bob seemed to be two halves of a whole, two halves which fitted perfectly against each other. It made

510

her feel incomplete – which she was. Without intention – they would have been distressed to know just how she felt – their closeness to each other made her feel unutterably lonely.

'So what do you think of our little Sue?' Bob asked, holding the child above his head, his arms stretched towards the ceiling. 'Isn't she a corker?'

'She certainly is,' Becky said truthfully.

At a year old her niece was adorable, and that was something else which Becky found difficult to take, though she was ashamed of herself for feeling so. It was nothing against the baby, it was just that these days she so much wanted another child. She didn't know where the desire had come from, she had never been over-endowed with maternal instinct, but it was there in her, strong and demanding. It was one of the reasons she longed to have Roland home again, though it was not the chief reason. Most of all she wanted him home for his own dear sake.

She left soon after breakfast on Sunday, excusing herself by saying that she had things to do when she reached home, also that Pop would be looking out for her.

Back in her own home she unpacked her clothes, and the photograph of Roland in its silver frame which had travelled with her. Christmas over, she thought. Another hill climbed. Now there would be the whole of 1926, a further Christmas, a little way into the next new year, and that would be the end.

She picked up the calendar which stood on her dressing-table and crossed off the days which had passed while she'd been away. Then she counted those which remained. She didn't really need to count them. She knew that after today she had four hundred and twenty-seven days more to wait.

CHAPTER THIRTY

To Becky, the winter of 1926 seemed the longest and coldest of her life, warmed only by her monthly visits to Roland. But in February he said, 'We're starting the final year, my love. It's all downhill from now on!' And in March, walking in the park, Becky observed the first crocuses making a purple carpet over the grass. A year ago she would hardly have noticed them, but now every manifestation of nature was important because it could be relayed to Roland. He was hungrier for such news than for the world's important happenings.

Jenny had written, inviting Becky and Christopher to visit her in Brighton for Easter.

'She says the weather could be quite mild there, especially as Easter isn't until April,' Becky told Mr Layton. 'All the same, I don't think I'll go. Perhaps later on, but not yet.'

There was too much unrest in the country; talks of lock-outs, threats of strikes. It would probably all come to nothing, and even if it didn't, might never affect Akersfield, but it could be risky to be away from the mill, just in case. Brighton seemed so far away. Though she had been to London, Brighton was like another country, almost abroad.

'I want to go,' Christopher said. 'But I don't want to go at Easter. It's lambing time. Uncle Bob said I could help.'

'You and your farming!' Becky teased him. 'Well actually that suits me. Perhaps we can go to Brighton in Akersfield Feast Week — if that's agreeable to Auntie Jenny.'

Only one month after Easter the strike came.

'How will it affect Layton's?' Becky asked Mr Forsyth

in the final days leading up to it.

She knew she should be thinking in much wider terms than that, but she couldn't. It wasn't the good of the country, or of the strikers, it wasn't even her own personal position which was important to her. Her anxiety was for Layton's mill, Roland's mill, first and foremost – and everything else came after.

'It's difficult to say,' he replied. 'A lot of the men sympathise with the miners. I daresay most of them do. They reckon the miners have had a bad deal. And they're working men themselves, don't forget. But they don't want to strike because they can't afford to. They've got wives and children to keep, rents to pay.'

'Well, if it happens, maybe it won't last long,' Becky said.

He shook his head. 'I wouldn't vouch for that, lass!'

When the strike did come, early in May, the impact on Akersfield was less than people had been led to believe. The fact that the trains didn't run meant there were some shortages in supplies, though, apart from perishables, not all that many. The shopkeepers of Akersfield were a canny lot; they always kept plenty in stock against a rainy day. The trams stopped, but it didn't matter much. Most people lived within walking distance of their work and the rest could use shanks' pony. Climbing the West Riding hills would be good exercise for some.

It was the newspapers people missed most. To everyone's surprise the *Record* disappeared almost at once. Some copies of the *Daily Mail*, printed in Manchester, found their way to Akersfield, as did the government's own paper, the *British Gazette*, and a few copies of the defiant *British Worker*. So what newspapers there were passed from hand to hand and were eagerly read until they fell to pieces. There was the wireless, of course, all those news bulletins; but it was what you could hold in your hand, actually read, that mattered. You could believe what you saw in print.

'There's a report here that the police in Leeds actually had to use their batons on the crowd,' Becky told Mr Forsyth. 'It says people were trying to hold up two trams

513

and one of the drivers was hit on the head with an iron bar! How terrible!'

'Well, that's Leeds for you!' Mr Forsyth said phlegmatically. 'They allus were a lot of hotheads i' Leeds. It couldn't happen in Akersfield, not that sort of thing. And the world hasn't stopped turning, lass. Steve Donoghue won the two o'clock at Chester, and it was rain stopped Lancashire playing at Manchester, not the strike!'

He turned away, seeming to dismiss the whole incident, though he was less easy in his mind than he pretended.

In the end, most of the people in Akersfield continued to work. At Layton's, and in many other places, they took up a collection for the miners. Perhaps more would have joined the strike, Becky reckoned, if it had gone on longer, but it was all over in a week. All those injunctions like 'Don't hoard food', 'Don't light fires', 'Don't send unnecessary letters', 'Keep off the streets', went by the board almost before they were noted.

Roland thought it was a good idea that Becky and Christopher should go to Brighton at the end of July.

'It will help to pass the time while the mill's closed,' he said. 'And I'm sure Jenny'll be pleased to see you.'

What neither of them said, though Becky was certain it was as much in Roland's mind as in her own, was that in Brighton she would be far away from the scene of what had happened at the same time last year. Not that she wouldn't think of it – how could she not? – but in different surroundings it might be more bearable.

'Look at it this way,' Roland said on one of her visits. 'If I earn my full remission, and I don't see why I shouldn't, it's the last summer holiday you and I will spend apart. By next summer we shall be together for always.'

He was so brave, Becky thought. He kept so cheerful, at least in her presence. She knew that the prison regime was telling on him, even though now that he was working in the garden he had more fresh air and exercise. Each time she saw him he was thinner, with a few more premature grey hairs at his temples. He looked considerably older than his thirty-four years. She also realised that he would cut his tongue out rather than complain to her. Sometimes when she went on a visit she did so feeling at rock bottom, struggling with herself not to show it. But out of his own meagre store he never failed to give her new strength to go on.

She and Christopher travelled to Brighton on the Saturday before the Feast week. He was all excitement. He had seldom been on a train before and never for a long journey like this. Then there was the crossing of London, from King's Cross to Victoria, in a taxicab. That was another excitement, especially as Becky requested the driver to take them by way of Buckingham Palace. Christopher was a bit disappointed in that.

'It's a nice big house,' he said. 'But not really like a palace, is it?'

Jenny was there to meet them at Brighton station, standing by the barrier, waving at them as they followed the porter down the crowded platform. She looks different, Becky thought. She looked better. She had lost the haunted expression she had had for the last year or two and had put on just enough weight to plump out her cheeks and add curves to her figure under the cotton dress – not that curves were fashionable. Clearly Brighton suited her better than Akersfield.

'Oh Becky, how lovely to see you!' Jenny cried. 'And you too, Christopher. I swear you've grown inches! Come along and we'll get a cab. The house isn't all that far, and there is a bus, but you must be quite tired.'

'I'm dying for a cup of tea,' Becky confessed. 'We left home soon after breakfast and I haven't had a hot drink since. We didn't have time in London or we'd have missed this train.'

'I gave you a drink of my dandelion-and-burdock with the sandwiches,' Christopher protested.

'Well, never mind,' Jenny said. 'I'll make a large pot of tea the minute we get home.'

The taxicab took them past the Royal Pavilion before turning to go along the seafront.

'*That's* a proper palace!' Christopher cried out,

'We'll go there one day,' Jenny promised.

The terraced house she rented was in a small street off the seafront. It was narrow and high, with one small room on each of four floors. Outside it was painted white, with blue window frames. It was totally unlike the houses in Akersfield, more like a house in a picture book. To Christopher's delight he was given the room at the very top of the house. When he looked out of the small dormer window, beyond the rooftops, there was a glimpse of the sea, though it was not a bright blue sea as he had expected, just the same grey as the sea at Bridlington.

'I'm so glad you came,' Jenny said later that evening after a very weary Christopher had been put to bed. 'I felt bad, leaving Akersfield just when you might have needed me. It seemed so selfish. But I had to, I had to get away, take this chance. Do you understand?'

'Not the details – and those I don't need to. As for being selfish, that's something you never were, even as a child. I was the selfish one; everybody knew that!'

'You were the glamorous one! Breaking away from home, joining the Bluebirds, travelling around. Oh, how I admired you, envied you!'

'So has it worked out, coming to Brighton?' Becky asked.

A smile illuminated Jenny's face as if a light had been shone on her. But not shone *on* her, Becky thought, for she was lit from within. She had not seen her youngest sister look like this before. Jenny had never been the one for strong passions, great enthusiasms, or perhaps she had and I was too taken up with myself to notice them, Becky chided herself. She had seemed a quiet, contained person, contented enough – and then when she took up nursing, dedicated to her work.

'Oh it has, Becky! It has! I could never have believed that it would be like this.'

There could surely be only one reason for her sister's bright eyes, glowing face?

'And am I going to meet him?' Becky asked.

'Of course! Later this week. He's away at a conference at the moment, but I very much want you to meet him.'

'And you're going to tell me all about him?'

'No. His name is Harry Lawrence and he's an anaesthetist at the hospital. That's all I'm telling you and you can judge the rest when you see him. He doesn't need any advance boosting from me!'

'I can hardly wait,' Becky said.

'Oh Becky, I'm so fortunate!' Jenny was suddenly serious. 'I never thought this would happen to me. But never mind me – how are you getting on? How is Roland? I've thought about you both so much.'

'Roland is wonderful,' Becky said quietly. 'He's brave and strong beyond anything you could imagine. As for me, I do my best. I'm getting through because I have to. And I'm helped by working at Layton's. With remission it will be only seven more months now, but I've a feeling they'll seem longer than all the rest put together.'

Jenny had taken a week of her summer leave and into the next few days she and Becky and Christopher tried to pack everything that Brighton had to offer. They bathed from the nearby beach, which Christopher complained about because it was entirely shingle, nothing like the firm golden sands of Bridlington, and the pebbles hurt his bare feet. They went a little further east along the coast and at low tide explored the rock pools, which he did enjoy, carrying home small creatures in a bucket of seawater and then, at Becky's insistence, returning them the following day. They went on both piers, tried all the amusements, visited two shows. There was never a spare minute between the day they'd arrived and the last evening before they were due to leave again.

'I *like* Brighton!' Christopher announced. 'Though it isn't better than Bridlington,' he added loyally. He had weighed down his small suitcase with specially selected pebbles for his grandparents and for Billy, and Becky had packed the obligatory sticks of rock in hers.

It was on this last evening that Becky at last met Harry

517

Lawrence. She liked him from the first moment, from his dark good looks – such a contrast to Jenny's fair beauty – to his quiet but confident manner. Most of all she liked his obvious care for her sister. He was a man to be trusted, to be relied upon, she thought – but not dull, as that might make him sound. Not in the least dull. He had a ready wit and a keen humour, which more than once had Becky laughing out loud; she, to whom laughter didn't come easily these days.

'So what do you think?' Jenny asked anxiously, when he had left, a little after midnight. 'Oh Becky, do you like him?'

'Of course I do, love! And I think he's exactly right for you, which is more important than me liking him.'

'But all the same you do like him, don't you?'

'I've told you! I really do! I shall be pleased and proud to have him for a brother-in-law. Am I going to have him for a brother-in-law?'

'I think so. I love him very much, but I have to be so very sure.' She had to be doubly, trebly sure. It was no more than a year ago she had thought that she could never fall in love again. There were days when she could hardly believe that it had happened to her.

'Don't tell Mother,' she said. 'I'll write and tell her myself. But you may tell Roland if you wish.'

Back in Akersfield, the holiday over, the mills working again, the black smoke pouring out of the chimneys and settling in a new pall over the town, Becky resumed her day-to-day life. Day-to-day described it exactly, for now more than ever she dared to live only one day at a time, doing what had to be done either in the mill or in the home in a mechanical fashion; something to be got through with the least possible trouble, though she was never less than conscientious.

Sometimes in these last few months she grew almost afraid, as if too much looking forward, too strong a feeling of optimism or even of complacency, might tempt fate, might cause something terrible to happen. Each night, in the first

518

stages of falling asleep, she was jerked back to wakefulness by a terrible enveloping wave of anxiety. It was an anxiety too strong to be placated by rational thought. She could only lie there trembling until it had passed.

To the outward observer none of this was apparent. It was a matter of pride with her that it shouldn't show. She seemed as strong and as capable as ever, especially in the mill. And it certainly seemed that fate was on her side there, for they were still taking as many orders as they could fill. Mr Forsyth made no protest at all when, at Christmas, she once again put extra money in the pay packets.

'It's going to be very much appreciated,' he said. 'My word, you've done a grand job here. Mr Roland will be very proud of you, and with good reason. Not long now before we have him back, and he'll be as welcome as the flowers in spring – but we'll not like to lose you, lass. We've gotten use to you.'

'Gotten use to you'. It was high praise indeed from this blunt Yorkshireman. Becky turned away, out of countenance with emotion.

'Perhaps you'll not get rid of me!' she retorted. 'Perhaps I'll be hanging about here until kingdom come!'

But she had other plans, God willing.

She went neither to Hebgyll nor to Longdale at Christmas. She wanted to spend it in her own home in Akersfield. The time was so short now. Mr Layton was glad of her company over the holiday. He seemed better than he had been for months, though he had almost ceased to go into the mill. He had instituted a regime of taking great care of himself, which if it had not had its sad side would have seemed comic. He refused to venture out in the bitter weather, avoided anyone who had the slightest suspicion of a cold or cough, took his iron jelloids by day and Sanatogen at night, watched his diet and got plenty of sleep. He was like an athlete in training, though his dedication had the sole purpose of being fit and well when his son came home. It would not be long now. When New Year's Day 1927 arrived, it was for Becky and her father-in-law a milestone. It was the beginning of a new life.

Early in the morning of a day towards the end of February, a bitterly cold day, with an inch of snow on the ground and the snow still falling, swirling in the wind, Roland stood in the room he had not entered since the first day he came into the prison. This morning he had discarded his prison clothes and had bathed, feeling, as he scrubbed himself in the hot water, that he was washing away the hurts, the indignities, the abasements of the last sixteen months. He had put on his own underclothes, his own dark suit – thought it was now too big for him – tied his tie with precision. Nothing could disguise the overall shortness of his hair, but hair would grow.

Now he stood before the desk, checking the contents of the cardboard box which had been handed to him.

'Everything in order?' the man behind the desk asked.

'Yes thank you.' He signed the receipt.

The man held out his hand.

'Then goodbye Mr Layton, and good luck!'

He was 'Mister' Layton again. With that one word he had been given back his identity.

It was not quite daylight when he went out, heard the door clang to behind him. At first the world seemed empty, nothing stirring. Then he saw her, no more than fifty yards away, a dark silhouette against the snow; and at the same moment she saw him. They ran towards each other, she more swiftly than he because it was some time since he had had an opportunity to run free and he had almost forgotten how to. Then they were in each other's arms.

'Oh Becky!'

'Oh Roland, my dearest love!'

By the time they noticed it they were covered in a powdering of snow.

'A fine thing if you celebrate your freedom with a bout of pneumonia,' Becky said, trying to speak normally. 'Get into the car at once. I'm going to drive you home.'

On New Year's Day, 1928, Eleanor looked around her

520

sitting-room at Whinbank. It was the first time in many years that everyone had been together in Hebghyll. Even Bob and Selina were there. Bob employed a farmhand permanently now, so they had been able to leave the farm for a day. Eleanor turned and spoke to the man who stood beside her.

'Do you find the whole of our family here all at once a bit overwhelming, Harry?' she asked. 'Jenny certainly has let you in for it.'

'Not a bit,' he said. 'It's marvellous to be here and I'm grateful you invited me. In any case, Jenny's told me so much about you all that I feel I know you.'

'Well, it is an important family occasion,' Eleanor said. 'And in future you'll be a part of those. It's a while since we had a christening, and this is rather a special one. I'm glad you're here to share it.'

Presently Harry moved away and Dick Fletcher came and joined his wife.'

'Everything all right, love?' he asked.

'Perfect!'

She directed his attention to where her daughters were standing together, the winter sun through the window catching the fair hair of all three of them as they bent over to admire Becky's small daughter, who was asleep in her mother's arms. Eleanor put out her hand and took Dick's.

'My golden girls!' she said. 'My dear golden girls!'

THE END

CARA'S LAND
by Elvi Rhodes

Cara Dunning first came to the wild and remote Beckwith Farm in the Yorkshire Dales as a young landgirl during the Second World War. Beckwith was isolated, sometimes beautiful, sometimes inhospitable, and had been owned by the Hendry family since 1700.

When Cara fell in love with Edward Hendry, it was not what her family had intended for her. Edward was fifteen years older than Cara, a pacifist, and a widower with two children, one of whom bitterly resented her new stepmother. But Cara was determined to make the marriage work.

Her greatest friend on the farm was Edward's mother. Edith, a loyal and wise daleswoman, was to see the young bride through many tragedies, many vicissitudes and the years of trying to run the wild sheep farm on her own. And as Cara's life began to change, so Cara changed too, finding a complete and utter happiness where she had never expected to find it.

0 552 13636 0

THE BRIGHT ONE
by Elvi Rhodes

Molly O'Connor's life was not an easy one. With six children and a husband who earned what he could as a casual farmhand, fisherman, or drover, it was a constant struggle to keep her family fed and raised to be respectable. Of all her children, Breda – the Bright One – was closest to her heart. As, one by one, her other children left Kilbally, so Breda, the youngest, was the one who stayed close to her parents. Breda never wanted to leave the West of Ireland. She thought Kilbally was the most beautiful place in the world.

The tragedy struck the O'Connors and the structure of their family life was irrevocably changed. Reeling from unhappiness and humiliation, Breda decided to make a new life for herself – in Yorkshire with her Aunt Josie's family. There she was to discover a totally different world from the one she had left behind, with new people and new challenges for the future.

0 552 14057 0

RUTH APPLEBY
by Elvi Rhodes

At twelve she stood by her mother's grave on a bleak Yorkshire moor. Life, as the daughter of a Victorian millhand, had never been easy, but now she was mother and housekeeper both to the little family left behind.

As one tribulation after another beset her life, so a longing, a determination grew – to venture out into a new world of independence and adventure, and when the chance came she seized it. America, even on the brink of civil war, was to offer a challenge that Ruth was ready to accept, and a love, not easy, but glorious and triumphant.

A giant of a book – about a woman who gave herself unstintingly – in love, in war, in the embracing of a new life in a vibrant land.

0 552 12803 1

SUMMER PROMISE & OTHER STORIES
by Elvi Rhodes

From Elvi Rhodes, bestselling author of *Ruth Appleby*, *The Golden Girls* and *Madeleine*, comes a collection of stories to suit the reader's every mood – tender, funny, romantic, ironic, bitter-sweet, nostalgic.

The couple in *Summer Promise* are, at first glance, placed in an appalling situation, but nevertheless in the warmth of southern France their relationship develops in an unexpected way. *Be Your Age, Dear* is a delightful tale of a generation gap, which, in one family, seems non-existent – or has it gone into reverse? *The Meeting* describes the ten-yearly reunion of a group of friends which, for obvious reasons, dwindles each time. The two members most closely involved come to a decision that was, perhaps, inevitable. *Model of Beauty* is set in a painting class, where the temporary illness of the generously endowed model brings about surprising consequences.

These enchanting stories are guaranteed by turn to entertain, soothe, intrigue and touch you.

0 552 13738 3

MADELEINE
by Elvi Rhodes

Sophia, spoilt pretty daughter of Helsdon's richest mill owner, lived a life of petted indulgence at Mount Royd, the Parkinson Home. Madeleine – daughter of a tyrannical and bigoted father who worked in the Parkinson mill – spent her time either at chapel, or working a fourteen hour day as housemaid at Mount Royd, a victim of Sophia's whims and occasional spitefulness.

But Madeleine who beneath her obedient and dutiful exterior was volatile, strong-willed, and rebellious – was not the kind of young woman you could overlook, and when Léon Bonneau – a younger son of a French wool baron – came to stay at Mount Royd he was, against his own inclinations, startled into noticing the dignity and beauty of the young housemaid.

0 552 13309 4

THE HOUSE OF BONNEAU
by Elvi Rhodes

The sequel to *Madeleine*

When ex-parlourmaid Madeleine Bates married the dashing French wool baron, Léon Bonneau, she felt that life would take on new dimensions. However, marriage brings a whole host of unforeseen problems to blight their future. Léon's family are deeply resentful of the girl who has captured his heart and drawn him away from them and their beloved France. Hortsense Murer, his childhood companion, feels that she should have been Léon's wife – and she uses all her feminine wiles to try and entice him back to her ever-welcoming arms. Madeleine, meanwhile, is haunted by the memory of the vicious curse issued by her arch-enemy Sophia Chester: that she would never bear Léon a son – a curse which, against all common sense, seems to be coming true.

These tensions seem set to destroy all that Madeleine and Léon hold dear, and it is not until Léon finds himself stranded in Paris during the siege that they realize what is most important in their lives.

0 552 13481 3

THE MOUNTAIN
by Elvi Rhodes

Jake Tempest spent the first twelve years of his life on the canals. Then, when his grandfather died, everything changed. His mam and he moved to Skipton, Mam worked in the mills, and they lived as best they could. It was there that she bought the picture of the mountain, and when she died it was one of the few things he took with him.

But the mountain was more than just a picture. It was a real place – Whernside – set amidst the rugged hill country of Yorkshire, and it was to Whernside that Jake was drawn, especially when he found they needed men to work on the new railway lines, cutting valleys, building viaducts, and carving a tunnel right through the great mountain itself.

As he settled into the new harsh life amongst the rough shanty villages of the railway workers, one woman lit his very existence – Beth Seymour. Beth was strong, brave, compassionate – and she was also married. Once she and Will had loved one another, but life for the rail builders was savage and coarse and Will Seymour was rapidly becoming brutalized by the manner in which he lived. Beneath the shadow of the mountain, in all its seasons, the passionate story of Beth, Will and Jake was played out to a dramatic climax.

0 552 14400 2

SPRING MUSIC
by Elvi Rhodes

Naomi had been contentedly and, she thought, happily married for nearly all of her adult life when her husband Edward explained kindly to her one day that he had fallen in love with a twenty-six-year-old and wanted a divorce. She had to leave the comfortable home she had shared with Edward and their three children, now all grown-up, and move into a small flat in the middle of Bath. The dramatic change in her lifestyle threatened to overwhelm her.

But gradually Naomi began to appreciate the changes, and even to enjoy them. For the first time in her life she could do what she liked, and make her own friends. If these included men friends – well, why not? Unfortunately her children could think of many reasons why not, and Naomi began a battle to establish her own independence, and to persuade her family that she had moved into the springtime of a whole new life.

0 552 14655 2